Praise for .

What a wonderfully poignant, hea̶ and cried a little while reading tale oɪ ɪɛʀɪndled love.... This was such a feel good book to read. I loved all the characters. They were genuine and thoroughly likeable. Family was a strong theme running throughout.

~ **Melanie M., a Goodreads reviewer**

~ ~ ~

Kallypso Masters creates characters so vividly that you feel you are living the experience.

~ **Nikki H., an Amazon reviewer**

~ ~ ~

The only reason I put it down was to sleep!! I have said it before and I'll say it again, I've never read a Kallypso Masters book I didn't love. This one is no different. I love her character styles, the way she ties one person to another with shared histories.

~ **Megan J., a Goodreads reviewer**

~ ~ ~

I have always loved Kally's books but I must say this is one of my favorites. I have laughed, cried, screamed and cheered with Kate and Travis. This story makes me think that there is really a second chance for people—in this realm and on a higher level.

~ **Roni B., a Goodreads reviewer**

Kate's Secret

Kallypso Masters

Copyright © 2017-2019

Ka-thunk! Publishing

Kate's Secret
Kallypso Masters
Copyright © 2017-2019
Ka-thunk! Publishing
Print Edition
E-book ISBN: 978-1941060292
Paperback ISBN: 978-1941060308
Original e-book version: August 8, 2017
Original print version: August 23, 2017
Last revised for e-book and print: February 24, 2019

ALL RIGHTS RESERVED
Developmental Edits by Meredith Bowery and Dana Delamar
Content Edits by Meredith Bowery, Barb Jack, and Jacy Mackin
Line Edits by Dana Delamar and Jacy Mackin
Proofread by Laura Combs, Barb Jack, Angelique Luzader, Carmen Messing, Eva Meyers, Lisa
Simo-Kinzer, and Christine Sullivan Mulcair
Cover design by Linda Kuhlmann of Two Trees Studio
Cover photos by DepositPhotos.Com
Cover photos graphically altered by Linda Kuhlmann
Formatted by BB eBooks

To discover more about this book and others, see the *Books by Kallypso Masters* section. For more about Kallypso Masters, please go to the About the Author section.

Dedication

This book is for all who have lost someone to spirit. I see your loss and your pain daily on Facebook. But I'd like to mention one woman by name—**Karen Henderson**, whose recent and unexpected loss of her husband, **Kenny**, brought tears to the eyes of many in the Romance writing and reading world. And yet her strength and courage—not to mention an incredible faith that tells her he hasn't left her and sends her signs daily of his presence—have inspired and encouraged me and countless others. Always watch for the signs because our loved ones never truly depart from our sides!

Acknowledgements

Kate's Secret has been my heart's delight to tell. I can see this series taking shape and form, going in an entirely different direction than I originally intended. As with all of my books, I don't write in a vacuum. In order to add all the layers I like having in a novel, I feed off of a lot of people, some of whom I'm about to name below. Whether they be beta readers, professional or volunteer editors, proofreaders—the questions they ask and the experiences they bring to the table make for a much more enriching story.

First of all, let me thank my subject experts who assisted me in getting my facts straight—or tried to anyway. As always, all errors are the author's. **Fiona Thomas** and **Christine Mulcair** provided EMT and other medical information. For American Saddlebred information, I was helped immensely by fellow Romance authors **Lynn Raye Harris** and **Jan Scarbrough**, as well as by **Kathy Brodie**, who gave me and my husband a personal tour of the Saddlebred farm where she works and provided me with answers to many of my questions about the differences in English and western style tack and much more! For Army and Army National Guard expertise, I was aided by veterans **Shannon Dale, Cody Mackin**, and **Karen Henderson**. Karen also inspired the apple pie moonshine references in the story.

My deepest gratitude to **Meredith Bowery** and **Dana Delamar** who helped me brainstorm and flesh out the book during developmental edits earlier this year. They sent me back to fill in the gaps at which point, the book went into content edits whose suggestions helped me fill out the story even more. Content editors **Meredith Bowery** and **Jacy Mackin** always challenge and encourage me to dig deeper and to discover the hidden gems in the story. They're tireless and always willing to take one more look at something. At that same stage, beta readers **Barb Jack** and **Lisa Simo-Kinzer** also see it. Barb catches inconsistencies and continuity issues, and offers suggestions that spark me to try different things with the story. Lisa, with her social work background, helps me flesh out the characters more deeply. Although Lisa occasionally wants to go *Dexter* on some of them, she hasn't killed off any of them yet. And then the book goes to the line edit stage. Because of editing schedules and my inability to write a book to a deadline, we had some interesting challenges with this one, but my thanks to **Dana Delamar** and **Jacy Mackin**, plus the incredible volunteer proofreaders who picked up the ball in the end zone and took the book to the goal—**Laura Combs, Barb Jack, Angelique Luzader, Carmen Messing, Eva Meyers, Christine Sullivan Mulcair**, and **Lisa Simo-Kinzer**—made sure the new typos I made at the last minute as well as any remaining inconsistencies or inaccuracies were corrected and wouldn't jar you from your enjoyment in reading this book. They also had some intriguing story questions that helped me iron out some confusion.

Of course, despite all of my amazing editorial, proofreading, and beta-reader teams, all errors left behind are solely mine to claim. If you see something you think needs correcting, never hesitate to let my assistant, **Charlotte Oliver**, know by e-mailing her at charlotte@kallypsomasters.com or messaging her on Facebook. She will share them with me, and if I agree it's a problem, I'll correct it in later versions. (Unless you're contacting me within the first few days of release, you might want to make sure your book is updated to the latest version available because I try to correct the file often during the initial weeks.)

As you may know, I often go to readers for answers to questions (too many to name here) but one that stood out this time was **Candy Wrenn Sapp**, who along with others on my timeline post, helped me get into 12-year-old Chelsea's head and motivations. There were countless other questions posted on Facebook, either on my timeline or in the *Bluegrass Spirits* discussion group, that also sparked ideas, so my thanks to all joined in to help.

Also on my team are my fabulous cover artist, **Linda Kuhlmann**, and formatter **Paul Salvette**, who make everything look good.

Last, but never least, to my amazing personal and executive assistant **Charlotte Oliver**. She recently came up in conversation with a text group where four team members congregate to help me in a crisis or to simply chat. Words like "angel," and "zen" came up to describe her. All I know is that to me and Mr. Ray, she's like family. The way she does everything so smoothly and without complaint makes her a joy to work with, too!

Author's Note

Dear Reader, welcome back to this second book in the new Bluegrass Spirits series. While writing this one, I started to feel I was hitting my stride. While I love Jesse's Hideout, there's something special about Kate's Secret, too. Perhaps it's that I'm once again writing about a military veteran or that I'm sharing more of my Kentucky roots with you.

This story touches on some subjects that have elicited strong opinions that didn't always mesh with what my facts were while doing research. Kate has Type I diabetes, for instance, and everyone seems to know a family member or a friend of a friend with the condition who don't match up with Kate's experience, but let's all agree that this is fiction and I'm satisfied as long as I can back up her experiences with at least one person's case. For instance, Kate follows a lot of the principles and diet rules in **Jasinda Wilder**'s *Big Girls Do It Running*. I am a Type II diabetic and have found the diet transformative in my own life and in lowering my A1C. But this is in no way a how-to on living with diabetes. Please be responsible and talk with medical professionals about yours and your family member's situation.

The same with the American Saddlebred horses in this book. Most of the people working on the book are familiar with western tack and horse terms, but not so much English. To cut down on the number of messages about so-called errors, I've probably gone a little heavy-handed with detail.

Lastly, a secondary plot in this story deals with a potential suicide. If you or someone you know needs to talk with someone who can help, contact the Suicide Prevention Lifeline (suicidepreventionlifeline.org) or an organization in your area for help.

Lastly, this is one of those books that has left me drained. Yes, there are more books to come in this series, but I'm going to write them on my schedule, not to a preorder date or deadline. I'm very excited about the next book—*Danny's Return*—and anticipate there will one day be a book about some other secondary characters within these pages. To stay informed about my progress, please sign up for my e-mails and/or text alerts!

kallypsomasters.com/newsletter

And now prepare to be immersed in the world of *Kate's Secret*. I welcome your heartfelt reviews if you're so inclined at the bookseller where you made your purchase, as well as at Goodreads and anywhere reviews are accepted. Thank you for picking up this book!

Prologue

"What's your greatest regret?" Obadiah asked.

"Not letting Gail back into Kate's life when she wanted to return." Depriving Kate of her mother had placed Ben Michaels in this cold, dark corner of Heaven where he would remain for all eternity if he didn't fix the mess he'd made in life. "What can I do about it now?"

"All depends on how badly you want to make amends."

The white-garbed spirit guide standing next to him then forced Ben to watch the replay of his life yet again in tediously slow motion. Every. Agonizing. Moment. Ben had been a selfish piece of work all right by choosing to keep Kate all to himself. He'd convinced himself he'd done so to provide Kate stability and to bring up his only child in a wholesome environment on the family farm. The fear of losing Kate had remained foremost in his mind for the rest of his life, in part because he knew he didn't deserve to have her. He'd gone through life paralyzed by fear that Gail would remarry and decide she wanted joint custody, now the desire to see his daughter reunited with her mother burned inside him. From what he could tell by a recent visit, his wife, Gail, had settled down. But was it too late?

Man, if his grandparents could see how badly he'd screwed things up…they hadn't raised him to be like that. He'd shortchanged his daughter in so many ways.

"Your grandparents—and even your parents—are fully aware of everything you've done," his guide assured him.

Ben sighed. "Yeah. Probably why they keep their distance up

here." Well, his parents had done the same on earth. He'd been cared for and raised by his grandparents, who had loved him unconditionally. Kate was the only other person to love him that way, but he'd killed any chance of that love continuing if she found out what he'd done.

"Your parents have their own work to do, but they have advanced beyond the level you've been stuck at for ten years."

"I had my reasons for doing what I did," he said, raising his chin defiantly. "But Kate and I didn't go anywhere. If Gail had straightened herself out and wanted to see our daughter, she knew where to find her."

"What if your wife didn't have the money to come back to Kentucky? Did you ever think of that?"

Ben conceded the possibility. Gail had never been able to hold a job for more than a few months. She'd been too much of a free spirit, flitting off to find herself every other month. He'd warned her when she'd left the last time that he wouldn't allow her to swoop back in when the urge to return overcame her. He'd seen firsthand several times that she'd only leave again in a few months and break Kate's heart all over again. Inevitably, Gail's need to wander always resurfaced over the course of their six years together. That wasn't fair to Kate. A five-year-old couldn't process the disappearances of her mother for weeks and months on end.

But Kate had been devastated anyway when Gail didn't return.

"How'd that decision work out for you?" Obadiah's question caught him off guard, reining in his thoughts.

"Not so well." In Ben's last year or two in the physical world, he'd begun to have regrets about depriving Kate of having both parents in her life. Gail had loved Kate in her own way.

Obadiah flashed several images across his mind, forcing him to face what he'd done. Some depicted events he hadn't even witnessed in life. Kate calling to her mom when she came home from school that first day only to discover Gail had left again. That went on for a heartbreaking number of days before Kate became silent and withdrawn. Why didn't Ben remember that? He'd probably been out in the fields or the barn working.

The next images showed Kate crying into her pillow each night for months. She'd put up a strong front around him. Often, she'd consoled him for his loss, not revealing the depth of her own heart-ache.

"She blamed herself, you know," Obadiah said.

"For what?"

"Sending her mother away."

"That's ridiculous."

"Children aren't rational about these things. In her mind, she did something that led to her mother's leaving. Furthermore, she thought you blamed her, which is how she explained why you never talked to her about her mother after the age of five. That's part of the reason she hasn't actively pursued trying to find her. She expects to be rejected again."

"I had no idea." Ben sure had been a selfish bastard.

The final image played out before him of one of the hottest days of the year. He'd been cutting tobacco all day and, after taking his shower, Gail took him by the hand, along with four-year-old Kate, and led them to the springhouse. Earlier, she'd stashed a picnic basket for them, along with a small cooler with cold drinks. They'd played "Ring Around the Rosie" with Kate. He could still hear her laughter filling the…

Ben blinked rapidly before turning toward the spirit beside him. "Why are you wasting your time on a despicable soul like me?"

"Because by helping you, I'm gaining spiritual growth without the pain and suffering of going through the physical plane again. Lord knows I tried to guide you for decades, but you weren't open to suggestion in the physical world. You've always been a challenging one for me to convey truth to."

Obadiah had been attempting to get Ben to do the right thing since he was a small boy on the earthly plane. Of course, Ben hadn't been aware he'd had a spirit guide while he was alive. He'd chalked up Obadiah's mental badgering as coming from his own conscience, which he readily ignored.

When introduced to Obadiah in the afterlife and learning the truth, Ben hadn't expected to develop such a close rapport with him. Never one to deal with messy emotions in life, Ben knew he couldn't sidestep them here, despite his stubbornness. But he was still a work in progress. Obadiah assured him not to give up hope.

Ben sighed, focusing on the problem at hand again. "Every birthday and Christmas, Kate expected her mom to come home any day for months and months."

Poor Kate. His trying to hoard her love had left her a fearful, untrusting woman making the same mistakes with her daughter, Chelsea.

"Certainly not the wisest decision you ever made," Obadiah observed. "I think you might have been surprised at how Gail would have grown into the role of mother, if only you'd given her one more chance. Poor woman didn't have an easy life before or after you, that's for sure."

Guilt washed over him. From this side of the veil, he could see the effects of his actions and how they'd affected both Kate and Gail. He'd justified what he'd done by saying Gail's desertion time and time again was proof she wasn't fit to mother Kate. Why had Gail given up so quickly?

"Benedict,"—Obadiah's stern voice put Ben on notice—"don't delude yourself. Gail continued writing letters to Kate for years after she left that last time. But you already know that, don't you?"

"You're right. I returned most of them. All but one."

"Is it in a place where Kate might find it?"

Ben shrugged. "Not without a little manipulation from this side, unless she decides to repaint the room it's in." He was still learning the rules of engagement in the afterlife, despite having been here for a decade in Earth years. "Would I be able to wriggle the letter loose from where I hid it?"

"I'm sure that power could be arranged if it's for a good cause."

"It's tucked behind a mirror above the fireplace in my old bedroom. Kate uses it as a guest room now. Well, more like a junk room, if you ask me." She rarely had people staying there, making the likelihood of the letter being discovered by anyone else even more remote. "It's summertime," Ben pointed out, "so there's not much chance of her accidentally finding it while laying a fire."

"True enough. Let me consult with my superiors to see what can be arranged. Moving physical objects isn't quite as easy as having the living see and hear us." Not that he'd managed to succeed there with Kate, either.

"Tell me, Benedict, are there any other actions you need to correct?"

"None that I know of."

"Are you sure?"

He sighed. His spirit guide didn't miss a thing. "Okay, I suppose I could see how Chelsea's father turned out and whether he's good enough to be a part of her life."

"Is that for you to determine?"

Probably not. "I guess that's for Kate to decide. Could I do something to bring Kate and that Cooper fella back together for a second chance?" Ben was getting his own second chance to correct actions that had played a role in keeping Kate away from her mother, but the situation with Cooper hadn't been his offense. Kate had asked him to keep Travis away.

"Travis Cooper has a friend who entered the spirit plane prematurely and is now making it his mission to help Travis move on with his life."

"A spirit guide?"

"Not in the true sense. This one shared a strong bond with him on Earth and that has carried over to the afterlife. Danny will be the perfect one to lead Travis out of the darkness he's experiencing these days, because Danny's actions led Travis into that state. I think the best thing you can do is to not stand in their way."

"I hope Travis is more open to listening to his friend in spirit than I was with you."

Obadiah rolled his eyes and smiled. "Almost anyone would be more open-minded than you were." The old soul's long-suffering patience had been the stuff of legend up here. "Now, are you ready?"

An overwhelming feeling of protectiveness for his daughter overcame him. Maybe he hadn't been a good parent while alive, but dammit he was determined to get it right now that he knew what his daughter had become because of his actions. Ben nodded. "I'm going to fix this. Thanks for giving me a chance to make amends, Obadiah."

He shrugged. "It wasn't up to me to allow you to interact with the earthly plane, but I have a lot riding on the outcome of this pursuit as well. While time means nothing to those of us on this side, the consequences of your actions—and inactions—have severe ramifications for those you've harmed. Do not delay further in rectifying this wrong."

Ben nodded, but something in the spirit's tone gave him a sense of unease. Why the sudden pressure, after all these years? Did Obadiah know something he didn't? Well, of course he did.

God, he hoped Obadiah wasn't hinting that his sweet Kate also might be in danger of crossing over prematurely. She took her chronic illness seriously, but everyone could mess up from time to time. Or was it Gail? She'd appeared frail to him on his last visit.

"I can tell you nothing," Obadiah said, "other than the time to act is now."

Ben hadn't been granted the gift of seeing into the future, so he'd have to take Obadiah at his word. It was time to right a grave wrong and reunite Kate with her mother as quickly as possible.

Chapter One

Kate Michaels came into the kitchen from the barn just as the phone went to the answering machine. She rarely made or received calls on the landline, but had heard it ringing when she reached the porch after her morning chores. Probably a telemarketer.

She walked to the sink, not expecting the caller to leave a message. Then a voice she hadn't heard in more than thirteen years filled the air, piercing her soul.

"Katie? It's Travis. I'm headed your way and should be in Midway in a couple of hours. Pick up, if you're there."

Travis Cooper? Back in Kentucky? Why? She remained frozen to the spot until the water became so hot she yanked her hands away. Still, she couldn't move toward the phone, merely standing and staring at it as if it had grown six ugly heads.

None of which belonged to Travis, the most handsome man she'd ever known.

"Listen, I know this is out of the blue. Just wanted to see you again. To talk. We left a lot of things unsaid."

If you only knew.

"I need answers, Katie."

Why now? There'd been years in which she'd dreamed of Travis returning to ask her what happened and to tell her nothing mattered except her. But she'd closed the door on Travis ever coming back into her life long ago. After an extended silence, she heard his sigh before the click of the phone reverberated around the room like a shot from a rifle.

A couple of *hours?*

Kate grabbed a paper towel to dry her hands as she glanced around the room. Chelsea's softball and outdoor gear was in the crate near the door. She picked up the entire bin as she raced from the kitchen, down the hallway, and up the stairs. In Chelsea's room, she nearly stumbled over her daughter's piles of discarded clothes. She'd vowed not to touch the mess in here, but now she needed to at least make it look like a guest room in case Travis ventured this far.

Why would he? She had a bathroom downstairs. With any luck, he wouldn't even come into the house.

But she couldn't take any chances.

Making her way to the closet, she tossed the crate inside before clearing the single bed of a truck bed full of stuffed animals. Thank heavens Chelsea was gone all week at summer church camp. Kate only had to worry about erasing all evidence that the twelve-year-old existed in this house.

And send Travis packing—again.

Where did he live these days? He'd grown up in Louisville, and she hadn't expected him to be happy living in the country. He'd had high ambitions. They'd broken up just before he'd left for a prestigious internship with a civil-engineering firm in Manhattan following their junior year in college. For all she knew, he still lived in New York.

She'd learned of her pregnancy two days after he'd received his internship acceptance letter. At the time, Kenny Chesney's "There Goes My Life" kept running through her head nonstop, only with a more realistic ending. Life wasn't a fairy-tale country song. She'd made the right decision to let him go to pursue his dream, though she'd chickened out of telling him in person and had left Travis a voicemail saying that she no longer felt about him the way he did about her. Then she blocked his number on her cell phone and let her father turn Travis away at the door when he'd come to the farm to try and win her back, she supposed. Coward much? *Totally.* But she wouldn't have been able to remain steadfast in her decision if she'd had to face him.

Acting had never been her forte and neither had confrontation.

Keeping the secret had nearly crushed her. Eventually, though, Travis had moved on. He hadn't returned to the University of Kentucky that fall and never tried to contact her again.

So what was bringing him into her life again after all this time? His dream of being a big-city engineer still didn't fit in a tiny farming and artisan community like Midway, Kentucky. Despite dating for more than a year and his insistence that he was interested in helping her rebuild her family's horse farm the way she'd talked about, Kate hadn't wanted to hold him back. One day, he'd have resented being tied down with her and Chelsea and would have left, just the way her mother had.

Chelsea didn't deserve to go through life feeling the way Kate had when her mother had abandoned her as a child. Better that Chelsea not know her father at all than to know him and lose him.

There had been times when Kate wanted to cave in and contact Travis's mother to ask where he was, but her father had explained that no man would want to be saddled with an unplanned baby just when his career was taking off. Daddy had been right. When she and Travis had talked about the possibility of marrying and having a family one day, they'd agreed it would be best to wait until they'd established their careers so they could give their children the best start possible in life.

So the decision to keep the secret from Travis had been relatively easy—and devastatingly difficult at the same time.

Later, when Chelsea started school and began asking about her father in earnest, Kate had been tempted again to contact him. How hard could it be when she knew where his parents lived? But by then, Chelsea had become her whole world. The thought of Travis demanding to have Chelsea for visits that would take her away terrified Kate.

Maybe her own mother hadn't wanted her enough to fight for her, but Kate wouldn't let anyone come in and steal her daughter. Had Travis somehow found out about Chelsea? Was that why he was coming back after all these years? Did he intend to take Chelsea away from her?

Over my dead body.

Kate glanced around the room, spying a pink zebra that must have dropped when she'd cleared off the bed. Frustrated, she kicked it in the direction of the closet. No hiding the fact this was a preteen girl's bedroom with the posters on the walls and ceilings, but she'd never be able to put them back in the right order if she took them down. Chelsea cherished her space and her privacy at this age.

Could this pass as Kate's own childhood bedroom? She shook her head. Not with Katy Perry, Luke Bryan, and Taylor Swift plastered above the bed.

But Travis wouldn't have any reason to come upstairs.

Calm down. Think!

A wave of nausea hit her as she bent to pick up a discarded bag of chips Chelsea had left on the floor. Her hamper was filled with dirty clothes as well. Kate had asked her to clean the room before she left.

Worry about the messy room later.

At the moment, she needed to settle the chaos in her mind. She simply wouldn't let Travis beyond the kitchen or living room. No way would he be sticking around long if she made it clear she didn't want him here. Kate would give him whatever answers he said he needed and send him back to wherever he'd come from in a matter of hours, if not minutes, with no conceivable chance of his ever laying eyes on this room.

Kate went room by room upstairs finding a few more things to hide from prying eyes before realizing she wasn't being rational. If she truly intended to keep him downstairs—or outside—then she needed to be working in those areas. How close had Travis been when he called? Heck, when had he called? Eight-thirty? Nine? She'd lost track of time in her panic.

It had taken her a lifetime to stop wishing for the impossible after losing everyone she'd ever loved—except Chelsea. She wouldn't let Travis shatter the carefully controlled world she'd made for her and her daughter.

Kate had reached the top of the stairs when a bout of dizziness caught her off guard. *Damn.* She grabbed onto the banister but didn't slow her progress to the hallway below. She still needed to make sure the living room, dining room, downstairs bathroom, and kitchen were free of any evidence of Chelsea's existence.

First, though, she'd better drink something to counteract the drop in her blood sugar. When Travis had called, she'd been about to fix breakfast, but he'd put her into such a tailspin she'd forgotten all about eating. Not something a person in her shoes should do—ever.

Kate reached the kitchen with a hollow feeling in the pit of her stomach and her heart racing as though she'd run the Derby Festival's miniMarathon. A quick glance at the clock over the fridge told her at least two hours had passed.

Oh no! The fridge was covered with pictures of Chelsea. She opened a drawer and tossed the photos and mementos into it haphazardly. She'd straighten it out later. When the white fridge was bare except for a few local business magnets, she breathed a sigh of relief and opened the door.

A blast of cold air hit the sweat dampening her forehead, making her shiver despite the warm June day. With a shaking hand, she removed the quart-sized Mason jar of homemade apple juice from the fridge. Just a few swigs, and she'd have this hypoglycemic episode under control. Food could come later. While running around like a crazy woman this morning, she'd also almost missed lunch, too. The juice would work faster anyway. She'd grab a protein bar before tackling the living room.

Gravel crunched on the lane outside, turning her shiver into an uncontrollable shake. He was here!

Now she had one thing and one thing only to worry about—*getting rid of Travis.*

* * *

"Go back to Katie. She needs you."

Travis Cooper had been awakened from a dead sleep last night when his best friend Danny came to him in a dream. Travis didn't believe in ghosts, but the urgency in Danny's voice had gnawed at Travis's mind for hours. Despite being dead for months, Danny had seemed as real as if he were there in his bedroom. He'd also been frantic that Travis needed to get up here to see Katie. Why? Danny had never even met her. Katie had kicked Travis to the curb months before he'd enlisted in the Army National Guard and met Danny in boot camp.

Travis had let Danny's words dog him for most of the morning before he'd given up working and hit the road. He was well beyond the Tennessee-Kentucky border before he called the number he had put in the contacts of every phone he'd owned since the last time he'd seen her. He just hadn't dialed it before today. Good thing she'd kept her landline.

Katie Michaels wasn't going to leave that farm for anything. Sure enough, when he'd called, he'd recognized her voice immediately on the answering machine. As he exited the interstate, an old Kenny Chesney song came on the radio. Travis had bought Katie that single the Christmas before they'd broken up. How he'd loved listening to her sing along with Kenny, her voice a bit off-key but music to his ears anyway.

What he wouldn't give to hear her singing along with it again.

While he had no intention of sparking an old romance, the urgency in his friend's voice had him worried that maybe something might be wrong. Did Katie finally need something from him?

You're pathetic, you know?

Danny had called him pathetic more than a few times, especially when Travis had too many beers and started talking about the girl he'd lost. Hell, that he'd even think Danny had made some kind of ghostly visit to him in a dream was ridiculous. Must be his subconscious talking or wishful thinking. He'd still like to have some answers from his friend about what had happened the night he'd died, but he hadn't been able to ask them during the brief dream.

As he drove up the gravel lane to the Michaels' circa 1900 farm-house, he took in the new white siding, replacement windows upstairs and down, and a green metal roof instead of the shingles he remembered. Saddlebred horses grazed in the nearby field with freshly creosoted fences. They'd even built a new barn as well as an arena. At one time, he and Katie had talked about working together here—him handling maintenance and construction while Katie gave riding lessons and took care of the horses she loved. Travis had offered to build her an arena like that one. Instead, a few months later, Katie had abruptly broken off their relationship. He'd been so stunned it had taken him a couple of months to figure out how to go on without her.

The place was thriving. Old Man Michaels had bragged that they'd make a go of it without any help from the likes of Travis. Had he been the reason Katie had broken up with him? Ben had never been particularly fond of Travis, that was for sure.

And from the looks of things, the cantankerous old man had been right. Katie didn't need Travis at all. The notion of coming all this way to the aid of someone who didn't need him irked Travis.

Why was he here in Midway again when, from the look of things, Katie was doing fine?

Oh yeah. Danny had sent him on this mission.

"Stop messing with my head, Danny boy." The loss of his friend had consumed him day and night for months. If only Danny had reached out to him that night…

Don't think about that now. Figure out why you're here, fix whatever it is, and head home to Tennessee where you belong.

Stepping onto the back porch, Travis thought he heard someone inside. Good. He wanted answers only Katie could provide. He hoped Ben wasn't home. That ornery old coot had interfered in his and Katie's business more than enough during their fourteen months together. What Travis had come here for had nothing to do with him.

But was there a husband in Katie's picture now? He hoped that wasn't who opened the door when he knocked.

He rapped sharply, only to be answered by the sound of breaking glass inside the kitchen. Peeking through a slit in the door's curtains, he saw a woman—*Katie!?!*—lying face down in a spreading pool of amber liquid and shattered glass. Passed out? *What the…?*

He tried the handle. Locked.

"Katie, it's Travis! Can you hear me?"

Silence.

Looking around the porch, he grabbed a baseball bat, of all things, and broke out one of the window panes. Reaching inside, he unlocked the ancient double-cylinder deadbolt. Why would she leave a bat on the porch and the key in the lock? He'd worry about her lapse in security later, because if he hadn't been able to break in this way, he'd have busted down the door somehow.

Once inside, he knelt beside her. "Katie!"

Nothing.

He felt for a pulse in her neck, letting out a breath when he found it. She wasn't dead at least. Pulling his phone from his back pocket, he dialed 9-1-1 and relayed what limited information he could to the dispatcher. He didn't have an address, having come here by memory, so he said the Michaels Farm. The woman said she knew where the farm was.

"Is Chelsea okay?"

The woman must be confused. "I'm calling about Katie Michaels. She's lying in her kitchen in a pool of apple juice of some kind." *Or was it apple-pie moonshine?* He and Katie had had a little too much of a friend's home brew one Thursday night, which had been the last time he'd touched the potent liquor. He'd thought they'd both learned their lessons then, though.

"Is Kate breathing?" So the dispatcher not only knew the location of the farm, but Katie, too. That was one thing he liked about living in a small town; everybody knew everyone else.

"Yes."

"Is she having a problem with her sugar?"

"What?"

"Did Kate faint because of her sugar?"

Hell, he didn't know Katie had health problems. Is that why Danny told him to come here? "She has diabetes?" His mother had been diagnosed with Type II diabetes five or six years ago, and before she'd found the right balance of diet, exercise, and medication. Mom had had a couple of close calls where her sugar had dropped too low. Was that what was wrong with Katie?

There was a pause on the phone before the dispatcher said, "Who am I speaking with?"

"Travis Cooper."

"Are you one of her students?"

Would the woman ever send the damned ambulance and quit asking all these questions? He was afraid to move Katie, but if they didn't get help here soon, he'd take her to the hospital himself.

"No. Just an old friend." An old *boy*friend to be exact. He'd noticed the riding lessons sign out front before pulling into her driveway, so that must be one of the ways they kept the place afloat all these years.

A distant wail of a siren came through the broken pane of glass. *Finally.* Apparently, the dispatcher had sent an ambulance while keeping him on the phone asking questions.

"Make sure she stays breathing and don't put anything in her mouth." What would he possibly put in her mouth? "We'll have someone there in a few minutes. They'll take very good care of her."

"Thanks. I hear the siren now."

Katie moaned, and Travis disconnected the phone without thinking. He stroked her hair. "It's okay, Katie. Help's on the way."

Her brow wrinkled, but her eyes remained closed. She faded out again, and her forehead relaxed once more. He continued to touch her there and along her cheek, hoping he was soothing her and that she knew he was with her.

"I'm sorry, Katie." Sorry he hadn't come back sooner. Or that he hadn't sought the answers he wanted back when they'd first broken up. He'd let his bruised ego rule him then, refusing to come groveling on his hands and knees to a woman who'd made it clear she didn't want him.

And yet he'd never wanted to make any other woman his wife.

Why the hell had she broken up with him in the first place? He still had no clue.

The siren cut off nearby, and he ran to the door so he could show them where she was. They drove up the lane at a good clip and stopped near the path to the kitchen door.

"She's in here. Passed out. Possible complication of diabetes."

When the hell had she gotten the disease? She wasn't overweight, but then neither was his mother. But Katie was only thirty-three—thirty-four in September. Did she have a family history? Her father didn't have it, as far as Travis knew. He only knew what she'd told him about her mother—that the woman had died when Katie was five.

The EMTs grabbed their equipment and followed him inside. Katie still lay pale and motionless in the same spot. Damn, he could have at least cleaned up the juice around her. He wasn't thinking clearly.

As they worked on Katie, he found the waste can under the sink and a pile of old newspapers on the floor near the door and began picking up the glass from the window he'd broken. He glanced at Katie and the EMTs every few moments to see what was going on. They worked in near silence, only asking each other for what they needed and what they found. One did a finger stick, and Travis thought he read the number as twenty-six on the monitor. *Damn.* No wonder she'd passed out.

If the dispatcher was aware of her condition, then Katie wasn't new to diabetes. So why wasn't she taking better care of herself?

Too many questions he didn't have answers to.

When one of the EMTs went outside again, Travis moved closer.

"How is she?"

"We're administering glucose but will need to transport her to Georgetown for observation."

Georgetown. After confirming where they intended to take her, Travis pulled out his phone and programmed the map app to the regional hospital. It was about half as far there as to the hospital in Frankfort, given that her farm was east of Midway. "I'm going to check on her horses and will follow you."

They quickly loaded Katie into the ambulance and left. Knowing the hospital wouldn't let him in to see her until she came to, Travis mopped the stickiness off the kitchen floor before going out to the barn to check on her horses, which appeared to be fine.

Katie had been the one to spark his interest in horses. Even though he'd never owned any of his own, he'd gone to a number of Saddlebred shows and had helped out on the horse farm of his foreman in Franklin, Kentucky. He'd check on Katie's horses more carefully later tonight after bringing her home. If she was released. Where the hell was her dad?

Five minutes later, with her purse in the passenger seat to give to the hospital staff, he drove the hilly, winding roads as fast as he safely could, relying on the GPS to get him to Georgetown Community Hospital.

Once there, he quickly learned only family could go back without her consent. He provided them with her driver's license and insurance card, feeling strange to be rifling through her wallet this way. He exhaled in relief when he found no photos of a husband or boyfriend. Only a few of a blonde-haired girl who looked to be a preteen, but too old to be Katie's daughter. A friend's kid, maybe? Or a godchild?

Every few minutes, he tried again to find out her condition, but they said they couldn't tell him anything. Would they at least inform him when she was being discharged so he could take her home? He had no clue who else to call for her.

"Mr. Cooper?" He looked up at the woman in the receptionist's window. "Ms. Michaels is asking to see you."

Seriously? He carried Katie's purse to the door where the woman buzzed him inside. A staff member met him and guided him to Katie's bedside. She was still far too pale, her hair plastered to her forehead, and she was avoiding eye contact with him, perhaps from embarrassment about how he'd found her—and yet she was the most beautiful sight he'd ever seen in too damned long.

When she finally looked up at him, his stomach did a funny little flip, and he grinned at her like a fool.

"Glad to see you're awake, Katie."

Chapter Two

K ate couldn't believe she'd woken up in the hospital after having a rare diabetic episode. But hearing the deep, soothing voice from her past made the experience even more surreal. It had to be him. No one had ever called her Katie but Travis.

Why was he grinning at her like that? Was he amused by her predicament? She looked away. "You found me?"

"I did. How are you feeling?"

"I'm fine." She avoided his gaze for as long as she could without coming across as an ungrateful bitch. When she looked his way again, his hazel eyes stared back at her with the intensity that had haunted her dreams for more than a decade. When Travis Cooper looked at her, she felt like she was his whole world.

Not that she wanted to feel that way anymore.

"Thanks for being there." Much as she hated to admit it, if he hadn't been there, Chelsea could be left motherless. "Um, I don't have my phone to call anyone for a ride home when they discharge me."

"No worries. My truck's parked outside, unless your dad will be back in time to take you home."

Travis must not have kept up with her from afar. Thank heaven. *He probably doesn't know about Chelsea, either.* She released the sheet she'd been holding onto for dear life and smoothed her hand over the wrinkles she'd made. "Daddy died ten years ago."

Travis came a little closer and squeezed her hand. "I'm so sorry, Katie. I didn't know. That had to have been hard on you."

"He was very weak from heart disease those last couple years, so it was a blessing."

"If I'd known, I'd have been in touch sooner."

She shook her head. "It's not necessary. I've been doing fine."

"I'll say. The farm looks great." He *almost* sounded as though that made him happy. "What happened this morning?" he asked as he pulled a chair closer to the bed and sat down. "You scared the hell out of me."

His eyes were more mature than she remembered. No, sadder. The newfound crow's feet added more character and made him even more distinguished looking. Where'd he gotten that tan? Travis loved being outdoors, but she'd pictured him primarily working behind a desk as a civil engineering, given his field of study.

Those carefree college days seemed like a lifetime ago.

Chelsea's lifetime, to be exact.

With sudden clarity, Kate remembered the chain of events that had landed her in the hospital. He'd asked her a question. "The day got away from me..." *after you called.* "I forgot to eat breakfast."

"Were you recently diagnosed with diabetes then?"

She shook her head. "No, I've had it for more than a decade." He raised an eyebrow, as if questioning her sudden inability to take care of herself. This had been her first major lapse since she'd been diagnosed as Type I when Chelsea was about fourteen months old. While she'd developed gestational diabetes in her seventh month, it had been easily controlled and went away, or so she thought, after giving birth. Then, about a year later, it was back with a vengeance that scared her and Daddy both. Most women who contracted diabetes post pregnancy ended up as Type II—able to treat it with exercise, diet, and perhaps oral medications. But Kate hadn't been among the luckier ones and required daily insulin injections. "Oh, I usually am much more in control of it. When I stick to my routine, everything's fine. To-day...well, things didn't go as planned."

"My mom's been Type II now for almost six years. She had a hard time of it at first. Have you thought about getting an insulin pump?"

"After weighing the pros and cons of the pump, I decided monitoring and doing my own injections was the way to go. I don't want to freak out my students or their parents if they see one strapped around my waist." Not to mention that her insurance company wouldn't cover the cost.

"Still, if it can help…"

She waved away his concern, not wanting to talk with him about her body's moment of weakness. Travis obviously still liked to fix things, and the last thing she needed was to have him hovering over her. "My endocrinologist said I was doing a great job of controlling my A1C. She agreed that the pump was more a convenience than a necessity for me, and I couldn't afford it. Trust me, today was just a glitch and won't be repeated."

"I couldn't convince Mom to get one, either, although it probably was overkill in her situation. She doesn't require injections any longer." Travis grinned.

Her heart fluttered the way it always had around him. The hint of a five o'clock shadow burnished his jaws and chin, and she couldn't help but remember the feel of his whiskers on her…

Kate blinked back to the present. What had they been talking about? Whatever it was, it was lost now.

Even though Travis had been the cause of this hypoglycemic tailspin, she needed to show a little gratitude. *Be fair.* All right, while she'd like to blame this episode on Travis, she alone bore the responsibility for her lapse in care and judgment today. No one else. "Thanks for calling for help. I might be facing a much longer stay in here if you hadn't found me when you did." She refused to think about what might have happened to Chelsea if he hadn't found her in time.

She shuddered, and Travis glanced around the room. "Want me to ask a nurse for a warm blanket?"

"No, thanks. I'm fine." Thank heavens her daughter hadn't found her. Chelsea already fussed over her too much. A twelve-year-old shouldn't be obsessed about her mother's health the way Chelsea was.

Just getting her to go to camp this year had taken a promise she would take care of herself this week. Now look at her.

"Any idea when you'll be discharged?"

Kate shook her head. "Soon. I think they want to test my glucose again in half an hour or so just to be sure." She glanced away. How was she going to get rid of him when they got back to the farm without appearing ungrateful?

"Good idea. I'm sure you'll be happy to get back home."

She nodded, finally ready to ask the question that had plagued her after his call. "What brings you back here, Travis? Where are you living now? Louisville? Or did you stay in New York?" He'd been so excited about his internship she wouldn't have been surprised if he'd stayed there.

He ran his fingers through his short brown hair, much shorter than he'd worn it when he was younger. "Not a chance. There's such a thing as a city that's *too* big. That place is on steroids twenty-four seven. And the noise with all those horns honking and sirens blaring—well, one summer was enough. But I'm glad I went. It changed my life, for sure." Without explaining what he meant, he grinned. "I live in a small town south of Nashville called Nolensville. Mostly residential and very quiet."

"I would have expected you to stay in the city." *Definitely not some small community like mine.*

He shrugged and looked away, a sudden solemnity settling over him. "I've changed. I avoid crowds and seek solitude more now."

Had something happened? Something more than a noisy summer in Manhattan? This Travis wasn't like the easy-going one she'd met and dated while going to school at UK. He'd always been driven, but pretty much went with the flow.

"I see you've done a great job with your farm, Katie. How'd you manage all that in such a short time?"

She'd had no choice. "It's been a long time since you've been there." He still hadn't answered her question about what had brought him back here. "I'm sure you didn't come all this way to check on how my farm was doing."

He stared at his hands a moment then met her gaze again. "I needed to see you again, Katie."

"Why now, after all these years?" Her voice grew husky and ended on a whisper. For a time—years, if she was honest—she'd longed to hear him say he cared about her even though she'd sent him away. Then she'd become too busy taking care of Chelsea, the farm, her father, and her students to give Travis another thought.

That so?

Not even close.

Who was she trying to fool?

"I wanted to make sure you were okay. I had a feeling you needed me. Call it a premonition. Or whatever."

"I never knew you were tuned into that kind of stuff."

After several moments, he grinned. "You'd think I was nuts if I told you where it stemmed from."

Judging by his cryptic statement, it definitely wasn't because he'd heard about Chelsea. She sank against the narrow bed, finally letting herself fully relax. "Try me."

"It's not important."

"If you leave it to my imagination, I'll probably come up with something a lot crazier than what really happened."

He rubbed his chin. "Just a crazy dream. Didn't make any sense at the time, but it made me think you needed me, and here I am."

"Well, I'm thankful for your not-so-crazy dream. But I'll be okay."

Lying flat on this hospital bed made it difficult for her to convince him she was fine and send him on his way. She tried to sit up, wanting to regain some of her equilibrium, but when he jumped up and wrapped his arm around her back to assist her, she realized what a mistake that move had been. Her heart came close to bursting at the feel of him touching her again. Kate shut her eyes and took a deep breath before swinging her legs over the side to face away from him.

Until she remembered she was in a backless hospital gown. Could this day get any worse?

Then Travis gave what sounded like a soft whistle, and heat rushed to Kate's cheeks.

*   *   *

Touching Katie, even innocently like this, did nothing to keep Travis's libido in check. When she seemed steady, he pulled his arm away. Her long brown hair had been gathered into a ponytail, and the gaping hospital gown revealed the peaches-and-cream skin of her toned back and her lacy pink panties peeking through. No tan line. She probably spent most of her days in the barn or in the arena training horses.

He let go a whistle of appreciation and winced at himself. *Juvenile much, Cooper?*

He'd barely caught a glimpse of the expanse of skin before she reached around and tugged the flaps of the gown closed, but that would be enough to fuel many new fantasies about her for the next sixty years, give or take a decade.

Clearly, Katie was trying to put some space between them by turning away. He walked around the bed to where he could face her again. Better, although he missed the previous view.

Her cheeks had grown rosy from embarrassment, no doubt. She stuck her chin out, which surprised him because she used to be self-conscious about it, saying it was too pointy. He'd always thought it was adorable.

"Really, I'm fine. I'm sure you have a busy life and work to take care of, so please don't feel you have to stick around. Well, once I impose on you to take me home."

Apparently, his hopes of rekindling something with Katie wouldn't be realized. She definitely wanted him gone. Perhaps things weren't as perfect at her farm as he'd thought on first glance. "I have some vacation time coming, and I want to help out in any way I can. For starters, I need to repair the window I broke to get inside to you."

"Oh." Her gaze avoided him. "Wouldn't you rather sightsee or visit your family in Louisville?"

The old spark returned to her chocolate-brown eyes. She'd always been full of life, unlike the way she was when he'd found her, which had scared twenty years off his life expectancy.

Time to change the subject. "So what have you been up to since college?"

"Working. Running the farm."

"What do you do for fun?"

"My horses are my fun."

"Are you running the place alone these days?"

"No, I hired someone to handle the breeding program and help at foaling season, but he's on vacation while things are slow."

Bingo! "While you're single-handed, I'd be happy to muck stalls. I'm going to guess you haven't taken a vacation yourself in a long time."

Her chest rose and fell as her eyes shot daggers at him. She didn't like being maneuvered into a corner, but she'd walked right into that one.

"I can see I'm not going to convince you that I'm fine until you've stuck around for a few days to see for yourself. But only a few days. I have plans for Sunday and all next week."

Clearly, they didn't include him.

"I'll sleep in the barn. I've missed being around horses. I may need a refresher, though, in taking care of them." He needed no such thing, having been up at Jackson's farm to help his foreman any number of weekends over the years. But having Katie working beside him would make this time all that much sweeter and give him a chance to get to know her again. "But tonight I think I ought to sleep in the house, just in case you have any more issues."

"I can set my alarm and test my sugar in the middle of the night. I've been dealing with this an awfully long time."

"If you promise to do that, then I won't come up and pester you.

But I still think I ought to sleep on the couch. That way, I'll hear if you call out to me." *Or fall again.*

She hitched the corner of her mouth, as if biting the inside of her lower lip. "Well, maybe tonight. Tomorrow, you can move into the small apartment in the barn. Miguel Salazar, my breeding manager, has the one in the arena."

She sure didn't want him under the same roof. What was she afraid of? "I'm sure the barn apartment will be a lot better than some of the places I've slept."

Concern flashed in her eyes. "What kinds of places—"

"Time for another finger stick." A much-too-cheerful tech came in carrying a small case and pulled out the testing supplies that reminded Travis of the ones that went with his mom's glucose meter. Just as well they were interrupted. He'd prefer to tell Katie more about his life over an uninterrupted dinner. Right now, he didn't want to delay her getting out of here.

"One-forty-two," the tech said.

"Does this mean I can go home now?"

"I'll let the nurse know, and she'll bring in the discharge papers as soon as they're ready."

Forty minutes later, he was guiding Katie by the elbow from the wheelchair to his truck, which was parked next to the hospital entrance. "Let me help you up."

"No, th—"

Ignoring her, he wrapped his hands around her waist and lifted her onto the bench seat. Man, it felt good to touch her again, and when he took his seat behind the wheel, he wished she'd scoot over and sit by him the way she did when they were dating.

Dream on.

"Why don't you close your eyes on the drive home?"

"No, I'm fine."

Regardless of whether he believed that, he let it go. "We can stop for dinner. You're probably hungry, and we don't want your sugar to tank again."

"Oh, yeah, I don't really have anything in the house to feed you. Let's stop at Lee's and grab some chicken."

Not exactly what he'd hoped for. "Why don't we eat there?" If she didn't want to invite him in to join her at the house, at least he could prolong their time together a little while longer.

"If you don't mind, I'd rather just have takeout. It's been a long day."

"Sure. No problem."

They rode in silence until he pulled into the drive-through line. He reached for his wallet. "What would you like?" After ordering their meals, she pulled out her wallet, but he insisted on paying. Soon, they were on their way, the smell of chicken filling the cab of his truck, mingling with the scent of apple juice on Katie's clothes. Wholesome in its own way, but he remembered back to the time they were dating when she wore a scent she called lemongrass. He'd found some of the Asian herb in the grocery one time and bought it just to remind himself of Katie.

All too soon, he was pulling into her lane. Again, he checked out the place. "I still can't get over all the changes you've made to the place. And, yes, I'm assuming it was you. Your dad didn't like change all that much."

Katie laughed. "No, he didn't. But if I hadn't done something, we'd have probably lost the place before...too long." What was she not telling him? "Sometimes, I find myself being resistant to change now, too."

"You always had a good head for business, Katie. I can't wait to check out that arena—but not tonight. You need to eat and then get some rest."

Through clenched teeth, she gritted out, "I said I'm fine."

Okay, apparently Katie still didn't like being told what to do. Never had, although she'd certainly let her father boss her around.

"Please excuse my manners." She took a deep breath and glanced at the bags of food on the seat between them. "Why don't you come in the house and eat before we head out to the barn to bed down the horses? I'll show you the arena in the morning."

While the two of them soon would be sharing the same roof, he'd rather they shared a bed. She might have gotten over him without a backward glance, but he still wanted her desperately. Even though her resistance toward him made it clear nothing was going to come of it, he looked forward to being with her for a few more days before heading back home to Tennessee.

He followed her across the yard to the back porch until she stopped short after spotting the broken window. "I'll fix that tomorrow!"

"Why did you have to break the window? The door wasn't locked."

"Like hell. The deadbolt was locked because I reached in and turned the key."

"Why would I leave the key in the lock on the inside of a double-cylinder deadbolt? Wouldn't that defeat the purpose of having one?"

"Well, now that you mention it, I was wondering the same thing."

She must have forgotten that she'd left it in there. Confusion was common after an episode like she'd had.

"I was surprised you didn't replace the door with the siding and windows, too."

"It's original to the house and gives it a lot of character," she said, preceding him inside. He'd still like her to update that lock. Damned things could get people killed.

He followed her into the kitchen, his feet sticking to the floor near the fridge. "If you point out where your cleaning supplies are," he began, "I'll mop again around the fridge. It's still sticky from the apple juice that spilled."

"I can do it."

"You need to take it easy."

She stared at him a long moment before pointing to the pantry near the hallway. "Thanks. You'll find what you need in there," she said.

They worked side by side with their separate tasks, and she pulled out a can of Zevia-brand ginger ale. "Sorry I don't have anything but diet soda sweetened with stevia. Would you prefer I make some tea?"

"No. I'll try that stuff."

"If you're used to drinks with sugar or artificial sweeteners, stevia's an acquired taste. I learned about it in Jasinda Wilder's *Big Girls Do It Running*. The Wilder Way helps me regulate my glucose. Although I don't follow it strictly, it's helped a lot."

"Never heard of the soda or the book, but nothing ventured, nothing gained." They sat across from each other at the oval table by the window, and he watched as she removed the breaded coating from her chicken breast. He took a sip of the soda and tried not to cringe. The bubbles tickled his nose, but on the second taste, it started to grow on him. "Not bad, but having been raised on sweet tea, it might take a little doing to win me over completely."

"I'll make a pitcher for you tonight that you can drink tomorrow. And have your mashed potatoes and gravy. I avoid white starches now, but it won't bother me to watch you eat them."

She did seem to be making healthy choices in her diet. Maybe today had been a fluke. Had his phone call thrown her off? He remembered Mom getting a call from Tanya that she was getting married, which sent her into such a tailspin she'd had an episode, forgetting to eat or take her meds regularly. He hated to think that Katie had been that upset by his returning.

"So how many students do you have?" He wanted to know more about how she'd turned this place around.

"I have eight who are serious, and a couple of others who just like coming out for recreational riding. I'm also boarding horses for several others, which helps."

"How do you run this place with only one hand?"

She averted her gaze, making him wonder if he'd ventured into an area that was off-limits. Did she have unpaid help, too—someone she was serious about? "Never mind. None of my business."

"Oh, it's not that. Miguel and I manage. So if you're hinting at whether I'm seeing someone romantically, this farm doesn't leave me any time to date."

Good. "How many horses do you have?"

"After this spring's foals, thirty-seven."

"That's amazing, but a lot of work to keep up with." How did only two full-time people handle it all? "For at least the next several days, put me to work. Anything that needs repairing or maintenance besides the window over there?"

She nibbled on her lower lip, making him want to do the same. "A fence was damaged in a windstorm Saturday night. I'd love some help with that. And I've learned not to turn down help mucking stalls. It's a never-ending chore, and..."—she glanced away—"...the, ah, student who helps me with things like that when Miguel's away is at camp this week."

"I'm sure anyone who loves horses is happy spending as much time as possible around them—either end."

She laughed, her eyes lighting for the first time since he'd seen her awake in the hospital. "This one does it under duress from her mother at times."

"Ah, a mom needing to help pay for riding lessons, maybe?"

The smile faded as quickly as it had come. "Something like that." She finished her chicken and green beans and took her plate to the sink. "Thanks for mopping up the juice and, again, I'm glad you arrived when you did."

They were back to being formal. Maybe over the next few days, he'd get her to relax with him again. He intended to try his damnedest to see that smile and maybe even hear her laughter once more.

Lordy mercy, he'd missed that.

He finished his supper and joined her at the sink, feeling the warmth of her body and inhaling her intoxicating scent. The scent of lemongrass came through now, with a lingering hint of apple juice. "Before we head out to the barn to take care of the horses, why don't I put some cardboard in that window pane until I can fix it tomorrow? Just be sure you don't leave the key in the lock again, because cardboard will be even easier to break through than the glass."

Katie put her hands on her hips and glared at him before giving a pointed look at the door. "If I'd left the key in the lock, wouldn't it still be there?"

He glanced over at the lock and shook his head; the key was indeed gone. "Strange. I didn't remove the key in all the commotion." He gave a mental shrug and turned his focus on her again. "Still, I wouldn't leave a baseball bat on the porch, either, if I were you. When on earth do you find time to play sports?"

"Um…" She wouldn't look at him. "It belongs to one of the kids who rides here. Sometimes they like to practice in the field out back."

Her fields were too hilly for anyone to play ball on. That was the second or third time she'd appeared to lie or leave something out of her answers. Not the old Katie at all.

One thing was certain. He planned to stick around long enough to find out what she was hiding.

Chapter Three

A buzzing sound infiltrated her sleep. Kate's head throbbed as if squeezed in a vise. She rolled over and squinted at the alarm clock. A little after seven o'clock.

Seven!?! She should have been up two hours ago. She'd never finish her chores before her first lesson started at nine.

Kate tossed off the blue chenille bedspread and sat up on the side of the mattress, but the room swam before her, keeping her from standing. Memories of yesterday, with Travis Cooper invading her space, her home, her life, came flooding back.

The emergency room had been bad enough, but she'd been too exhausted to deal with the guilt of asking him to sleep in the barn apartment after all he'd done for her yesterday, so he'd slept on her couch. She'd managed to send him out to the barn first last night, which gave her time to rid the living room of photos and other items belonging to Chelsea. Had he snooped around anyway? He'd called upstairs to her in the middle of the night to make sure she was okay when he'd no doubt heard her alarm, but she'd assured him her sugar was fine. He'd have had no reason to have seen Chelsea's room.

You need to tell him about her.

No, I don't.

Since when did her conscience start sounding like Daddy?

What she needed to do was show him around the new buildings today. He'd seen the barn last night when he'd helped her bed down the horses, but her goal today was to give him so many jobs to do that she'd hardly see him.

In the beginning, her greatest worry was that Travis wouldn't be able to give up his dreams to be a father, but her dad had been the one to plant ideas of custody battles and such in her mind all those years ago. She feared him taking Chelsea away. If Travis opted to fight for custody, a judge might allow a twelve-year-old to choose which parent she wanted to live with.

Lately, Kate and Chelsea had been having the typical mother-daughter conflicts, mostly over cleaning her room and doing her homework without waiting until the last minute. At least Kate assumed they were the norm. Her own mom hadn't stayed around long enough for Kate to know, but the parents of her students hinted at similar issues at home.

Travis might decide to have nothing to do with Chelsea. But if he did want to be a father to her, would he be content to see her on the occasional weekend or vacation? Or would he want her all to himself, shutting Kate out?

What makes you think the worst, Kate?

She shivered. Good heavens, she could swear Daddy was in the room with her, talking to her. She hugged herself and looked around.

"Daddy?" she whispered then shook her head. She was officially losing it. Besides, even if her father's spirit could talk to her, he sure wouldn't be encouraging her to think well of Travis. Her father had been one to fuel the flames of her fears, not to douse them.

She rubbed her arms and took a deep breath, mentally prodding herself. Her real worry—the thing that kept her up half the night—was her fear that Chelsea would find out about Travis and become so angry at her for keeping her father out of her life that she'd reject her.

The only way to keep Chelsea to herself would be to send Travis away before he learned about her existence. Kate still knew nothing about him or why he'd really come here. Was he settled now? Dependable still? Did he keep his commitments?

She was sure her mother had been all those things at first, and still, she'd abandoned Kate and her father. Life carried no guarantees. While

Kate might be able to handle abandonment again, Chelsea was just a kid.

She needed to show Travis that she didn't need his help and send him on his way. But that was the opposite of what she'd planned to do last night by keeping him busy. Her head hurt from trying to consider every angle.

Drawing a deep breath, she walked into the bathroom and tested her glucose. Two-forty-four. Way too high. The low blood-sugar episode reversed itself to the extreme. She needed to get her body under control again—sooner rather than later—so that Travis's time here could come to an end.

I want my calm, boring life back, please.

Normally, controlling her diabetes was relatively easy.

Downstairs, she saw little evidence of Travis when she walked into the living room to see if he was still sleeping. He'd folded up the sheets she'd given him to make his bed and left them over an armrest. She didn't remember him being so neat in college. While she could have let him sleep in Daddy's old room, which was now her guest room, she didn't want Travis to get too comfortable. She wanted him gone.

How had he fared on the sofa last night? At over six feet, no doubt Travis would have had his feet hanging over the armrest of her sofa, or he would have slept propped up with pillows on the other end. In college, he slept in his boxers.

Don't picture what he slept in while he was in your living room.

Of course, the memories of waking up beside him the last month and a half that they'd dated had been imprinted indelibly on her brain.

Wondering where he might be, she returned to the kitchen and glanced through the window over the sink. His truck remained parked in the circular drive, so he hadn't left. Supposing he'd turn up sooner or later, she injected her insulin into her upper abdomen and decided to deal with him later. She had stalls to clean and horses waiting to be fed.

The cardboard on the door's window reminded her of last night.

He'd wanted to barricade the door with the heavy butcher block, but she'd convinced him that the deadbolt would suffice—without the key in it. He'd lived in the city too long. Oh, sure, there was crime in rural areas, too, but far fewer thugs per square mile out here as Daddy used to say.

She had to admit having Travis downstairs had given her an odd sense of security. She'd slept soundly, without a care.

Inside the barn, she entered the tack room only to stop abruptly. *Have mercy.*

Grinning widely and eyeing her from head to toe, Travis carried a bucket filled with oats, his bicep straining the sleeve of his plaid shirt and looking ready to burst the seams. "Mornin', darlin'." That smooth-as-whiskey voice rumbled over her, and Kate swore she was twenty years old all over again.

Travis's short brown hair stuck up every which way, as though it hadn't been brushed or he'd run a hand through it, the way she wanted to right now. He sure did fill out his western-cut shirt perfectly, and the light green tone of it made his hazel eyes stand out. His tight pecs gave way to a trim waist and an abdomen that no doubt looked like a washboard. He'd always been attractive, but he'd honed his body to perfection. Not to mention working in the sun, judging by his tanned hands. Maybe he didn't delegate from his engineering office.

A heaviness pooled in her lower belly. Was it a reaction to her insulin shot in the abdomen or the potent man standing in front of her? Her body responded in ways it hadn't in years. No man had ever turned her on as much as this one had, but she needed to fight that attraction. *Darlin'?* No one but Travis had ever called her that. "I'm not your darling. What are you doing?"

"I've mucked all the stalls," he began, making his way toward her. She fought the urge to take a step back, standing her ground instead. "Time to feed the horses their breakfast. How're you feeling? Have you eaten?"

She'd be better if he wasn't in here, although he'd kept her on schedule today. "I'm fine. You didn't need to do that, but I appreciate it. I overslept." She reached for the bucket, but when she tried to take it from him, their hands brushed. A jolt of electricity flashed up her arm.

Simmer down.

When he didn't relinquish his hold, she backed away and watched as he walked back into the aisle between the stalls. She shouted how much to feed the first horse.

"You already have the instructions on each stall."

Oh yeah. She'd done that because Chelsea had trouble remembering the amounts and she sometimes had her friends Jason and Lidia Brodie help out.

Kate retrieved a currycomb and headed to Buttercup's stall, since Travis appeared to have been up long enough to cancel out her tardiness. Momentarily rid of him, she let the calming strokes relax her as she talked to the most senior horse in her barn. The chestnut mare had been a gift from her father when Kate had turned ten. In turn, Kate had continued that tradition by giving Chelsea her own horse, Jasmine, at the age of six.

During Kate's teen years, she'd taken to calling the horse B.C., thinking Buttercup sounded too childish. The horse hadn't seemed to mind the name change and had served Kate well all this time as a brood mare. Now, at twenty-five, she made a wonderful, calming companion horse and a pleasure mount for novice riders.

B.C. shuffled gingerly around her stall, arthritis apparently doing a number on her joints this morning. "Looks like your day is off to a rocky start, too, old girl." Kate nuzzled her mane and neck, closing her eyes as she relaxed into the horse.

"I was happy to see you still have the old girl." At the sound of Travis's voice, Kate went back to combing the mare. While Travis hadn't felt comfortable being on her farm when they'd dated, mostly because of her father's dislike of him, B.C. and the other horses had accepted him.

Travis circled around the front of the horse and stroked the mare's nose. "Good morning again, girl."

She whinnied and nuzzled Travis's cheek. *Traitor.*

"Sorry I don't have any carrots with me, but I promise next time I'm in here, I'll stock up first." Ah, so he was still bribing her horse for its affection, same as he had back when he'd first visited the farm while they'd dated. Well, "bribing" was perhaps a bit harsh. He'd actually always had a rapport with B.C., more so than with the other horses on the farm. He'd had no background with horses, having grown up in a large family in South Louisville that couldn't afford the luxury of owning and boarding horses, but he'd been a natural.

Kate had to look away from Travis's strong hand caressing the mare's coat. The way he used to trace his fingers along her skin… "My foreman has a couple of horses on his farm in Franklin, Kentucky, an hour or so north of Nashville, but we haven't ridden in way too long."

"So, other than the times we rode here…"—*Oh, that didn't come out right*—"…you're saying your riding experience is still pretty much limited to those trail rides your family took during your summer vacations?"

He grinned, meeting her gaze. "I make up for my relative inexperience with a strong dose of enthusiasm." Considering how little he'd ridden, he'd always impressed her with his innate skill. "And I'm a very quick learner."

Kate ducked her head, avoiding that amused twinkle in his eyes. Was he reminding her of their first time together? Heat stole over her cheeks and throat. Yes, Travis Cooper was definitely a very quick learner.

There had been a time when she'd thought the two of them might one day run this place together, before Travis had left for his internship in New York and she'd given him his freedom.

Don't reminisce about impossible dreams.

If Travis ever found out about Chelsea, he'd want nothing more to do with Kate anyway.

*   *   *

Seeing his daughter so torn pained Ben to the core. When she discovered what he'd done, she would no longer be able to maintain the tight rein on her emotions that had helped her to cope with so much already. The crushing ache in his chest was worse than what he'd felt in the physical world, including the heart attack that had ended his life. She'd followed in his footsteps, almost to a T. How was he going to fix this without losing her love forever?

Perhaps there was a way to help Kate see that she didn't have to go it alone, even though he'd modeled that type of parenting to her for her entire life. He needed to fix this. Despite having done more than his fair share of meddling during his physical life, Ben wasn't clear on what he was allowed to do from here. Surely he could do something to help these two wake up and smell the coffee.

"Obadiah, why don't you spell out to me what the rules of engagement are from this side?"

"Damn the rules. All's fair in love and war." At the intrusion, Ben turned to find another spirit sitting next to him on the barn truss, much younger in appearance although he had an old-soul feel about him. "I didn't follow rules in life, and I sure as hell don't intend to start now."

"Who *are* you?"

"Danny's the name. I'm a former explosive ordnance disposal specialist with the US Army National Guard." He projected an image of himself dressed in his fatigues. "I used to be anyway."

Ben had been drafted into the regular Army, but didn't remember anyone by the name of Danny in his unit. "Did we serve together?"

"When were you in?"

"1968-1971."

"Not likely. I wasn't born yet."

Ben glanced down at Travis petting Buttercup and chatting with Kate and remembered Obadiah's words. "You served with *him* then."

"I did indeed. He was my sarge and later my best friend in the world. He made staff sergeant by his third tour, but I was medically discharged by then. I'd have followed that man to the ends of the earth. And beyond, obviously." Danny narrowed his eyelids, and his gaze bore right through Ben, not that there was any barrier to stop him. "You've got your work cut out for you, man, if you expect to get Trav to help reach your daughter. He's not very receptive to messages from us disembodied spirits."

"What have you tried so far?"

"Came to him in a number of dreams."

"No response?"

Danny shook his head. "None, except for the very last one. The one that got him to finally check on Katie yesterday—and not a moment too soon, either. He chalked all the others up to wishful thinking—or the nightmares of a grieving man." Danny sighed. "That man thinks about me *every* day, but I don't visit him in his dreams nearly that often."

"How'd you know I'm hoping he'll help me with Kate?"

"The Army's grapevine has nothing on the one up here. We don't even have to speak to know what's going on. I think the Powers That Be want us to find connections amongst ourselves so we'll have better success at whatever mission we're working on. Anyway, when I heard the name Travis Cooper, I knew I had to check you out. I'm trying to piggyback on your mission."

"Why?"

"Well, when I came to Trav in a dream a couple of days ago—urging him to come check on Katie—he finally listened. Or followed through, whether he heard me or not."

"She goes by Kate."

"I know you call her that, but I've only ever heard Trav call her Katie."

What difference did it make to Ben? "Well, whatever you said, he listened that time."

"Not because he actually thought it was me talking. Maybe he thought he was having a premonition." Danny shrugged. "In Iraq, he kept us out of harm's way a number of times by trusting his instincts."

"I think a lot of us had those kinds of experiences in combat. How many tours?"

"Two—until I was sent home with a Purple Heart and an empty boot. Trav completed three."

Danny remained quiet for a moment then pointed to the two of them below. "Anyway, here he is."

"So that explains why he showed up yesterday out of nowhere."

Danny nodded.

Ben sighed. "Unfortunately, I'm not sure Kate's all that receptive to *him*, embodied or not. She's one stubborn, independent woman."

"Sounds like Trav's perfect match, if you ask me."

They watched in silence a moment. "Why do you need to get through to him so bad?"

"He thinks I killed myself."

"You didn't?"

Fire spit from the spirit's eyes. "I'd never do anything like that."

"Sorry, but I hadn't met you until a few minutes ago. What makes Travis assume you did?"

Danny sighed. "Damned pain—both physical and mental—was too much that night. I self-medicated. Trav found me with a half-empty bottle of pain pills, but he didn't seem to figure out how much tequila I'd finished off in the kitchen before that. Autopsy said the combination killed me, but it wasn't intentional. I was actually having more good days than bad by then, mostly thanks to Trav and the guys at work. They gave me a sense of purpose again after losing my damned leg to an IED."

Ben glanced down, but the man appeared to be whole to him.

"Of course I'm whole. Why would I spend eternity with that broken-down body? I've been restored to an earlier model."

Ben smiled. He'd chosen to knock a couple of decades off his appearance, too. Not that the ravages of illness on the physical body were carried over into the afterlife anyway. "You know, he probably blames himself." Ben had lost more Vietnam vet friends to suicide than he wanted to count. He'd harbored that guilt about a couple of the guys who'd killed themselves—ones he'd been closer to than most. He should have been there for them, too.

"Oh, I know he does. Has some kind of savior complex that makes him think he can be there to rescue everyone who needs it. But having him believe that bullshit is killing me all over again."

"Why don't you try to get his attention with a scent? My Kate knows I'm around when she smells pipe tobacco. What scent would he recognize as being from you?"

Danny chuffed. "Nothing he'd likely want to smell again."

Ben laughed. He liked this fellow. Too bad Kate hadn't met some-one like him. Although if he had been heavy into booze and pills, well, maybe Travis was a better match. That man had a tight rein on himself that would be more what Kate needed. Strong, stable—why hadn't he seen that in him when the kids were dating?

Danny must be ignoring Ben's thoughts, because he continued, "Trav's not one to go to a psychic medium, either, so I can't reach out to him that way."

"It's too bad the spirit world and the physical one have to be so separated." Ben sighed. "Kate doesn't see me, either—and thinks it's her subconscious or her memory when she hears me—so I don't think I'd be able to relay a direct message to her to pass on to him." Both looked down on the earthly plane again in silence.

After a long while, Danny said, "I managed one change to the physical world and got that deadbolt key into the lock so Trav could make a hero's entrance to rescue the girl all Hollywood style. Maybe I can do something else like that."

"That was you? I wondered why she'd even locked it, much less left the key in the lock. I often reminded her to lock the door at night, but she rarely did so during the daytime."

"So any suggestions for how we can fix this?"

"We may not be able to."

"With all due respect, bullshit, sir. I've never backed down from a fight. Not even one with my best friend there." Danny laughed. "Drove Trav nuts when we first met in boot camp, but he managed to straighten me out enough to make it through." He sobered. "Trav needs to know the truth."

"What difference does it make if he knows it wasn't suicide? You're still dead to him."

A pained expression crossed his face. "Yeah, but as long as he keeps blaming himself for my death, he's never going to get on with his life. Right now, there's something he needs more than anything else." He cast his gaze down at Travis. "That woman—your daughter—holds the key."

Danny was right. Ben's determination had never been greater than in this moment. "Now we just have to figure out how to make that happen."

Chapter Four

K ate didn't know why she started thinking about her dad, but she did. Shaking off her melancholy mood, she tried to regain her focus on her primary goal. "Thanks for your help this morning and yesterday, Travis, but there's no need for you to hang around any longer. I have everything under control again."

"If I didn't know you so well, I'd think you were trying to get rid of me, Katie."

Obviously, he didn't know her as well as he liked to think he did. "Everyone calls me Kate."

"You'll always be Katie to me."

Sadly, she'd never be anything to him. She'd blown that chance when she'd made her decision about Chelsea. But hearing him still calling her by the nickname melted her to the core. From his lips, Katie felt like a special endearment.

"Listen, I have work to do before my first student arrives and a busy day ahead." Of course, he'd already taken care of most of her chores out here—and he knew it.

"Have you eaten breakfast yet?" he asked.

Damn. She'd forgotten all about it. If she kept this up, she'd be back in the hospital by this afternoon. The man had her rattled, for sure.

"I plan to eat as soon as everything's done here."

"What else needs doing?"

"Do all the horses have their feed?"

"Yep."

He'd already mentioned cleaning all the stalls. "Well, it sounds like you've taken care of most of it."

"What did I miss?"

Begrudgingly, she conceded the point. "Nothing, I guess."

A smile lit his face, making his eyes twinkle in a way that caused her heart to ache for the future that she'd denied them. And now she intended to deny herself again, because any chance of a happy life for them was long gone.

"Great, because I'm half-starved." Unfazed by her sour disposition, he came around B.C. and took her hand. Even though she wanted to avoid further close contact with him, the man's nearness short-circuited her brain. Without any resistance on her part, he led the way out of the stall, bolting the door behind them.

"What would you like for breakfast?" she asked. She'd be going heavy on the fats and proteins today to get her sugar back under control.

"Omelet sound good to you? I checked the fridge earlier, and you have the makings of a pretty good western one. I'd be happy to help."

Having someone cook for her sounded like total bliss. "I usually just scramble eggs and fry some bacon or sausage patties and call it a meal. When did you start cooking so fancy?"

"I know this is going to sound strange, but in the Army National Guard."

"When were you in the Guard?"

"I joined on the anniversary of 9/11." She wanted to ask him what had prompted that decision, but he continued. "Had to be self-sufficient in the barracks, and my buddies didn't seem to care whether they ate MREs or real food."

"MREs?"

"Meals Ready to Eat, but don't let the name fool you. Might be good while you're sitting on a sand dune in Iraq, but on base, I preferred something closer to Momma's cooking, so I learned to do it myself while on leave."

She met his gaze when they reached the porch as he waited for her to precede him up the steps. "You did a tour in Iraq?"

"Three, actually." The smile faded from his face, and she decided not to ask him for fear she'd hear the horror stories. The thought of Travis being in harm's way made her lose her appetite.

But she found herself curious about his time in the service. "Where did you train?"

"Fort Leonard Wood in Missouri."

"You're still active duty?"

He shook his head. "Reserves."

"That means you could get called up again."

"If I'm needed, I'd gladly serve. That's what I've trained for all these years."

"I never knew you were interested in military service. You seemed so set on a career in civil engineering." She squeezed his arm. "I'm glad you made it home." She meant it, but the thought of him deploying again scared her to the core.

"A lot of guys didn't. And nobody comes back the same." She wondered how the war had changed Travis. Outwardly, he appeared to have more confidence, and his service probably explained the changes in his physique, which had been pretty hot when she'd known him in college, but was smokin' now.

"I'm sorry anyone had to go through that, but thank you for the sacrifices you and your buddies made for us all." Trite, but she hoped he knew she was sincere. "My dad served in Vietnam, and it affected him for the rest of his life."

"So did my dad."

"Daddy never talked about it to me."

"Mine only opened up after I'd done my own time overseas."

"Too bad they never met. I bet they could have helped each other by sharing some of those experiences." Too late she realized her actions had kept the two vets from meeting.

That thought must not have been lost on Travis, either. He glanced down at his work boots before meeting her gaze once more. "Let's go eat before your first student arrives."

She walked through the door first. Both washed their hands at the kitchen sink before she started pulling ingredients out of the fridge. She flashed back to just a day earlier when she'd passed out on this spot.

"Thanks again, Travis. I'm glad you were here yesterday." The words came out before she thought about how they might sound, but honestly, if he hadn't found her so soon, she might not be having this conversation with him. The thought of Chelsea having to deal with her death gave Kate nightmares.

Then take better care of yourself, Kate.

Her daddy's voice echoed in her mind. He'd been on her daily during that first rocky year, and she could almost hear him again now. Monday's episode was reminiscent of some of her lapses during the first year she'd been diagnosed after it came back postpartum.

While she fried the bacon, Travis chopped mushrooms, a tomato from her windowsill, a bell pepper, and half an onion.

"How many eggs for each omelet?" she asked.

"Three."

She retrieved the eggs and a block of cheese from the fridge and broke six eggs into a bowl. Being domestic with Travis made it feel as though they had been doing this for years.

Stop it. Just stop it.

She began scrambling the eggs. Kate didn't want or need a man. She'd let her father control her every move the first twenty-three years of her life, and she didn't intend to give any man that much power over her again.

"Katie?"

She stopped and looked up. "Yes?"

"I think those eggs are about pulverized." He grinned, and she glanced down to see that she'd nearly whipped them into oblivion.

"Sorry." Needing a diversion, she went to the stove to turn the bacon. "Soft or crispy?"

"Extra crispy, please."

Just the way she liked it.

Stop finding ways you're still compatible.

With the bacon finished, he took over and sautéed the veggies and mushrooms in the bacon grease while she pulled the cheddar through the slicer and set the plate next to the skillet.

While setting the table, Kate said, "So tell me what you've been doing since the last time I saw you."

"That's a lot of territory."

"I'm in no hurry." She wanted to know what his life had turned out like.

"I joined the Army instead of returning for senior year."

All this time, she'd thought he'd transferred to a university in New York to finish his degree.

"Then I started a construction firm in Nashville."

That, too, surprised her. "Following in your dad's footsteps?"

"More or less, but far enough away from his business that we're not in direct competition. I hire fellow vets, and we do a lot of school and community projects in addition to high-end homes."

She remembered him mentioning being there while in the ER. "Why Nashville?"

"One of the men in my combat engineer squad talked nonstop about how wonderful it was there." A shadow came over his face. "When he didn't come home, I…" His voice drifted off with a catch.

"I'm so sorry." Travis would have felt each casualty personally.

He waved off her concern. "At first, I wanted to be around to help his wife and kids if they needed anything. Well, one thing led to another."

Had he married her? Or was he referring to sticking around and starting his business? He didn't wear a ring, but a man who worked with machinery often didn't.

What do I care? If he's married, then he's off-limits, which will make it even easier to send him home.

Travis cooked the eggs on one side before flipping the omelet and filling it with veggies and cheese.

"I see you like your omelets well-cooked, too."

"Just like my bacon and my steaks."

She smiled. "I remember how you like your steaks from all our cookouts." Growing serious again, she had to force herself not to pursue a line of questioning concerning his marital status. Instead, she asked, "How many people does your firm employ?"

"Thirty-two at the moment, including some subcontractors. Small potatoes compared to what I'd planned on in college, but turns out I prefer it this way."

He actually sounded happy. Her throat closed up. Had she ever known Travis at all? She'd gotten everything wrong. *Everything.* And she'd ruined all three of their lives. Her eyes grew hot, burning with unshed tears. She should have told him about the pregnancy instead of pushing him away and deciding what was best for all of them. While that might have kept him from going into the military, and who knows how his absence would have affected the lives of so many in his squad, at least Chelsea could have grown up having her father present. And what about the degree he'd worked so hard for? Had that also been cast aside?

There was no undoing her actions now, but how could Travis or Chelsea ever forgive her?

How could she ever forgive *herself?*

His hand warmed the small of her back. "Hey, what's wrong?"

She blinked a few times to clear away the tears. "Sorry. I'm just happy you found something you obviously love doing." What was one more lie between them?

"Apparently, we both have."

She nodded. "I put in a lot of effort into making my mark on this place." *But I wish you'd been beside me, too.*

He flipped half the egg mixture over to cover the insides and let the cheese melt. "The farm appears to be doing great. Good for you on offering riding lessons. I remember you wanted to make that happen."

He'd been the only person she'd shared that dream with back in college. That he remembered it all these years surprised her.

"Yours is almost ready."

She needed to get moving. "What would you like to drink?"

"Coffee."

"Still drink it black?"

He grinned. "Is there any other way?"

While starting a pot, she said, "I have two promising pupils. The older one is going to the Lexington Junior League in July to compete in several performance classes. That will be the highest level she's competed at."

"That's great! You must be really proud."

"I am. Melissa and her horse started here when she was seven. She's really put her heart into it." She wouldn't mention that the younger of the two was their daughter. Chelsea would have loved to compete, but Kate couldn't afford to give her one of the better horses. Those needed to be trained and sold to keep the farm afloat. Instead, she'd given her Jasmine, a competent mount, but one that would never make it to the level at which Chelsea dreamed about competing.

He scooped an omelet onto her plate and started on the next one while she filled two cups with coffee and carried them to the breakfast nook overlooking the arena barn. On her way back to retrieve her plate, he asked, "Would you like any fruit with yours?"

"Nah, I'm good."

She didn't want to mess up her sugar, so she'd stick with the omelet. "Melissa's my first student of the day. She'll be here in about twenty minutes." Kate would keep an eye out for her through the window.

"Don't rush your breakfast."

"I always eat fast anyway."

They ate in silence until curiosity got the best of her.

"Do you have any regrets about the way your life turned out, Travis?"

He set down his fork but continued to chew, then took a leisurely sip of his coffee. She couldn't eat or drink another thing until he answered her.

"Only one."

* * *

Travis let those two words hang in the air as he watched Katie's eyes open wider before a telltale blush crept into her cheeks. She knew darn well what he was going to say, so he didn't give her the satisfaction.

Her newfound independence ought to please him. He'd always thought her father had used a mixture of strong-arm tactics and guilt to keep her from standing on her own two feet. She'd blossomed since then. Clearly, she didn't need him any more than she had needed her dad. She'd just lacked the opportunity to make her own decisions without any bossy men telling her how to live.

He hadn't really seen himself as domineering, though. He'd tried to encourage and support her in any decision she'd made—except the one to dump him.

So if he wasn't needed, why didn't he leave today and go home where there were guys who did need him? As a big brother to Clint and his triplet sisters, he'd gone through almost his entire life being called on by one person or another for something. Not that he wanted Katie to lean on him in the same way his siblings did. And he still hadn't gotten an answer about why she'd cut him off in the first place.

"How about you, Katie?" She blinked as if she didn't know what he meant. *Come on, baby. Give me a bone. Tell me you regret breaking up with me.* "Any regrets?"

She shrugged and glanced away. "It's hard to grow up without having more than a few."

So much for that lame attempt at getting her to admit what he wanted to hear.

"It's nice being able to catch up on old times, and I don't need to be back home until Sunday night." He really had no specific time to be back, but wanted to find out if she'd really kick him out on Sunday morning. "My foreman, Jackson, can handle just about anything that might come up, and I'm only a few hours away in case of an emergency back home."

The momentary scowl she shot his way told him she didn't want him to stick around even that long. While she might not need him to help run this place, after yesterday's episode and today's nearly missed breakfast, he wasn't sure she was taking care of her health yet. She did need him; she just didn't know it.

Yet.

"I don't mind sleeping in the apartment in the barn that we talked about last night, but I'd love to hang around a few more days."

"Why?"

He shrugged, trying not to let on how much it hurt him that she still wanted nothing to do with him. Wishful thinking? Did he really hope to win her back in the next few days? Given how she'd resisted him until now, there wasn't much hope of that happening.

But dammit, he had to try. "Why not?"

Picking up her plate with the half-eaten omelet without responding, she scraped the remainder into the trash bin and refilled her mug. Had she eaten enough to fuel her until lunch? Her back turned to him still, she said, "You've pretty much seen everything there is to see."

No, she definitely wasn't going to invite him to stay. That was neither here nor there. He didn't have to leave Midway until Sunday night. He just hoped she wouldn't bar him from the farm. Not only did he need to be near Katie, but being around her horses had a healing effect on his soul.

And after losing Danny to suicide five months ago, he needed a change of routine to help keep the nightmares at bay. Danny had been doing so well and working hard on the latest build. How had Travis not seen how depressed his buddy had become?

"There's that window to fix," he said, pointing to the door. She nodded, reluctantly. "Consider me unpaid labor. I'll work for a place to sleep and meals." He didn't intend to have her slaving over the hot stove for him, though. Some of those meals would be in romantic booths at local restaurants. "Katie, I know this may not make sense, but this place will be therapeutic for me. I could use some downtime."

She turned to face him, cradling her mug. "Horses can be great therapy. If that's what you need, Travis, then please use the barn apartment for the next few days. It's air conditioned. But I'm sure you'll want to be in Louisville Sunday for Father's Day."

"The apartment sounds perfect." He wouldn't say anything more about Sunday. He'd been with Dad a few weeks ago, so they weren't expecting him to show up physically so soon. His plans depended on how things went here the next few days, but he wouldn't tell her that. Meanwhile, he'd prove himself useful around here.

He stood, gathering up his dirty dishes. "Keep me busy. Make a list of what needs doing." Travis didn't know how to be idle. He rinsed his plate and mug and left them in the sink. "First thing, I need a tape measure to order a replacement pane."

She glanced at the cardboard he'd placed in the broken window on the door. "Get receipts, please. I'll reimburse you."

He had no intention of charging her. Hell, he'd broken the window. "I'm also happy to take care of feeding the horses and cleaning the stalls, and I think you mentioned a fence needing repair. That's always easier with two people than one. But if there's anything else you need, just say the word."

Katie nibbled her lower lip, making him hard. He hadn't kissed her in so damned long, other than in his dreams. How would she react if he tried?

She'd probably punch him at this point. But he still had five days counting today—six, if he played his cards right and stayed on until

Sunday—to win her over.

"There *is* that fence to repair after a storm over the weekend. I've been putting it off until…"

It was a start. "Say no more. I'm your man." *And I will be again. Mark my words, Katie Michaels.*

"Besides the fence, I also lost a section of roof on the storage barn in the storm. I was going to wait on Miguel to help me fix that. Not to mention that I have an ornery stallion in the corral that likes to kick down fence rails. When he has his run of the pasture, he usually burns off that extra energy. So the sooner we can mend that fence and get him back out there, the better for my corral."

Travis couldn't wait to meet the beast. "Is he trained to riders?"

"Somewhat. But if you haven't ridden in a while, I might suggest one a bit easier to handle."

He grinned. "I'm sure I can manage. Hey, while you're doing your morning lessons, I'll head to town to pick up supplies. You need fence rails?"

"No. I keep plenty in the old barn for repairs."

"Good. I look forward to going for a ride, too. Maybe this evening?"

"Maybe. I have a lot of work to do."

"Don't forget you now have an extra pair of hands." When she glanced at his hands, he wondered if she remembered his touch on her skin. Were her cheeks growing pinker? He smiled. "Be thinking of anything else that needs fixing. It's only Tuesday. I'm at your service for the next several days."

"Until Sunday morning."

He shrugged noncommittally. She sure wanted him out of here by Sunday.

At first, she hesitated then nodded abruptly. "I'd better head out to the arena." Her gaze wandered to the doorway into the hall as though expecting someone to walk in.

"Sounds good. See you in a couple of hours."

After they finished the repairs, he'd show her he knew how to handle that stallion of hers—just like he knew how to handle a feisty woman like Katie.

Chapter Five

K ate wasn't Travis's boss—or his anything, for that matter. But she'd sure as hell make sure he was off this farm come Sunday morning. Chelsea was due home around suppertime, and no way could the two of them meet.

But was that really what was best for her daughter? How many times had Chelsea asked about her dad only to be told he was a fellow college student who had been out of the picture by the time she was born? Kate's stomach knotted. Was that really fair to Chelsea? To Travis?

She just didn't know if she could upset life as she knew it. While Travis still seemed like a good man, and a responsible one, she knew next to nothing about him. He could have a wife and children down in Nashville. Then again, he'd given her looks no honorable married man would.

Again, none of her business, and she had no intention of bringing up the subject with him. She needed to think of him as the unpaid handyman he wanted to be—nothing more, nothing less.

Melissa and Miss Pickles worked tirelessly in the morning session. Her top student had hopes of winning at their third qualifying event in Ohio and going on to the Junior League and maybe even Louisville this summer.

Next came Abbie, one of her infrequent students. Having Travis watch Kate put the girl and her horse through their paces after he returned from the store to get the window pane was intimidating at first. But Kate found her focus, and they had an intense session working on a bad habit Abbie had developed of allowing her horse to duck out, or cut corners, in the arena. At the end of the session, Abbie's mother indicated that she wanted her daughter to start showing Moonbeam this summer.

"I'll work out a training schedule and see if there are some beginner's classes in any regional shows for her to enter." Kate would ask Travis to install tailboards in Moonbeam's stall to prepare for the horse's tail training. After all, one of the hallmarks of Saddlebred horses in the arena was their long flowing tails standing erect. She didn't want to undo all her hard work in bracing their tail muscles by having them rub them against the walls of the stalls.

Abbie and Moonbeam had a long way to go, but with determination, they'd make it. Chelsea wouldn't be happy to hear a riding friend close to her age was going to be doing performance competition. Kate wished she could afford a decent show horse, too, but it wasn't going to be possible unless Kate trained or bred a world champion and her reputation went through the roof.

When Abbie led her horse out of the arena, Kate turned toward her office.

Travis stepped away from the fence rail he'd been leaning on. "You're very patient."

She'd somehow managed to block out thoughts of Travis during Abbie's lesson. She'd had a lifetime of experience in shutting out things she didn't want to deal with or face. She turned to him and smiled. "Thanks. It takes patience by the boatload some days."

"Melissa worked hard to please you during that first session."

"She wants to win her class in two weeks so badly I think she'd walk through fire if I asked her to."

"When's your next lesson?"

"Not until two. We should have plenty of time to repair the rails in that fence beforehand."

"Sounds like a plan." He placed his hand on his stomach. "That omelet is sitting here like a rock right now. I can use a workout."

No doubt his abs were rock hard, too. *Stop picturing his abs.*

"Hey, if you think we can spare a few minutes first, I'd love a quick tour of the arena before we get to work, unless you need to eat something now."

"I was just about to go test." She pulled a protein bar out of her pocket. "I keep these with me when I'm on the go. I can grab one for you, if you'd like."

He shook his head. "I couldn't eat another bite. But if we have time after doing the repairs, how about we head to Midway and grab some lunch? I don't want you missing any more meals on my watch."

The last thing Kate wanted was to be seen hanging around with Travis in Midway. "Please, yesterday was a rare lapse in control. Stop worrying about me. Besides, it's best if I eat at home, at least until my sugar's stable again."

"Oh, I didn't think about that."

"Restaurants can be a minefield." She'd long ago grasped what to avoid when eating out, but he didn't need to know that. Drive-through was one thing as far as visibility, but sitting in a local eatery would be too risky. Chelsea had a lot of friends from church and school as well, and she didn't want to embarrass her daughter by having anyone asking nosy questions about the man Kate was with.

After excusing herself to go to the arena kitchen to test, she returned to his side with two bottles of water in hand, giving him one. "Thanks." He opened it and took a drink while she watched his Adam's apple bob.

"Your sugar okay?"

"Hmm?" She needed to stop ogling the man. "Oh, yeah. Fine." Wanting to steer the conversation away from her health, she said, "I guess you've seen most of the arena while watching me teach students this morning."

"Yeah, but I'd love it if you'd tell me about how it all came about, in case I someday have a client wanting one."

As they walked through the arena Katie gave Travis a quick overview of the construction materials used, her choice of footing, and time frame. She even offered to show him the blueprints and specs, if he wanted that much detail.

He could talk about construction for hours, but she needed to begin the work on the fence repair. Time to move the tour along. "Let's go up to my arena kitchen slash office slash award room." She led him to the opposite end of the arena and up the stairs to the multifunction area. "Some of the parents with children wait here during lessons." She pointed toward the table and chairs, but he was drawn to the trophy case.

"Impressive awards."

"I've had some fine horses come out of these stables—both in breeding and training—and a number of my students have gone on to be regional winners. One even made it to the World's Championship Horse Show last August, but didn't ribbon in her class."

They moved toward the case. "Who's Chelsea?" His question caught her off guard, and she stumbled, nearly falling. "Whoa, there!" Travis caught her by the elbow to steady her, which didn't help the alarm bells going off in her head.

"Why do you ask?" What had she missed? She hadn't come out here yesterday when she'd been eradicating evidence in the house, but the trophy case didn't have anything identifiable as Chelsea's. Besides, he was still too far away to read anything in the case if by chance Chelsea had put something in there.

"Yesterday, the dispatcher asked if Chelsea was okay when I called 9-1-1. I've been meaning to ask you ever since who she is."

"Oh, she's another student of mine." That wasn't a lie because she had been giving Chelsea lessons since she was four. She hoped he wouldn't wonder why the dispatcher—no doubt Sally, a friend since middle school—would only ask about Chelsea.

Breathe, Kate.

"Is she good?"

"Very. But…her mom can't afford a competitive show horse, or the costs of competing at the level she deserves. But she's shown at the county fair and done well. I don't think she's developed the fire in her belly, either, to train at the level she'd need to in order to do the show circuit." Still, Kate trained Chelsea as hard as the others who had better horses. If Kate could ever sock away enough money to keep an excellent horse for Chelsea to compete on, not to mention pay the exorbitant costs associated with showing it, Chelsea would at least be prepared.

While Jasmine was a wonderful companion horse, conformation issues with her forelegs toeing out would never make her competitive beyond the 4-H or academy beginner's levels. She could let her show on Chula, perhaps, but the last time Kate had sold one of Chelsea's training mounts, it had led to more hostility from her daughter than Kate wanted to deal with.

"It's frustrating to desire something that's out of your reach." His eyes smoldered as he stared at her, his gaze dipping to her lips.

Her skin started to tingle, and her mouth went dry. She knew that look. Was no topic safe between them? "Let's load up the supplies in my truck and head out to fix that damaged section of fence."

"We can take mine, if you'd like."

While his truck must be a dream to drive and certainly was half a dozen years newer than hers, she balked. "I have half the supplies and my toolbox in the backseat already. And I need to be back in time for my next lesson." Without waiting for him to argue, she started toward the house.

"Sure thing." He fell into step beside her.

"I'm just going to grab my hat. You might want one, too, given how high the sun is."

Twenty minutes later, they had loaded up the treated rough-cut rails and topper boards she'd creosoted last Sunday. Her cordless power tools and drill bits were already in the truck. Minutes later, they were surveying the damage. All three boards in this section had been split in half by the falling branch.

He wore a blue Kentucky Wildcats ball cap, which shaded his face somewhat. She'd picked up her straw cowboy hat to keep the sun off her face and neck.

Luckily, her hat hid her face somewhat, too, as heat crept into her cheeks as she remembered the time Travis visited one weekend at the end of spring break. They'd gone to the springhouse, ostensibly to check on fence damage from another storm. Instead, that night they'd dipped into the apple-pie moonshine her roommate Lidia had made and that Kate had stored in the springhouse. And then...

Don't think 'bout that night now.

As they worked together carrying the boards, supplies, and equipment off the bed of her truck, Kate couldn't help but notice the way Travis's biceps strained. When he walked back to retrieve her drill, she was riveted by the curve of his butt filling out his tight Wranglers. She nearly stumbled twice in the next few minutes because she couldn't take her eyes off him coming or going, but caught herself before he could wonder why she was so clumsy.

They removed the broken rails and screwed the first of three replacement ones into the creosoted posts. He insisted on setting the screws while she held the board. Her breath caught in her throat when his elbow brushed the side of her breast. She took a step back, knocking over the box of screws.

Sweat trickled between her breasts from the intense early afternoon sun, but Travis hadn't even broken a sweat. How could he look so cool in this muggy weather?

"Sure is a scorcher today," he said. He unbuttoned and removed his shirt, totally short-circuiting what was left of her brain. Oh yeah, he'd definitely spent some quality time in the gym. Hard, flat pecs gave way to a ripped eight-pack of abs, and all that taut, rippling muscle was covered by smooth, lightly tanned skin she longed to touch. "I didn't bring an endless supply of shirts. Can't have it getting too sweaty before I can do laundry," he explained as he hung it over a post away from the area where they were working. He grinned at her wickedly as he strutted back to where she stood, fully aware she was staring.

"Feel free to use my washer and dryer if you need to. They're in the garage."

"Thanks."

Travis was well-tanned so probably had little chance of getting a sunburn out here. Watching him work was a thing of beauty, but why was she acting like a teenager ogling a hunk's beefcake poster? For all she knew, he had a woman back home who got to enjoy this sight every night. Was he divorced? Single? Of course, no harm in her looking as long as she didn't touch. And no problem there because she had zero intention of acting out her mind's runaway fantasies.

She tried to limit her staring and chose to cast sidelong glances his way instead. A sheen of sweat finally glistened on his chest as he measured and cut the last board. So he wasn't superhuman and was equally affected by the heat and humidity. She held one end of the board for him as he screwed it into the post, trying not to notice the way his pecs bunched. Her battery-operated boyfriend might need some replacement batteries tonight. When was the last time she'd even had a desire to release any sexual frustration? Despite her feeble attempts to look away, like steel to a magnet, she was drawn back by his asking her to hand him another screw, a new bit, the tape measure. Every time their fingers touched, electricity sparked between them.

The sooner he put the topper boards on to finish off the repair, the better. While he didn't need her to stand so close, Travis insisted that she hold the board long after he'd placed enough screws in it that the board wouldn't possibly budge an inch. Again, his arm brushed against the side of her breast, and her nipple tightened in response. She prayed he couldn't see the effect he had on her.

Kate held her breath, waiting for him to finish before she filled her lungs again. He seemed to be taking his sweet time, and she finally let go. "I'll start packing up."

Half a minute later, he set down the drill. "There. All done." Travis picked his shirt off the post but didn't put it on.

Why didn't he wipe off the sweat, or at the very least cover his bare chest? "I have some clean, dry towels in the truck." She picked up the saw and loaded it into the backseat of her pickup before handing him a towel.

He grinned at her in a way that told her he'd caught her looking more than once and was well aware of the effect his body had on women.

On the drive back to the house, he said, "I'll need to take a shower while you're giving your next lesson. I didn't see one in the barn apartment, though. The claw-foot is nice, but I'm not much on tub baths."

Why she hadn't bothered to install a shower, too, was beyond her now. When she'd renovated the bathroom in the house, she couldn't part with the antique tub and had it installed in the barn apartment. She even snuck out and occasionally took baths in it when she was feeling particularly nostalgic.

Kate tried to remember if any of Chelsea's things had been left in the upstairs bathroom after her sweep of the house yesterday. "Let me just make sure you have some fresh towels and a washcloth first."

He nodded. "How many lessons do you have this afternoon?"

"Just one. Melissa's returning for another lesson to go over some problems she's having, but it might last a little longer than ninety minutes. I should finish by three-thirty, four at the latest."

"Great! I thought we could have a cookout tonight, but I'll need to go to the grocery. What do you feel like eating?"

"I'll make a list."

"I have a good memory as long as you don't go over twenty items."

Impressive. "I have rib eyes and sirloins in the deep freeze and tomatoes, peppers, and squash in the garden."

"I'll get fresh ones since it's late in the day to thaw them naturally. How about corn on the cob, baked potatoes—"

"I try to go easy on starches, but you go ahead and get anything you'd like."

"Sorry. I wasn't thinking." The cockiness from earlier disappeared.

"I don't expect you to remember all the finer points of a diabetic's diet."

"I didn't live with my mom when she was diagnosed, but try to be aware of her preferences when she comes to visit. Why don't we grill some steaks and veggies tonight?"

She was touched that he was so accommodating.

"Sounds delicious." All the more so because she didn't have to prepare and grill it. She checked in the garage and found she needed charcoal but not lighter fluid.

He grinned. "Maybe we can take that horseback ride after dinner. I'm looking forward to meeting that stallion you were talking about."

"Always up for a ride." He winked, which did strange things to her stomach.

Images of riding Travis flitted across her mind. Why did everything he asked or said come out with a double meaning? *Because my mind is on one thing and one thing only.*

She brought her focus back to him. "But if you haven't ridden in a while, are you sure you're up to the challenge? Angus is far from well-behaved, and he hasn't been ridden in ages."

"I'm always up for a challenge, darlin'." Somehow, she didn't think he was talking about Angus at the moment.

Travis left for the store. Kate tested, grabbed another protein bar to tide her over until their early supper, and met Melissa in the arena promptly at two. The lesson went by fast, keeping thoughts of Travis at bay. Her energy level low from not eating a proper lunch, she called it quits promptly at the ninety-minute mark. They had plenty of time to prepare for the Junior League.

While Melissa cooled down Miss Pickles, Kate crossed the yard and came inside the house to find Travis sitting at the table chopping veggies for the grill. "I'm starving," she said, reaching over his shoulder to grab a scrubbed button mushroom and pop into her mouth.

"Nibble on some cheese," he said, motioning toward the counter. "You need protein."

"Perfect." She nibbled on a few bites of cheddar to curb her hunger. "Let me hop in the shower then I'll help with whatever you need." Her clothes had become soaked with perspiration, despite the arena being air-conditioned. "I had to get a little physical with Miss Pickles to show her and Melissa what I want them to do differently."

Travis chuckled. "Sorry I missed it. I'll start the charcoal at four."

Having survived on protein bars all day, she was glad they'd be eating supper early. Kate went upstairs. After her shower, she tested her sugar then dressed in Wranglers and a form-fitting blouse, pausing to check out her reflection in the mirror. When was the last time she'd checked herself out like that?

You've got it bad, girl.

Nonsense. She simply wanted to look good for a guest.

When she returned to the kitchen, Travis was nowhere to be seen. She nibbled on some cheese until the door opened and he came in carrying an empty platter that he placed in the sink. Her mouth watered in anticipation. She hadn't taken time to grill in a long while. She and Chelsea would have to do this more often when she came home.

"Anything I can do to help?"

"Wanna pour the drinks? Sweet tea works for me. Lots of ice."

"Coming right up."

Fifteen minutes later, he brought in the steaks and vegetables. They sat down at the table, and he asked, "So your sugar's running steadier today?"

"It was a little high this morning but it's been under control since we came back from the pasture. Doctor said it could take a day or two to settle down after having a major drop like that."

Wanting to steer the conversation away from her health problems, she told him about some of the more amusing incidents with her students in the ring. When she ran out of stories, he said, "You looked like you really enjoyed yourself in the arena today."

"Training is one of my favorite things." Realizing she wasn't learning anything new about Travis, she asked, "Tell me a funny story from work." He often had some good ones about working summers with his dad.

He stopped chewing, growing serious. "I'm afraid it hasn't been a lot of fun the past few months." Suddenly, a smile spread across his face and his eyes lit up. "Last year, though, one of my crew pranked me good. We'd laid the brickwork frame for a new porch, and he asked me to go back to my truck for a nail set so he could hang the front door. I had the damnedest time trying to find it and finally gave up. When I returned to the front of the house, he and another guy were hanging the door using the same nail set I'd been looking for. Being a little pissed at them for wasting my time, I stepped onto a drop cloth spread across the porch and promptly fell about two feet into the hole we'd prepared for pouring concrete later on. Didn't even occur to me the hole was there I was so ticked off. Needless to say, the two of them were howling, especially Danny, who undoubtedly set up the prank."

"I'll bet there's never a dull moment with him around. Is it safe to leave him on his own at your worksites?"

Travis's smiled faded immediately, and he glanced away. "Yeah, well, I'd give anything to have him around again. He died five months ago."

Kate reached over to cover his hand and squeeze it. "I'm so sorry, Travis." She wondered if it had been a construction accident, but didn't want to pry. No wonder he hadn't enjoyed working these past few months. Memories of his crew member must haunt him.

"Me, too. Sorry to put a damper on the conversation, but I'd forgotten all about that day. Thanks for getting me to talk again about the good times we'd had."

"Anytime at all. Sometimes it helps to talk with someone who isn't as closely involved."

He gave her a pained expression, and she realized he might think she was referring to him and her, rather than her and his friend.

Hoping to change the subject, she said, "I'm looking forward to our ride tonight." She rarely had the opportunity to indulge except during the winter months.

Her anticipation of the ride probably caused her to eat too fast, but when she finished the perfectly cooked meal, she practically jumped up from the table. "Give me ten minutes to run upstairs and get ready. I just need to check my messages first," she said, pulling out her cell phone. "A student thought she might have to cancel tomorrow."

Travis chuckled, apparently amused at her enthusiasm. "Take your time. I'm going to get my boots out of my truck. I'll meet you in the tack room."

"You brought riding boots?" Daddy had called Travis "Cowboy" after he'd showed up in fancy western boots one weekend to take her out to dinner. Did he still wear the same style?

He grinned, melting her insides. "Let's just say I was hoping to get a chance to ride while I was here."

Horses. He wants to ride your horses, *not you.*

She wanted to ask him about his marital status, but that would only make him think she was asking because she was interested in pursuing something with him.

And she wasn't. She really wasn't. She couldn't be.

Because she'd lied to Chelsea. And Travis.

Taking a deep breath, Kate headed upstairs, listening to voice messages on the way. Good thing Chelsea wasn't allowed to call her except in an emergency. No news was good news.

After she finished checking her voice mail and changing into her riding gear, Kate went to the corral where she'd been keeping Angus until the fence could be repaired. He detested being cooped up in a stall. "How'd you like to go for a ride, boy?" He whinnied and shook his head, his luxurious black mane flying. "Promise me you'll be nice. Travis may not have a lot of experience with a devil like you. Now, you wait here while I saddle up Neptune."

Chelsea had been learning the solar system when Kate had brought the gelded bay to the farm, so Neptune it was.

Travis joined her in the tack room, and she stared down at his boots. If not the same pair from thirteen years ago, they were awfully close.

"Something wrong?"

Yeah. I'm in big trouble.

Travis's well-worn boots peeked out from his bootcut Wranglers, and a black cowboy hat ramped up his sex appeal even more. Nothing hotter than a cowboy fantasy, even for this Kentucky girl. "I'm used to jodhpur boots around here."

"Sorry. These are all I've got." He grinned at her, clearly not sorry at all. Did he remember her fascination with those boots all those years ago?

"Is Angus trained to a western saddle?"

"Both western and English, actually—and he hates them equally."

"Figures."

"If you'd rather ride a better behaved horse—"

"No. Angus'll do fine. Besides, I've ridden western mostly."

She pointed out the gear for the black stallion while gathering her own saddle, bridle, and bit for Neptune. She'd never have gotten Angus into a stall for this ritual. She hoped they'd have no trouble with the spirited horse. "It might be best if you and Angus had a little time together before you attempt to saddle him."

Travis picked up the tack. "Good idea."

"He's in the corral now, so at least you won't have to chase him down over seventy acres."

Travis laughed as he walked out of the barn.

Kate remained in the stall to saddle Neptune and led him outside about fifteen minutes later. Angus had fire in his eye, none too happy about seeing the bridle and reins no doubt. She was surprised to see the two of them in what appeared to be a standoff as Travis spoke softly to the horse. "You don't want to make me look bad in front of the lady, do you? Surely you've tried to impress a filly before."

She couldn't help but grin at his silliness. So Travis was trying to impress her? He seemed not to have changed a whole lot since they dated.

If so, that must mean he was single, right? And that maybe her cowboy fantasy could come true…

But first she needed to be certain she was right to bring him into her and Chelsea's lives before allowing him to get any closer. This time, her heart was part of a pair—inseparable from Chelsea's—and she wouldn't let them come away with a broken one.

She had to know for certain about the woman he'd moved to Nashville for. She couldn't risk assuming anything. "Travis, did you marry the widow you went to Nashville to check on?"

Oh heavens. That hadn't come out the way she'd intended at all.

Chapter Six

W/*hat?*

Travis turned to find Katie with her saddled horse, both ready to go. "Beg pardon?" *Married?* Only once before had he found himself close to getting engaged, much less married—and that was with this woman. He'd hoped to ask Katie after he'd completed that internship in New York. No way would he have asked her to give up this place, but he'd had some thinking to do that summer about whether he could be happy in a backwater town like this.

But she hadn't given him the time to sort that out.

And now she was questioning his character? Did she think so little of him that she'd suspect him of cheating on a wife? "Whatever gave you the impression I'm married?"

She shuffled her feet, avoiding his gaze at first, then squared her shoulders. "Well, you said you went to Tennessee to take care of your buddy's widow and kids. And that one thing led to another, so I just assumed…"

His laugh spilled out before he could catch himself, unable to be angry at her when she looked so serious yet still so adorable. Angus danced away from him, but Travis grabbed and held onto his halter.

She placed her hands on her hips and glared at him. "What's so damned funny?"

The stallion continued to try to take advantage of the distraction and escape, but Travis held firm before answering her. "No, I didn't marry Megan. Can't a guy watch over someone without getting married? Look at us." Okay, that might not be the best example, because he wanted her under his body in the worst way. Or on top. He wasn't picky.

"Since when were you looking after me?" The blush in her cheeks was too sexy for words.

"I'm doing it right now, darlin'. Making sure you're okay after what happened yesterday."

Her body relaxed. Why would she care if he was married or not—unless there was still some hope? Travis grinned. *Oh yeah.*

"Ready to ride?" she asked.

Now he needed to show her he was still good with horses so maybe she'd realize he'd be good for her, too. "Just got to get this bad boy saddled up."

"Whenever you're ready, I can help." She took Neptune's reins and wrapped them around the slats in the corral fence.

"No need. I've got this."

Careful, Trav. Don't get too cocky now.

Travis froze. Danny's voice was so strong he expected to be able to turn around and see him standing there. But he'd been fooled by his brain too many times to fall for his delusions today.

"You okay? You look like you've seen a ghost."

No, only heard one.

"I'm fine." Securing Angus with a lead rope to the same rail Neptune was tied to, he picked up the blanket and placed it on the stallion's back. The horse danced away from him again, but no way was this four-legged beast going to get the better of him in front of Katie.

"Simmer down now. We're just going for a ride. Nobody's gonna hurt ya, boy."

Angus eyed him suspiciously but, oddly enough, settled down for him. Piece of cake.

You never learn.

Travis shivered. He could *swear* Danny was right next to him. He glanced over his shoulder, pretending to focus on the saddle on the fence, then looked quickly back at Angus. Nothing. Always nothing.

What did he really expect? He had to stop doing this to himself. Danny was gone.

Moving slowly, Travis turned to lift the saddle off the fencepost and continued to speak softly to the horse as he swung it over its back. Angus started to buck. Travis grabbed his halter with a firm grip, and gently patted Angus's rump to calm him down, but that only riled him up more. Remembering how Jackson usually patted his excitable horses on the shoulder and down the flank, he tried that, which seemed to do the trick.

"Atta boy. Good boy."

Although Katie remained silent, probably not wanting to interfere with his budding dynamic with Angus, Travis was conscious of her presence. He reached under the horse's belly for the cinch and tightened it incrementally hoping not to rile Angus up again. So far, so good. With the saddle in place, he put on the bridle and reins, unclipping the lead rope holding from the rail. He turned to Katie for the first time. Did her wide-eyed expression indicate her appreciation for his ability to tame the beast?

"Now, let's go for that ride. Open the gate after I get up on him, Katie."

"Are you sure that saddle is on tight? Angus has a tendency to—"

He cut off her words with a shake of his head. "Nothing to worry about. I've got this."

She seemed dubious, but hadn't he already shown her that he could soothe the spirited animal? Maybe she'd even see parallels in the gentle hand he'd used with her, assuming she let things advance to that point with him again. He grinned and put his boot in the left stirrup, holding onto the saddle horn as he raised up and swung his leg over.

At last, Angus had accepted the unfamiliar weight on his back, and Katie shook her head in awe as she unbolted the gate. Suddenly, Angus screamed and began to kick with his hind legs as he tried to buck Travis off.

"Watch out, Travis!"

As if in slow motion, he felt himself sliding off the horse, saddle and all. He hit the clay ground with a thud.

"Are you okay?" she asked, coming to his side.

Nothing hurt but my ego.

"I tried to warn you. Angus tenses his abdominal muscles when being saddled, which expands the width of his chest enough it can make it difficult to get a tight cinch."

That's what you get for showing off.

"Stop trying to bring Danny back," Travis muttered to himself. He stood up, brushing the dust off his jeans. Taking the leather lead, he tied Angus to the rail again and readjusted the saddle.

"Talk to him again in soft tones. You might even walk him around a little to let him get used to having the cinch tightened under his belly."

He did what Katie suggested, wasting several more minutes of riding time to walk the horse and then retighten the cinch. But when he mounted, the saddle held him. Angus still wanted nothing to do with having his weight on his back, though and began kicking and bucking instantly. Travis white-knuckled the pommel with one hand while attempting to maintain his seat in the saddle.

"Whoa, now! I thought we were buddies." Leaning back to counterbalance himself against the horse's bucking, he spoke softly, trying to maintain a sense of calm. "Simmer down, Angus. We're just going for a ride with your mistress over there. Don't embarrass yourself." *Or me.*

But his words fell on deaf ears as the horse did his damnedest to throw Travis to the ground. A shrill whistle brought the beast to a sudden standstill, nearly toppling Travis anyway. He could have managed the horse without having Katie interfere.

"Wow. How'd you know to whistle like that?" Katie asked.

He turned to her, still trying to remain prepared for any sudden movements from Angus. "What do you mean? Wasn't that you?"

She furrowed her eyebrows and shook her head. "Maybe it was instinctual, but you clearly whistled. I heard you, and obviously, so did Angus."

He thought he heard Danny's laughter in his ear, as though he were on the saddle right behind him. Yeah, right. Either he was losing his mind or Katie was pulling a trick on him.

Listen here, Danny boy. If that really is you messing with me, why don't you do something useful like help me look good in her eyes instead of trying to get me killed on this horse?

Danny laughed again. *I whistled, didn't I? Calmed him right down.*

Delusional. Not only was he still talking to Danny in his head, but now he was carrying on two-way conversations.

Travis rubbed his eyes. Angus had calmed down, so he'd best show him who was in charge.

"Travis? Ready to go?" Katie asked.

He nodded. She motioned him through the gate before mounting her own horse, eyeing him cautiously. She probably thought he was nuts, too. "What's your horse's name?"

"Neptune."

"I always thought the planets were considered female."

"Don't judge. I let…one of my students name him. His white blaze reminded her of a celestial body, which got her thinking in that direction."

"Ah." She was really good with her students. Almost like a second mom. Katie would make a good mom someday. Thoughts of all the fun they could have attempting to achieve that status made him stir in places a little too tight to be comfortable in this saddle.

Within minutes, they were riding uneventfully across the meadow. The grass was drying up in the midsummer drought. At six o'clock, the air was still muggy and hot. Not that his maneuvers with Angus hadn't raised his body temperature a little, too.

"Thanks for suggesting this ride." Katie brought him back to the moment.

"My pleasure. I've missed it."

"Well, obviously, you haven't lost your touch."

It might have looked like he had Angus under control, but maintaining the illusion wasn't easy. The muscles in his forearms bunched as he continually fought to keep Angus under his thumb. *No more outbursts like that earlier one, old boy.*

"You're handling him better than anyone has before, including me. I usually give him his space and just let him earn his keep in stud fees."

"He's definitely more of a handful than that horse I used to ride out here—what was his name?"

"Cisco Kid."

"How could I forget?" He launched into a bad rendition of the seventies' song about how Cisco was a friend of his and soon had her laughing. When he saw they were approaching the spring, he let the song trail off. He glanced over at Katie, who appeared to be haunted by old memories, too.

Had they arrived here by accident, or by design?

Travis pulled up on the reins and grinned as the memory came back to him from that warm mid-spring night so many years ago...

* * *

"I don't think we should do this," Katie whispered. "Daddy will..."

"You're an adult, Katie. Don't let your dad control you for the rest of your life." Travis eased the shirt off her shoulder and placed his lips against her warm skin. They'd been dating for months now, but she'd always put the brakes on before going too far.

He wanted to bury himself inside Katie in the worst way. Her dad might call it raging hormones, but what they had was a lot deeper than that. She'd been driving him crazy since he'd sparred with her during a classroom debate in English Composition freshman year. That proved this attraction wasn't only physical, didn't it? The fire in her eyes and the way she'd managed to sway him and most of the others in the room to her cause had sparked something in him. Being a jock, he hadn't exactly surrounded himself with intelligent girls before, but Katie…well, she was different. It took him a year to convince her to go out with him, though.

Katie tugged on his belt loop, and he nearly came in his pants.

Have mercy!

His fingers undid the rest of the buttons on her shirt, and he peeled it down her arms, exposing her high, firm breasts encased in a chaste white cotton bra. His breathing became shallow as he took in the sight. Never had he wanted anything—or anyone—this badly.

Reaching behind her, he unclasped the hooks and pushed the cups away from her peaks only to replace them with his hands. She filled them nicely. Nothing wasted.

"Daddy's going to k—"

Placing a finger under her chin, he tilted her head back and covered her lips with his, not wanting to hear another word about her domineering father. The man hadn't thought much of Travis when she'd brought him out here for a first visit last month. Made Travis feel like manure under the old man's boot, in fact.

But, dammit, he and Katie loved each other, whether her father liked it or not. They were both twenty and didn't need anyone's permission to be together. If only she didn't kowtow to the man so much. She needed to stand on her own two…

Hell, he needed to quit thinking about Old Man Michaels. With his sweet, sexy Katie here with him on this hot spring night and a raging hard-on that had tormented him off and on since he'd met her, he had more important things to concentrate on.

Travis lowered Katie onto the old quilt they'd borrowed from the barn. He hoped it would cushion her from the smooth but hard limestone.

Sometime later, drunk on love this time, he stretched out beside her and stared up at the stars. He hated that he'd hurt her this first time, but hearing her scream his name as she'd exploded for him seconds before he'd come was just about the sweetest sound in the world.

"So beautiful," he said.

"I love how many stars you can see in the sky out here. Not like when we're on campus in the city. I hate being cooped up there."

"I'm not talking about the stars." He leaned on his elbow and traced a finger from the side of her forehead, down her cheek, around the curve of her jaw, and lightly over her lips. She smiled and kissed his fingertip.

"That was amazing," she said, but then her smile faded. At least he hoped there'd be a next time—and soon. He bent to kiss her. When he pulled away again, he whispered, "You surprised the hell out of me."

Katie's brows wrinkled. "You don't think I'll get preg—"

He shut off the thought by pressing his finger firmly over her lips. "It's our first time and we only did it once. I can't believe the condom broke." That had never happened before. Had he accidentally torn it in his haste to rip open the pouch with his teeth? "Don't worry. I'll get some new ones tomorrow."

She grew silent.

He curled a strand of hair behind her ear. "We'll be fine, Katie, but if you do get pregnant, you know I'll marry you."

"We already talked about waiting until we get our degrees and you establish yourself in your field first."

He grinned. "I like being established in *your* field."

She rolled her eyes and grinned. "You're so corny."

At least he'd stopped her worrying about the possibility of getting pregnant tonight. They had already discussed how it was best to wait and have children later, once their careers were solid and they could afford them. Not that he really thought in a million years she'd come out of tonight with a baby. Some people had no success even when all the calculations were right and the stars aligned.

She glanced away. "I'm going to have an uphill battle getting Daddy to like you. He isn't happy with anyone I date."

"He'll have to let go of you one of these days. It's not like you're going to abandon him or the farm. You love this place too much to leave it completely. I know and respect that."

She smiled, her body relaxing. "He'd love the offer you made to improve the outbuildings, if only he'd be open to making a few changes. Perhaps the place could turn a profit someday if we spruced things up some."

"And I built you an indoor arena to do everything you want to do," he reminded her.

She sighed then smiled. "Horses are expensive, so finding ways to offer services like riding lessons make sense."

"You're a natural instructor. No one can sit a horse as well as you, either."

Even in the moonlight, the blush in her cheeks was visible. She didn't have enough confidence in her abilities.

"I love to teach, especially kids. Who knows? Maybe that will be my calling, although I'll still need to do all the other things around here. Daddy isn't getting any younger, and his heart's not as strong as it once was."

Travis would never get her to leave this place so his best bet was to win over the old man.

Easier said than done.

$*$ $*$ $*$

Angus snorted, tossing his head, and Travis blinked back to the present hot summer evening, shifting in the saddle to hide his hard-on. Katie seemed to be lost in thought, too, and still stared at the spring-house. More so at the entrance steps, where they'd made love with the wild abandon of youth. Not that he wouldn't like to have another go on those steps. Damn, they'd been lucky she hadn't wound up pregnant that first time Today, though, he wasn't carrying protection. What would Dad say if he found out all those lessons during Travis's teens about being responsible had been wasted? Not that he'd wanted to be with a woman in a long time.

But he could control himself; he was a grown-ass man. And it wasn't as if she was sending out vibes inviting him to do anything with her anyway. Quite the opposite, actually.

Travis dismounted and tied the reins to an iron ring on the door before turning as Katie tightened her grip on Neptune's mane and swung her leg over the rump of the horse. Her legs and ass encased in tight denim were as sexy as all get out. *Sweet!*

She'd barely set foot on the ground before saying, "We should head back. I'm sure the horses in the barn are getting hungry."

"Aw, come on, Katie. Let's stay a bit. For old time's sake."

Her gaze darted toward the steps again, her cheeks growing pinker, before she reached for Neptune's reins and tied them on the same ring. She looked up at Travis, meeting his gaze momentarily. A spark of something hot flashed across her eyes. Or was it just wishful thinking?

"Katie, I…" The time for talking was over. He placed one hand on her back and tipped her chin back with his other.

"Travis, I don't think this is a good—"

He'd wanted to kiss her from the moment he'd seen her at the hospital. To touch her and be touched by her. Cutting off her words, his mouth crushed her lips before he eased off and tried to use a little finesse. All the years apart faded away, and it was as if they were both up here that first time again. She moaned, and he cupped her head before reining in his passion slightly. Didn't want to scare her off, but he didn't want to stop, either. He nibbled at her lower lip until she opened for him, and his tongue darted in and out playfully seeking…something. Perhaps the part of him that had been missing for thirteen years.

Katie coiled her arms around his neck—whether to keep from falling or to prolong the kiss, he wasn't sure—but it certainly wasn't the response of someone wanting to put an end to this kiss. He spread his legs before wrapping his arms around her waist to lift her short frame slightly and pull her against the length of his body as he deepened the kiss.

"Oh, Travis," she whispered against his mouth, still holding on rather than pushing him away.

Her tongue met his at last, wrestling a bit before she made circular motions in his mouth. He sucked her tongue deeper, and she gasped. But he captured her sigh in his mouth. Her fingers ran through his hair. Katie moaned again, lighting a fire within him he needed to extinguish.

Sweet Mother of God, I've missed you, Katie.

Suddenly, her body stiffened. Sensing this moment might be coming to an end, he trailed kisses along her jaw and down her neck hoping to prolong the pleasure. Her hand stroked his cheek at first then lowered to his shoulder, but as quickly as she'd melted into his kiss, she pushed him away.

Both of them spent a few moments catching their breath without making eye contact.

"You still make me crazy, Katie."

She waved away his words. "Let's head back to the house."

How could she just shut down her emotions like that?

She released the reins of both horses, handing him his, and was mounted and riding away before he'd even gotten back into his saddle. Angus danced around a moment at the indignity of being ridden again, but Travis controlled him more easily this time and took off after Katie, watching her hair lift and fall as she hightailed it back to the barn.

You can try to run, Katie, but I'm not letting you go as easily this time.

If she had a good reason not to explore something with him again, then she'd better spell it out. But she'd kissed him back just now. Yeah, she wanted him as much as he wanted her. Whatever had happened all those years ago couldn't be undone.

But he'd come back here for answers, and he damned well intended to get them.

Chapter Seven

K ate rode Neptune hard and fast back to the barn, as if putting some distance between herself and Travis would erase the way her traitorous body had wanted to ride him fast and hard as well when he'd kissed her moments ago.

The blood still rushed through her body from the adrenaline of the gallop—okay, that kiss was probably responsible for most of the rush. Her lips tingled as though his were still crushed against them. Their tongues had entangled as their bodies pressed against one another. And she'd wanted more.

At the barn, Kate pulled up on the reins and gripped Neptune's mane as she dismounted.

How am I going to convince him I want nothing to do with him when my body responds that way?

The pounding of Angus's hooves against the hard, dry ground told her she'd better get her emotions in check immediately. No way could she explain away her reaction to his potent kiss, so she'd simply ignore it.

He'd taken her by surprise. She'd been lost in the memories of her first time with him there on the steps of the springhouse. No doubt, he'd been caught up in the same flashback. The visceral memory of his body heavy on hers all those years ago as they'd given in to many months of frustration, of depriving themselves of the pleasure and fulfillment only sex could give. Why had they waited so long back then? Well, she—not they. Travis had been wanting to deepen their relationship a lot sooner than she had.

So if sex was so great, why hadn't she found anyone else she wanted to be with in that way since? Someone who was worth taking a little time away from the farm?

Because you use Travis as your measuring stick, and everyone else falls short.

Kate could excuse her body's response to him back then as being young and inexperienced, but she was thirty-three now. Okay, still relatively inexperienced when it came to sex, but her practical, prudent mind had no justification for deserting her this evening in almost the same way it had back then. At least she did have the wherewithal to stop him tonight with only a kiss. But oh, how her body now ached for more!

How had they gone from a pleasure ride to coming close to riding each other in such a short time? Her attraction to him had been intense from the moment Travis had entered her cubicle in the emergency department at the hospital yesterday, but that didn't mean she had to act upon those renegade emotions. She knew perfectly well how to relieve sexual tension on her own, but frankly, that didn't appeal to her tonight.

I want Travis.

She loosened Neptune's girth and removed his saddle, walking the horse to cool him down by the time Travis rode up. If only it were as easy for her to expel the excess heat from her body.

"Tell me you didn't feel what I felt," Travis demanded as he dismounted nearby.

Kate stumbled, holding onto the reins to keep herself from taking a tumble. "How would I know what you're feeling, Travis?"

"Oh, I think you know exactly what we both just experienced at the springhouse." Travis loosened the cinch on Angus's saddle and fell into step behind her. No doubt he was looking at her ass.

She kept placing one foot in front of the other without further mishap, intent on getting into the barn without answering his question. "The horses need to cool down." *And so do I!*

But nothing was going to ease the ache Kate felt to her core short of making love with Travis—and that was out of the question. She had her daughter to think about this time.

After about ten minutes of walking their horses, Kate led Neptune into his stall and removed his tack to continue the cool-down process with a rubdown while Travis took Angus to the box stall near the tack room. She listened as Travis carried on a conversation with Angus as though speaking with another person. They seemed to have hit it off.

Why not? The man was definitely likable. Other than Travis's cockiness and a tendency to be impulsive, she could find no faults in him. She picked up a currycomb and went to work on Neptune. The methodical rubbing motions soon had her lost in thoughts of what to do about Travis. And Chelsea.

What a mess she'd made of all three of their lives.

She hadn't been fair or honest with either Chelsea or Travis, and the truth was going to come back to bite her in the ass—sooner than later. What would Travis say or do when he found out about Chelsea? How would Chelsea react to finding out who her father was? Would Travis want to be a part of Chelsea's life?

Undoubtedly. He was as responsible as the day was long, always wanting to protect and look after those he loved. On the other hand, what if for some unimaginable reason he chose not to remain a part of Chelsea's life after meeting her?

I don't want her to go through life feeling rejected by a parent the way I was.

The old tape ran through her head even though she'd found no basis in reality for the thought. Still, what if she'd misjudged him? She'd been all wrong about what Travis wanted in terms of a career and where he wanted to live. She'd dated him for months and hadn't understood him at such a basic level. And now after a day, did she think she knew him any better? Until she could be one-hundred percent sure that Travis would be a stable presence in her daughter's life, she needed to wait.

And there was still the very real possibility she could lose Chelsea in a custody battle. What if Chelsea turned on her and decided she wanted to live with Travis because Kate had lied to her all this time?

"Want me to put Angus back in the pasture, now that the fence is fixed?"

Kate jumped at Travis's intrusion into her thoughts about him, but nodded. "I'm sure he'd be in heaven. He's missed being able to run around with free rein."

"I've missed riding. Haven't been since I took my buddy's kids up to Jackson's place when their mom remarried last year."

"Jackson?"

"My foreman. The one who lives near Franklin, Kentucky."

"Oh yeah." Travis had an entirely new life in Tennessee.

"Megan's kids loved riding there, but she wound up marrying a man who has a couple horses and a small farm south of Nashville, so they're overjoyed."

"I'm glad she found someone to be with and to help raise her kids, but it sounds like you were a substitute dad to them for a while." Would he have picked up parenting skills that would help with Chelsea?

"Hardly that. More like an adopted uncle. Megan's done an amazing job raising them on her own, but it's good she has someone again. Craig can rest in peace now."

What did she say to that? Fortunately, Travis had been there to come to the rescue.

"I'm a bit thirsty after that ride. Mind if I come in for another glass of your sweet tea, Katie?"

She couldn't think of a way to say no that wouldn't appear the height of rudeness. "Not at all." They headed into the house, and Travis took a seat in the kitchen while she poured his tea and her lemon water.

They sat at the table and drank in silence a moment, until the solitude shattered when Travis asked, "Why are you so reluctant to admit we still have chemistry?"

She nearly choked on her water. Staring at him while trying to find a reason that made sense, she said, "Because nothing could come of it other than a one-night stand, and I'm not interested in that."

"Says who? I mean, about nothing coming of it."

"You live three or four hours away."

"Four, but what difference does that make?"

"Might as well be four days. You have responsibilities there, and I'm never going to give up my farm. I don't think a long-distance relationship would suit either of us."

Not that she hadn't gone all these years without any relationship whatsoever. But she wasn't going to get involved with Travis. She couldn't.

"You'd be surprised what someone would do out of love for another."

Please don't talk about love.

Both had sacrificed a lot from the decision she'd made in college. "Sometimes it just doesn't work out. Let's not complicate things by trying to rekindle what we had before."

Travis sighed and stood, carrying his glass to the sink. "Need me for anything else tonight?"

Did she ever! But she had Chelsea to worry about. Becoming intimate with Travis again would only make their parting in a few days that much harder. She already had enough memories of him to haunt her for the rest of her life, not to mention any new ones.

But what if he didn't leave? One minute she wanted to tell him about his daughter, and the next she wanted to send him away again before Chelsea came home.

She'd sleep on it again before doing something she might regret. "No. I'm fine. Good night, Travis."

"Nite, Katie."

She watched him walk out of the kitchen and then across the drive to the barn. Maybe a good workout would relieve some of this tension. Kate dressed in her sports bra and leggings before heading to the garage where she'd set up a gym to help stay fit on days when the extreme temperatures in summer and winter kept her from exercising.

Only tonight, she'd be working out for a very different purpose. When she finished, she wanted to be able to hit the shower and then drop into bed without another thought of Travis.

Good luck with that.

* * *

"They both heard me!" Danny whooped and did a fist pump in the air to celebrate his victory. *Yes!* His vibration must be getting stronger or something. "Did you see that, Ben?"

Ben shrugged. "See what?"

How could he have possibly missed it? "A little while ago, before they went for their ride," he prompted. "When I whistled to bring Angus under control to keep Trav from getting killed, not only did the horse listen, but Katie thought Travis had whistled and vice versa."

Ben harrumphed. "Well, I wouldn't have minded it one bit if Travis had been trampled by Angus. Then he wouldn't be taking advantage of my daughter the way he just did."

Danny stood stock-still as the smile faded from his face and glared at the old man. "What do you mean, taking advantage of? From where I hovered, Katie kissed him back."

"She's vulnerable, young, and impressionable."

He shook his head. "Sorry, but that woman's in her thirties and well beyond the age of not knowing what she wants. She wants him, all right."

"Then why did she hightail it back to the barn?"

"Because she's stubborn—like you are."

"I like to call it using her head," Ben argued, crossing his arms.

Danny shook his. "Why do you want her to be alone and miserable the rest of her life? Trav would be a fantastic husband to her, the best there is."

"Doesn't matter what I think. She doesn't want him around and, apparently, isn't going to tell him about Chelsea."

"I'd lay odds that she comes around before Sunday. She's wavering because she can't find any reason not to tell him."

"Well, that doesn't mean she wants him in *her* life, just that she might allow him in Chelsea's."

"It'll be pretty hard to separate one from the other."

"Which is probably why she hasn't confessed yet."

"You sure are a killjoy, Ben. Not just with me, but wishing the worst for Katie, too."

"That's a matter of opinion what's best or worst for her. I'm not saying I don't want her married. Every woman needs a husband."

"Tell that to an independent woman." Danny grinned. "And Travis has a lot of strong, independent women, from his mother to his three sisters alone. He also knows how to find balance in control. I'm sure, if he had to, he'd relinquish authority in some areas."

"Kate's as independent as they come. She isn't going to let some cocky man come in and tell her how to run things."

"Oh, Trav's not going to take over running her farm. I'm just saying he likes to be in charge in the bedroom."

"What are you talking about? He's not getting anywhere near Kate's bed."

Danny chuckled. *Dream on, old man. Dream on.*

Despite Ben's being blind to what was happening right in front of them, Danny continued to celebrate having gotten through to both Katie and Travis, even if they weren't completely convinced yet that it was truly him.

More work to do. One way or another, Danny intended to make Travis see he needed to go after what he wanted in life—Katie Michaels.

*   *   *

Sleep didn't come quickly to Travis that night. Katie's refusal to acknowledge the undeniable chemistry between the two of them had left him beyond frustrated. He'd never be able to relax enough to get any rest. Not to mention trying to figure out why she was fighting the attraction. Was there someone else? Did she have a date Sunday with whoever it was?

Hard to believe she was all that serious about the mystery guy because she damned well participated willingly in that kiss. So why the brush-off right after?

He'd never fallen for any woman like Katie in his entire life. Oh, there had been others he'd dated—mostly the ones Danny had thrown in his path who were looking for a man to settle down with and have kids. He hadn't been ready for anything permanent at the time, and eventually, Danny had quit trying to fix him up.

Hell, even though it had annoyed him, he'd love to have Danny try one more time to find him someone because that would mean he wouldn't be gone. Would Danny have approved of Katie for him? Travis had certainly talked about her enough, especially when the two of them were awaiting their next move in Iraq and had time to kill. Travis wished he could have introduced the two of them before...

Once upon a time, he'd dreamed of settling down with Katie, having kids, and building a good life together. He'd tried to pretend—to himself, at least—that he'd gotten over her long ago, but those old wounds had been split wide open the moment he laid eyes on her.

Why had she sent him away in the first place? He ought to ask her, but she seemed so evasive about anything personal that she wouldn't tell him anyway.

Travis rolled over and punched the pillow, taking out some of his frustration—but not nearly enough. On top of being haunted with thoughts of Katie, his Danny delusions were getting worse, simply adding to what kept him awake long into the night. This sure as hell needed to come to a stop.

Danny's death was the most devastating loss Travis had suffered in his life. Yeah, he'd been heartbroken when Katie dumped him, but as this week was proving, that couldn't be repaired. Danny, on the other hand, wouldn't be coming back into his life again. No wonder his mind wanted to hang onto him, but Danny was dead and cremated, for Chrissake.

Let the man rest in peace.

Giving up on getting any sleep—or anything else—Travis decided to do something worthwhile. He should clean the saddle he'd used today. He tossed off the sheet, pulled on his jeans, and headed to the tack room next door. Flipping on the light, he laid out everything he'd need on the workbench.

The slow process of applying saddle soap and conditioner to the leather soothed his nerves. He'd missed riding and being around horses. Not that he was ever going to consider getting a horse of his own. He had more than enough to handle running his construction firm and taking care of his employees. But maybe he ought to find a riding stable nearby doing what Katie did and take lessons once a week for equine therapy or something. Or drop in on Jackson's farm more often. Being around Angus today, despite his orneriness in the beginning, had been a balm to his soul.

The barn door opened. He waited for Katie to make her way to where he had the light on. Was she having a tough time sleeping tonight, too? Maybe the two of them should talk over what went wrong in college and whether there was any hope for working it out now. They could then make better use of these sleepless nights.

Grinning as he thought about those possibilities, Travis entered the barn aisle, glancing toward the door he'd heard opening, but neither that one nor the one at the other end was open. A niggling sense of concern sent him checking on each horse. He'd walked up one row of stalls and had started down the other when the smell of smoke bombarded his senses.

Fire being the biggest fear in any horse barn, he checked out the stall closest to the smell—Neptune's. The horse whinnied at him when he looked between the holes in the grill on the upper part of the door. The horse's gaze was intent upon the opposite corner from where the horse stood. Travis saw nothing but an oat bucket hanging on the wall of the stall.

He sniffed again. Vanilla pipe tobacco? Old Man Michaels was the only person he'd ever known to smoke a pipe, and that was his favorite flavor of tobacco.

"Mr. Michaels?"

Sheesh. Still talking to dead men much?

"Everything all right?"

Travis nearly jumped out of his skin at the voice then realized it was Katie, not another ghost.

"Sorry," she said. "Didn't mean to scare you, but I came downstairs for a drink and saw the light on out here. Wanted to be sure none of the horses was having a problem."

No, she wouldn't come out here to check on your sorry ass.

She wore a long T-shirt and a pair of tennis shoes. She must have dressed in a hurry because he could swear she wasn't wearing a bra or shorts. Had she been sleeping in the nude? As if he'd given himself away by staring, she crossed her arms in front of herself.

Too late, darlin'.

But had she just come into the barn? If so, where was she when he'd looked in the aisle a few minutes ago? "Do you smell tobacco?"

She sniffed the air. "No."

"For real?" Maybe he was going nuts. "It smells just like your dad's pipe tobacco." Travis didn't believe in ghosts, either, but needed a rational explanation for what he was experiencing if not a ghost.

She gave him a wistful smile. "I used to sense him in here when he first passed. He loved the horses so much. Maybe he's hanging around still."

Seriously? "So you think he's haunting the barns?"

"Oh, no. Haunting sounds creepy. But I'd like to think he'd pay a visit every now and then as more of the benevolent spirit of a loved one."

Then why wasn't he letting her smell it? Old Man Michaels wasn't exactly what Travis would consider his loved one.

But who wouldn't think it nice to pretend their loved ones never really checked out? Travis would be the first in line to see or talk with Danny again, mainly to ask him why he'd done it. But he didn't intend to give in to any more wishful thinking.

Her smile faded. "Daddy didn't expect me to be able to do as well with the farm as I have. I can't imagine him coming around anymore."

"You've done an amazing job, Katie. I'm sure he'd be proud of you. I know I am."

She glanced at the dirt floor and muttered, "Thanks." Why wouldn't she believe him? She met his gaze again and added, "Listen, don't worry about Daddy. He won't bother you out here."

"Knowing him, he's probably doing it just to freak me out." *Or keep me in line around his daughter.* "He never did like me much."

She grinned lopsidedly. "He wanted to be top dog—not only in my life but on this farm. If he met you today, I think he'd love you."

"Why's that?"

"For one, he was intensely patriotic. You served your country when you could have easily focused on building your business skills rather than giving up those prime years to the Army."

"The Army only improved my skills."

Her eyes twinkled in the dim light. "Daddy would have liked hearing you say that." She shuffled her feet and stifled a yawn.

"Back to bed, missy." He took her by the shoulders to turn her around and send her back to the house, but touching her sent his good intentions out the window. Staring down at her like this, all those emotions from up at the springhouse came back with a vengeance. When she didn't shrug out of his hands, he pulled her closer. Still no sign she wanted to bolt.

He lowered his face to hers, and her eyelids fluttered closed. *Have mercy!* He might regret this for the rest of his life, but he pressed his lips against hers—tentatively at first, giving her one last chance to get the hell away. Instead, she snaked her arms around his neck, tilting her head and opening her sweet mouth to him.

Once again, he took what she offered. How could he resist? Who knew when her mood would shift again, and she'd push him away?

She tasted of mint. The woman turned him on like no other had. He wrapped one arm around her waist, pulling her curves into his body. Grabbing her hair, he pulled her head back until her mouth opened more completely to him.

The kiss grew deeper, and he lost himself in her until her passionate moan was followed quickly by her hands pushing him away. Again. Her eyes showed passion…and confusion. Damned if he'd apologize for this kiss, either.

"Why?" she asked.

Why what?

Why'd he kiss her?

Why'd he come back to her?

Why'd he stop kissing her?

He fought to control his breathing. "I think you'd better go back inside, Katie." *Where you're safe. From me.* Not that he'd ever hurt her, but he hadn't had a chance to go to the drugstore for protection, and he respected her too much to let things get out of hand unless he could be responsible. He wanted her more than ever, but for keeps this time. Until he understood her reason for breaking it off all those years ago, he'd better not fan the flames.

"You don't need to be losing any more sleep." This time when he grasped her shoulders, he turned her around and gave her a gentle shove in the direction of the barn door. He couldn't resist smacking her pert little ass for good measure. "Don't come anywhere near this barn in the morning until *after* you've eaten breakfast. I'll take care of the horses."

She stopped and turned to face him, tilting her chin back. "They're my responsibility."

"Maybe so, but while I'm here, consider me another hand. Allow yourself to wake up naturally, rather than to the sound of an alarm at the crack of dawn."

He pictured her eyes opening for the first time tomorrow morning. Would her hand search him out in her bed after dreaming about him during the night?

Yeah, dream on.

His groin tightened imagining it. In his fantasy, she didn't have on a stitch of clothes, either. If he kicked his morals to the curb right now, he'd be the first thing her eyes would light upon when they opened in the morning.

Don't go there.

She sighed as if disappointed in his resolve to send her away. "I can't believe I'm admitting this to you of all people, but I'm exhausted. I'll set my alarm for an hour before the first lesson—but don't expect me to start following orders like I'm one of the troops you're used to bossing around."

"What makes you think I gave orders?"

She shook her head and grinned. "Because you're a natural leader and a take-charge person. Even if you barely outranked them, I have no doubt the men in your squad followed your direction."

"I could say the same about you—being a take-charge person, that is."

"You do what you have to." She pivoted around before tossing back over her shoulder, "Get some sleep yourself. Breakfast will be about eight-thirty. Join me."

He grinned as he watched her walk away. "I'll be there." In his mind, he stripped off her shirt. But that fantasy wasn't going to come true until she trusted him again. To that end, he'd continue to share meals and other times with her.

I'm not giving up on you so easily this time, Katie.

Chapter Eight

W hen she heard the knock on the kitchen door at eight-thirty sharp, a sleep-deprived Kate emptied the rest of the sausage patties onto the platter beside the well-done scrambled eggs. A bowl of cubed cantaloupe she'd harvested from her garden the day before yesterday was all she could find to go with it.

"Door's open!"

"Smells wonderful." Travis sounded as cheerful as ever.

"I'll bet you're starving after all the work you did this morning. I'm just glad I set that alarm for eight or I might still be snoring away."

"You never snored." She'd only slept at his place a few times after they'd become intimate before she'd called off the relationship.

"I'm older now, and the Ohio Valley takes a toll on your sinuses over the years." Chelsea let Kate know in no uncertain terms that she snored like a freight train, although her daughter slept lightly and might have exaggerated a tad.

The two sat across from each other at the oval table. Kate still wondered why her dad had visited the barn last night. Probably to scare Travis off. Funny that even in the afterlife he didn't trust Travis around her.

"What are you grinning about?"

She wasn't aware she had been. "Oh, just thinking about…last night." When he beamed at her, her insides melted making her forget what they were talking about. Then she realized they weren't on the same wavelength. "Did Daddy give you any more trouble after I left?"

He sobered. "Oh, no. And he wasn't any trouble in the first place.

A little alarming maybe. You never want to smell smoke in a barn. Once you confirmed it was your dad, I didn't allow him the satisfaction of bothering me." Apparently, Travis hadn't forgiven Daddy for all the slights while she and Travis had dated, either. "How'd you sleep, Katie?"

"Like a baby." *A colicky one.*

"Glad to hear it."

She took another bite. Should she invite Travis to stay in her guest room instead? Why didn't the thought freak her out as much as it had two days ago? *Oh, Katie, be careful.*

She was calling herself by Travis's nickname for her now. Sounded right to her ears.

"The apartment isn't too bad, is it?" she asked. She'd spent a few nights out there before hiring Miguel. Now he handled most of the long nights waiting for a foal to be born, unless multiple mares were in labor at the same time.

"Not at all. Don't worry about me." He took another bite of his eggs and asked, "So which is more lucrative—breeding and selling horses or training horses and riders?"

"I really need to do both to stay afloat. Each has its season. I'm slowly making a name for the stables with a number of excellent performance horses sold in recent years, but until I have that coveted World Champion, I won't be in high-enough demand as a breeder to stop training. Plus, I love working with young students."

"Maybe Melissa's Miss Pickles will be the one."

"I didn't breed that one, but I did train her, so perhaps that would help my reputation in that regard."

"How many stallions do you have?"

"Three. A fourth will be on loan from another stable next month, though. He's a two-time World Champion. I'm hoping he'll give me some fine foals that will be the break I need to make it to the next level."

"When does the breeding season start?"

"We bred the first mares about a month ago and will continue throughout August. I should have several in heat in a couple of weeks, so this was the best time to give Miguel some time off before things get crazy around here." She wouldn't get into the details of semen collection and her mail-order program. "Breeding is extremely high-tech these days with artificial insemination and dummy mares. I even keep a centrifuge on hand for when a stallion's…output…isn't quite as potent as I or my clients would like." She looked down at her plate, blushing for some reason. Why couldn't she use the biological terms around him, especially when talking about horses? He'd taken a livestock class once to be closer to Kate, and all this had been taught then.

Kate focused on eating her breakfast for a moment. It was best to let this discussion fade away.

Travis shook his head, the corner of his mouth quirking up. "Why do they always find a way to take the fun out of everything?"

Her chewing came to a halt, and she stared across the table at him until her cheeks grew warmer. Once again, she tried to concentrate on her eggs, but the words hung there until he spoke again.

"Poor Angus having to be around the mares in heat and being given dummies to do the deed with, having his output measured. Great way to take the romance out of it. Maybe that's why he's so frustrated all the time."

She nearly choked on her coffee. Was he going to talk about horse sex all morning? No way was this coincidental. And why couldn't she come up with another topic of conversation to save her soul? All she could think about was that night long ago at the springhouse…and last night's kisses.

"Any other students competing at the Lexington Junior League show?"

Finally, a new topic.

She shook her head. "Just Melissa on Miss Pickles. They're signed up for three performance classes."

"I think I'd have enjoyed going to horse shows, but only to help out in the background. I wouldn't know the first thing about training and competition."

She relaxed into her chair, thankful for this new direction in the conversation. "I'm sure your crew in Nashville would miss having you on the job there." *Hint, hint. Go home!*

For a flash of a second, though, she wondered what life might have been like if she hadn't broken up with him. Would he have been content to work in a small city like Frankfort or Lexington, both within easy commuting distance of her farm?

Stop thinking about what might have been.

They finished eating in silence until he wiped his mouth and set his napkin beside his plate. "Thanks for breakfast, Katie. What time will you be finished with lessons today?"

"About noon."

"How about going to the gorge to do some hiking this afternoon? Supposed to be in the nineties, but it'll probably be a little cooler there than here."

She hadn't been to Red River Gorge in forever. The one time she'd taken Chelsea there, the memories of her hikes with Travis had been too overwhelming. After that, she'd taken Chelsea to other state parks and nature preserves Kate hadn't been to with Travis before.

Feelings from long ago flooded over her, and she longed desperately to recapture them. Perhaps going with him again one more time would erase the earlier images embedded in her mind. It was a wonder they hadn't been arrested for some of the things they'd done in that place. She grinned. Not that he was any less potent now, nor were his kisses.

Even though she didn't think it was a sane decision, she heard herself saying, "I'd like that. We can pack a lunch to eat on the way and hit the ground running—well, hiking."

"Let me worry about lunch. And I'll clean up in here if you want to head out to get ready for your lesson."

"You're going to spoil me, Travis."

He grinned. "My pleasure. Besides, I'd go nuts sitting around with nothing to do."

"I don't think I have enough picnic stuff on hand, though."

He grinned. "No problem. I need to pick up some things at the drugstore anyway, so I'll stop and get bug spray and sunscreen, too."

"I have plenty of sunscreen." Her insect repellent was with Chelsea at camp, though.

"Great. If we leave here by twelve-thirty, we'll be there by two."

"Perfect." He began clearing off the table as she hurried out the door to greet her first student of the day. It was going to be a long morning. She hadn't looked forward to anything as much as their hike in a long time.

Once again, that inner voice tried to caution her to take things more slowly and not let her guard down too far.

Nonsense. I'm not going to do anything stupid. I'm still in control.

*   *   *

Travis watched Katie leave the kitchen, his gaze riveted by her cute ass encased in tight jeans. Man, he felt like a horny teenager, but Katie was even hotter now than she'd been in college, if that were even possible.

He washed the dishes and glanced out at the barn, imagining Katie with a riding crop in hand as she guided one of the horses to do her bidding. He shook his head and grinned at the direction his mind was going. He needed to get his mind off sex and head to the store. Not that condoms weren't at the top of his list. He doubted they'd need them today when the Gorge would be filled with hikers, but damned if he'd be caught unprepared again if the moment was right and Katie was willing.

He surveyed the contents of her fridge to see what they'd need that he hadn't bought yesterday and found an open jar of green olives. Since when did Katie start eating those? She'd only been interested in black ones on their pizzas, and she'd had a real aversion to the green. She also didn't strike him as someone who had time to entertain much.

He shrugged it off. Katie had changed in a lot of ways. Maybe she acquired a taste for green olives since they'd dated. Hmm.

Armed with a mental list of what he'd need, including the sprouted grain bread she liked so much, he went to the store in Georgetown. They wouldn't have to worry about supper tonight, because he planned to take her to their favorite country kitchen in Clay City. Her diet didn't keep her from enjoying meats and most vegetables, and as much as he'd hate skipping it, he wouldn't order a piece of their fabulous pie to eat in front of her.

An hour later, he loaded up the truck with enough food that he wouldn't have to worry about her sugar tanking again. They'd be doing some serious hiking.

Back at the house, he organized the fixings and condiments for the sandwiches in one section of the fridge, including those mysterious green olives. All they had to do was make their sandwiches and hit the road. He pulled out his phone and checked the browser for the best trails to hike. They ought to go with a moderately tough one, although they both seemed to have enough exercise in their daily routines to be able to handle something more. With the perfect one chosen—a challenge, but not overwhelmingly so—he wondered what else he'd do to occupy the next couple of hours.

Not wanting to be accused of snooping around beyond the kitchen, he headed out to the arena. Katie was so wrapped up in instructing her student that she didn't notice him entering. *Good.* He hunkered down behind the fence slats to keep it that way but still give him a decent view.

"Much better, Abbie!" Katie yelled. No riding crop. There went that fantasy. "That's what I've been talking about."

She must be on her second lesson at least, since Melissa had been scheduled as the first. Closer to finishing up. The girl's gray horse stepped over a series of six long poles lying on the ground at ten or eleven foot intervals. The goal seemed to be to get the horse to maneuver over them while carefully watching the placement of its hooves. He had no idea which gait they were going for.

"You're doing great. Now, bring Moonbeam back to a walk, Abbie. Don't let him fall back to pacing." Ah, pacing must be bad. The young rider held on tightly to the reins, her face beaming yet serious at the same time. "Give him a 'good, boy.' You've both done a great job, Abbie. Now before you take him back to the barn to cool him down, I want you to do two sets of serpentines and work on the bending and circling techniques."

The horse and rider made their way back through the poles as Katie continued to offer advice and praise. As they finished the second round, Abbie shouted, "We did it, Moonbeam!" She patted the horse's neck and leaned forward to say something only the horse could hear. Moonbeam nodded his head vigorously, as if in agreement.

"I'll see you tomorrow, Abbie. Great job."

While the girl led her horse out of the arena, Katie went to pick up the first of the poles.

Travis was out of his quasi-hiding place in seconds. "Here, let me help with those."

"Oh!" Katie jumped and dropped the end of the pole. "I didn't see you there."

"Didn't mean to scare you." Travis lifted two of them at a time. "Just wanted to watch you work. You're amazing with both the horse and the rider."

"Well, they're a team. Besides, I love what I do."

"It shows." He followed her to where she dropped the first pole and placed his beside hers, and then they went back for the other three. "Listen, if you want me to stop watching, you'll have to give me something else to do."

"You've already been to the store?"

He nodded. "And the dishes are done. Everything's ready in the fridge to make sandwiches for lunch."

"If you'd like to take Angus for a ride while I finish my last lesson, feel free. You're the only person I trust with him."

"Sounds good. See you in ninety minutes."

Like a kid at Christmas, he headed out to catch the stallion, but would be counting down the minutes until he saw Katie again. How'd he go from not giving her much of a thought over the years to having her consume his every passing minute?

Boy, have I got it bad. Again.

How would their story end this time? Did he and Katie have a chance at something moving forward, despite their past history? They both had homes and livelihoods four hours apart from one another. Travis wasn't ready to give up the company he'd worked so hard to put together. But Katie was equally entrenched here. In fact, that had been a concern of his even back then, although he would have started a business in Lexington or even nearby Versailles if she'd let him be a part of her life.

Ever since Katie had woken up in the hospital, she'd been so serious—almost fearful of him or something—but maybe he was managing to get her to lighten up some. She wasn't the same person he'd known in college, but then neither was he. They'd both been through a lot, suffered significant losses, and worked like hell to get where they were.

Would she ever open up about what had happened to them over a dozen years ago? And why was she so eager to get rid of him now? Only one way to find out. That meant spending more time here on the farm with her.

He couldn't help but chuckle to himself. She ought to love that.

Chapter Nine

Kate washed up in the arena kitchen wondering if she'd done the right thing to agree to a hike in one of their favorite places. When she came into the barn in search of Travis, he was nowhere to be seen. She entered the house to find he'd nearly emptied the fridge and had filled the table with sandwich fixings.

"Angus has been cooled down and put out to pasture again," he said as he made himself a ham and Swiss sandwich with all the fixings.

There was no turning back. "That's more than I can eat in a week," she told him.

"I plan to give us both a workout, so you'd better go prepared."

Ignoring the heat infusing her face, she walked over to the table and made a dressed turkey and provolone sandwich and slid it into the storage bag.

"Want me to put some olives in a plastic container?"

"If you want some," she said as she waited for the microwave popcorn to finish. "I can't stand the things." Obviously, he didn't remember everything about her.

"Then why'd you have a half-eaten jar in the fridge?"

Kate's hands stopped in mid-motion. *Drat!* How was she going to explain the vile things away since he thought she lived alone? Why did Chelsea have to love them so much?

"Oh, *olives.* Sure. Bring some. Not too many, though," she cautioned. "I have enough here to fill me up."

"I love them, too." Is that where Chelsea inherited her taste for them? Could something like that be genetic?

Kate watched in horror as he dumped the juice from the jar and filled a pint-sized container with every last one.

Two hours later, thoughts about having to eat a few disgusting olives had faded to a dim memory as they took in the beauty of the Red River Gorge together. They'd eaten sandwiches in the truck on the way here, but hadn't bothered with the messy, nasty olives.

As they climbed a ridge, Kate tried her best to find a foothold on the steep stretch of the trail. "You sure don't believe in letting me ease back into hiking, do you?"

"Hang in there." He wasn't breathing hard. The man must be in superb shape, something she wished she hadn't become so aware of lately. "We'll rest at the top of this hill. There's a great view, as I recall. Not that this one's all that bad, either."

"Stop staring at my ass, Cooper."

He chuckled, but didn't deny her accusation.

If the trail wasn't so narrow here, she'd allow him to go ahead, but knowing where his attention was focused only gave her the determination needed to surmount the hill as quickly as possible. On the top of the ridge, all thoughts of Travis flew out the window.

"Oh my! It's amazing! I'd forgotten how beautiful it is here."

Travis joined her on her right and took in the view with her. The sandstone cliffs and limestone rock faces on the other side of the Gorge opened up before them.

He cleared his throat. "I can't tell you how much I've missed this place. It always gave me a sense of humility when I started thinking that I actually had any control over anything."

She understood exactly how he felt. "Makes your problems simply fade away, doesn't it?"

"That it does." They stood in silence, taking it all in for a few minutes, until he whispered, "Maybe if I'd brought you here, Danny, you wouldn't have…" His words tapered off.

Danny? The crew member who had died recently? Kate turned toward him and caught a glint of a tear welling in his eyes before he turned away and lifted his hand to his face to rub his eyes. Kate tried to find words to comfort him, but decided that, if he was fighting so hard to keep her from seeing his emotions, he'd prefer his privacy. So once more she remained silent.

After a moment, he cleared his throat again. "This would be a great place to grab a bite. I'll share the other half of my sandwich with you, if you'd like."

"No, thanks. I couldn't eat another bite."

"Well, I don't want to eat in front of you. You can have most of the olives."

Her stomach turned at the thought. They sat on limestone out-croppings and he pulled the food out of his backpack, handing her the container with the vile things. She opened it and held it out to him. "You should try some on your sandwich."

He stared at her as if she'd grown horns.

"No, thanks. Really. Have all you want."

Steeling herself, she opened the lid and was hit by the vinegary smell. Her stomach lurched again, but she took a plastic fork and speared one, bringing it to her mouth. When he glanced out at the view, she tossed it behind her head, hoping that wouldn't be consid-ered littering and wouldn't endanger any wildlife.

But eating them might endanger her!

She was in the process of tossing a handful more over her shoulder when Travis turned toward her. She had no recourse but to put them into her mouth. Oh, dear Lord. She began chewing and fought down her gag reflex as she picked up her water bottle and washed them down without chewing for the most part.

"You okay? You look as green as those olives."

Not sure she could speak yet, she nodded. She handed him the container, unable to stand the smell any longer. "Here, you can have the rest. I've made a pig of myself already."

She watched as he brought the container to his lips and tilted his head back to down the remainder. Kate shuddered. At least they were all gone now.

Travis stood and gathered up their trash and belongings into his backpack. He handed her another bottle of water. "We'd best keep going. Otherwise, the sun will set before we get back to the truck."

They hiked along the ridge a ways until he indicated the spot where they should branch off on a new trail leading to the parking lot. Going down went much faster than hiking up had taken, and they were back at the truck in under two hours from when they'd stood on the cliff.

Kate smiled up at him. "What an amazing day. Thanks for suggesting we come here, Travis."

"Day's not over yet. We're going to Clay City for supper."

"I wonder if our favorite restaurant is still around."

"Wonder no more. I looked it up, and it's doing a thriving business. Even expanded since the last time we ate there."

"Catfish and fried green tomatoes, here I come."

"A woman after my own heart."

She closed her eyes a moment before turning to stare out the passenger window. If he knew what she'd kept from him all these years, he'd think differently.

Because he'd insisted on driving today, she was able to enjoy the scenery as they drove into town shortly after sunset. While central Kentucky had beautiful rolling hills, the eastern part of the state's mountains were awe inspiring.

"It's gorgeous here, isn't it?" His question pulled her back.

"Very." But being in the area again also bombarded her with memories of when things had been good between them. Back when their futures held so much promise and hope.

Arriving at the restaurant a little after seven, they found that the dinner crowd had begun to thin out, but Travis asked if she minded being seated at the table in the corner near the kitchen. "Just like old times."

"There's no bad spot in here." Settled in, they began looking over the menu, which hadn't changed much since their college days. "She serves all the things I don't like to cook. This is going to be a treat."

"I hope you can find items that won't mess with your glucose, but with all this protein, I doubt you can go wrong."

"Hardly. The amount of breading is negligible." She had her heart set on fried catfish, hush puppies, kale, and fried green tomatoes.

"You look so healthy that I sometimes forget what you're dealing with."

She shrugged off his concern. "You can get used to anything when you have no choice." Just like she'd had to adjust to not having Travis in her life.

But you *had a choice.*

After he ordered pork chops, mashed potatoes, and cornbread, he reached across the table to squeeze her hand. "Katie, I'm sorry I wasn't here for you when you needed me over the years."

So am I.

"Actually, Monday aside, I haven't had that much trouble with it. Besides, you were here the other day—arrived just in the nick of time, I'd say."

"I only did what anyone would have done in an emergency."

"But no one else was around to do *anything*. If you hadn't shown up…" She couldn't even say the words. Chelsea could have been left motherless or left with a mother lying in a diabetic coma. Her neighbors and good friends, Lidia and Jason, had agreed to be Chelsea's designated legal guardians and would have stepped in immediately in that event. But the thought of Chelsea growing up without her mother made Kate nauseous.

"You okay? You look a little pale. Should you check your sugar?"

She shook her head. "I'm fine." Her close call gave her all the more reason to tell Chelsea about her biological father. He should be the one taking care of her if something unthinkable happened to Kate.

Soon. But she didn't want to ruin tonight by revealing it now.

"I certainly don't want a repeat of the day I showed up," he said. "Man, you scared the life out of me. At first," he looked down and grinned before meeting her gaze again, "I wondered if you hadn't been hitting the apple-pie moonshine again."

"Heavens, no!" She laughed. "Once was enough for that. Remember how sick we both were that weekend? Daddy thought I had the stomach flu. That was the last time I touched the stuff, though Lidia still makes it as potent as ever for her friends."

While they waited for their food, she tried to come up with other dinner conversation. She hadn't been on a date in a long time. Wait. Was this really a date? Flustered, she asked, "What kinds of things do you do for fun in Nashville?"

"Boating. Fishing. Hiking. Being out in nature is phenomenally relaxing. I inherited Danny's golden retriever, Sadie. She keeps me company and commiserates with me."

"Why didn't you bring her with you?"

He chuckled before taking a sip of his sweet tea. "Poor thing gets carsick on long trips, although she manages up to an hour or so at a time. My foreman, Jackson, is taking care of her while I'm gone. She's hung around the crew so much that she's content being with any of us. Sadie's an amazing dog, though. There's something calming about being around animals. She can turn a bad day around in no time, and lately, she's been alerting me to problems on the work sites as if she were a service animal."

"You take her to work with you?"

He nodded. "I have long days and wouldn't want to leave her alone that much. I think she has a few demons of her own to battle. I'm sure she misses Danny, too."

Her heart went out for him, but before she could offer further condolences, he sat back in his chair. "Anyway, it's good having her around the workplace. She can sense when one of the guys is having problems. But I don't try to put her on duty all the time. Mostly we go for hikes, go fishing, or just lay around my house. She loves it when we sit side by side on the couch and I pet her or rub her belly."

Don't even think about getting jealous of his dog, Katie.

Not wanting to take him back down a sad path, she brought up the time he'd taken one of her livestock classes with her.

"You know I just wanted to be close to you," he admitted unnecessarily. "But you could have warned me they would be castrating pigs during one class."

Okay, maybe she chose that topic because it might keep them from becoming too amorous tonight. Her heart was dangerously close to melting with affection for him. Kate shook her head. "You turned as green as the olives I ate earlier; I thought you were going to pass out."

"Let's just say you sure know how to test a guy."

"Me? The course description in the catalog was very clear. You just didn't look."

"Guilty as charged. I was only out to impress upon a country girl that I could handle life on the farm."

"Well, you succeeded, didn't you? I was so taken by the fact that you'd go through that class with me that I invited you out to the farm soon after."

"I'd been out there lots of times before that."

She leaned closer to whisper, "But we both know what happened the weekend after that particular class up at the springhouse."

His eyes smoldered, and before she could retreat, he closed the gap and placed a kiss on her lips. She hadn't expected to have this become a romantic dinner, especially with the topic she'd brought up. Thankfully, their kiss was interrupted when the server brought them their dinners. Her lips tingled where he'd touched them. Before things went too far, she needed to get a grip.

They ate in relative silence, except for moans of appreciation. Travis was easy to be with, something she hadn't fully appreciated back when they were young. They'd both been so intense then, wanting to live life to the fullest and do everything imaginable in as short a time as possible.

They managed some chitchat and laughed about other college memories, but all too soon, the meal had come to an end. It was pitch dark when they got back on the Mountain Parkway to return to Midway.

"Think your dad will pay another visit tonight?" He must still be trying to sort out what to make about Daddy's visit last night.

"Can't say."

"Well, I don't intend to lose any sleep over it, even if he does. As long as he doesn't change tobacco flavors, I'll assume the smell of vanilla pipe tobacco is his and not a barn fire."

She laughed. "Daddy was set in his ways on this side of the veil, so I can't see why he'd bother to change over there. But I do have cameras and smoke alarms all over the barn that would pick up any hint of a real fire."

"Glad to hear it." He glanced her way a moment then back to the road before asking, "Did it bother you when you became an adult that he still treated you like a kid? You always had great ideas for how to run the place, but he disregarded each one out of hand."

She sighed. "Of course it annoys me now that I waited so long, but I was a different person before he got sick than I am now. So afraid of everything, especially responsibility and losing his respect and approval. I was willing to let him control my every move because that meant I wouldn't have to make the wrong decisions and live with the consequences."

"Was it hard on you when you had to start running the place?"

"Was it ever! I still had him around for guidance during those first couple of years. While bedridden, his mind was as sharp as ever almost to the end. I tried to learn everything I could before the day came I could no longer ask him anything. But I do things so differently than he did that it's hardly the same place."

"Trust your instincts," he said as he drove up the lane to her house. "They haven't failed you yet."

Oh, but they had.

But to Travis, she said, "Thanks." Although she'd often wished she'd had Travis with her to share the successes and failures, it was probably for the best that he hadn't been forced to live out his life on her small farm in the country. He'd made a difference in a lot of people's lives. Still, he could have changed hers and Chelsea's lives, too. "If only I hadn't sent you away." *Oh, God, no!* As soon as the words tumbled from her mouth, she cringed inwardly. Her heart pounded as she prayed he hadn't heard her. How could she let her guard down like that?

He cut the engine and turned toward her. "Why *did* you call it quits between us?" No such luck. "Especially in an impersonal voicemail. Then you refused to take my calls or to see me when I came back from New York the next weekend." She heard the pain in his voice, felt it viscerally, but couldn't speak. "I'd thought what we had was good. We could have made a great life together."

He waited for her to say something, but still she had no words. What excuse could she give him that wouldn't reveal Chelsea's existence? How could she justify depriving Travis of knowing their daughter—and Chelsea of forming a close bond with her daddy? Travis would have made a wonderful father.

He still can.

"It's complicated," she blurted out. Lame answer, but what could she say.

"I'm not going anywhere."

Did he mean tonight or forever? *Oh, dream on.* Obviously just tonight.

"Would it help if I said I was wrong about the reasons?"

He thought a moment. "Not particularly. I should have pressed you for answers a long time ago, but why can't you just tell me?"

Perhaps a half-truth? "I didn't want to tie you down."

"What's that supposed to mean? We were in love. That doesn't result in tying someone down. Just the opposite."

"You have an ideal view of marriage, but in my experience, it doesn't always work when two people come from different background and personalities."

"You're basing that theory on what, exactly?"

She'd never told him the details about her mother, either, too ashamed to. Instead, she'd hinted that Mom had died rather than tell him she'd deserted her and her father. How could she possibly explain her lies of omission?

But exhaustion overcame her, so she didn't intend to get into that tonight. "It doesn't matter now." She reached for the door handle and escaped briefly until he met her again at the side of the truck as she pulled the backpack from the backseat.

"I'm really tired. We'll talk more tomorrow." Not about these topics. Again with the half-truths. What was the matter with her? "Good night, Travis."

His hand warm on her cheek nearly brought her to her knees. "Someday, Katie, I hope you'll give me the courtesy of telling me why you ended the relationship. Why you threw away what we had—what we *could* have had." With a shake of his head, he turned and walked toward the barn without giving her a chance to respond.

Her throat closed up, and her eyes welled with tears as she started toward the kitchen door. She'd hurt him. Tonight, she needed to do some thinking. Maybe by tomorrow, she'd know what she should tell him.

Kate was in for another sleepless night, for sure.

Chapter Ten

Travis thought about what Katie had refused to tell him the entire next day. Apparently, she had no intention of revealing what went wrong with their relationship back then. If she couldn't open up to him, did he even want to try to rekindle anything? How could he avoid the same pitfall if he didn't even know what had happened?

Today, she'd mostly avoided him, immersing herself in training sessions. Forty-five minutes ago, he'd heard her come into the barn, saddle up Neptune, and leave. While he'd love to go for a ride, he stayed in the barn apartment, not trusting himself around her.

So how was he supposed to fix things and move forward if they couldn't talk to one another?

He'd spent the afternoon installing the tailboards on the walls of Moonbeam's stall at Katie's earlier request, opting to drive the nails by hand in an attempt to relieve his frustration. Despite being physically tired at only six o'clock, he was far too restless to stay cramped up in the apartment. Maybe he'd take a ride on Angus after Katie returned so he could expel some of this pent-up energy burning inside.

Frustrated, and with no sign of Katie returning, he decided to go for a good run. Not on the road, but in the fields where no one would bother him and the hills could kick his ass. He might run into Katie, but so be it. Even if she wouldn't give him the time of day, he could make sure she was all right. Okay, so he was worried about her. She'd been gone a while now.

He'd left his good running shoes and workout clothes at home, but could make do with his tennis shoes. He removed his button-down plaid shirt altogether—draping it around his neck for later—and changed into a pair of shorts. Danny would have busted his chops for wearing cotton to exercise. He gave a mental shrug and set off up the hill behind the barn.

Travis hadn't been much into running unless he had to, but his buddy insisted it was a great way to escape the demons. Not that Travis's problems were anything compared to the ones Danny had tried to outrun on his blade prosthesis. But he'd have done anything to get Danny off his pity pot at that point.

One thing was certain; Travis needed a rigorous physical outlet tonight. When he dropped into bed this evening, he didn't want to be haunted by thoughts of Katie. And the physical release he wanted most—with her—was out of the question.

Maybe it was time to give up and head home tomorrow.

Nah. Like Sadie with her rawhide bones, he wasn't giving up until he'd gnawed it down to nothing. He deserved answers.

Travis set out toward the hill behind the barn. By the time he reached the crest, his legs and lungs burned, but at least the pressure in his chest had decreased. He picked up the pace, and soon his mind went numb.

They used to challenge each other to sprints and longer races while in boot camp, Iraq, and after Danny had come to work for him. Running helped them both cope better.

Why didn't you ask me to go for a run that night, Danny?

Travis blinked the sweat from his eyes. He had to stop thinking about him. Slowing to a walk, he glanced down at his watch. He'd been out for more than an hour. Looking around to get his bearings, he saw the springhouse at the bottom of the hill with Neptune grazing near the steps.

Don't go near there, man.

Too many memories. Of the past. Of that kiss the other night. Travis couldn't help himself, though. Always a sucker for punishment, he walked toward the limestone block building with its silver metal roof. After the heat of the run, he could use some cold water and a place to cool off. Then he'd head back to the barn. Maybe he'd be able to sleep now.

As he came around to the front of the building, he saw Neptune's reins trailed through the gaping doorway into the springhouse. Likely, Katie'd secured them to the rusty ring on the wooden plank door. She was nowhere in sight, though. She had probably sought relief from the heat of the evening, too.

"Oh, Chelsea. Will you be able to forgive me?" Katie's voice, raw with anguish, echoed from inside the springhouse.

Who was she talking to? Wasn't Chelsea one of her students? He was fairly certain Katie had ridden out here alone tonight, and there was no sign of another horse. Maybe he ought to leave—or at least make his presence known.

Worried about her, he called out. "Katie? You in there?"

Duh. What do you think?

If he hadn't been thinking about Danny during his run, he doubted he'd be plagued with hearing his buddy's voice right now. Would he ever be able to stop his mind from playing these sadistic tricks on him?

The door creaked open wider. Katie stepped closer to the opening, but didn't reveal her face to him. "Travis? What are you doing out here?" The wariness in her voice made him wonder what she feared he'd do or say.

"I was just finishing up a run. Thought some spring water might hit the spot." Not a complete lie.

She avoided his gaze and waved him inside. "It *is* a lot cooler in here."

He walked down the limestone stairs and into the ancient structure where the temperature dropped about twenty degrees. Passing by her and acting as though he'd only come for a drink, he knelt on the foot-high wall surrounding the trough of cold water and picked up the dipper. Might not be the most sanitary way to get a drink, but he'd made do under a lot worse conditions. After drinking his fill, he swished the dipper in the water and hung it back on the wall hook before standing and smiling at her.

"I haven't been in here in forever." Other than in his fantasies.

Silhouetted against the door's opening, Katie's body was ramrod straight, her chin held high. No warm smile, no softness in her gaze. Was there no spark left of the old flame between them?

"Thanks for the drink. I'll leave you to your…thoughts." He didn't want to say conversation because that would clue her in that he'd listened outside a few minutes ago.

The longer his eyes had to adjust, the easier it became to make out her features in the dim lighting. Her eyelashes were clumped. Had she been crying? He wanted to…no, he *needed* to ask. This might be his last opportunity to get the answers he'd come to Midway for. He'd never been one to run away from a problem.

"Katie, we need to talk." The wall surrounding the trough of water appeared to be dry, and he indicated that she should take a seat.

After some hesitation, she complied, sitting several feet away. He stepped closer before sitting down, and she wrapped her arms around her waist.

Where should he start? Danny, maybe? "Katie, I didn't fully explain why I chose to come back and see you now, but…" *Lordy mercy*, let the words come out sounding better than they did when he'd practiced in his head. "The night before I arrived, I had a dream in which an Army buddy of mine came and told me I needed to find you again. He didn't say why, but indicated it was urgent. Hell, I still don't know why. Maybe he just wanted me to think about someone living for a change and let him rest in peace."

"Wait. You mean this buddy in the dream is…no longer alive?"

He shook his head then answered, "No," in case she couldn't see him. "It's the Danny I told you about."

She closed the gap between them, and her hand squeezed his forearm. "I don't want to pry, but if you want to talk about him, I'm here. You said he died five months ago."

He nodded, his throat closing with emotion. He hadn't even talked to his family about Danny yet, although they'd been at his memorial service and understood.

"Did it happen stateside or during a deployment?"

"We haven't deployed in more than three years." While he didn't want to say the ugly word, he did so anyway. "He died at his apartment. Appears to have been a suicide, although the medical examiner couldn't rule out accidental death."

"Oh, Travis! How awful for his friends and family, doubly hard not knowing with any certainty what happened."

More than you can imagine.

He nodded. "I should have tried harder to get him off the painkillers. I thought we were making progress and that he was moving in the right direction toward a new life after...But opioids eventually killed him." Travis didn't intend to go into the details of all that Danny had suffered after the deployment that sent him home prematurely.

"I can't imagine how hard it is to go back to civilian life after all you experienced over there. Sounds like the two of you were close."

He nodded. "He was closer to me than my own brother, if that makes sense. And Clint and I are pretty damned close."

"I'm sure the bonds forged in combat supersede blood ties many times."

That she didn't judge him for making a statement like that helped relax him a little more. He couldn't explain why he'd listen to a ghost in a dream, but wanted her to understand what had brought him to her doorstep.

When she laid her head on his shoulder, all thoughts of Danny escaped him. "I'm glad you made it back, Travis."

Almost sounded like she meant back here to her farm—and her. This place felt more like home than anywhere he'd been since they'd split up. Then he realized she simply meant home to the States. "Yeah. Me, too." What else was he supposed to say? He'd been so glad to return from that disastrous second deployment and hadn't wanted to go back for a third, but did.

When she shivered, he moved closer to wrap his arm around her at the exact moment the door slammed shut without warning, blocking out what little daylight there had been. Neptune nickered outside.

Katie jumped up, out of his arms. Her feet scuffed along the dirt floor as she headed for the door. She probably welcomed the intrusion, wanting to break contact with him. The squeak of the rusty, cast-iron handle confirmed her whereabouts as she pressed the latch repeatedly, without success it would seem.

"I can't get it to open." Frustration in her voice coupled with a bit of panic told him she didn't find the notion of being locked in here a particularly welcome predicament. He, on the other hand, saw the possibilities of his playing the hero for the only woman he'd ever loved. A good tug ought to open it up, but why rush?

"What are we going to do, Travis?"

The rising panic in her voice quashed his libido, so he turned on the flashlight app on his phone. "Let me take a look." Keeping his voice calm, he stated the obvious. "Neptune must have spooked." With his reins tied to the ring on the door, the horse likely inadvertently pulled it shut. Standing, Travis closed the gap between them and placed his hand over hers on the handle before she jerked away. "Probably just jammed from the humidity swelling the wooden planks." He gave the door another tug. Nothing. Several more attempts offered the same results.

"I can't figure out why it's still stuck," he said, shining his light around the edges of the door. He could still see some light coming through from the outside near the hinges. "Darnedest thing I've ever seen." He tried the handle again but couldn't get it to budge.

Katie brushed his hand aside and began yanking in earnest. Apparently, being stuck in the springhouse with him wasn't high on the list of her favorite things. "Is there someone we can call to help us out of here?" he asked. "I have my cell phone."

"Yeah. My neighbors, Lidia and Jason Brodie. But I doubt we'll get a signal from in here."

He glanced down at the face of the phone. "You're right. No service."

Quit your worrying, Trav. I'll let you both out in time.

He heard Danny as clear as day, but Katie didn't react at all. Hallucinating again.

Instead, she grabbed the cell phone from him and held it aloft, trying to find a signal in this dead zone.

What if he told her he sometimes thought he heard Danny talking to him? Would she think he'd lost his mind? But if by some miracle his friend *was* around, then he wanted help getting them out of here. Katie couldn't remain stranded up here without food and insulin for long. "What the hell are you doing?"

Katie lowered the phone, but saw her cock her head in the phone's illumination. "Sometimes I can get a signal in other places on the farm if I move the phone around."

He didn't realize he'd spoken aloud until she answered. "Sorry. Good idea." Danny was going to make him look like an idiot yet.

Lighten up. Damn, if I was locked in here with a sexy woman like Katie... I'm just trying to help things along. You sounded like you were giving up. But if things go the way I planned, you can name this one after me.

The Danny voice wasn't even making sense anymore. What the hell did he mean by *this one?* And who'd he think he was calling Katie sexy? Not that she wasn't, but a friend wouldn't come right out and say it. Travis tried to shake off the delusion and went to the door to try it again. After multiple attempts, he gave up.

"Why don't we sit down?" she suggested. She took a spot on the stone wall surrounding the water trough again, and he followed suit, taking the phone from her hand just before she lit into him.

"Did you set this up? Is someone out there holding the door closed? Travis, if this is your idea of a joke—"

"Whoa! Don't bust *my* chops. I had nothing to do with this." Man, she didn't trust him as far as she could throw him. "The way I figure it,

Neptune yanked the reins attached to the door, and it shut." No way was he going to tell her they might both be the victims of a supernatural prank, because he didn't want to believe that, either.

Still concerned about Katie's health, though, he asked, "When's the last time you ate something?" She'd been working all afternoon. Had she eaten supper before going for a ride?

"Supper—an hour or two ago."

Damn. She couldn't go too long without eating or her sugar would tank again.

She pulled some pouches out of her pocket. "Don't worry about me. I have fruit gummies on me at all times, just in case. These'll last me all night, if we have to wait for someone to come looking for us tomorrow. I can even share."

"I'll be fine. I trained for situations like this." Well, the not eating part. "We have plenty of water. I'm more worried about you."

After being locked in the springhouse only a short time, Travis was beginning to feel as stir-crazy as he had before his run. "Don't worry. I'll get us out of this mess."

Danny, boy, if you're really responsible for this situation, you'd better resolve it PDQ. If not, I'm going to come after you when I get to the afterlife.

"How? No one's going to come looking for us until tomorrow when my first student arrives. I just hope they think to search up here. They may not realize Neptune's missing, too. But with our trucks in the drive, surely they'll get suspicious. I've never been late for a lesson."

Travis wasn't about to take advantage of the situation or Katie's anxiety, but when she began trembling and wrapped her arms around herself again, he took the shirt from around his neck and handed it to her. "Here, put this on. It's not very heavy, but another layer is better than nothing."

"N-n-no, I'm fine."

"Like hell. You're shivering."

"Well, I wasn't expecting to get locked in here tonight. And it's hot as Hades outside, so I thought I was dressed appropriately." She let him drape the shirt around her shoulders and tugged the flaps tightly closed in front of her chest. For good measure, he wrapped an arm behind her and pulled her against his chest. Lord knows *he* was anything but cold at the moment. Her lemony scent filled the air, making him long to steal another kiss, but he put the brakes on the impulse.

"Travis?" she whispered.

"Yeah?" His voice had become husky.

"You're like an oven."

He grinned. "You're welcome."

"You aren't wearing an undershirt, are you?"

He chuckled. So she'd noticed. "Nope. Not a chance during a muggy Kentucky summer—not during a Tennessee one, either."

She groaned. "I was afraid of that."

She started to wriggle away from him, and while he didn't hold her all that tightly, he hoped she'd reconsider. "I'm just trying to keep you warm, Katie."

"It might be best if I scoot over here a while."

"What's the matter? Don't trust me?"

"No, it's not you. I don't trust *myself*."

Seriously? Was there hope yet?

With the pounding of his heart in his ears, Travis cupped her chin and guided her face toward his. The pulse in her neck jackhammered against his pinky, telling him she was at least as excited as he was. Travis only hesitated a fraction of a second to give her time to say no, but when he heard no protest, he lowered his lips to hers. A sigh puffed against his lips. He teased hers by flicking his tongue playfully, giving her every opportunity to push him away if she didn't want this to go further.

When she wrapped her arms around his neck, he lifted her onto his lap without breaking contact with her mouth, placing her just where he wanted her to be.

Chapter Eleven

A torrent of emotions flooded through Kate. Most of them told her to push him away, but the strongest voice in her head insisted she hold on tight. So she did.

Opening her mouth, her tongue clashed with his until he drew hers deeper into his mouth, releasing and sucking it back even harder. This kiss had gone from zero to one hundred much faster than their prior ones. She melted to the core, throbbing in places that left her unable to think or breathe. The tightening of long-buried frustrations pooled low in the center of her body. In the past, she'd been slow to surrender to him, but not tonight. This might be their last time together, and frankly, she'd missed him. She knew why she'd avoided him all day, but there would be no denying him tonight. They were trapped, and at the moment, she didn't really want to be rescued.

When his hand slipped under the two shirts she wore and cupped her breast, a wimpy warning bell chimed once, twice—but she ignored them both. The feel of his hand over her bra reminded her of all she'd missed out on. None of that mattered now. Years of loneliness and regret evaporated. In this moment, there was only this man and a grown-ass woman with a burning need for him.

He parted the flaps of the shirt he'd just put on her and lifted the hem of hers above her breasts. Her hand raked through his hair as he broke away from her mouth and trailed kisses down the column of her neck. Her breathing became shallow. Thank heavens he supported her back or she might have fallen into the trough behind them.

Perhaps a good dousing's what you both need.

Kate froze. *Daddy?*

Ridiculous. Ignoring her annoying conscience, Kate trailed her fingertips lightly along Travis's neck to his pecs. She stroked the muscles there, playing with the dusting of hair in the center of his chest and pinching one of his nipples at the exact moment he did the same to hers. She drew in a sharp breath as a zing of sensation bolted to the core of her sex.

A moan escaped her. "Oh, Travis." She came close to telling him how much she'd missed *this*, but what if he rejected her after finding out about—

Travis cupped her breast and lowered his lips to her nipple, sucking and biting on the sensitive peak through the silky fabric of her bra. She wanted to remove the thin barrier, but instead clasped her hands behind his head, delighting in his sensual adoration of her body. No man before Travis had made her feel like this, and there had been none since.

Tell him.

Kate wished the nagging voice in her head would mind its own business. She'd tell him about Chelsea. Soon. But not now. Not until—

The door opened and crashed against the wall, startling them both. As abruptly as they'd fallen into each other's arms, they pulled apart. Travis groaned. *No, wait.* She did, too.

More. She wanted so much more! Kate drew a ragged breath, ready to scream in frustration before coming to her senses.

"Your timing sucks," Travis said.

She tugged down her shirt and removed the one he'd loaned her, handing it back to him. "I didn't hear any complaints earlier," she said. Embarrassed suddenly, she wondered if he'd seen the stretch marks on her breasts and belly here in the darkness. She'd remained mostly covered, so probably not. Still, would this happen again, possibly where she wouldn't have the benefit of darkness?

"I wasn't talking to you, Katie." Following his gaze toward the open doorway, Neptune stood staring at the two of them.

He was talking to her horse? She almost giggled as the pent-up energy dissipated.

He planted a chaste kiss on her cheek. "Katie, I still go a little crazy whenever I'm around you."

"Yeah well, in case you missed it, the feeling is mutual." Was he trying to give her a graceful way out of the situation? It might be best that she take it. "Let's forget what happened in the panic of the moment," she said.

Easier said than done.

Smiling down at her and cupping her cheek, he said, "Not a chance, woman. I wasn't in a panic at all. Why don't we head back to the house and find us a comfortable bed?"

"I don't think that would be wise." She stood, wringing her hands. "The bed part, that is. But before we get locked in again, let's get out of here."

Travis chuckled. "No doubt I'll lie awake all night finishing what we started."

Her face flamed at the image he'd planted in her mind. She focused on the situation at hand instead. "Funny how the door came unstuck so easily for Neptune. He must have kicked it in."

Travis glanced at the horse then the door, but seemed skeptical. "I thought horses kicked with their back legs."

She looked over at Neptune who had gone back to munching on the tufts of ultra-green grass near the spring's runoff. If not the horse, then who or what would have busted open the door at just that moment?

Daddy?

Oh, come on, Kate. He'd never manipulated the physical world like that before. Sure, there had been a couple of instances where she'd smelled his pipe tobacco, but nothing like this.

But she'd heard his voice chastising her during that kiss. Could it be?

No. The thought of her dad spying on her with Travis mortified her. Didn't souls have important spiritual work to do on the other side rather than interfering in their daughters' love lives?

She closed her eyes, not believing what she was thinking at the moment. After a deep breath, she said, "We'd better be heading back to the barn before it gets too dark."

"Good idea."

Her nipple and lips still tingled where he'd touched her, kissed her, sucked on her…

"You go ahead and ride back," he suggested, cutting off the memory. "I'll see you in the barn."

Before she left him, she said, "I appreciate your concern about my sugar levels when we thought we might be locked in the springhouse overnight." That he'd been worried about her welfare affected her in equally troubling ways.

"Be careful."

She left the cool interior, untied Neptune's reins, and remounted. Staring down at Travis a moment, she made a decision that had been a long time in the making. "Why don't you come to the kitchen after I cool Neptune down?" Only Kate was the one needing a cool-down tonight. "I made some brownies." She wasn't sure her black-bean version would be to his liking but the high dose of cocoa would certainly calm her jangled nerves.

"Sounds good." His smile warmed her all over again, but then he grew serious. "God, Katie, I've missed you."

She couldn't bare her heart to him yet. "Oh, I doubt you've given me much more than a thought or two all these years."

Fishing for compliments much, Kate?

"I'll plead the Fifth then." His grin once again made her stomach flip-flop. If things had continued in the direction they'd been going, she and Travis would have been making love in the springhouse again. Would they have had sex if Neptune—*or the ghost of her father?*—hadn't called a halt to their passionate embrace? Lord knows she wouldn't have had the self-control to stop herself.

Thank God someone or something had, though. Think of the regrets she'd add to the list if they'd gone any further tonight without her being fully honest with him! All hell probably would break loose as early as tonight, assuming she got brave enough to confess over the brownies. Despite the niggling feeling she was courting disaster, she asked, "Would you like to ride back with me on Neptune?"

His eyes smoldered, heating her up all over again. He grinned. "No thanks. I doubt I could keep my hands off you, and we both need some time to sort out where we're going. That might best be done separately."

She nodded. At least one of them had a clear head. Inviting him inside her house again might also have colossal ramifications, but she wouldn't rescind the offer. She pressed her knees against Neptune's sides, clicking her tongue as she trotted off toward the barn.

As the clapboard farmhouse came into view, doubts assailed her once more. How was she going to tell him about Chelsea when the time came? How could she explain to him why she'd done what she'd done? Worst of all, how was he going to react to the life-altering news?

She was still wiping down Neptune when Travis popped in to say he was going to grab a quick bath. No doubt, he'd prefer a cold shower after what just happened in the springhouse, but he'd have to settle for the hand-held nozzle he'd installed this week in the apartment's tub.

After he left, she finished with Neptune and started doling out oats to the horses. When Travis finished bathing, he came back to help haul water. He'd dressed in tight jeans and a denim shirt, his hair still wet from his bath. She fought the inappropriate urge to run her fingers through it. And now she was wet, too. How the man could elicit such responses from her long-dormant body with his mere presence or a casual glance was beyond her.

Get your mind off the unattainable.

"Oh, I ought to warn you about the brownies," she said as they made their way toward the house together after the horses were taken care of. "They're made so as not to trigger a sugar spike."

"I wondered how they could be part of your diet. What's the catch?"

"A secret ingredient. But if I told you what it is, I'd have to kill you." She grinned at his stunned expression as she opened the kitchen door.

"Sounds serious. Is it legal?"

She laughed out loud. "Not *that* ingredient! This is Kentucky, after all. And, yes, it's perfectly legal, just not one you'd associate with baked goods." She went to the sink to wash up, and he followed suit.

While he poured the bottle of Fairlife milk, she carried the container of brownies to the table. "Let's dig in," she said.

She waited for him to take his first tentative bite, chew, and swallow. As if not quite sure yet, he took another bite, this one even bigger. Then he smiled at her. "These are some of the best brownies I've ever tasted."

Her gaze shifted to his mouth where he'd been tasting *her* less than an hour ago. When he licked a crumb of brownie from the corner of his lips, a heaviness pooled in her lower abdomen. She remembered his tongue entangled with hers…

Once again, Travis made her experience emotions she hadn't allowed herself to feel since their breakup. Her mind conjured up any number of sensual scenarios featuring him in the starring role of each, but she tried to quell them. Most likely, none of them would come true.

"Aren't you going to eat yours?"

Picking up the brownie, she took a bite. They did taste good, but she'd had them lots of times. "I've gotten good at finding ways to enjoy the treats I love with a few necessary substitutions among the ingredients."

They were coming to the end of the brownies and their last evening together before she would tell him the secret that most likely would end any chance at their having a future together romantically. Oh, he'd probably be a part of her life forever as they shared the parenting of

Chelsea, but she wanted to enjoy these last moments with him without acrimony.

After he took a swig of milk, he asked, "What's on the agenda for tomorrow?"

That all depends. "Um, I have a light day with lessons because half my students are at church camp. I should finish up by lunchtime."

"Perfect. Play tour guide for me tomorrow."

Tell him tonight.

She ignored the nagging voice in the back of her mind. The thought of spending another idyllic day with him like yesterday's time at the Red River Gorge was too tempting.

Don't be selfish.

"Aren't your folks expecting you Sunday?"

"I was just up there for Memorial Day weekend two weeks ago. Besides, they don't even know I'm in Kentucky." He'd been close to his parents back in college, so she wondered why he hadn't told them about this journey into the past. Did they harbor any resentment toward Kate for calling it off with Travis? How might a meeting with his parents and siblings go when they found out about Chelsea?

"Do you want to split one?" he asked, reaching for another brownie.

"No, but you go ahead. Two's my limit."

He bit into another and grinned. "Man, they're good."

She couldn't watch him eat without another carnal side trip, so she picked at the crumbs on her plate. "How are all the Coopers doing?" He hadn't said much about his family up to now.

He reached for his fourth brownie, the last on the plate, and swallowed before answering. "Mom's trying to convince Dad it's time to join her in retirement."

"I can't believe *she's* retired."

"Well, it was partly due to her health after getting diabetes. Being office manager at his company was too sedentary. To keep her A1C down, she quit to become more active." He took a drink of milk before continuing. "Clint's poised to take over the firm whenever Dad steps down. He's married now with two little kids. His wife, Susan, helps out with the books, working from home."

"And your sisters?"

"Tanya moved to Chicago to work for a major tech firm. She travels a lot. I'm lucky if we cross paths twice a year anymore. And Shania and Emmylou started their own business together."

She had to smile at the way Joe and Loretta, Travis's parents, had named their five children after the country-music stars they loved. The boys for Travis Tritt and Clint Black, and the triplets for Shania Twain, Tanya Tucker, and Emmylou Harris. His mom told Kate years ago that she'd been named for Loretta Lynn and wanted to pass along the tradition.

"What kind of start-up?"

"They find missing people."

Well, that certainly was an unusual career choice. "Sounds interesting. As long as those people want to be found, I suppose."

Kate used to fantasize about tracking down her mother, but then reality clicked in. She didn't want to risk another rejection if her mom didn't want to be found.

"They're a whiz at reuniting adoptees with birth parents and long-lost siblings and such. And they love what they're doing. They get to travel quite a bit, too. All three of my sisters have a touch of wanderlust. Emmy and Shania still live in Louisville, but they could work anywhere given the majority of what they do happens online."

"Fascinating. Those two always seemed closer to each other than with Tanya."

"Yeah. Tanya's a bit of an introvert and a loner."

Travis stood. "I'm going to call it a night. Why don't you sleep in again tomorrow? I can handle the horses and stalls."

"Thanks, but I'm already back on my schedule of rising at the crack of dawn."

He smiled at her. "I won't complain about having you working alongside me."

Memories of ogling his half-naked body while they fixed the fence flashed across her mind. Her carnal thoughts had set her body on fire and had probably led to that kiss and their eager fumblings in the springhouse a little while ago.

With mere days before Chelsea came home, her conscience told her it was time to tell him. Travis would need to come to grips with the news before he'd be ready to meet his daughter for the first time. So why weren't the words coming to her?

"Good night," Travis said, walking toward the door.

She followed him. "Night, Travis."

As she watched him walk back to the barn, she thought about calling out and offering to let him sleep in the house again. But, no. Chelsea didn't need to come home to find that her mom had a hired man sleeping down the hall from them.

Be fair, Kate.

Okay, not a hired hand at all, but Chelsea's dad. She closed and locked the door and made her way upstairs to prepare for bed.

On a whim, she bypassed her bathroom and walked to the end of the hallway to where her father had slept. She'd thrown out the mattress he'd died on and had totally redone the space into a guest room, although she rarely had anyone stay over. Lidia and Jason had stayed a few months when their house was undergoing extensive renovations, but that had been years ago. It had become more a storage room for winter things in summer and vice versa. The room used to smell sweet from her father's pipe, and she often came in here in the weeks and months after his death to feel closer to him.

Oh, Daddy, I miss you.

She wiped at her stinging eyes and moved toward the mantel over the fireplace. When Kate was little, Daddy had stripped off layers of paint and stained it to match the walnut bedroom suite that had once belonged to her great-grandmother.

Kate looked at some of the photos of Michaels family ancestors, most of whom she'd never known. There were side-by-side pics of Daddy—one with infant Kate on his chest while they both slept and another of him in the same pose with his granddaughter as a baby. Kate had wished at the time to have been able to place Chelsea on Travis's chest to carry on the tradition, but that hadn't been possible.

Kate and Chelsea had missed out on having connections with extended family members. Bringing Travis into the family would change that for Chelsea, opening her up knowing a slew of aunts, an uncle, and grandparents who would dote on her every move.

If Daddy had lived longer, no doubt he'd have made a profound impact on Chelsea's life, too. Her eyes swimming with tears, Kate picked up the picture of Daddy holding her daughter. Travis should have been the one in that photo. They'd all been robbed of so many years together.

Sometimes life just wasn't fair.

Only it was her actions, not random fate, that had deprived Travis of having those moments with his baby girl. Her heart ached at being the reason he didn't know his daughter.

Wiping at her eyes, Kate turned and left the room, flipping off the light switch and making her way to her bedroom. It had been a long time since she'd felt this alone. Sitting on her bed, she opened the drawer to her nightstand and pulled out three photos. If her father had known she had them, no doubt he'd have destroyed them along with all other evidence of her mother's existence.

She didn't know why she'd kept these hidden away to this day. *Yes, you do.* Even after all this time, her chest ached to look at them. They evoked thoughts of the fictitious relationship she pretended to have had with her mom before she'd left soon after Kate's fifth birthday. While she had vague memories of the woman, nowadays she wasn't sure how much was real and how much she'd conjured up.

Kate's favorite image was taken on that last birthday together. Her mother's eyes were animated and her smile beaming, lit from some-where inside, and she appeared ready to help Kate blow out the candles, if need be. Kate's smile was radiant, too. She couldn't remember being that happy for the rest of her childhood.

The tears were back, flooding her eyes and rolling down her cheeks. How could she still long for something she'd never really had?

Kate dashed away the tears and tucked the snapshots back into the drawer before heading to the bathroom to shower. Tomorrow would take a toll on her, this time with memories of a different part of a past filled with regrets. She needed to be mentally prepared for the afternoon with Travis. No more excuses.

The time to tell him about Chelsea had come.

Chapter Twelve

"What the hell do you think you were doing locking them in there like that, Danny?" Ben kicked a porch post, not unlike the way he'd kicked open the springhouse door a short while ago.

Danny balled his hands into fists. Ben was fit to be tied, but Danny had no intention of caving in to his bullheadedness. He had a mission and limited time to achieve success. Trying to exhibit a cool exterior, Danny pointed out, "I didn't notice either of them complaining."

Realizing their earthly charges had parted ways for the night, Ben and Danny wandered around to the front porch, settling in the swing after Katie went upstairs.

"That's my daughter you and your buddy are messing around with."

"And Travis is my best friend," Danny said, giving a nod toward the barn where Travis had disappeared. "Don't tell me you didn't see the sparks flying between those two. They're perfect for each other. He never stopped loving her, if you ask me."

Ben scrutinized the barn before turning toward Danny and staring through narrowed eyelids. "That may be, but locking them in the springhouse to force them together isn't the way to go about making them see that."

"How do you know? You showed up and kicked open the door just when things were getting hot and heavy," Danny grumbled.

"Dammit, the last thing Kate needs is another baby with him."

"Maybe that's *exactly* what she needs. And I know Travis would jump at the chance to be a father from the get-go this time."

"He doesn't even know he's a father the first time yet. How can you be so sure?"

"Because I've seen him around kids. The man's a natural."

Ben remained silent a moment. Had he made any progress in winning the older spirit over?

"Just how do you expect to get through to him? Haven't noticed you having all that much success."

Danny shrugged, fully aware the old man had changed the subject rather than concede that Danny had a point. Hell, Ben was right. He hadn't convinced Travis he was with him at all. Katie seemed slightly more believing that she'd heard her father.

"If you've got any better ideas, I'm all ears," Danny said.

Ben became silent again. Danny could hear the June bugs and see the yard lit up with lightning bugs. He missed the little things he'd been enchanted by as a boy that he'd lost the ability to enjoy later in his miserable life.

"Getting those two together isn't my primary mission," Ben said. "I'm here to undo the mess I created between her and her mother."

Danny remembered the scene he'd witnessed earlier tonight in Katie's bedroom, which left a bitter taste in his mouth. "Yeah, those tattered photos she saved broke my heart. You really were a dirtbag, you know?"

Ben stiffened then nodded. "You're right. I sure was."

"Well, admitting it is the first step. Her mom's still alive, right?"

"Last I checked, she was. Living in Oregon. Don't know how she wound up there, but she's always been a drifter. That's how I met her. What worries me is that her health isn't all that good."

"Terminal?"

"Not like cancer or anything. She doesn't take care of herself, though. Her diabetes is out of control, too."

"Does Katie know her medical history?"

Ben shook his head. "Not for that side of the family, anyway, because I had no idea myself. Kate and I didn't talk about her mom at all. I let Kate think I was just too torn up about Gail's deserting us. Truthfully, I just wanted to keep Kate all to myself. Selfish bastard, I know."

"I'll say."

Ben turned toward him. "You sure are an agreeable sot."

Danny held up his hands. "I haven't had a drink in five months."

"Because you've been *dead* for that long."

Danny shrugged. "We aren't here to talk about my mistakes. And I'm sure I haven't said anything you haven't told yourself a hundred times since you crossed over."

With a sigh, Ben said, "A million times maybe."

"You taught Katie to hoard her own daughter, just like you did with her. At least I can see her wavering before it's too late to redeem herself. She'll come around, once she knows she can trust Travis. And there's no better man to be Chelsea's dad than my buddy. So how do you plan to get Katie to search for her mom?"

Ben seemed to think on it an awfully long time. "All I can do is try my damnedest to pry that last letter from Gail loose and get it in front of Kate's face. She came darn close to it tonight, but she'll never find it on her own unless she takes down that mirror over the fireplace. Not sure how much kinetic energy I can muster."

"You sure had no trouble with the springhouse door."

"Getting Neptune to bump his head against the door helped."

"Well, maybe between the two of us we can gather enough force to nudge the envelope out of its hiding place." Danny thought a minute. "If that doesn't work, how about a visit to your wife? Or widow, I guess you'd say now."

"I tried to visit her soon after I crossed over, but she cussed me out."

Danny laughed. "Think maybe you deserve it?" He sobered. "Wait. She could see and hear you?"

"Oh, yeah. Even when we were together, she'd told me she communicated with spirits who had crossed over. I never believed her back then, but man, I do now."

"If she's so intuitive, then convince her she needs to come back here."

"Tried that that first time. She refused. I guess she has some things in her past she's not too proud of. Doesn't want Kate to be ashamed of her."

Danny shook his head. "Crazy how humans in the physical world worry about the stupidest shit, isn't it? We sure don't care about any of that over here."

Danny had made the same mistakes on Earth. His own parents had disowned him long before he wound up in juvie and later joined the Army. His father was on this side of the veil now, but Danny hadn't reached out to him yet. Danny did visit his sister once after his death. She seemed aware of his presence, but became frightened of him, so he decided to keep his distance after that.

His mom, on the other hand, was so closed down spiritually he couldn't even visit her in a dream without her writing it off as a delusion. He didn't want her to think she was going bonkers, so he'd left her alone, too. As for his dad, well, maybe some grudges did carry over to this side. Neither had sought the other out in the past five months.

But Travis was a different story. Not that he hadn't dropped everything to come up here after that dream visit from Danny. "Travis'll come around. He's just too logical with that engineer's brain of his. Eventually, my melodic voice will make an impression on him."

"You mean nagging voice, don't you?"

"Well, that, too." Danny laughed. "Tonight, I saw some wavering in his disbelief."

"You think so?"

Danny shrugged. He hoped so because that would help in his mission to get Travis to understand what had happened the night he died. "Perhaps Katie would be a little more open than he is, though.

Of course, they both heard me whistle at Angus, before convincing themselves it had been done by the other one. One way or another, I'm going to get through his thick skull."

Ben nodded. "I believe you will. Now, if you'll excuse me, I have an equally stubborn woman in Oregon to pay a visit to." He slapped Danny on the back. "If I strike out with Gail and you do with Travis, however, we'll go to plan B."

Whatever that is.

*   *   *

After pulling himself away from Danny, Ben had instantaneously found himself in the kitchen of Gail's Portland bungalow. She looked worse than the last time he'd been there, dark circles under her eyes and a row of pill bottles scattered across the beat-up tabletop. She wasn't staring at those, though. Instead, she had a photo in her hand. He drew closer to see who it was, having a feeling he already knew.

Kate.

Strangely enough, it was from the same day as the birthday photo Kate had held onto all these years and had taken out tonight. Their daughter wore her Sunday best and a smile as wide as Kentucky. The joy in her eyes as she looked up at her mother in this one gave him another pang of regret.

"I was so wrong, Gail."

"About time you figured that out, you bastard. A little late, though."

"Bullshit. Kate will welcome you back in a minute."

"We went over this last time. I'm not going to mess up her life at this stage in the game. She probably thinks I'm dead by now, anyway."

"No, she doesn't. She's just afraid to get her hopes up and search you out only to be rejected." He almost said *again*, but caught himself in time. Gail had never rejected their daughter. *She's just been a lost soul herself.*

Gail stood, the maple chair scraping against the linoleum as she made her way to the sink to fill a glass of water from the tap. Her blonde hair was held up by a clip. She'd always worn it loose when they were married. He'd loved her hair. While Kate had inherited his brown hair, Chelsea's was exactly like her grandmother's.

"Write her another letter," he begged. "You can find her address on a computer somewhere. It's not a rural route address any longer but has a road and house number. I promise no one will intercept this one."

She shook her head as she carried the glass back to the table and started opening the pill bottles. "I wouldn't know where to start. It's better she hates me for deserting her than to be ashamed of me for what I did to survive."

He didn't like hearing the despondency in her voice. She'd always been lighthearted and carefree. "Don't do anything stupid with those." Danny's story about mixing pills and booze made Ben nervous, although she didn't seem to have any alcohol nearby.

She grinned wryly. "These are just for diabetes and high blood pressure, you old coot. I'm not planning to off myself, if that's what you're worried about."

"Good, because I met up with a fella on this side—a fellow Army vet—whose death looked like a suicide to his friends. Says it wasn't, but the folks left behind don't know that."

A thought suddenly occurred to him. Would Gail's death trigger a next-of-kin notification for Kate? He was afraid to ask, but if he couldn't get her to reconnect with Kate while alive, he didn't want Kate to get word from her mother only after Gail had crossed over to this side.

Dammit, he needed to get the two of them together sooner than later. "Don't you even want to see your granddaughter? She looks more like you every day."

Gail stared at him, wrinkling her brow, and he caught the first spark of light in her eyes. "I didn't know Kate married."

"She didn't, but she has a twelve-year-old daughter who's the spitting image of you."

Her eyes grew bright. "That's incredible. I would love to see her. Is she on Facebook?"

"What's Facebook?"

"An online social media thing."

He drew a deep breath. She only wanted to see her on a computer screen? "How the hell would I know? I never even used a computer. But I'd guess most of her social life is at school and church."

Gail shook her head. "You never could keep up with the times." She stared at her hands a moment, then whispered, "I've tried to find Kate there, but she must not be into that stuff, either."

"Too busy running that farm."

Gail gave a lopsided grin. "She surely didn't inherit my vagabond genes, did she? You were always so connected to that land. Her roots run deep there. I'm beginning to think having roots isn't a bad thing anymore."

"I wish you'd get in touch with her. You don't need to spend your last years all alone when you have family out there to love you. You moved around too much."

"I've been here in Oregon for eight years and nine months." Apparently, she could settle down in one place if she wanted to. "Only reason I'm here is that I held my last job here. I can't work anymore but got on subsidized housing."

Ben sighed. "I bet your daughter would put you up in our old bedroom and take care of you the rest of your life." Were her days numbered? Obadiah had hinted that someone's were, and Kate looked a lot healthier than Gail did.

Gail waved him away. "Go back wherever you came from, Ben. Leave me alone."

How was he going to be able to convince Gail to reunite with her daughter in case time was running out? Kate didn't have much to go on, either, to locate her mother. As a kid, she'd only been taught that her parents were Gail and Ben Michaels, in case of emergencies. Her birth certificate in the bank box would give Kate her mother's maiden name, but the damned woman stopped using that when she left Reno years ago. Of all things, she went by the made-up name Serenity Chula now.

"Take care of yourself, Gail. But don't be surprised if you hear from Kate one of these days." He needed to lay some groundwork, though, to get the girl to embark on the search. Travis had mentioned having two sisters who found missing people. Maybe they could help—not that Kate was one to ask anyone for help.

He and Danny would just have to shake loose that last letter. Perhaps Kate would pick up on the clues to Gail's current identity if she read between the lines.

As he receded back into the limbo he was stuck in, she faded away.

His first attempt at manipulating the physical world was busting down the springhouse door to slow things down between Kate and Travis. Danny was probably right. He needed to butt out. At least this time, he'd be doing something for good. What could be more noble than to reunite one lonely daughter with her mother?

Chapter Thirteen

The night before what would be one of the most monumental days of her life, Kate was restless. She flipped her pillow and punched it several times before trying once again to fall asleep.

"Trust him."

Kate jumped at the sound of a strange man's voice in her bedroom and reached for the nightstand to turn on the light, wishing she had a weapon she could use against the intruder. If only Travis was sleeping down the hall, she'd scream. But when she turned on the light, the room was empty.

"Trav's the salt of the earth. You won't find any man better."

The disembodied voice seemed to be coming from near the window, but she was on the second floor, and that window was shut tight while the central air ran.

Had she fallen asleep without realizing it?

"Who's there?"

"The name's Danny."

Who on earth was…wait. Danny? Travis's friend? His *dead* friend?

Clearly, she was losing her mind…or dreaming.

Kate lay down again and closed her eyes. First, she'd thought she heard him in the springhouse, and now this. Perhaps if she focused on something else, her imagination would stop playing tricks on her or she'd switch to a more interesting dream. For a moment, she tried to work out how to implement a new technique she planned to show Melissa and Miss Pickles tomorrow.

"Travis will make a great dad. You have nothing to worry about."

Short of stuffing her fingers in her ears and chanting *lalalalala* the way Chelsea used to do, Kate didn't know how to block out the disembodied voice. Maybe she could test him to see if he truly was Travis's Army buddy haunting her bedroom.

"Sure you can. My left leg was blown off above the knee by an IED in Iraq. Just ask Travis. He'll tell you it's me, because I know he didn't reveal that to you the other day when he talked about me."

He was reading her thoughts? She remembered back to that conversation. Travis had mentioned Danny's recent suicide, but nothing about an amputation. How was she supposed to ask Travis something like that without a good reason—something more rational than that a ghost had told her.

"Correction. It wasn't a suicide," the disembodied voice interrupted, again as if reading her thoughts.

"*I* didn't say it was," Kate argued, then shook her head. Now she was talking to herself...or whoever this "Danny" was.

"I know that's what Trav told you, but he's dead wrong. You can help him understand I didn't think it through. Just needed some relief from the pain and mixed booze and pills."

"I've never met you before. Why would he believe anything I said?"

"He trusts you. I can tell."

She'd done nothing to earn his trust and was about to shatter any chance of him trusting her in the future.

"Look, you're good for him. I'd seen him around my buddy Craig's kids, and well, when I saw how miserable Trav has been blaming himself for my death, I decided he needed a distraction."

Is that what she was?

"When I found you and Chelsea, I knew you two would help him to move on."

Danny had been spying on them? For how long?

"You have to tell him about Chelsea, Katie."

She sat up in bed and shouted to the wall across the room. "My name is Kate, and I don't have to do anything." Apparently, he couldn't read her mind, because she'd already made that decision.

"No disrespect, ma'am, but you're running scared and basing your decisions on some things your dad told you that, well, weren't completely true."

"How could you possibly know anything about him? I've never met you before in my life—or yours." Did souls gain universal knowledge of life events while on the other side?

"Let's just say your dad and I have talked a time or two."

"Prove it." She couldn't believe she was challenging a ghost.

"He uses the smell of his pipe tobacco to let you know when he's near. Most recently, he did that in Neptune's stall."

Okay, there's no way he could know that, was there? Still, she wasn't ready to concede that he really communicated with Daddy on the other side. "What was the name of his first childhood horse?"

"Hmm. That hasn't come up in our conversations. Hold on. Let me ask him."

He was silent a moment. Was he gone? She hoped so. She couldn't believe he actually had gone off to consult with her father on this. Until he said, "Tigger."

How could he have known that? Who *was* this guy?

"Is that right?" he prompted.

"Yeah. Tigger bounced around and bucked him off so much at first, that's the name he gave him." Daddy had shared lots of stories about his first horse. Sadly, the horse had suffered a ruptured aorta when only five years old. Daddy had mourned that horse a very long time.

"Now will you listen to me?"

"What exactly do you want?"

"I want you to give Trav a chance. Take a leap of faith. Tell him the truth. He deserves to know about his daughter."

"Did Travis send you up here?"

Danny laughed out loud. "Hardly. He's like you, trying to pretend

I'm not really talking to him."

Not unlike her father's spirit in the springhouse earlier. "So was my daddy trying to talk to me in the springhouse tonight?"

"How should I know? I had other things on my mind."

"I just thought all you ghosts hung out together and could read each other's thoughts."

"Sometimes, but I don't belong on this side. I wasn't finished with my life contract there. So the less time I spend with dead people, the better."

Her head hurt trying to figure out what he was talking about.

"But Travis truly knows nothing about Chelsea. You need to tell him. Just like you need to tell him I didn't off myself."

"Why don't you tell him yourself?"

"Tried, but he ignores me." As an aside, he said, "Give me another minute, Obadiah. This is important."

Who was Obadiah? "Okay, tell me what really happened that night, Danny."

"New contract? All right, all right." He sighed. "Sorry, Katie, but apparently, I'm needed elsewhere. Remember what I said. Tell Trav about his daughter. No more delays or excuses. And about me, too!"

"I already planned on telling him tomorrow." The silence in the room was deafening. "Wait! You can't just disappear like that! We weren't finished talking!" Still nothing.

Kate plopped back onto the pillow, wide-eyed and staring at the ceiling. "I can't believe I was just yelling at a ghost to come back so we could talk more."

What just happened? Could she have dreamed it? Was she hallucinating? His knowing about Daddy's tobacco smoke didn't really prove anything she didn't know herself. This could all be some elaborate half-awake dream her mind had cooked up to handle the stress of the last few days.

But there was one piece of information she didn't know already that Travis could corroborate—did Danny lose a leg to an IED in

Iraq? Which one did Danny say it was? Left? Regardless of whether she remembered that part correctly, she could try and get that information from Travis to find out if she was losing her mind or had actually been visited by a ghost.

She rolled over, stared at the empty pillow beside her, then reached out, and placed her hand on it. Having him here the past few days gave her a glimpse at what might have been if she hadn't broken it off with him. Travis should have been here next to her all these years.

And would have been, if she'd told him about Chelsea when she'd gotten pregnant.

Tomorrow, the safe, predictable world she and Chelsea shared would be blown apart when Kate confessed her secret.

* * *

Kate had slept fitfully the night before and had gone through the morning's lesson on automatic. She'd begged off taking Travis sightseeing, knowing she couldn't put off the inevitable any longer. But, after checking to be sure she could eat out, Travis suggested they go to Midway for a late lunch.

Now that she'd decided to tell Travis about Chelsea, she wasn't as concerned about people in Midway seeing them together, so she jumped at the offer. But she had no intention of creating a scene in public.

Coward.

The sound system played an old Sinatra song in The Grey Goose as they were guided to a secluded table in the back. Travis held her elbow as she took her seat. She'd expected him to take his on the opposite side of the table, but instead, he chose the chair next to hers. Trying to study the menu and pretend she wasn't aware of their arms brushing each other's blew her concentration. Good thing she knew by heart what she wanted, because all she could think about was his scent and the warmth emanating from his body.

"What do you recommend?"

That you sit on the other side of this table.

"Um, they're well-known for their burgers. I usually have mine without the bun, but I'm not in the mood for one today. I'm going for one of their unique pizzas. The pesto one is delish." Her glucose was under control, and their pizzas were thin crusted, so she should be fine. "Or you might prefer a steak, Travis. No matter what, though, we're getting their beer cheese as an appetizer." She was rambling, but couldn't shut up.

"You've hardly looked at the menu. Did you memorize it?"

She laughed. "I've missed coming here, but I guess when something works, it doesn't need to change."

"Why don't we share a pizza then?"

"Sure. And the beer cheese." She loved that stuff.

He grinned. "I think we can manage to polish off both. We worked hard this morning."

He ordered a beer and she a water with lemon as she tried once more to calm her nerves.

"I've had a great time with you this week, Katie."

"It's been nice." Her fingers nervously rearranged her silverware.

"Spending time here with you has given me more peace than I've had in a long time."

She'd enjoyed herself, too. Much more than she'd expected to when she'd first learned he was on his way here. His phone call seemed like ages ago. "I haven't allowed myself to go for a hike or a horseback ride or even out to lunch like this in a very long while."

"I'd love to keep stealing you away from work." He wrapped his arm around the back of her chair, and she sat ramrod straight. Her body warmed as her breathing became shallow. Tucked away in the quiet corner with him, she wanted nothing more than to rest her head on his shoulder. But this wasn't a date, even if he was treating it like one. Also, she wouldn't send out signals like that just before telling him...

They sat in silence a few moments. Then he said, "Do you have any students headed to Louisville in August to compete during the Fair?"

"That depends on how well Melissa does in Lexington. She'll have enough points, and her parents certainly can afford it. She might at least ribbon if her class is split into three groups of twenty-five, which has been the case in recent years. Still, that's only nine ribbons for seventy-five riders. A lot of expense for such a risky outcome."

"It's a shame that girl you told me about the other day can't afford to compete at the level she'd like if she's that good," he said.

Kate held her breath, not knowing where this conversation would go or why he kept bringing up Chelsea. But he continued, seemingly unaware of her nervousness. "Some kids don't get a chance while others who may not be as good are front and center for everything simply because their parents have more money." Did she detect some resentment in his voice?

"It's the way of the world, I'm afraid." Kate had gotten used to disappointment early on, so perhaps her view was skewed. "I'm sure there were things you wanted that your parents couldn't afford to give you."

"Hell, yeah. With five kids, they had to scrimp just to feed us. In seventh grade, I wanted so badly to go on a class trip to New York City, but it might as well have been the moon."

"But you don't seem any worse for wear to have missed it." Was Chelsea going to have similar regrets many years later about not being able to do everything she wanted?

"The perspective of age and understanding lessens the disappointments. Besides, I've been there numerous times now." The server came and took their orders, but he stuck to the same topic. "So what's your biggest childhood disappointment?"

She didn't even have to stop and think. "Not having my mom at my graduations." Or Christmases, Easters, birthdays. "And all the other special occasions a parent should witness." Having shared those joys with her own daughter, Kate saw clearly how much her mother had missed out on, and what she'd stolen from Travis.

"It has to be rough losing a parent when you're young."

Kate had never told Travis the truth about her mother before, choosing instead to spout a lot of half-truths about losing her and her being gone. She hadn't intended to do so now until the words spilled out. "I lost her, but not to death. She left my father—and me—to make a life of her own somewhere out West."

Travis cupped her chin to turn her face toward him and look into her eyes. "Why didn't you ever tell me that?"

She tried to avoid his gaze, but he was relentless. The intense concern in his eyes melted away her indifference to her mom. "It isn't something I share with anyone."

"But we were closer than anyone else. I wouldn't expect you to keep something like that from me."

Oh, Travis, if you only knew the secrets I've hidden from you.

His face began to blur before her as her eyes welled up, and she tried to give him a lopsided grin to lessen the pain. "You took me to see your mom when we first started to date. She treated me like another daughter from the day I met her. I felt motherly love for the first time I could remember." Not that she'd feel that again if she ever returned to the Cooper household after having kept Chelsea from her father and his family all these years. She hoped they'd want to finally get to know their granddaughter and niece, though.

A rogue tear trekked down her cheek, and Travis bent down to kiss it away. Then another on the left cheek, which he took care of the same way.

Kate broke away, fighting the urge to bury her face against his chest in order to hide her raw emotions. "It's water under the bridge now. I hardly ever think about my mom anymore."

Liar.

The beer cheese arrived, although he didn't pay it any mind. "What's your mom's name? Where did she go when she left? How old would she be now?"

Kate blinked away any remaining tears and met his gaze. The same old fears reared their heads again. If she'd done something to make her mother leave forever, what made her think the woman would accept her now? "You can't fix this, Travis. I know your sisters find missing people, but Mom has always known where I am. If she wanted to see me again, she could have done so at any time. It's been almost three decades, and she hasn't reached out to me. That's all I need to know." She reached for a carrot stick and dipped it into the soft, sharp cheddar cheese.

"What if she didn't stay away by choice? What if circumstances, or even someone else, kept her away? Could be she didn't return because of a financial or physical barrier."

"There are phones, emails, letters. To have zero contact with me whatsoever is quite telling."

He fiddled with his fork a minute. "Are you sure she's still alive?"

A dagger-like pain ripped through her chest. As much as she didn't want to seek her mother out, the thought that she'd *never* be able to see her again tore her apart. Could that be why she'd never made contact with her after leaving?

No. Somehow Kate believed she'd have sensed it if her mother had died. She refused to contemplate the finality of death. "I can still remember that last goodbye. She said she was going to visit family or friends in San Diego. Said she'd be back—but that was almost twenty-nine years ago. I never saw her again."

"How'd your parents meet? They sound like total opposites."

She supposed it wouldn't hurt to tell him what little she knew. "Mom was selling her handmade jewelry as a vendor one Christmas at the Kentucky Horse Park. Dad had brought up one of his horses for a demonstration there. A more unlikely pair would be hard to find. But for some reason, they hit it off."

"Apparently, or you wouldn't be here." Travis's attempt at levity brought a smile to her face, too. "Background doesn't determine who you'll be attracted to. Look at us. I was city, and you were country, but we had a lot in common and no trouble connecting."

They certainly had. "That's because you loved the same country things I did and spending time with me outdoors. Mom, on the other hand, was never into the horse farm or rural Kentucky living. She was rather…bohemian. A true California hippie. Sometime after my fifth birthday, she chose to go back to that lifestyle, it seems."

"She was here for more than five years, though. If she were truly that flighty, wouldn't she have deserted you and your dad long before?"

"Daddy said she was a dreamer. That wasn't the first instance of her wandering off. He said she felt the need to roam a couple of other times. I don't remember them, but I was awfully young. But she didn't come back that final time."

"I still think you ought to find out why."

Kate nibbled on a celery stick and gave his words more thought.

"Let me ask Shania and Emmy to see what they can find. If you have your birth certificate, it would give them enough information to start."

Her heart pounded at the thought of finding the answers to questions she'd kept buried inside her entire life. Should she give him what they'd need? Deep down, though, she did want to know the truth, despite her fears. "The certificate is in my safe-deposit box at the bank down the street." She hadn't any reason to look at it in all these years but supposed it would have her mother's maiden name on it. All she remembered was Gail Michaels, but doubted her mother kept the Michaels family name if she wanted nothing to do with Kate's father— or her.

Would seeing the name written on that piece of paper churn up memories she'd rather not remember?

"We'll go get it after lunch."

"I don't have the key with me."

"Okay, then we can get the key and come back into town." He seemed more anxious to get started than she was. "She may have remarried by now," Travis pointed out.

Could Kate have a whole other family? Half-siblings, maybe? Did she really want to know?

"My parents never divorced, but I doubt someone who'd abandon her husband and daughter would be all that concerned about committing bigamy. What I can't figure out is why Daddy didn't file for a divorce. Any court would have granted one on grounds of desertion."

"You're sure he didn't?"

She nodded. "I asked him once why he didn't date a woman from church who seemed interested in him, and he said he was still married."

"What if she didn't desert him but was pushed away?" His words echoed what Kate had done to Travis, not that they'd been married.

"It doesn't affect my relationship with her, if there ever will be one."

Travis squeezed her forearm. "I'm sure it's scary to think about confronting her or even meeting her amicably again after all these years, but maybe it will give you peace of mind and closure."

"What if I don't like what your sisters find out about her?" And worse yet, what if her mother still wanted nothing to do with her?

"No one is going to force you to do anything you don't want. Let's see if they can locate her first. Then you can decide how you want to pursue it after that. They've worked miracles before, so be prepared for a result—positive or negative."

The server brought them their pizza. Not wanting to continue this conversation, Kate dove in. But her mind swirled at all the possibilities before shifting to what she planned to tell Travis tonight. No more stalling. Danny was right. Her stomach knotted up, and she could barely finish one slice of the pizza. She'd forgotten about last night's encounter, but needed to talk with Travis about him, too. That's something they could do here this afternoon.

Hoping to steer him to Danny, she said, "Tell me more about your time in the Army." Would he be like her father and remain closed-lipped about it?

"I worked with a great group of soldiers. Our job was blowing things up."

She grinned, shaking her head. "You sound as though you enjoyed that." Or was he merely sugarcoating it for her? She needed to guide the conversation to his deceased friend. "I'm sure there were tough times while you were over there."

He shrugged off her observation. "We had a job to do, and we did it. You have to focus on your mission at all times and never forget you're a target. There's lots of hurry up and wait, monotony and boredom, but you can't let your guard down for a second. Then all too soon you're back home in civilian clothes trying to make a smooth transition into the normal world again." He glanced down, peeling the label from his sweating beer bottle. "Some never quite make that transition."

Like most people, she'd heard the statistics. She swallowed hard and asked, "Like your friend Danny?"

He nodded, but didn't say anything. *Keep him talking.*

"Any chance you'll be deployed again?" The thought of him being sent overseas and having something happen to him instilled new fears in her. How did military families handle the stress? Her heart ached for the widow and her children he'd told her about the other day, too.

"Sure. While we're most often called to handle local problems in our state and surrounding ones, there's always the potential for a reservist with needed skills to be called up." He was quiet a moment. Then he whispered, "After losing Danny, I don't know if I have the desire anymore. I know that sounds pretty pitiful—"

She placed her hand on his forearm, ignoring the spark of electricity arcing between them. "Hardly. Deployments are incredibly disruptive, not to mention terrifying. Besides, you've taken on a new mission now—helping your veteran brothers and sisters transition stateside again." All too soon he'd have another mission—fatherhood.

"Funny you should call it that. It's always seemed like a mission to me, too."

She realized she hadn't managed to get him to say anything more about Danny. Needing to find out if his friend truly had found a tear in the veil long enough to make contact with her, she asked, "What happened to Danny that made it so hard for him to…deal with life?"

He sighed. "He made it through the first deployment without any problems. Danny didn't have an ideal childhood, so he could handle more trauma than many others could."

She hated picking at the wound, but… "Then what happened after the second deployment?"

Travis drew a deep breath. "Craig was right next to me when he was killed. The explosion tore off Danny's leg above the knee." Her heart pounded. He'd described what Danny had told her had happened, without the IED detail. Given that they were in an explosives unit, she could have surmised another type of explosive. "He had a severe period of depression after that," Travis continued. "After he got out of the hospital, I hired him so I could keep tabs on him. He seemed to be doing okay, then had to have another surgery, and dealt with pain management issues after that. Hit painkillers pretty heavily." He dragged his fingers through his hair. "Found him dead five months ago, but you already know about that."

Tears in her eyes, she said, "Travis, there's something I need to tell you about Danny's death."

Chapter Fourteen

What could Katie possibly know about Danny or his death, other than what Travis had already told her? Before he could ask, she continued.

"Last night, I heard a man talking to me in my bedroom."

Travis's body went on alert. Someone had gotten into her room? Had he—

"He said his name was Danny," she continued before he could ask.

Travis relaxed. He didn't know what kind of game she was playing here, but decided to play along. "And just what did he say to you?"

"Well, he told me about his leg being blown off by an IED."

How could she know that it was an IED? He'd only said he'd been injured the same day Craig was killed. Lucky guess?

"That's not all he revealed." She glanced down and fiddled with her napkin. "He wanted me to assure you that..." When she met his gaze again, her eyes were bright with unshed tears. He steeled himself for whatever she was going to say. "Travis, he said he didn't kill himself. Not intentionally, anyway. It was some kind of horrible accident."

Travis gritted out, "Downing half a bottle or more of pills is no accident."

She chewed on the inside of her lower lip. "He didn't go into any details. But what about the alc—"

The server stopped to check on them, and Travis asked for the bill. To Katie, he said, "Look, I really don't want to talk about this anymore. If you're ready, we can head back to the farm. I'd like to repair the roof of the old barn before the hay gets wet or moldy."

"Listen, I know it sounds ludicrous that your friend would come to me, but he said you were ignoring him. I'm telling you exactly what he told me."

He nodded, put his credit card in the vinyl holder, and then turned toward Katie. "I know you're trying to make me feel better and help me stop dwelling on what happened to Danny…" *More like what Danny did to himself.* "But I'd rather not talk about it."

Her brows knitted, but she kept quiet.

Back at the house after another run to town for her birth certificate, Travis hauled the metal roofing onto the top of the old barn, determined to repair the section that the recent windstorm had torn off. But *he'd* been blown away over lunch by two things—Katie's confession about her mother, who may not be dead, and her claim to have been visited by Danny, who was.

He didn't know how to begin processing it all. Clearly, Katie wanted to make him feel better and tell him what he wanted to hear about Danny. Not much more to think about there. So he'd focus on the issue of her missing mom.

You are one stubborn cuss.

Travis ignored the Danny voice in his head and focused on reality. To grow up without a mom was bad enough, but believing that she'd chosen to live her life without her kid in it had to be devastating. Danny had been estranged from his mother, too, and Travis believed it was part of the reason he'd had a tough time after that last deployment.

Maybe that had something to do with how Katie buried or hid her emotions. She'd had to learn early on to suck it up and move on. That she bore any shame as a result of her mother's abandonment flat out disgusted him. Why hadn't she trusted him enough to tell him the truth back when they'd dated? No matter. She'd told him now.

As soon as they came home from the bank, he'd taken a photo of the birth certificate and texted it to Emmy and Shania asking them to report back as soon as possible with any news. He didn't know which of his sisters would take up the case, but told them he wanted to get the search started today or as soon as possible. Because his sisters weren't too fond of Katie after she'd dumped their big brother, he'd told them all communication should go through him.

As suspected, her mother's maiden name was on there, but the biggest revelation was Katie's middle name—Katherine Serenity Michaels. He would guess that her dad had chosen the first name, but Serenity undoubtedly had been her free-spirited mother's contribution. Not at all surprising that she'd never told him her middle name before. He grinned. Not exactly a common one here in Kentucky.

"How's it coming?" Katie called up to him from the ground. He glanced down at where she stood, one hand shielding her eyes from the sun that had sunk low on the horizon.

"Almost finished."

"Great." She glanced away but didn't leave until she met his gaze again. "I wondered if you'd like to go for a horseback ride this evening?"

"Sounds good to me." His time here was growing short, and he still hadn't a clue if there might be a chance in hell of their seeing each other again after this.

She didn't smile, as though she'd perhaps wanted him to say no. "Okay. In about an hour?"

"Sure. I ought to finish here in about half that time." Tonight might be his last opportunity to rekindle something with Katie. He had to make the most of it.

"Thanks for taking care of the roof for me. I was going to wait until Miguel came back. I've never been fond of heights."

"Don't mention it."

True to her word, an hour later, they were saddling up Angus and Chula, a palomino mare Katie had chosen to ride this evening. "What kind of name is that?" he asked.

"A Spanish one. I looked it up. Means pretty."

"Where'd you come up with that?"

She shrugged. "I have no idea. But I needed to name a bunch of new horses, and that one just stuck in my head for her. Odd because you don't think of a Spanish beauty being a blonde, but…"

The only Chula he'd ever heard of was Chula Vista near San Diego. Had her mother mentioned it? Was it a clue as to where she'd lived or disappeared to? He'd mention it to his sisters, but didn't say anything to Katie. Didn't want to get her hopes up until he had something positive to report.

Grabbing the saddle horn, he hoisted himself up and waited for Katie to mount Chula. "Where to?"

"Why don't we ride the perimeter of the big field to make sure there's no delayed damage to the fence? Then we'll head to the springhouse for a drink."

He nodded. The two of them gravitated toward that covered spring just about every time they rode. Katie remained quiet the first twenty minutes, as if deep in thought. Something seemed to be on her mind. Had stirring up memories of her mother caused her change in mood since lunch?

When they reached the springhouse, they tied the horses to a near-by tree branch rather than the door, to avoid a repeat of the last time. He motioned for her to precede him down the stone steps and inside. When she didn't go straight for the dipper, he took it down and filled it, handing it to her.

"No, thanks."

Shrugging off her melancholy, he drank his fill and replaced the dipper on the wall. "What's up, Katie? You seem preoccupied."

She nibbled at her lower lip, short-circuiting his brain. "I think you should have a seat, Travis. There's something I need to tell you."

She wrung her hands together, and the hairs at the back of his head stood on end. Was he about to get the brush-off again? Face to face this time? Here he'd thought they'd been getting along better than ever, despite a few rocky patches.

"I haven't been honest with you about something."

Something besides her mother? He faced her. "What's going on?"

She retreated to the other end of the damp, stone building. Without turning to face him again, she whispered, "There's someone you need to know about."

What on earth could she be talking about?

Hold onto your britches, Trav.

He was being bombarded with an overload of sensations—and Danny hallucinations weren't going to help anything.

Sudden clarity hit when Katie began pacing. Travis remembered the dispatcher asking if Chelsea was all right and Katie having an odd reaction whenever he'd talked about the girl. Why would the dispatcher be concerned about only one of Katie's students, unless…

Before he could express his suspicion, Katie blurted out, "We have a daughter together."

"Chelsea," Travis said. It wasn't a question. He knew.

She nodded and turned toward him. "When I found out I was pregnant, I'd already decided not to hold you back when your dream was to be a big-city civil engineer."

Her words didn't make any sense. "So when you ditched me, you knew you were pregnant with my baby?" Why hadn't she notified him all those years ago when he could have been here for her? Hell, why hadn't she told him on Monday? Or Tuesday? Or any day this week, for that matter?

Still reeling from hearing that he had a daughter, he sat down on the side of the spring trough. Clearly, she hadn't wanted to share Chelsea with him. At some point, her words crashed into his brain. "…no intention of you finding out about her, because I didn't want to put my daughter through what I'd been through."

Who the hell did she think she was to unilaterally make that decision? Heat flooding his chest and face, Travis stood again and took his turn at wearing a trench in the old floor, avoiding going anywhere near Katie. He clenched and unclenched his fists, wanting to pound the wall, but not particularly wanting to inflict any more pain at the moment. He felt as though his heart had been ripped out of his chest and stomped on. His mind alternated between numb and overwhelmed with questions.

How had he ever thought that he and Katie were meant to be together? He didn't even know this woman. Lying about her mother was trivial compared to lying about their own daughter.

"She's at a vulnerable age now. She can't be taken away from everything she knows."

Taken away? What would a confirmed bachelor do with a kid? The last thing he intended to do was take Chelsea away from her mother—but that didn't mean he wouldn't want to get to know his daughter.

"Travis, she's all I have in this world. Please don't take her away from me." The fear in Katie's voice was palpable. If he'd been able to speak right now, no doubt there'd be a bunch of fear in his own voice, too.

He raked his fingers through his hair. A kid? And he was a father?

"I wanted to tell you so many times, and I've been riddled with guilt every time I chickened out."

Good. You ought to rot in the guilt for what you've taken from me.

He stared out the doorway, then started to pace again. He probably only caught half of what she said, but his mind couldn't get over the fact that they had made a daughter together—and he was just hearing about it. How the hell was he supposed to process something out of the blue like this?

"Where is she?" His words came out in a croak because his throat had tightened up.

"At church camp. She'll be home about suppertime on Sunday."

He blinked rapidly and turned to stare blankly at the flow of water into the spring's trough. He was days away from potentially meeting his only daughter and it would happen on Father's Day. How appropriate.

You'd better stick around for that, Trav.

Even his subconscious wasn't giving him any credit for being a decent human being. Then he remembered that same internal voice saying something that made no sense whatsoever at the time.

"You can name this one after me."

Holy hell. Apparently, he wasn't hallucinating Danny's voice at all. Is this why Danny had visited him in a dream and sent him up here? His buddy had known about Chelsea all along. Must be nice to have such a clear picture of someone else's life—after you chose to no longer be a part of your own.

"Some friend you are."

"I'm sorry, Travis."

He realized he'd said the words out loud and that Katie thought he was speaking to her, but he might as well have been. Katie certainly was no friend to him. Or anything else, for that matter.

Wait. He still couldn't figure out why Danny would doubt that Travis would stick around. While Travis had given up on having children and his own family long ago, he'd made his crew at work an extended family of sorts and had been an uncle to his brother's kids, as well as Craig and Megan's. After seeing all they'd been through raising theirs, there'd been times he'd been thankful he hadn't had to deal with any of that. Having kids was a scary amount of responsibility.

Guilt washed over him. *Yep, you sure are father of the year material, Cooper.*

"Say something, Travis."

His mind was going a mile a minute. Did he care that she was nervously awaiting his response? Well, given he'd only known about being a father for all of five minutes, tough shit.

He scrubbed his face with his hand. "I don't know *what* to say. What do you expect me to do with an announcement like this? How the hell did this happen?"

She glanced toward the springhouse steps, taking him by surprise again. *Seriously?* "How can you be sure it was that first time?"

She shrugged. "It was a couple more weeks before we…did it again. According to the doctor, conception was earlier than that."

"What I want to know is how we get to where she's, what—twelve? Thirteen?"

"Twelve and a half. Her birthday's in January."

Her name was Chelsea, and she was born in January. Where had he been then? He'd finished boot camp and was headed to Iraq for the first time, that's where.

"And you couldn't bother to tell me in all these years? Why the hell not?" he shouted then gritted his teeth, angry that he'd lost control of his emotions.

"I was scared." Her voice was barely a whisper.

"Of what?"

She shrugged. "Of you not being able to make a commitment to us for the rest of your life without having regrets and resenting me for killing your chance at your dream."

"Just what did you base that fear on?"

Tears shimmered in her eyes as she faced the open doorway. "I didn't want Chelsea to suffer from having a parent who didn't want to be a part of her life. In time, you'd have grown sick of this place and deserted us. Her."

To be compared to a woman who deserted her family only burned his gut more. In a hushed whisper, he said, "I'm not your mother, Katie. I take my responsibilities a lot more seriously than that."

She nodded. "I know, and I'm sorry. I screwed up. While I can see that now, having seen you again and hearing the turns your life took, hindsight is twenty-twenty."

"My character didn't change. You'd have seen that if you'd given me half a chance."

Unable to bear looking at her any longer, seeing tears streaming down her cheeks, he turned away and stared out the doorway at the horses grazing near the tree.

"What do you plan to do about her, Travis?"

"I have no clue." This changed everything. Hell, how was he going to be a significant part of her life when he lived four hours away?

They'd need to work out some kind of visitation schedule. "I need to think."

Katie was up in his face like a drill sergeant in a minute, sparks flying from her eyes. "If you can't commit one-hundred percent to being a part of Chelsea's life, I want you to leave her alone. It's better she not know her father at all than to know him and be abandoned by him later."

Clenching his fist, he took a step backward. "Look, you just sprang all this on me not five minutes ago. Don't expect me to start behaving like some perfect dad in a matter of minutes. All I'm saying is that I need time to think. Then we can decide what's best."

Katie began shaking and wrapped her arms around herself. "I'm sorry." She sounded slightly contrite, but he wasn't looking for apologies at this point. "Take all the time you need." But her inner Mama Bear reared its head again. "Just don't make any promises to her until you're ready to commit. I don't want to see my girl hurt. She's never had a father figure around, other than Daddy, and she barely remembers him."

At least Ben hadn't been overbearing and overprotective toward Chelsea, the way he had been with Katie.

A sudden sense of…something he could only describe as protectiveness came over him. *Now I'm someone's father.* Travis wanted to meet the girl, to get to know her, but would he make the same mistakes Old Man Michaels had? He didn't know the first thing about parenting. Yeah, he'd been raised in a loving family and had a lot of knowledge to draw from, but the potential for screwing up such a precious life was more than he could deal with right now. What if he messed up her life or wasn't there for her when she needed him most, the way he hadn't been there for Danny?

"I need some space to figure this out. I'm heading home tonight."

Her body visibly relaxed—from relief, perhaps? Is that the answer she'd expected? Wanted? "Take all the time you need, Travis. Be sure before you come anywhere near her that you're ready to make a lifetime commitment."

Clearly, she had no intention of telling Chelsea without that assurance from him. He could see she was simply protecting her daughter.

His daughter, too. *His* little girl.

Oh, lordy. He needed some time alone. "I'll call you when I'm ready."

Ready to what? Talk? Tell her to leave him alone? Or head back up here and meet his responsibilities—ones he hadn't even been aware of—at long last?

No damned clue.

$$*\quad*\quad*$$

Kate sank onto the cold, limestone wall as she watched Travis walk out of the springhouse, untie and remount Angus, and ride out of sight. She'd told him. Finally.

As expected, he'd chosen to leave, his anger at her barely controlled. Not that she blamed him.

Would he return? There might be no hope that she and Travis would have any future together as a couple, but would he want to have anything to do with Chelsea? It sounded as though he just needed time to come to grips with becoming the father of a twelve-year-old. But could he handle that role?

If not, he needed to steer clear of Chelsea altogether.

Kate waited about twenty minutes before following Travis, hoping to give him time to clear out before she made it back to the house. Mounting Chula, she chose a meandering path back to the house to give him even more time. She continued to shake, not a hypoglycemic episode, but perhaps from shock or relief at finally getting the news out there. She didn't want to face him again in this state.

When she crested the last hill and looked down on her farmstead, his truck was no longer parked in the lane, and she missed it already. He'd been out of her life all these years. What difference would his absence make now? She'd known all along he wouldn't be staying.

Life would go on as it had before for her and Chelsea, no doubt.

So why did her heart ache tonight as though a piece of it had been carved out?

She must be missing Chelsea, now that Travis wasn't there to distract her. Even though the girl had been a handful lately, her acting out was simply the tween personality rearing its ugly head. Deep down, Chelsea was a wonderful daughter and would grow up to be a good person.

How would things change for Chelsea if Travis became a part of her life? Not that she intended to bribe her daughter to keep her happy here, but maybe it was time for Kate to give her more freedom. She'd be thirteen on her next birthday. Why not let her go to the school dances she'd begged to go to, as long as they were well-chaperoned?

Stop acting like Daddy.

Her father hadn't let her do any such thing until she was sixteen. He'd even forbidden her to go to the senior prom with the boy who had asked her, telling her he wasn't good enough for her.

Kate needed to let Chelsea experience some independence, or she'd never know how to take care of herself when Kate wasn't around. She'd laid a firm foundation all these years and had to trust that Chelsea had a solid head on her shoulders. The time had come to loosen the reins a little and let her grow up.

Would that include allowing her to spend time in Nashville—Nolensville, specifically—with Travis if he decided he wanted Chelsea to be a part of his life? She'd want to check out his place first to make sure it was suitable for a twelve-year-old girl. After all, she had no clue what kind of lifestyle Travis led.

Trust, but verify.

But she had no real reason to doubt that Travis would keep their daughter safe and protected while with him. She shook her head at the notion of his doing anything else. An alpha male like Travis would be no different than Kate's own father, growling at any boy who came anywhere near Chelsea and swiftly neutralizing any threats—real or imagined.

She smiled for the first time in hours. Yes, Travis would be Papa Bear on steroids. Chelsea would be a lucky girl.

If he accepted the challenge to become an active participant in Chelsea's life.

After taking care of Chula, she went into the house to check her glucose. Finding it elevated, she administered her insulin, ate a light snack, then prepared for bed. No sleeping in anymore, even though she hadn't exactly expected Travis to do her morning chores. She had stalls to muck, horses to exercise, and riders to give lessons to.

Life was going to go back to normal.

It sure was going to be lonely around here until Chelsea came home.

Chapter Fifteen

Travis woke up Saturday morning with a hard-on and a hangover. One helluva combination, but supremely fitting. Staggering to the bathroom, he reached for the naproxen bottle and filled a glass with water. The headache and nausea wouldn't abate fast enough, but maybe he'd remember next time not to overdo it with liquor.

Please, don't let there be a next time.

He hadn't tied one on like that since the night of Danny's memorial service. Booze hadn't helped then, so what had made him think it would be the answer now? Both times, he'd indulged at home rather than with his buddies. In the kitchen, he emptied the remainder of the fifth of Jack someone had given him for Christmas down the drain to remove further temptation. Two pity drunks a year were two too many.

His phone buzzed in his sweatpants. Would Katie be calling to find out what he intended to do? A mix of dread and, oddly enough, anticipation filled him as he pulled it from his pocket. *Jackson.* He hadn't let his foreman know he'd come back home last night. With his hand-eye coordination slightly off, it took him two punches to hit the answer button on the screen.

"You okay, man?"

Jackson worried too much about everyone. Not unlike Travis.

"Yeah. And you?"

"Can't complain. What are you doing back so soon?" He must have driven by the house, which wasn't exactly on his way to or from anywhere given that he lived an hour on the other side of Nashville.

"Find what you were looking for?"

"And then some." When he'd taken off last Monday, he'd only let on to his foreman that he needed some time away to come to grips with Danny's death and that he'd be gone at least all week, but hadn't mentioned anything about visiting Katie. "Listen, there's a whole lot of other shit going on with my life right now."

"What can I do to help?"

"Nothing, but thanks. I have to sort this out on my own. So if everything's okay at work, I don't think I'll be in today."

"I wasn't expecting you back until next week anyway. Everything's under control so well it's downright boring." Jackson paused a moment. "You been drinking?"

The man knew him well. "Was last night. But I'm sober now." Not that he'd pass a blood-alcohol test. "No more booze for me." Especially not if he was going to set any kind of example for his daughter.

"Good. That stuff'll kill you, too."

"Too?"

"You know. Danny."

"What about him?"

Jackson was silent a moment, then said, "His toxicology reports showed he had a lot of alcohol in his system on top of the opioids."

Since when? Of course, he'd never actually looked at those reports. Hell, hadn't he been the one who'd found the pill bottle on the bed with Danny? What more did he need to know? Although, as disgusting as the thought was, if Danny had used his sidearm instead, Travis wouldn't have been left with so many doubts.

Suddenly, the memory of that night flashed before his eyes and he remembered the kitchen table as clear as day when he'd come in. A nearly empty but capped bottle of tequila, no glass, had been sitting there. Had he blocked that out, not wanting to believe Danny would mix alcohol and pills?

But who was he to judge? Travis didn't have uncontrolled physical pain like Danny had. His own post-combat issues had been mild in comparison, and he'd managed to keep them under control most of the time. Poor Danny had the double whammy of injuries from the IED attack and all the surgeries that involved on top of his PTSD shit. Turned out to be a deadly combination.

Oh, Danny boyyyyyy, the pipes, the pipes are calling.

The piss-poor rendition of the song Travis used to taunt Danny with sounded as though it came through the cell phone. "What are you listening to?"

"Nothing. I'm trying to figure out the books and can't have music on while I'm concentrating. Whatever you hear must be on your end."

He wasn't imagining what he'd heard. "Never mind." He didn't want Jackson to think he was ready for a shrink.

"What's going on, Trav? I'm worried about you." Jackson said.

"Nothing."

It's you, it's you, must go, and I must bide. Again, the haunting "Danny Boy" lyrics seemed to be coming through the phone, taunting him as though Danny were serenading him.

Hold on a minute. Hadn't he been pissed at Danny for not being honest with him about his final days? He owed Jackson the truth. "Actually, Jackson, a lot's going on. I went to Kentucky to see an old college flame." She'd meant a lot more than that to him at one time, but with all her secrets, those feelings were gone now. All he could summon up now was a healthy dose of anger.

Jackson laughed. "Good. You needed to get laid."

Travis shook his head then cringed in pain. It was hard to be mad at his happy-go-lucky friend. How did Jackson keep his crap together when the world was falling apart around them? He'd done two tours in Afghanistan with the Marines.

"Sorry to tarnish my reputation, buddy, but I didn't get her into bed. Good thing, too, or I might have wound up with another kid."

"What are you talking about? You don't have any kids."

"Oh, on the contrary, congratulate me, Jackson. I'm the proud father of a half-grown twelve-year-old girl."

"Come again?"

"You heard me. Turns out I left my college sweetheart pregnant."

A brief silence greeted him, followed by Jackson howling with laughter. At least one of them found some humor in the situation. "Dayum. What's she like?"

"No clue. I didn't meet her." The silence on the other end this time was deafening and prolonged. Jackson's old man had been absent from his life, and Jackson remained bitter about it to this day. "Don't worry. I'm going to meet her eventually. She was away at camp this week."

His laughter suddenly gone, Jackson cautioned, "If you can't commit to being a major part of her life, then stay out of it altogether. Don't get her hopes up."

"You sound like Katie."

"That your girlfriend?"

"*Former* girlfriend."

"Does the kid know about you?"

"Not as of when I left."

"Good. All I'm saying is, if you aren't going to make a solid, life-long commitment to her, she's better off not knowing you exist."

"Listen, I know I can't screw this up, Jackson. I just needed a little time to figure things out. I'm heading back up there later today." *As soon as I can keep my bleary eyes open and not blow an illegal Breathalyzer if I get pulled over.* "But I'll probably be back at work Monday. If I need even more time, I'll let you know."

"Don't sweat it. Take all the time you need. This is the first vacation you've taken since you started the business."

"Look who's talking."

Jackson huffed unapologetically.

Travis thanked him for holding down the fort before saying goodbye and wishing him well, leaving Travis alone once again trying to sort out what the hell he was going to do. He ran his hand through his hair and stared at a wad of gold fur on the floor. Hell, he hadn't even asked how Sadie was doing. He shook his head in disgust. Before setting the phone down again, he texted Katie.

TRAVIS: Send me her picture.

Katie didn't respond right away. After ten minutes, he was reduced to begging.

TRAVIS: Please.

A few more minutes passed. Still nothing. Maybe she was busy with a lesson or driving or something. Then again, maybe she didn't intend to share Chelsea with him at all.

You'd better not go there, Katie.

He'd give her a little more time. Then…

KATIE: Here's one taken a few weeks ago.

Travis's heart stopped a moment before pounding back to life so hard his chest ached. The sweet face staring back at him was his daughter's. *His* daughter. He flashed back to the hospital where he'd been looking through Kate's wallet for her insurance card. Same girl, although this shot was a candid one unlike those that had been school pics most likely.

She'd practically grown up without knowing him at all. Why the hell hadn't Katie reached out to his mom and dad at least to let them know. Maybe even ask them for information on where he lived? If she'd wanted to find him, she could have.

Clearly, she hadn't wanted him to be part of either of their lives.

Chelsea's long, blonde hair had streaks of sunlight glinting off the strands on one side. Where'd she gotten blonde hair? No one in Travis's family was light-haired—he and Katie both had brown.

Maybe she wasn't his after all.

He looked closer. Those green eyes staring back at him were definitely his mom's. And that high forehead? Just like Clint's. Not a chance he could deny the girl was his.

But Chelsea's smile—well, that was pure Katie—although it seemed somewhat forced, as if she might have been annoyed at her mom at the time she'd snapped the photo.

A kid with an attitude. Now *that* she got from Travis, especially at that age.

He was grinning down at his phone like a sop, but couldn't bring himself to stop staring at her picture. Every time the screen dimmed, he touched it to bring her face back into the light.

"Chelsea, you don't know me, but I'm your dad." His voice sounded hoarse from emotion. What would he say to her when he met her face-to-face the first time? It would be kind of lame to say those words to her over the phone. He'd definitely need to tell her in person.

How did someone start a parental relationship with a preteen? Travis dropped into a chair at the kitchen table. He had no clue. But he'd better figure it out. Fast. He had no other choice.

When Chelsea returned home late Sunday afternoon, he intended to be there to greet her. No, *meet* her.

Congratulations, Mr. Cooper. It's a girl.

"Tell me about it, Danny." If Danny hadn't come to him in that crazy dream, Travis still wouldn't know about Chelsea. Would Katie have *ever* contacted him to tell him? If she hadn't done so in the thirteen years since she'd found out she was pregnant, there wasn't much of a chance she would have.

Thanks, buddy.

One thing's for certain—nothing in this world would stop him from returning to Kentucky to meet his little girl. He rubbed the back of his neck to try to relieve the tension. Or was it fear? *Shit just got real.*

* * *

Kate stumbled as she entered the barn. Her mind reeled from the thought of having to prepare Chelsea for the real possibility that her father could suddenly show up on their doorstep.

Would he come back? Or would the photo assuage his curiosity?

Travis was an honorable man. He'd be back once the hurt and initial shock wore off. She tried to run through the scenario of how she'd tell Chelsea about him, but kept coming up blank.

As though pulled by an invisible string, she made a beeline to Chula's stall and spent the next hour giving the horse a brushing she would come to expect every time. The comforting repetitive motion calmed Kate's nerves a tad, but every time she pictured Travis here in the barn, her peace was shattered once more. He'd almost become a fixture in here in a few short days.

How could she both miss him and never want to see him again at the same time?

Knowing she probably should have done this first, she set down the curry comb and asked anyway. "Chula, honey, how about a ride?" The horse nickered and nodded her head. Taking the saddle and bridle from the tack room, she readied her and soon led her out of the barn.

The noontime air was as hot as ever, but Kate planned to ride fast, at least for a while after her mount was warmed up. When she had Chula up to a canter, the breeze cooled Kate down immediately. "I promise you another rubdown when we get back to the barn, girl, but I really need this." As if aware of her mistress's words, the horse ran even faster. Kate's hair came loose, and she ripped the band out to let the strands fly like Chula's mane.

Exhilaration washed over Kate. After about twenty minutes, she slowed the horse to a trot then a walk. Stopping, she surveyed the farm she'd been granted stewardship of. Had she instilled that sense of love and responsibility in Chelsea? One day, if she chose to remain here, this farm would be hers.

The rolling hills and creosoted fences stretched out far beyond her own borders—all the way to the Brodies' winery toward the east.

She hadn't visited Jason and Lidia in forever, but needed to talk with someone. Maybe they would be around, although it was rare to find them idle on a Saturday. Her two best friends in the world might be able to help her sort this mess out, though, so it was worth a try. She'd grown up with Jason as a neighbor and had met Lidia Mercado in college, later introducing the two of them. They'd been married for a decade now.

An hour later, after seeing that Chula received her second rubdown of the day, Kate drove the two miles to the gate of Chambourcin Winery. For years, Kate had provided peaches from her orchard to the winery for one of their fruitier blends. While by necessity, she wasn't much of a sweet wine connoisseur, Kate did enjoy their dry reds.

Seeing how the couple had transformed his family's beef cattle farm into a popular vineyard and winery had given Kate some of the courage she'd needed to make changes to her own place.

"Get in here, *amiga!*" Lidia greeted her at the door. "You have to solve a dispute between me and Jason."

Finding both of them home on a Saturday afternoon was unheard of. Jason spent a lot of his weekends traveling to promote their wines and weekdays working at his advertising firm in Lexington. Lidia was the brains behind the vineyard and winery, putting her love of agriculture and chemistry to work.

"Here, taste this." Inside the kitchen, Lidia handed her a wine glass half filled with a sparkling red. Lidia knew Kate's limitations, so she accepted and took a sip without blinking. The full-bodied wine burst with flavor on her tongue. She detected no strong grape flavor, and the sugar level was minimal, but there was a hint of something…she couldn't quite name.

After swallowing, Kate asked, "I like it, but don't ask me to describe it. The bubbles are a nice touch, though."

Lidia glanced at Jason. "I told you!" To Kate, she added, "He doesn't think we should expand our line of sparkling wines, but there's something about this one that just sings to me." Narrowing her eyes, she leaned toward Kate as if seeing her for the first time. "What's wrong? You look like hell."

She'd always been able to count on Lidia to be honest. "Gee, thanks."

"Take a load off," Jason said, pulling out a bar chair. "I'm going to leave you two ladies to talk. I have a feeling it's going to get all emotional in here." He gave Kate a peck on the cheek. "But you know how to reach me if you need me."

Lidia gave him a look of exasperation. "Go! But I'm pursuing this new line."

He waved her away. "Do what you want. You always do."

She grinned at him, but her smile disappeared when her focus returned to Kate. "Is Chelsea all right?"

Kate nodded. "She's at camp until late Sunday afternoon."

Her friend leaned back in her chair, her shoulders relaxing. "Good. So what's going on?"

Drawing a deep breath, Kate dove right to the heart of the matter. "Travis was here this week."

Lidia's eyes opened wider as she leaned closer and reached for Kate's arm. "And you didn't invite me over to gawk?" Lidia smiled. "That man was molten sex on a stick."

Kate remembered the nights she and Lidia had spent in their dorm room freshman and sophomore years talking about the boys in their lives. Lidia always gave it to her straight on which ones to ditch, but she'd thought Travis was a keeper. Of course, he wasn't the one who'd called it quits. Not the first time, anyway.

Kate shrugged, reining Lidia in. "For obvious reasons, I didn't want him to stick around too long."

"So he's gone already? Does he know?"

Kate nodded, drawing a deep breath.

"*Bueno.* I never agreed with your decision to shut him out. He would have been a great help to you in raising her."

"We've been over this before. He had a career to build. I was certain that eventually he'd resent being stuck here in sleepy Woodford County. I didn't want to chain a baby around his neck."

Lidia shook her head. "Kate, a baby is such a blessing! How could anyone feel burdened by such a beautiful thing?"

Too late, Kate remembered how badly Lidia wanted a baby, but the couple had been plagued by fertility issues and had given up.

"I'm sorry, Lidia. I wish my own mother had shared your enthusiasm."

"Leaving you was her loss, and I'm sure she's suffered every day since then."

Kate didn't want to talk about her mother.

"You still could have given him the information to make that choice for himself."

"That's basically what he said—that I unilaterally made the decision for him." Even though a part of her knew Travis and Lidia were right, she said, "I just didn't want to put Chelsea through what I'd been through." She held out her hand like a stop sign. "And before you say anything, yes, I'm fully aware that's come back to bite me in the ass."

Lidia had fought many times with Kate about calling Travis, even before Chelsea was born. But Lidia hadn't brought it up since Daddy passed. "You knew this day would come eventually. That man was crazy about you. So what did he say about becoming an instant dad to a preteen?"

"Needless to say, he wasn't all that thrilled at the news. Said he needed time to think."

"How'd you expect him to react?"

Kate sighed. "Honestly, a lot worse than he did. He left late last night—I suppose to return to his place near Nashville—less than an hour after I told him, he was gone." Drawing a deep breath, she tried to veer off the subject of Travis. "Look, what I'm here for is some advice about how to talk to Chelsea about him."

"When are you going to tell her?"

"As soon as I know he intends to be a part of her life."

"Careful, Kate. She has the right to know her father, even if he doesn't choose to meet her or step up to the plate."

"She's going to be shocked, to say the least. She's already angry enough at me for normal mother-daughter stuff. I don't want our relationship to deteriorate any further." Tears welled in Kate's eyes. "I don't want her to hate me for this," she said in a whisper.

"She needs to be told—and soon."

Kate wasn't so sure. "Chelsea hasn't asked me about him since third grade. She's accepted the fact that he isn't around. Why stir up all that emotion again?" Lidia glared at Kate. "Okay, okay. I'll tell her Sunday. Or Monday, maybe." Kate added, "I've always been honest with her—up to a point. I assured her that he didn't know about her, so that he hadn't made the choice to abandon her." *Unlike my mom.*

"Just because she hasn't talked to you about him doesn't mean she's not still thinking about him. A little girl needs her daddy, Kate. Who's to say part of the reason you two are going through a rough patch lately isn't because she's begun to realize that you've kept him from her?"

Feeling a bit defensive, she said, "But this is the first I've heard from him since that summer we broke up."

"You mean, since you broke it off."

Kate shrugged. "Semantics."

"Kate, you need to be truthful with her—and yourself."

"I've already told her that her father and I thought we were in love and made a baby but that circumstances split us up."

"That's a cop-out. *You* were the only circumstance that split you two up, Kate."

Guilt washed over her at the enormity of the secret she'd kept from Chelsea—and Travis.

"Tell her the *truth.* Tell her about your own mother and your reason for doing what you did. She's old enough and has enough compassion and empathy to understand that even parents are human and make mistakes—sometimes enormous ones. Explain that our feelings aren't always logical or rational." She paused then added, "But the sooner you tell her, the better."

"I could have at least shown her photos of him."

"Shoulda, coulda, woulda. Forget the past. You need to move forward. I know why you did what you did, but now you need to fix it."

I'm too scared.

"We've been through all this before, but you chose not to tell him, even when you could have notified his parents that you needed to speak with him. I bet he'd have come back to you in an instant."

"It's not like he's been in hot pursuit of me all these years—and I didn't move around at all."

Lidia shook her head. "I'd say there isn't much chance of any kind of romance developing between you two now, but it's not about you and Travis anymore, Kate. You need to make amends to Travis and Chelsea and do whatever it takes to bring *them* together as father and daughter."

"I know."

When Kate's chin quivered, Lidia stood and closed the space between them, wrapping her arms around her. "Don't worry. He'll do the right thing."

"I have no doubt that he'll be back, once this all sinks in. He shoulders responsibility like a general. Earlier today, he asked me to text him a photo of her."

"Did you send one?"

Kate shrugged. "Of course."

"Okay, that's a good start."

"I just don't want him to take her away from me, Lidia." She choked on the words. Kate returned Lidia's hug and buried her head in her friend's side. After giving in to tears for a few moments, Kate nudged her away and drew a deep breath. "I'm sorry, Lidia. I didn't mean to lose it like that."

"Maybe it's time you let out some of those pent-up fears you've let rule your life. Besides, I'd have been insulted if you hadn't come and talked to me. You can't keep shit like this bottled up, *amiga*."

"You're the best friend a girl could ever have. Thanks for listening." Kate might not be able to look her friend in the eye for a while, but she'd needed to hear these things before Chelsea came home tomorrow.

Lidia rubbed Kate's arm before returning to her seat. "Now, back to business. Let's practice what you're going to say to Chelsea."

She sighed, shrugging. "The truth, I guess."

"Which is…" Lidia prompted.

She met Lidia's gaze despite her recent weak moment. "I suppose I have to tell her my reasons for sending Travis away, selfish though they might have been."

"*Mierda*, Kate. What's selfish about wanting to let a guy follow his dream? However, what you need to admit is that it was awfully presumptuous of you to decide you knew better than Travis did about how he'd handle the situation."

"Well, nothing turned out the way I thought it would. He didn't stay in New York City. Didn't even complete his civil engineering degree. Instead, he joined the Army National Guard and served three tours in Iraq. Then in between deployments, he started what appears to be a successful contracting business in or near Nashville."

"Three tours? That's intense. What's his temperament like? Is he someone you'd want Chelsea to be around?"

That sounded like Lidia's polite way of asking, without coming out and saying it directly, if he had post-traumatic stress issues. "He seems to have it together." *More so than I do at the moment.* "He even helps other vets get back to work and regain control of their lives after deployments. I can't think of a single negative thing to say about him."

"Remember, you barely know him anymore. Spending a couple of days with someone isn't enough time to reveal their true character."

"Actually, he was here since Monday—five days."

Lidia leaned forward. "We won't go into how miffed I am that you didn't call me over for coffee to share a little of that eye candy."

Kate smiled. Lidia had certainly lifted her spirits. "Anyway, you know how you can get a vibe about someone, positive or negative, the first time you meet them?" Lidia nodded. "Well, I don't have a single negative feeling about him. He's a genuinely nice guy, as far as I can tell."

"Good. Then go ahead and tell Chelsea. Expect for this to be hard on her—harder than it is on you and even Travis—but in the long run, she's going to love getting to know her dad. I think half her problems are that she doesn't have one to straighten her out."

"Hey, I've done okay as the disciplinarian."

"Yeah, but a girl just needs her dad sometimes. Moms are too close to what they're feeling, if that makes sense."

But talk of turning Chelsea over to someone else to parent her threatened to send Kate into another tailspin. "What if she decides she'd rather live with him than me? I can't lose her. She's my whole life."

Lidia grinned. "That kid loves you. She's just being a typical tween. She'll come around once the initial shock wears off."

"I hope you're right," Kate said. Soon after, she said goodbye and left Lidia's kitchen. She still didn't know how she'd broach the subject with Chelsea, but she probably needed to do so almost immediately after the bus dropped her off at church tomorrow.

After returning from Lidia's, Kate found herself in Chelsea's bedroom. She put the room back to rights after the mad dash she'd made through it Monday. Needing to feel close to her daughter, she crawled onto the twin bed and hugged a stuffed dragon to her chest.

"Oh, Chelsea, please don't hate me for what I didn't do."

Chapter Sixteen

Travis parked his truck in Katie's drive and sat staring between the house and barn a while, not sure why he'd decided to surprise her this time rather than call and tip her off. But here he was. He glanced at the seat beside him and the five-foot stuffed pink and purple unicorn he'd purchased on a whim for his daughter. Hell, was this one taller than she was?

Man, I hope Chelsea likes stuffed animals. Giant ones. Otherwise, I'm going to look like a damned fool.

Already he regretted the impulse buy. A twelve-year-old was probably into boy bands and jewelry more than stuffed animals. How would he know? He was going into this cold. But he didn't want to screw it up, either.

Opening the door of the truck, he left the critter there until after he asked Katie about it. Right now, he needed to find out more about his daughter. He knocked on the kitchen door. No response. After a few minutes, he headed toward the arena. Sure enough, he found Katie working with a young student and decided to watch.

Katie's love of the horse, rider, and the sport showed through in every gesture, every encouraging word.

He wished he hadn't noticed, but Katie had a body that became hotter with age. She'd always turned him on, but at a time when he ought to have more self-control, she totally did a number on his libido. How was he going to come to terms with his feelings about her—and the secret she'd kept from him—if he couldn't separate one head from the other?

He tried to imagine what Katie had looked like with her belly swollen with his child. *Lordy mercy, I've missed out on so much.* Before he let the anger boil up inside him again, he checked out her ass instead. Yeah. That should help him separate the carnal from the maternal.

Keep it carnal.

Because anytime he thought about her mothering his baby, his *daughter*, without him, he had a tough time suppressing intense feelings of resentment toward her. Would he ever be able to forgive her for the years of knowing Chelsea she'd robbed him of?

One thing Travis had learned a long time ago was not to waste time worrying about things he couldn't change or control. He needed to focus on the present and try to carve out some kind of future with Chelsea.

"That's it, Melissa! Just like that!"

The girl rode down the long side of the arena, glancing his way as she passed, smiling, and saying, "Hi!"

With his cover blown, he came out of where he'd tried to remain hidden. Katie glared at him one hot moment before studiously ignoring him for the next ten minutes as she finished the lesson. The student was a few years older than Chelsea. She drove herself here. He tried to imagine what Chelsea would look like riding. Lost in his thoughts, he didn't realize Katie had dismissed the girl. He watched her dismount and lead her horse to its stall.

Without missing a beat, Katie's boots squeaked on the rubber-mulch as she made a beeline for him. "I thought I told you Chelsea wouldn't be back until tomorrow evening."

So that's going to be the way of it. What did she expect him to do, just show up at the door and introduce himself to Chelsea cold turkey?

"You did. But we have some things to discuss before she returns."

She narrowed her gaze, but remained silent. What the hell did *she* have to be angry about? Without another word, she turned to follow the student. At loose ends, he walked up into the kitchen that also served as the trophy room and found himself drawn to the case filled with ribbons and photos of horses and riders competing. Were any of them pictures of his daughter? With their helmets on and the focus being more on the horses, it was hard to tell. These looked like bigger shows than at a county fair.

But…her mom can't afford a competitive show horse, or the costs of competing at the level she deserves.

He remembered talking about Chelsea with Katie before he'd realized she was referring to herself. Was the farm not quite as lucrative as it would seem? Was she in debt too far to give Chelsea the things she should have?

And still she hadn't tried to get in touch with Travis to help?

He drew a deep breath and blew it out, trying to get a handle on his anger once again. He'd been cheated out of something he couldn't get back. And what about his folks? They had a half-grown grand-daughter they didn't know about. His parents weren't getting any younger. What if one or both had died before Travis had introduced them to Chelsea?

The number of check marks in the column of Katie's unforgivable deeds would have continued to grow exponentially if that had happened, but he needed to stop thinking that way.

I can't change the past.

Lord knew he wished he could on a number of fronts. But one thing he could do was be a part of Chelsea's life—for the rest of her life—*if* she wanted him there.

That might be a big *if*. What if she thought he'd abandoned her? Katie had a lot of resentment toward her own mother and definite conflicting feelings about finding her. If what Shania and Emmy found wasn't too devastating, he'd share it with Katie.

First things first. The time had come to learn more about Chelsea in preparation for their first face-to-face tomorrow.

He drew in a deep breath. *I hope I'm ready for this.*

∗   ∗   ∗

Kate said goodbye to Melissa in the stall after her horse had been rubbed down, but couldn't bring herself to go back to the arena and face Travis just yet. The cowardly part of her had hoped he'd stay in Nashville rather than choose to become part of Chelsea's life. No such luck. Not that she really expected anything less.

What did he want to discuss, beyond the obvious?

You aren't going to find out hiding in this barn.

She blinked and looked around, expecting to see Daddy standing there. He'd always been one to say what he thought in life, so was he now encouraging her to pursue Travis? She chuffed. That would be the day, especially after all the unflattering things he'd said about him when she was dating him in college.

Walking into the kitchen and waiting area of the arena a few minutes later, Kate found Travis staring into the trophy case. Perhaps this could be common ground. "This one's of Chelsea competing at the academy level at a show on the Shelby County Fairgrounds in May. She'd been begging me to compete so I let her enter some beginner's academy classes that Saturday morning."

So he'd been looking at her all along and didn't know it. She looked a lot more professional than some of the riders in more advanced shows. "How'd she do?"

"Blue ribbon in one class and a red in another."

"First and second. Not bad."

"She was fabulous. You should have seen her." The words were out before she could halt them. She cringed inside, but tried not to groan outwardly. He didn't say anything. "She earned both of those ribbons under a tough, but fair, judge."

"Impressive. I'm sure having you as her trainer made a big difference, too."

She shrugged. "I work hard and demand that my students, including my own daughter, do their best at all times." Sometimes Chelsea accused Kate of pushing her harder than the others, but she tried to be fair. "She's been wanting to do another show, but, well, we haven't found the right one yet."

"What other things does she enjoy doing?"

"Typical middle-school stuff—lip syncing to her favorite songs, being on her phone chatting or texting with friends, reading voraciously, and playing softball when she's not riding her horse, Jasmine. Temperamentally, she's mostly sweet. Likes to get involved in charity projects at school and stands up to bullies. This past school year, she volunteered with kids in elementary school to tutor them in math." Kate paused, turning her body fully toward Travis. "She definitely didn't get math skills from me."

"I've always loved math."

I know. On more than one occasion, Kate had thought of Travis when she'd watched Chelsea quickly figure out some complicated math problem.

"I should warn you that she's also in the midst of raging hormones. She can be giggling one minute and bursting into tears the next."

His smile widened. "Man, I go from not being able to wait to meet her to being terrified, all in a matter of seconds." He paused a moment before asking, "Would you mind showing me her room?"

She shook her head. "I don't want to invade her space without her permission. If she wants to invite you in to see her room, fine."

The light faded from his eyes. "Yeah, I understand. My sisters were super private at that age, too. I just want to know everything about her and don't know how to go about it."

That he had taken an interest in Chelsea should please her. Travis hadn't asked for any of this, but he appeared ready to accept his role as Chelsea's father.

"Have you had dinner yet?" she asked.

He shook his head. "Can I take you out somewhere?"

"Thanks, but I'm having trouble controlling my sugar levels today, so I need to eat here tonight." The stress she'd been under had totally spiked her glucose. "But there's enough for two if you'd care to join me. We can talk more about Chelsea over dinner." She hoped they'd be able to stick to that topic and not venture into discussions about their future. For now, it appeared that the only future they'd have would be sharing the parenting of their daughter.

The smile reached his eyes again, and they lit up. "I'd like that."

She led the way to the house and washed up before beginning to prepare the chicken cacciatore while he chopped vegetables for the tossed salad. She'd put some dinner rolls in the oven for him, too.

"Would you prefer penne or rotini pasta with your chicken?"

"Either sounds great. Whatever you're having is perfect."

Kate found being amicable took a lot less energy. She intended to make this a stress-free meal. Afterward, perhaps she'd show him some of the photo scrapbooks she'd made of Chelsea over the years.

* * *

So his kid took after him in math, huh? Hearing that there might be some of him in Chelsea, other than the family resemblances, made him feel like a king. He wanted to know more.

While he chopped the carrots into disks, he cast sidelong glances at Katie. The lines around her eyes had relaxed some since he'd first arrived. Maybe she'd come to realize he wasn't the enemy.

"Is she a good student?"

Katie shrugged. "She's not consistent. She can go from straight As to mostly Bs and Cs from one semester to another. Getting her to do homework can be a chore worse than mucking stalls."

He nodded, grinning. "Sounds a lot like me at that age. Maybe she'll outgrow it once she starts to think about college and her future. What does she want to be when she grows up?"

"A medical researcher. She wants to find a cure for diabetes."

"Wow." Clearly, Chelsea cared about her mother's illness. Just how much did she know about it and how had it affected her?

"Yeah, tell me about it. But at her age, kids change their minds every other month. Last year, though, she wanted to be a doctor. So there seems to be a theme here."

Over dinner, he continued to ask questions about Chelsea until Katie said, "After dinner, why don't we sit in the living room and go through some of my photo albums?"

"I'd like that." *In some ways.* He also dreaded watching his secret daughter growing up before his eyes, knowing he'd missed out on so many years already. "Mom and Dad are going to be over the moon when they find out about her."

She glanced away. "When do you plan to tell them?"

"Not 'til after I meet Chelsea and see whether she wants to have anything to do with me and my family. I'd rather they not know she exists than find out Chelsea wants nothing to do with them."

Katie reached across the table and squeezed his hand. When he met her gaze, what looked like tears welled in her eyes. "Chelsea needs grandparents in her life. Trust me. She'll want to get to know them."

He sat back in the chair, and she pulled her hand back. "Hope so." But what about getting to know him? Before he sank in the deep end of the bitterness pool, he reined himself in. "What has she said about wanting a dad, though?"

She stared down at her plate. "When she first went to school and found out other kids had a mommy and a daddy, it was hard for her. But she hasn't really asked much about her own dad in the last few years."

"What does she know about me?"

Her gaze met his again, fierceness in her eyes. "That you didn't abandon her. That was really important for me to make her understand. I told her you just didn't know about her."

"Why didn't you give me a chance, Katie? What did I ever do to make you cut me off from your and Chelsea's life like that?"

She drew a ragged breath. "It wasn't you. It was me." Without explaining further, she stood and began clearing the dishes from the table. "Let's clean up in here, and you can start going through my photo albums." After loading the dishwasher, she poured him a sweet tea and herself a flavored water and carried them into the hallway. He followed her into the living room where he'd slept that first night he'd shown up here. Seemed like a year ago. His entire life had changed since then.

"Where would you like to start?"

"From the beginning."

"I probably have eight full albums."

"If we have to stop and take care of the horses, we can. I'm happy to sit and go through them by myself if you have other things to do. But I'd love to hear your commentary. To hear you tell Chelsea's life story as we go."

Katie sighed, but nodded. "Have a seat on the couch." She went to the bookshelf to pick up two huge albums and brought them over to where he waited. He'd left her plenty of space on the couch, but she sat much closer than he'd expected. Close enough to smell her scent. Nothing manufactured. Just Katie. A mix of soap, lemongrass, and leather.

Don't be thinking about leather in that way with sweet little Katie.

He fought back a grin, but at least the carnal thought had lightened his mood enough to begin this journey into a life he hadn't been a part of. His own flesh and blood had been front and center in most of the photos, none of which included him.

You can't undo the past.

He nodded at Danny's words. His buddy had said that to him the first time he'd visited after he'd rejoined his friend stateside while Danny lay in a VA hospital bed with his leg amputated. He'd been much more accepting of his condition than Travis had been at first. If only…

When Katie balanced the album between their laps and opened to the first page, his thoughts returned to the moment. The first photo showed an extremely pregnant Katie smiling at the camera, hands folded below her belly to show off her baby-swollen abdomen. He detected a touch of worry in her gaze. The photo had been taken in this very room, near the fireplace, which was blazing. Christmas decorations were still on the mantel.

Other photos on this page included sonogram shots of what he supposed was Chelsea in the womb. "Is she sucking her thumb?"

Katie laughed. "She was. I'm surprised you can make that out."

"Well, that's what it looks like, but I didn't know babies did that even before they were born."

"Oh, they have all kinds of tricks in there. Somersaults were her favorites. And kickboxing."

What would it have felt like for him to be touching Katie's belly when Chelsea kicked his hand? He tamped down his regrets and turned the page. He was bombarded with images of the tiniest baby he'd ever seen. Okay, so he hadn't seen many.

"She was born in Lexington on the 21st of January. It actually snowed seven inches a few days before. Daddy and I were worried we wouldn't be able to make it there if the roads weren't cleared. Thankfully, most of the snow melted by the time my contractions started. You know how it is on backroads when there's a heavy snow."

I should have been the one taking you to the hospital.

Most of the photos showed Chelsea bundled up tightly with only her little face sticking out. One of her having a bath surrounded by bubbles.

I should have been there to hold you, baby girl.

Would he have his guts ripped out with each turn of the page? Could he do this? The walls started to close in on him. When Katie reached to turn another page, he placed his hand over hers.

"I need some air."

Travis shifted the album to her lap, stood, and walked out the front door. He wasn't sure if he needed to run or to puke his guts out. He decided to try running first and broke out in a jog then an all-out run. The sun was lower in the sky, but still an hour or more from setting. He started down the lane. His eyesight blurred, but he veered to the left and onto the road. The heat of the day hadn't waned much, and sweat soon trickled down his neck.

"Why?" The sound of his scream made him realize he'd stopped before the word had been ripped from his chest. Why had Katie done this to him? How was he going to ever make up for what he and Chelsea had lost? Of course he never could.

A vehicle approached him from behind, and he stepped into the grass on the side of the narrow road to let it pass, but the damned thing slowed down instead. "Hey, can I give you a ride somewhere?"

He stared at the woman, but couldn't see her face because the sun was behind her. He shook his head.

"Travis Cooper. I heard you were back."

Who the hell would know him from Adam around here? Her Hispanic accent sounded familiar, though. "I'm sorry. Do we know each other?"

"I'm Lidia Brodie. Well, you might remember me as Lidia Mercado. I was Kate's roommate at UK." Her head turned toward the steering wheel momentarily before returning to his direction. "In college, you and my husband, Jason Brodie, used to shoot hoops together."

His mind wasn't thinking clearly at the moment, and he was in no mood for a stroll down memory lane. "Sure. I remember you," he lied. "Listen, Lidia, I appreciate the offer, but I need to finish my run and head back to Katie's."

Her grin told him she read more into those words than was based in reality. "No problem. I know how hard it is to get healthy around here when everyone stops to offer you a ride. I'm glad you came back." He remembered Katie mentioning Lidia when they'd been locked in the springhouse. Had she filled her in on this week, or did Lidia mean back as in since he and Katie had broken up? "We own the Chambourcin Winery down the road on Jason's old family farm. I know he'd love to catch up on old times with you if you ever want to stop by."

Travis nodded. "Thanks. I hope to be around for a while. If so, I'll do that."

She looked like she was about to say something else, but seemed to check herself before putting the SUV back into gear. "Have a nice evening. Tell Kate I said hi."

After saying goodbye, he watched her drive away slowly. Almost immediately, his brain locked in on a memory of the four of them having pizza while watching the Final Four. Jason Brodie. He hadn't been in classes with either of them, but they'd been friends of Katie's. Still were, apparently.

With the wind out of his sails and his courage back up, he turned and walked back to the house. He'd better get his shit together before Chelsea came home. He hadn't asked if he could stay the night at Katie's place, but he had a lot of albums to work his way through by tomorrow afternoon.

What if Chelsea didn't want him to be part of her life? The nagging thought wouldn't be resolved until they met and he could gauge her interest in having a father in her life. Still, he was beginning to feel like he knew her. To feel a connection to her that was heart deep, which sounded strange given the fact they'd never met.

Tomorrow. And then he'd either go home empty-hearted, or they'd find a way to mesh the rest of their lives together in a way that would work for all three of them.

Chapter Seventeen

K ate stared out the picture window and down the lane long after Travis ran out of sight. Why had his emotional response to the photos been so surprising? She'd cheated the man out of twelve and a half years of Chelsea's life. Over the last half hour, she'd come down off her high horse and started to see this situation from Travis's perspective.

Suddenly, she wanted to do whatever it took to make this work between them. It was inevitable that Chelsea would want to get to know Travis better. Chelsea had longed for a dad for years, even to the point of trying not so subtly to talk Kate into dating the divorced father of one of her riding students a few years ago. Perhaps not so coincidentally, that had been about the time she'd stopped asking about her own dad.

Raising Chelsea, Kate had had little time to think about bringing a man into their lives. Her sole focus had been on raising her daughter and running this farm. But like it or not, Travis was going to become a part of their lives. And honestly, she'd never forgotten him. Every time she looked at Chelsea, she remembered…

How could she make this easier on them both? She had no clue how to even introduce the two of them to one another. "Chelsea, I'd like you to meet your father," she'd practiced. Hardly. But it sure beat pretending he was a new hired hand or, worse, a man she'd begun dating in the last week and invited to stay here. No, she needed to tell Chelsea the truth from the start. She'd told too many lies already.

The thought of Chelsea's reaction and response almost made her sick to her stomach.

Travis entered the lane, walking rather than running. As he came closer to the house, the resolute look on his face made one thing clear. He'd come to a decision, too.

She walked out onto the front porch and waited for him. Hoping to head him off at the pass, she said, "You're welcome to spend the night inside. And I'll answer any questions you have."

His eyes opened wider for a second before he schooled his expression. "Thanks. I'll take you up on both offers. I'll probably be up all night going through the rest of the albums." He squared his shoulders. "If you don't mind, Katie, I need to do that alone."

Why did it feel as though he was already shutting her out of his and Chelsea's world? "I understand." She wasn't sure how to say this so she might as well just do it. "Travis, tell me what you need in order to be ready for tomorrow."

He squinted at her. "I haven't a clue."

"Well, just ask. Anything. Anytime. I'm sorry I've been treating you like the enemy. This must rank high on your list of the most difficult situations you've been forced to deal with outside combat."

His body relaxed. "That it does."

"I want to make it better for you both. Would seeing her room help? If so, I'll take you up there now."

He shook his head. "No, you were right. I don't want to invade her privacy. But I would like to see every last photo. You have enough captions that I'll be able to figure out what's what."

She nodded and waved him onto the porch, but didn't lead him into the house immediately. "The important thing is that she doesn't feel she has to choose between us." *Please, no, because I would lose.*

"We both want what's best for Chelsea. But I do have some questions." Travis indicated the swing. "Have a seat." As an afterthought, he threw in, "Please."

He joined her, and Katie moved as close to the armrest as possible, too aware of his body next to hers to be able to concentrate fully. He spent the next half hour grilling her for more information about Chelsea. Hobbies other than horses and softball. Childhood illnesses and injuries. Favorite foods, colors, TV shows, movies. The list went on and on until he asked, "Does she have a boyfriend?"

"She's only twelve and a half! Of course not!"

"Good, because I'd probably break the arms of any boy who tried to touch her."

Kate couldn't contain her grin, but turned away so he wouldn't see it. "You sound like Daddy."

"I have a newfound respect for your father's overprotectiveness."

Had Hell frozen over? Or had she been transported to some alternate universe?

"She does have a crush on one of the counselors at camp this week but he's in college and no doubt will have been thoroughly trained in how to handle preteen and teen crushes before being hired."

"Damn straight."

That they'd found common ground on something warmed Kate's heart. Chelsea might not be happy to hear she'd now have two protective parents making sure she stayed out of trouble, but having someone else play the bad guy for a change might cut Kate a little slack in that department.

Travis gently moved the swing back and forth with his foot as the silence dragged out. Was he running out of questions? Then he asked, "What position does she play in softball?"

"Pitcher."

"Good for her. When does the season end?"

"Already has. But she plays in the church league throughout the rest of the summer. Local games only."

This time several more minutes passed before he said, "I think I'm ready to start in on the albums again."

She nodded and started to stand when he gently grabbed her arm. The now-familiar electricity bolted through her body. "Katie?"

The lines at the corners of his eyes relaxed as a slow smile spread across his lips. Her gaze rested there, and for one bizarre flash of a second, she longed to feel those lips on hers again before she looked into his eyes. Pulling herself back to reality, she asked, "Yes?" Her voice was barely audible to her ears, and she cleared her throat after the fact.

He did as well. "Thank you for choosing to have her and for keeping her rather than giving her up for adoption. I know it can't have been easy to raise her on your own all these years."

I will not cry in front of Travis.

She swallowed past the lump in her throat. "I never considered anything else an option."

"I've heard some really sad stories from my sisters about clients trying to find biological parents, and I'm glad she's always been with one of us." Before she could apologize again for shutting him out, he added, "I'm not going to come between you two, but I do want to carve out some time to get to know her. Just father-daughter time. Will you be okay with that?"

No mention of the three of them, but what did she expect after the way she'd locked him out of their lives all these years? She'd regret that decision for eternity.

"Absolutely. No doubt she'll demand to have that time with you, too."

Kate didn't know yet what type of reception he'd receive from Chelsea, but that he was here and willing to become a part of Chelsea's life meant a lot to her. She'd make sure Chelsea didn't pick up any negative vibes from her toward him that might sway her opinion of her father.

A mosquito bit her, and she smacked it. "Let's go inside before we're eaten alive. I'll freshen your sweet tea while you dive back into the albums. Are you okay with sleeping on the couch, or would you prefer the guest room? It's not really made up yet and has become my storage and junk room."

He chuckled. "The couch is fine. Closer to the photo albums. But I plan to move back to the barn tomorrow. Don't want to give Chelsea the idea anything's going on between us."

Kate huffed, making light rather than letting those words seep into her soul. "Not to worry. I'm an asexual being in her eyes—a mom."

"I hear you," he said, smiling. "I still don't want to think about my mom having sex with Dad—and they're going on thirty-six years married this October with five kids." His grin faded. "I have a lot to learn to do this half as well as they raised us."

"It won't be so different from how you engage with other close family members. Mutual respect. Open communication. Love. Lots of unconditional love."

"You make it sound easy."

"I'm not saying I've succeeded all the time. I've made plenty of mistakes." *Especially when it came to being honest with my daughter—and you.*

"Hey, do you want me to go with you to pick her up tomorrow?"

Did she? No clue. "Let me think about it. Might be best for her to meet you here, or you might have a dozen teen and preteen girls drooling over you—and their mothers wondering what Kate Michaels has been up to while Chelsea was away."

"I doubt those girls would give an almost middle-aged man like me a second glance."

Oh, Travis, you never did see how the female set looked at you.

"But I see what you mean about wagging tongues. I don't want to make things difficult for either of you since you have to go on living here."

So did that mean he didn't have plans to take Chelsea away from her?

She shrugged, trying not to show her thoughts. "I try not to care much about what people think concerning me, but don't want Chelsea to bear the brunt of bullying or teasing."

"I can already tell I'm probably going to be worrying about both my girls anytime you're out of my sight."

Both my girls? The thought that he might still have feelings for Kate after this made her tingle in places best shut down, until she realized he'd probably been talking about Chelsea and his dog, Sadie.

Of course, Kate was the mother of his daughter, so he'd care about her in that way. But she couldn't expect him to have romantic feelings for her any longer.

How would it go tomorrow when they told Chelsea—and where and how did they intend to do it? While he pored over more photos, she went out to the barn to take care of the horses and do some thinking.

After their talk tonight, though, she was certain now he wouldn't run out on Chelsea. Her daughter's security and happiness was all that mattered.

Their daughter's. She needed to stop thinking of Chelsea as only hers.

* * *

Travis hoped he'd made some progress in getting Katie to trust that he was here for the long haul. She'd spent a lifetime in a black cave of distrust and resentment.

He sighed. It wasn't as though he didn't share some of that latter sentiment.

Don't let resentment seep into your bones, too, Trav. It will only fester and rot your soul.

"Easier said than done, Danny," he said. But damned if he intended to wallow in bitterness about the past. What's done was done. Time to move on.

Well into the night, he scrutinized every page of photos in every album. Katie had done a phenomenal job of chronicling Chelsea's life to date, almost as though she wanted to be able to show him someday.

Yeah, right.

He noticed the photos became fewer and fewer in the past couple of years, though. Had Katie become too busy, or was Chelsea avoiding the camera? Was Chelsea one of those girls who was self-conscious about her face and body the way his sisters had been at that age? How could she be? She was perfect in every way per the two-dimensional proof. Maybe they'd both grown too busy to chronicle her life, although there were lots from birthdays and Christmases. Winter months probably were a little less busy.

Travis recalled the one Katie had texted him where Chelsea appeared to be less than thrilled to be having her photo snapped. *Tough.* He wanted new ones by the thousands—and that was during the next few days or however long he would be here this time. For them, their life together would begin tomorrow evening.

There were several shots in the past year of Chelsea riding the bay named Princess Jasmine. He'd spent a good deal of time with that horse while cleaning her stall. Not temperamental, but spirited. Nearly sixteen hands tall. A lot of horse for a young girl to handle, but Chelsea seemed in control of her in these pictures.

He'd have to ask Katie whether Chelsea had raised the seven-year-old horse from birth. He could totally picture a young girl naming a pet after something fanciful like her favorite Disney princess. Come to think of it, he'd seen a Halloween photo from maybe six years earlier of Chelsea dressed as Princess Jasmine from *Aladdin.*

What did she plan to go as this Halloween?

Will I ever come to know her well enough to answer that?

Damn straight, he would.

Or had he missed out on her trick or treating years? She might still dress up for parties or something. He hoped so. Halloween had always been one of his favorite holidays.

Travis rested his head on the back of the couch and closed his eyes, imagining the moment when Chelsea would first learn he was her daddy. The backs of his eyelids stung, and he blinked away the moisture. A safer subject for his daydreaming tonight would be what might happen further down the road. What kinds of activities might the two of them enjoy doing together?

The enormity of what the future might hold took its toll, and he gave in to sleep only to dream about his blonde-haired princess riding around the arena as her mother gave sharp commands and effusive praise…until he realized Katie was holding a frying pan.

The smell of bacon wafted under his nose, and he blinked awake. Sunlight streamed in the window, and he jumped up as if caught with his pants down. An afghan had been spread over him. Had Katie seen him sleeping upright? She'd left him sheets and a cotton blanket before heading to the barn last night, but he hadn't budged from this spot since then. Unless he'd covered himself in his sleep, she must have done it. How'd he sleep through that? Usually he was a light sleeper.

Travis rubbed the stiffness from his neck. Man, there'd be hell to pay before he worked the kinks out today.

After a quick stop in the bathroom, he wandered down the hallway and into the kitchen. Katie removed strips of bacon from the skillet, placing them on a plate covered with a paper towel.

"Good morning." His voice sounded as if it had passed through sandpaper. He made a beeline for the coffee pot. "Sorry I slept so late. I don't even remember falling asleep."

"How far did you get?"

"Almost finished the last one." After making scrambled eggs and toast to go with the bacon, she sat at the table beside him ten minutes later. "Tell me about Chelsea and Princess Jasmine."

"The horse or the movie character?"

"Both, maybe. I'm curious. Did she name the horse?"

Katie nodded. "I gave the horse to Chelsea as a yearling on her sixth birthday, and Jasmine was her favorite princess at the time. Of course, she'd been around the horse almost nine months by then because she was born to one of my mares."

"Which one does she like now?"

Katie smiled indulgently. "She's not really into Disney princesses any longer. Sexy country music singers and famous Saddlebred horses are her rock stars now."

He needed to keep a cheat sheet. "How am I going to remember everything?"

She reached across the table and squeezed his hand. "You don't have to. It's not like you're cramming for the New Father 101 final exam. Just be yourself, talk with her about things you have in common, ask her questions, and let nature take its course."

He'd lost his appetite due to the sizable knot in his stomach. "I'm going to be a nervous wreck until you two come home this afternoon."

"Actually, I've thought about it, and if you wouldn't mind, I'd like for you to come with me to pick her up. I'd prefer that to having her simply happen upon you in the barn or something. And I'm certain she'll rush to Jasmine's stall first thing after we get home."

His heart hammered, robbing him of thought or breath. "Are you sure?" *Because I sure as hell am not.*

She nodded, then pulled her hand back, and moved her eggs around on the plate. "But let's not tell her who you really are un-til…until I'm sure." What could he do to assure her he wasn't going to desert Chelsea?

"Katie, I'm not like your mom. I'll never walk out on her. *Ever.*"

She nibbled her lip, anguish written all over her face. He wanted to wrap her in his arms, but held back.

"Trust me, Katie." If she believed he'd treat their daughter right, maybe she could relax. Given what happened with her mom, no wonder Katie hadn't been able to expect him to do the right thing all those years ago. He began to see that he wasn't the one facing the test of a lifetime—Katie was.

She drew a deep, ragged breath. "Wait for my signal as to the best time to tell her. Not in front of her friends at church, though."

"Agreed. But definitely tonight, right?"

The silence dragged out between them until she whispered, "Okay. Tonight. I know you two are going to hit it off and bond with each other quickly. I'll try not to get in the way."

He wished she'd included herself in that bonding scenario and that they could be a traditional family, but at the moment, Chelsea remained his first concern.

"I'll wait for your signal, but how will I know when you're ready?"

"She knows her father and I were college sweethearts, so when I tell her you and I knew each other at UK, she's probably going to figure it out herself. Then we can both follow her cues as to what she needs to know."

"Hey, wait. Will she recognize my name?"

Katie shook her head. "Not the name Travis. She asked once a few years ago, but I didn't think she needed to know your full name yet."

No, I guess you wouldn't.

"I promised I'd tell her when she reached an age where she might want to look for you. Of course, her last name is Cooper, too."

His fork clattered to the plate as his breath caught in his throat. "My daughter has my last name!" His heart swelled to nearly bursting. *Chelsea Cooper.*

"Of course. It's on her birth certificate." At least he hadn't totally been erased from Chelsea's life, even if the girl didn't know much about him. "I figured she'd see it on the birth certificate if she ever applied for a passport or something. And Lidia and Jason, who would be her legal guardians if anything happens to me, know——"

"We need to talk about revising your will."

Her face grew a little ashen. "Definitely. I'll get in touch with my attorney and have her draw up the new version this week. You'll want to do the same."

Until now, he'd left everything to his siblings and niece and nephew. Knowing his own daughter had almost been left out of his will—albeit inadvertently—made him sick. Would he ever get off this roller coaster of emotions?

He needed some time to himself, to prepare for what was to come. "I'll be ready by five to pick up Chelsea." *My daughter.* If he said it a million times, it still wouldn't sound real to him.

"Sounds like a plan," she said.

A lousy one, he thought, as he headed to the barn to check on the horses and expel some pent-up energy. He'd never have launched a mission in the military with so many unknown variables. Katie knew Chelsea better than he did, though, and wouldn't do anything to hurt her daughter. He'd follow her lead.

Trust your instincts, Trav. In Iraq, they got us all through a lot of shit.

But they hadn't survived everything. Danny had lost his leg. Craig, his life.

But nobody's gonna be shooting at you, man. That's always a good day.

Travis grinned, the tension lifting a bit. *You can say that again, Danny.* While a lot was riding on this, they'd all survive to go on and work out whatever their future would hold.

Chapter Eighteen

"By the way, Happy Father's Day."

Katie's words hit him like a blow to the solar plexus. He'd been so consumed with the discovery he hadn't remembered what day it was. He'd have to give Dad a call later on. He'd never forgotten the day before—and had never had reason to celebrate it as a father, either.

Travis watched from the passenger seat of Katie's truck as the kids and their chaperones poured out of the church bus, wondering which one was his daughter. Would he recognize her after seeing her grow up in the photos he'd gone through overnight?

Maybe he shouldn't have agreed to come here. His heart hammered so loudly he was sure Katie could hear it. He couldn't think of what to say to Chelsea when they first met. He had to be careful not to give anything away, because this wasn't the place to tell her. In a few hours, Katie's secret would be revealed.

Because I'm not losing another night's sleep without Chelsea knowing her daddy loves her and always will.

The fifteen or so girls were full of smiles and giggles, along with a few shy glances cast toward some of the boys, including one who must be that college-aged counselor Katie mentioned Chelsea had a crush on. But about a third of the bus's passengers were younger boys. When the hell did church camps go coed? Okay, he'd only ever done Boy Scout ones, so maybe these always had been. Still, wasn't that asking for trouble, especially with pubescent kids?

A few more kids exited the bus. Suddenly, all the air was sucked out of the truck's cab. He recognized her in an instant.

Chelsea. My daughter.

She was talking with one of the boys closer to her own age, although that gave him little comfort. Travis might have some twenty years on that boy, but he could remember those days and didn't like the idea of some punk kid making moves on *his* little girl.

And the look on Chelsea's face wasn't so different from the ones Katie had given him before they'd started dating. But Katie had been almost a decade older than Chelsea was now.

"I thought you said she wasn't interested in boys yet?"

As if she hadn't been paying attention, Katie cocked her head first toward him then homed in on Chelsea. "Oh, that's just Tony. They've been friends since kindergarten."

"Look at her. Tucking her hair behind her ear, glancing away with a coy smile, and then giggling at something he said. I'd suggest you find out what happened at camp this week."

Katie leaned forward as if that would help her see any more clearly what was right before her eyes.

"Wow, you're right. Something's changed between them."

"What are you going to do about it?"

She turned toward him. "Do? I can talk to her again about the dangers of getting too serious about boys at her age, but it's not as if she's going to start dating tomorrow. She's twelve! Even if they do start going steady, or whatever they call it these days, she's always stuck to any curfews I've set, and she and her friends are always chaperoned by one parent or another. I wouldn't worry too much."

"So you'll let her go on dates in a few years?"

Katie grinned. "I think you're going to need to pace yourself, Travis, or you'll have an ulcer before she turns thirteen."

He held up his hands in frustration before waving a hand in their direction. "I can't believe you don't see how badly this could go. She's definitely interested in that Tony guy as more than a friend."

"Girls get crushes on boys all the time at that age—and sometimes they last all of a day or two. When she left for camp, the crush was on that nineteen-year-old counselor over there. Let's just be thankful that one's blown over."

"Maybe. But if he's the one in the Wildcat T-shirt, then she's also been giving him looks." Could girls become pregnant any time after they hit puberty? He ran his hands through his hair. "I'm not sure I'll survive instantaneous fatherhood, much less the rest of her life. Maybe if I'd been a part of her life up to now, I'd have more confidence that she'll make the right choices."

"Are you saying you don't trust that I raised her right? That she hasn't learned the difference between right and wrong by now?"

Hearing the indignation in her voice, he faced her squarely. "I have no clue, Katie. All I know is that I can put myself in that boy's shoes right now, and I don't like what he's thinking."

Katie slumped against the seat back. "Once you get to know her better, you'll see that Chelsea has a good head on her shoulders. She'll make the right decisions."

"I'm sure your father said the same thing about you."

"I was a lot older when I got serious about anyone—and you know it."

Point made. Travis sighed. "Just promise me you'll have a talk with her about how to protect herself from diseases and unwanted pregnancies."

"I already have."

He squinted his eyes and stared at her in disbelief. "Seriously? She's still a kid." Okay, he was starting to sound unhinged.

"Make up your mind, Travis." Katie laughed, but he didn't see any humor. "Listen, I learned the hard way about the consequences of unprotected sex. So I started talking with her when she was far too young for me to be worried—and the talks have matured as she has. When the time comes, those words will come back to her. At the very least, she'll be prepared."

"Good." Katie had done most things right when it came to parenting. Would he have done as well?

"I even told her we'd talk about specific types of contraceptives when she began dating," Katie added, "even though she assures me now she's going to practice abstinence until she marries."

"Don't they all?"

Katie laughed. "Hormones being what they are, I agree that's not the safest mode of protection. An eighth-grade girl in her school got pregnant last year. That's scary stuff."

"Damn straight." A girl only a grade ahead of Chelsea had gotten pregnant? *Oh, hell no.* But Travis couldn't help but add, "I would never have put the blame or responsibility on you for getting pregnant, by the way. But thanks for letting me be your first, Katie."

Her cheeks grew red, and she avoided eye contact as they both refocused on Chelsea and the other kids.

When a man he assumed to be Tony's father came up and hugged him, Chelsea began searching the parking lot—looking for Katie, no doubt.

Katie opened the door and exited, shouting unnecessarily after the girl had already started in their direction, "Over here, Chelsea!" Katie practically sprinted toward their daughter, and Chelsea launched herself into her mother's arms. Watching the two embrace, leaving him out in the cold, made him even more determined to put this damned secret behind them.

When they broke apart and started toward the pile of duffel bags and luggage next to the bus, Travis got out and caught up with them by taking long strides. "Let me do the heavy lifting, ladies."

Uncertainty clouded Katie's face as Chelsea looked from him to her mother. Travis extended his hand toward Chelsea. "I'm Travis, an old friend of your mother's. Just visiting for a few days."

She accepted his handshake shyly. "Hello, Travis."

His heart thudded to a stop. Overcome with emotion, he couldn't force another word past the lump lodged in his throat. He was holding his daughter's hand for the first time. Travis wanted to blurt out right then who he was, but showed some restraint.

"I suppose we ought to be heading home." Katie broke into the sweet moment when she moved toward the stack of suitcases and duffel bags and lifted a lime-green one, and he released Chelsea's hand with reluctance.

No way. Travis put his feet and head into gear and took it from her. "That's what I'm here for." He took it from her and hefted it onto his shoulder. *Oof.* What on earth did the kid pack in there, anyway?

Katie wrapped an arm around her daughter. He didn't notice any strain between the two of them despite what Katie had mentioned. "Let's head home."

Home. To an outsider, they appeared like any other family picking up their kid from camp. But they weren't a family, not in the sense he wanted them to be, anyway. At the moment, he wasn't anything to Chelsea, so he'd need to remember his place.

Until Katie revealed his identity, and then they'd see what would happen with his relationship to his daughter.

*   *   *

Seeing Chelsea and Travis together for the first time did a number on Kate's psyche. In Chelsea's early years, Kate had fantasized about Travis showing up and the two of them forming a strong father-daughter bond, but as time slipped away without her doing a damned thing to precipitate that meeting, she'd all but ruled out any chance of it happening spontaneously.

Thank goodness he hadn't blurted out who he was. Kate hadn't completely trusted Travis to hold back. He seemed so proud to call himself Chelsea's dad. She wouldn't put it off too long, but at least wanted the announcement to happen at home.

Travis's good looks hadn't been lost on their daughter, either, judging by the shy grins and the blush that crept into Chelsea's cheeks when he shook her hand. She'd been unable to maintain eye contact with him.

All the more reason not to put off telling her.

Daddy wanted her to tell him? Well, that was certainly a turn of events. Had Danny been working on him from the other side? Okay, she'd decide when would be the best time to reveal his identity, but it needed to be tonight. The perfect Father's Day gift.

Their lives would never be the same again.

Back at the truck, Travis opened the rear passenger door and loaded Chelsea's bag behind the passenger's seat, leaving room for Chelsea to sit behind Kate—probably so he could look at her when they spoke to each other. Kate got in behind the wheel and started the ignition, asking Chelsea how her week had been.

"The usual."

"Did they keep you busy?" Kate asked, putting the truck in drive.

"Yeah."

Clearly, getting information out of her was going to be like pulling teeth. As they drove out of the parking lot, Travis asked, "What was your favorite thing about camp?"

"Sitting around the fire pit, roasting marshmallows, and talking way past midnight on our last night."

"That was always one of my favorite things to do when I went to Boy Scout camp."

"Rick told some really scary ghost stories."

"Rick?" Travis asked.

Kate heard the tension in his voice and bit her lip to keep from smiling. "Rick's the camp counselor I told you about."

"Oh." He sounded even more worried. *Poor Travis.* She'd warned him that Chelsea's crushes were fleeting, but given time, he'd learn to navigate the Chelsea waters soon enough. He was doing a great job at asking her open-ended questions, though. Kate could take a few lessons there.

"Rick's great. So funny. And kinda cute, too. He's going to be a sophomore at UK and is majoring in recreational studies." Turning her attention toward Kate, she added, "Hey, Mom. Tony's going to ask his parents if he can take horseback riding lessons from you. I told him how much fun it is, and he wants to try it."

Oh, my! Travis had been right about them, for sure. Something had changed between the two while at camp. He'd never been particularly interested in horses before.

"Sounds great," Kate said. "I'll wait to hear what the Mongiardos decide, but I have room in my schedule to take on a new student this summer, maybe even two." The upcoming winter months were her slowest times, but she predicted the boy would lose interest in horses—possibly Chelsea—long before then.

Talk of camp picked up again, and Chelsea entertained them all the way back to the farm with tales of the awful food and which girls snored the loudest in her cabin. Kate parked next to Travis's truck, and Chelsea asked. "Are you staying in my house?"

Kate's heart hammered until he answered, "No, in the barn apartment. I'm keeping an eye on things for your mom while Miguel is away."

Perfect answer, Travis. Kate relaxed, and her shoulder muscles screamed. She didn't realize how hard she'd been holding onto the steering wheel on the drive home.

"I thought he was coming back tonight," Chelsea said to Kate.

Kate turned around in the seat, wondering why all the questions. "Well, he was, but his dad isn't doing well, and he asked for another week off."

"How long will Travis be here?" Chelsea asked, not directing her words toward Travis. Kate had no clue how to answer that one.

Luckily, Travis chimed in again. "At least a couple more days."

Before Chelsea asked any more questions, Kate interjected, "Would spaghetti and meatballs be all right for supper?"

"Sure." Chelsea and Travis answered simultaneously. Chelsea added, "But not too much for me. I gained a ton at camp."

"Nonsense," Kate and Travis said. She smiled her appreciation to him. Chelsea, on the other hand, gave him an odd expression as if wondering why he'd have an opinion since he didn't know her.

"You look fine," Kate added. She hoped this wouldn't be the beginning of her daughter becoming obsessed about diets and weight. Chelsea was perfect in every way. Kate's focus had been on making sure they ate the right things. Perhaps having a father around to reinforce that she was beautiful would benefit Chelsea's self-esteem. The only body issue Kate cared about was having Chelsea eat healthy foods, hoping she'd avoid developing insulin problems. Not that Kate had gotten diabetes due to bad eating habits. Of course, Kate had no idea what her mother's family's genetics were, but why take a chance in case she could prevent Chelsea having to suffer?

What else didn't she know about her mom? She hadn't heard anything from Travis's sisters, but with Chelsea about to officially meet her dad tonight, Kate's desire to find out more about her mom was surfacing again.

One step at a time, Kate.

Kate and Travis opened their doors to exit, and he smiled as he reached behind his seat to remove Chelsea's bag at the same time her daughter—*their* daughter—grabbed it from inside. There was a momentary tug of war that Travis won. While Kate couldn't read either one's expression, Chelsea's giggle was unmistakable.

Having the conversation they needed to over the dinner table might be awkward, but soon the secret she'd kept from Chelsea would be revealed. Given how well they'd hit it off so far, Kate didn't expect there to be any problems with them forging a strong bond.

Please, Travis, don't take my baby away.

Kate pushed those old fears to the background. Chelsea was going to love having a father in her life, and he hadn't given any hint that he intended to take her to court for custody. Nothing of the kind.

If he did, she'd cross that bridge if she came to it, but right now, she wanted to make things go as smoothly as possible for all of them.

Chelsea jumped down from the truck and bolted for the barn. "I'm going to go say hi to Jazz!"

When she was out of earshot, Travis said, "I don't know how I could have thought my life was complete before today. But there's no way in hell it ever can be again if she's not part of it." He started toward the house with the bag, but made eye contact with Kate and mouthed the words, "Thank you," as though unable to get the words out.

Her stomach flip-flopped. Embarrassed by the sting in her eyes, she nodded and followed him toward the kitchen door. "Supper will be ready at seven."

"Wouldn't miss it for the world."

Kate's heart felt as though it were being squeezed in a carpenter's vise. She should be overjoyed that he wanted to be a part of Chelsea's growing up. And she was. But she also was terrified that she might lose her daughter to him?

Chapter Nineteen

N early half an hour later, Travis steeled himself to head back to the house for dinner. He'd carried Chelsea's bag as far as the porch before Katie had taken it from him and disappeared inside. He'd given Chelsea her space with her horse and occupied himself with loading up some hay bales from the old barn to bring down to the horse barn tomorrow.

Time crawled despite his having something to do until they ate. He'd called Dad to wish him a Happy Father's Day, and it had killed him not to tell him the news, but he needed to make sure this was going to turn out okay first. The work in the stalls afterward helped him expend some of his nervous energy, but it hadn't done a damned thing to help him come to grips with the enormity of the moment when he'd be introduced to his daughter as her *father* for the first time. Right now, as far as she knew, he was a total stranger.

Whether Danny's advice had changed his way of thinking or not, he'd been unable to resent Katie for keeping them apart. All he felt was immense gratitude to her for the awesome job she'd done raising Chelsea.

At seven, he knocked on the kitchen door and waited until he heard Katie invite him inside. Upon entering, Katie stood at the sink draining the spaghetti into a colander, and Chelsea was nowhere to be found.

"Anything I can do to help?" he asked.

She didn't look at him, her back rigid with her lips drawn in a tight line. He'd like to discuss more about the plan for tonight, but not when there was a chance Chelsea could overhear them. He'd hope for the best. "You can call Chelsea down."

The request was such a simple thing, so why did he suddenly have performance anxiety about doing it right? "Sure thing." He walked down the hallway and called up the stairs to Chelsea, "Dinner's ready, Chelsea!" He wasn't sure if she could hear him over the Luke Bryan music or whether he should wait for her here or in the kitchen. But she came out of her room and bounded down the stairs before he had to decide.

"I'm starved! My mom's the best cook."

"That, she is."

She stopped and looked at him. "How long have you been here?"

"Since Monday." *More or less.*

"Hey, if you live in Nashville, do you know any of the famous country music singers there?" Her initial shyness seemed to be wearing off.

"I'm friends with a number of them, actually." Okay, maybe *friends* was a strong word, but Travis desperately wanted to be seen as a hero in his girl's eyes. They discussed a few of her favorites, many of whom he knew. Arranging a meet-and-greet with one or two of them shouldn't be too hard. He'd helped build lavish homes for several stars. While he didn't hang out with them socially, they'd always given him an open invitation to grab backstage passes whenever he wanted. He'd never had the inclination to take them up on the offers—until now. "Maybe I can arrange for you to go backstage and meet one or two of them sometime."

The squeal she let out nearly shattered his eardrums in the enclosed area. Katie came running from the kitchen, staring from one to the other. By the glare she gave Travis, no doubt she suspected he'd already revealed his identity. Man, he hoped Chelsea's response would be that enthusiastic when the time came.

"Is everything okay?"

"Better than okay, Mom!" Chelsea said, rolling her eyes. "Travis knows lots of my favorite singers—and he said he could arrange for me to go backstage at a concert sometime."

Katie's scowl told him she was none too happy about *that,* either. In a matter of minutes—hours at most—Chelsea would know who he was. She'd better get used to him making long-overdue promises like these to his daughter. And some of those might include ones that would take Chelsea away from her for a day or two.

Chelsea's bombarding him with a list of the artists she'd like to meet had him grinning again despite Katie's dour mood. The two of them walked side-by-side down the hall and followed Katie into the kitchen.

"Can you believe Travis knows so many famous stars, Mom?"

"That's nice, honey," she said, dismissively. "Oh, I forgot the rolls. Chelsea, why don't you go out in the deep freeze and get a bag?" Chelsea sighed dramatically, but did as she was asked and went through a door he hadn't used yet but that he supposed went to the garage.

When the girl was out of earshot, Katie whispered to him, "How could you get her hopes up like that? As far as she knows, you're a complete stranger who's planning to haul her off to Nashville. What worries me even more is that she doesn't seem to have any qualms about going off with you."

"Lighten up, Katie! My 'stranger' status is about to change. Besides, don't assume I planned to meet all of them back home. I figure a couple or more will be performing in Louisville, either at the state fair or at the Yum! Center." They'd only be gone for the day and an evening most likely.

"Oh." Katie's shoulders relaxed.

"But when she finds out who I am, if she wants to visit me in Nolensville someday to see where I live, I sure as hell intend to take her there, too." Katie might as well prepare herself for that eventuality, because he had every intention of making that girl the center of his life from this day on.

Hearing Chelsea approaching as she hummed one of her favorite country tunes, Katie turned around to stir the sauce in the pot. "We'll discuss this later," she whispered.

Damn straight—and Katie had better be changing *her* tune if she wanted this to work.

"Smells wonderful," Travis said, hoping to ease the tension and not give Chelsea the impression they'd been arguing about anything. His parents had never argued in front of their kids—and possibly at no other time, either. Travis would like to model their behavior in front of his own child.

Katie asked them how many rolls they wanted and put four on a cookie sheet. He supposed those weren't on her diet, since she only included what he and Chelsea wanted. She then asked Chelsea to get the drinks. After pouring water for her mom and sweet tea for herself, Chelsea asked, "What would you like to drink, Travis?"

"I'll have sweet tea, too, please. Thanks." Katie had been making a pot for him, since he preferred that over soda or water, but knowing his daughter drank the same thing added to the growing list of similarities he'd noticed between the two of them.

"Would you rather wait for the bread or just dig in?"

"Dig in! I'm starving!" Chelsea said.

Smiling again, Katie served the spaghetti and meatballs from the stove and brought her daughter's plate over first, then Travis's. He waited to see where Chelsea would sit before taking a seat across from her but left the head of the table for Katie.

"Go on and eat while it's hot," Katie said as she returned to the stove for her own plate. Chelsea mumbled a quick grace and dove in, but Travis had been taught not to eat until his mother sat. While it wasn't his place to correct Chelsea's conduct—yet—he said pointedly, "No, I'll wait for you."

Chelsea looked over at him as she chewed slowly and swallowed before setting her fork down as well. *Good girl.*

Chelsea reminded him of his own sisters when they were that age.

He just wished he'd paid more attention to them when it came to their interests and obsessions at any given moment. He had trouble finding things to talk with Chelsea about.

Katie set her plate on the table and bowed her head. He'd gotten out of the habit of praying before eating, but sent up a few words of thanks to God, Danny, and whoever else was responsible for bringing Chelsea into his life. He supposed Katie deserved a great deal of his thanks, too.

Norman Rockwell couldn't have painted a more wholesome family dinner scene. If only it could last forever. While he doubted he and Katie would be able to mend the hurt her secret had caused, he didn't want to be bitter about it, either. Danny was right, and Travis pushed away the negative emotions again.

Atta boy.

Shut up, Danny.

Katie smiled in the direction of her—*their*—daughter, and he shoved all thoughts of his friend to the back burner. "So what else did you do at camp, sweetie?"

The telltale blush answered the question before the girl said a word, whether from what she did or what her mom called her in front of him, he wasn't sure. "They let us play in the creek more this year. A bunch of us spent a lot of time down there when we weren't playing those dumb group games. Mostly just wading and talking. I showed Tony how to catch crawdads."

He hoped that's all the two of them learned—although there probably were plenty of chaperones keeping an eye on things.

Lordy, I'm never gonna survive Chelsea's dating years.

But he was happy to hear she wasn't a girly-girl. If she could handle crawdads, then she'd probably like to go fishing. He didn't get his boat out on Center Hill Lake nearly enough since Megan's kids had a new father to do that with them.

Before he could ask more about this Tony kid, Katie asked, "So did you meet any new friends?"

"Not really. Our church's group was so big that we had two whole cabins to ourselves. But I saw some girls I know from Georgetown's softball team at the dining hall."

Travis focused on eating while the two of them discussed camp activities, but he didn't miss a word. When they seemed to have run out of things to talk about, a buzzer rang, and he practically jumped.

"I'll get the rolls," Katie said.

"Tell me, Chelsea, what are you going to be doing this week now that you're home?"

She blinked at him a couple of times before answering, again probably wondering what business it was of his. But she answered. "Some of my friends are going to the movies tomorrow night." He was happy to hear she wasn't going to the movies alone with Tony. As an afterthought, she turned to her mom. "Can I go?"

"Don't forget that you have some chores to catch up on," Katie reminded her as she placed two yeast buns on each of their plates.

Chelsea rolled her eyes. "I *know*, Mom."

He tried not to shake his head at the dramatic response.

"Do you need a ride?" Katie asked.

"Tony's dad is taking us."

"I'd be happy to give you a lift anytime you need one," Travis said.

Again, she gave him that odd "why should you care" stare. "That's okay," Chelsea said, taking a sudden interest in spreading butter on her roll.

He supposed it sounded strange for the stranger sleeping in the barn to be offering to run the neighborhood carpool. This farce wouldn't continue much longer, thank God. He was ready to hit the ground running and become Chelsea's dad—tonight.

"But maybe you can pick us up later," she suggested to him, which just about knocked him flat. "Tony's dad has to go to bed early to get up for his shift at Toyota, but we want to go out for pizza afterwards."

"I'd be happy to." He glanced at Katie, realizing he hadn't consulted with her first.

A muscle spasmed in Katie's cheek. "Thanks, Travis, but I'll be finished with my work by then. I'll pick them up and shuttle everyone home."

"But, Mom, I want to go in Travis's truck. It looks totally a-maz-ing!"

He had no clue why his truck was any better than Katie's, other than it was probably five or six years newer. Good thing he'd hidden the unicorn in the barn apartment before heading to the church earlier. But the disappointment in Katie's eyes tore at him. "Why don't we both go to get them?" And to Chelsea, he asked, "How many of you will there be?"

"Four, including me. They can fit in the back and I can sit in the front on the fold-down console seat between you two."

Not much got past Chelsea. Speaking of which… "How do you know so much about the interior of my truck?"

"Oh, I was looking online for a replacement for Mom's. It's getting old, and the Sierra is an awesome truck."

"Not to mention out of my price range, sweetie," Katie said. "Besides, this one should be fine for a few more years."

"Remember, this one gets more of a workout than my truck does," Travis said. Katie's shoulders relaxed. She'd been tensed up the whole ride home. "But I don't mind driving tomorrow night. That okay with you?"

Katie forced a smile. "Sure."

Dammit, he wouldn't apologize for wanting to spend every possible minute with Chelsea. While most parents probably hated having to run around dropping off and picking up their kids, it was a new experience for him. Long overdue, actually.

But he'd better text Jackson tonight and let him know he wouldn't be back for at least a few more days. Deserting his crew made him uncomfortable, but Jackson kept everything running like clockwork, and they were ahead of schedule the last time they'd talked shop. Not that Travis had ever been gone this long before, but Jackson had understood and had given his blessing.

When they'd finished eating and had run out of things to talk about—except for the one thing he'd *wanted* to discuss—he stood, picking up his plate. When Katie started to do the same with hers, he said, "Chelsea, why don't you and I clear the table since your mom did all the work fixing the meal?"

Chelsea looked at her mom and then at him and blinked. *What's with all the blinking?*

Katie shook her head, preparing to stand. "I don't mind doing it."

Travis hoped his expression to Chelsea conveyed how much he really wanted *her* to pitch in. After a moment, Chelsea took the hint and picked up hers and Katie's plate along with her own, carrying them to the sink.

Katie, unable to let them do it all, apparently, went to the stove to put away the leftover sauce. "We should have enough sauce for lunch tomorrow, if you all want it again. I'll make fresh spaghetti, but we did a number on the meatballs."

"Thanks for going to all the trouble and for having me over, Katie. Dinner was great."

"I thought you hated being called Katie, Mom?" *Dammit.* Leave it to Chelsea to pick up on that. And then her words made him smile. In college, Katie had told him she only allowed him to call her that. Looks like that hadn't changed. Maybe she'd held onto some feelings for him all these years, and not just the physical ones, either.

When Katie didn't appear to have a response, Travis said, "I've called your mom that ever since we went to school together at the University of Kentucky. She's indulging me, for old time's sake."

Katie's eyes opened wider. Too late, he realized that part about going to college together was supposed to have been her line, but his smile grew bigger. Enough messing around.

"You went to UK with my mom?"

"Sure did. For three years." The girl looked from him to Katie and back to him. Would she make the connection? She seemed to be scrutinizing him more closely, and they waited.

"So is Travis going to be eating with us all the time, Mom?" Chelsea asked, still looking at him.

He wasn't sure of the significance of the question, but taking the hint that she might not want him around for every meal, he was about to say he could take care of breakfast and lunch on his own when Katie said, "Yes, he is. Travis is more than an old friend from college, Chelsea. He's…" Chelsea shifted her gaze toward her mom and waited. They both did. His heart pounded as he waited for her to reveal his true identity to Chelsea. "…actually…"

Come on, Katie. Tell her.

Chelsea's big green eyes kept opening wider. Then she narrowed her gaze at him. "Are you dating my mom?"

Okay, that wasn't the logical conclusion he'd expected her to draw. "Not anymore."

Chelsea set the plates in the sink. "You dated her in college?"

He looked at Katie, who had taken a sudden interest in emptying leftover spaghetti into the pot she'd dump on the compost pile in the morning.

She hadn't asked him to lie about anything. "Yeah, I did. For more than a year."

He had the feeling Chelsea wanted to continue her line of questioning until Katie tried to put an end to it. "Chelsea, would you like to watch a movie tonight before you hit the sack?"

He was beginning to think Katie had no intention of telling her.

"No. I'm really tired. I'm just going to bed early." She looked at Travis again. "I guess I'll see you tomorrow." He wasn't sure whether she was happy about that prospect or not.

"I'll be here," he said.

The girl was down the hall and climbing the stairs double time. She'd probably be texting her friends in seconds.

Travis turned to Katie. "Why didn't you tell her? That was the perfect segue."

"I don't know. It was on the tip of my tongue, but…"

"That girl's smart. If she hasn't put it all together yet, she will soon. If you don't tell her tonight, I will. I've waited long enough." For him, the wait had only been two days, but it seemed like a lifetime.

Katie washed and dried her hands. "All right. I'll go upstairs and tell her now. Do you want to be there with me?"

While he couldn't wait for the news to come out, he was scared spitless, too. "I'll wait downstairs. There's something I need to get out of the barn first." Undoubtedly, at the snail's pace Katie revealed things, he'd be settled in the living room long before Chelsea heard the news.

"Do you need help with the horses…?" she asked.

Quit stalling.

He shook his head. "They've all been fed and taken care. Look, if you don't want to tell her alone, then I'll join you."

She waved him away as she walked toward the hallway. "No, I've got this. I'm going up to talk with her now."

To make sure he was seated in the living room when they came down again, he hightailed it to the barn apartment. If he could, he'd shout it to the world that he was that little girl's father.

A million thoughts vied for attention, but suddenly, thoughts of telling his family about Chelsea settled in the forefront. How long before they'd meet her? It was a question of when, not if, at this point.

However, there *was* one person he could share the news with now. Unable to keep the grin off his face, he said, "Danny, what do you think of my beautiful daughter? I can see now that she's the reason you sent me back here. Isn't she as sweet as pecan pie?" That had been a favorite expression of Danny's. He shook his head. "Can you freaking believe I'm a dad, buddy?"

What felt like Danny's hand clapping him hard on the shoulder blade nearly knocked him off his feet. That Danny had found a way to be around him still gave him a lot of solace, although he worried, too, that maybe he was one of those ghosts stuck in between Heaven and

Earth. He wanted Danny to find some peace now, if he hadn't been able to find it in life.

The fact that he'd never be able to introduce Chelsea to his best friend made his heart squeeze tight. If Danny had still been alive, the two of them probably would have shared a cigar right about now. "I miss you, man." If only Katie hadn't…

Fester, fester, fester.

Travis's mood lightened again. "Okay, okay," he said out loud. "At least I know you can see what's going on."

Now get your ass and that psychedelic pony in the house.

"Try to stop me," he said as he picked up the unicorn.

*　*　*

Travis surprised the hell out of Danny. There'd been a moment after Danny had clapped him on the shoulder where his buddy turned around and stared right through him before his gaze darted around to the opposite corner of the apartment's bedroom. Anymore, when he'd talked directly to Travis, he got responses. Having Travis aware of his presence meant he was making progress.

But why he hadn't told him about the misunderstanding from the night he'd died, Danny couldn't say. Maybe he didn't want to take Travis's eye off the primary mission. Getting him reunited with his two girls was of the utmost importance.

Too bad Travis couldn't see him, though. Whenever Travis addressed him by name, Danny was drawn back to his side, but the man seemed surprised every time he heard him. How could he not think Danny would stay around him, especially until this mission was completed?

But Danny was getting wind of something monumental in the works for him up here, an opportunity that would give him another chance at reaching the goals that died with him. Unfortunately, this meant he would no longer be able to hang around Travis as a spirit. The thought of leaving his best friend once and for all ripped Danny's heart out. But Danny's spirit guide said he'd need to make a decision soon.

If he stayed up here, he'd be able to hang out with Travis all the time. When the opportunity presented itself, he'd be ready. He'd have to weigh his options and determine quickly whether to finish out a life that had been cut short due to illness or injury. While he hadn't made a firm commitment yet, what other choice did he have?

Right now, though, he needed to focus on the mission at hand.

Despite the millions of souls floating around in the afterlife, Danny sure got lonely sometimes. "Ben, you around?"

Summoned by Danny's thoughts, Ben joined him in the barn's apartment.

"You should have seen that sappy man a minute ago," Danny said. "If I had any stogies, I'd share one with you."

"They told Chelsea, and I missed it?" He seemed disappointed.

Danny shook his head. "Not yet, but it's going down tonight if Trav has anything to say about it. If we hurry to the living room, we'll get a front row seat."

In a flash, they stood near the fireplace, watching Travis pacing back and forth, occasionally glancing upstairs in anticipation—or was it fear?

Danny grinned. "Never thought I'd witness the day when my best bud became a daddy. The way he's avoided relationships since the day I met him makes it just about impossible to make a baby, that's for sure."

"He sure had no trouble sniffing around my daughter's skirts in college." Ben didn't give Danny time to respond before he asked, "You reckon he'll make a good dad?"

"Hell, yeah. The best. He was always great with the crew's kids at the annual Veterans Day barbecue and Christmas parties. And he became a surrogate dad to the three kids of one of the guys we lost in Iraq, at least until their mom remarried. I always thought it a shame he didn't have any of his own, but he told me his reasons for avoiding women were none of my business, so I didn't push it. Now I can see he's been pining for Katie all those years."

Ben huffed. "I doubt that."

Danny stared at the spirit beside him as though he must be blind. "What's the matter with you? Don't tell me you can't see it every time he looks at her."

Ben shrugged. "Can't say that I do. They don't seem to like each other half the time."

Danny shook his head. "You're in as much denial as they are. Trust me. They're still in love. Your daughter has a stubborn streak to rival yours."

"Yeah, unfortunately, that's another trait she took from me. But she didn't have her mother around to balance out her personality any." Ben glanced toward the stairs, wondering when Kate and Chelsea were going to come down. "I suppose stranger things could happen. Being with Gail again has certainly stirred up feelings I once had for her, and I'd never have guessed that would come to pass in a million years."

"Well, something must have made you two fall in love with each other in the first place."

Ben nodded. "Don't laugh, but…I admired her free spirit." Danny's jaw dropped, and he waved away the reaction. "Ironically, that was the very thing that broke us apart in the end."

"Has Katie found that letter yet?"

"No. I was checking on it when you called me. I can try to pull it out a little farther, but short of yanking it out and dropping it in front of her nose, I don't know what else I can do. She rarely goes into that room."

Danny didn't know what to do about that situation, but his mission remained clear—reuniting Travis with the family he needed.

In the few minutes they'd been watching, Travis had sat down and gotten up several times, but still there was no sign of Katie and Chelsea.

"If they're smart," Danny said, "they'll figure out they're perfect for each other and do something about it before they throw away another opportunity to be together. Damned fools may not get a third chance."

It might be too late for Danny and Ben, but dammit, he wanted Travis to live the rest of his life to the fullest and to find love and happiness. What more could he do to help?

First, he wanted to witness the moment Travis entered Chelsea's life as her father.

What was holding up those girls?

Chapter Twenty

K ate walked up the stairs to Chelsea's room, surprised at how quiet it was. Normally, she'd be blaring music. Perhaps she actually *had* gone to bed early and wasn't texting friends.

"It's freaking me out. What if it's..." Her daughter's voice came through the door killing that idea.

Kate's knock cut off the last word. "Sweetie, can I talk with you a minute?" She waited.

"Hold on," she whispered. "It's my mom."

The door opened, and Chelsea stood there dressed in basketball shorts and a black night shirt emblazoned with a fire-breathing dragon. She tilted her chin up, but the worry in her eyes belied her attempt at bravery. Did she know?

"What's up, Mom?"

"May I come in?"

"Sure. Let me end this call first."

Chelsea picked up the phone from her bed. "I'll call you back in a few minutes." Her daughter listened to what the other person said before saying, "I am."

Kate wanted to tell her it might be more than a few, but didn't. Kate sat on the bed and waited for her to put the phone down.

"What's up, Mom?" she asked after setting it on the dresser.

No amount of rehearsing helped prepare her. Any scripts she'd planned with Lidia yesterday promptly flew out the window. "Baby, there's something important we need to talk about. Have a seat." She patted the mattress in front of her.

"Mom, I can get caught up on everything by tomorrow night. I really *need* to go out with my friends."

"No, that's not why I'm here." Chelsea stared at her as Kate tried to determine how best to broach the subject. "There's something I need to talk with you about." *Please let me find the right words.* "Honey, it's your father."

Chelsea's body tensed. "I knew it! Tony said I was wrong, but…Travis *is* my dad, isn't he?"

Thank God she hadn't put this off until tomorrow. Kate nodded, unable to say the words past the lump in her throat.

Chelsea stood up and began pacing the floor. "Why now?"

Good question. "He showed up out of the blue Monday. I hadn't seen him since we broke up. When he found out about you, of course he wanted to get to know you better."

"I'm just supposed to love him because you two had sex and accidentally ended up with me?" Her eyes grew bright as her chin quivered.

"Oh, baby, you were *not* an accident." Kate went to her, reaching out to hug her, but she stepped away and continued to pace, clenching her tiny fists. "Chelsea, look at me." The girl spun around, glaring at her. "Baby, it wasn't like that at all. We'd dated for a year and were talking about a future together."

"Then why didn't you tell him about me?"

"Sit down and let me explain what happened." Kate sat on the bed again, waiting. Chelsea cocked her head, hugging herself and looking so lost. Finally, she inched her way toward Kate and joined her, picking up a stuffed dragon to hug to her chest.

"Travis didn't know he *had* a child until Friday."

"I thought you said he came on Monday."

Kate drew a deep breath. "He did, but I needed to be sure he would be a good father and stick around before I told him. But it's important for you to remember what I told you before—he's never left you or rejected you."

"How can you be sure he won't leave me whenever he gets tired of me?"

"Because Travis Cooper isn't that kind of man."

Her eyes blazed. "Then how could you keep him a secret from me for so long? Why would you do that?" Her shrill voice pierced Kate's heart. "Did you even consider telling him about me at any point? Did you ever think he might want to know he had a kid in the world?"

She swallowed hard. "It's complicated." *I made a mistake.* "Calm down and—" Kate opened her mouth to try and respond, but the rapid-fire questions kept pouring out.

"Were you afraid he'd try to convince you not to have me?"

"Never!" she said, shaking her head. "He would *never* have asked such a thing."

"All the times growing up when I asked about my dad, you were vague. If he hadn't shown up here, he *still* wouldn't know about me, would he? Why didn't you want me to know him?"

Kate deserved Chelsea's tirade, and wanted to explain, if only she could find the words. "I planned to give you information to seek him out when you turned eighteen…" *and could better handle rejection if it came to that.* "Until this week, I didn't know where he was or how he'd turned out." *Not that I couldn't have found out quite easily.*

"But you loved him once, so he must not have been a bad guy."

"I did." *And still do in some ways.* "My reasons for breaking it off with Travis had nothing to do with his character."

"Then why?"

Kate closed her eyes and took a deep breath, unable to face the hurt in her little girl's eyes again. "We were dating in college, just like Travis said at supper. We'd talked about having a future together, but weren't engaged or anything. Travis wanted to make his mark in the world first." Chelsea didn't interrupt, so Kate continued. "He was studying civil engineering, and I was convinced he'd probably wind up working in a major city. Right around the time I found out I was going to have a baby, he took an internship in New York City." Kate finally met her daughter's gaze again, silently imploring her to understand. "He was so excited to go, and I was certain he'd be offered a position with them and would want to live there. Sweetie, I could never live like that, and I didn't want that for my baby, either. This farm is the only place I'd ever lived, except for college. I'm a country girl and always will be."

"But he doesn't look like a city boy to me."

"No, he doesn't, and that's part of what I've come to understand this week. Everything I thought Travis would do or become didn't happen due to other circumstances I'll let him talk with you about. I considered telling him about my pregnancy at least a dozen times that summer and fall, but always convinced myself I was doing the noble and right thing—"

"He had a *right* to know about *me*."

Her heart squeezed tighter. "Yes, he did. But I didn't want to interrupt his life or make him give up his dreams. He worked hard for everything he achieved, so when the opportunity came up to pursue them, I couldn't hold him back."

"Who were you to decide for him? For me, even? You should have told him and let him make the decision himself."

"I know now that would have been the best thing. Back then, though, I didn't see it the same way. Hindsight is twenty-twenty. It wasn't until I talked with Travis this week that I figured all this out."

Chelsea narrowed her eyes. "I think you were afraid of something. What did you think would happen?"

So many things.

Kate took a deep breath. "That the day would come when he'd resent me and choose to leave us." *Or, worse yet, take you away from me.* "I didn't want you to go through the pain of losing a parent after getting close to them."

"Like your mom did to you?"

Kate nodded, her throat constricting. She'd told Chelsea the truth about her mother long ago, but they hadn't really talked about her much since.

"Not everyone does that, Mom. Most kids know both their parents, and even if they divorce, they still see both their mom and their dad."

Leave it to Chelsea to bring a pesky thing like logic into this. She had always been excellent at debate and emotionally smarter than Kate had been—at that age or even now. "I wasn't thinking with my head, sweetie. Only my heart. You have to believe me when I say that, at the time, I thought I was doing what was best."

"Best for who? Not for *me*!" Chelsea bolted up again and resumed her pacing before facing Kate again. "Maybe not for Travis—my dad—either. I had every right to know my father."

"Yes, you did," Kate whispered.

"Mom, I still don't get why you did this."

As hard as it was to admit, she only had one response. "I'm sorry. I made a mistake. If I could go back and fix this, I would. I was wrong about everything. I never should have cheated him out of watching you grow up or you out of having a father in your life. I'll have to live with that bad decision for the rest of my life, but I can't change what's already done. All I can do is work to help the two of you build a relationship together." She drew a deep breath, feeling defeated. "Just don't take out your anger at me on Travis. Give him a chance. He's not to blame at all for what happened."

"No, *you* are."

Too drained to try and apologize or explain further, Kate nodded.

"Do you hate him?"

"Of course not! I could never hate him." Kate stood and closed the gap to cup Chelsea's cheek, relieved when she didn't pull away. "He gave me you. And it was because I loved him so much that I kept the pregnancy a secret."

"Love? That's not how love works, Mom!"

What did Chelsea know about love? Okay, that wasn't fair. She'd never known anything but love and support from Kate. "You don't know the pain of losing—"

Chelsea jumped up from the bed again. "You don't know that pain *I've* felt, Mom. I didn't let you know how much it hurt because I didn't want you to feel bad, but…I missed having a dad there to teach me how to pitch—"

"I taught you that."

"True, but what about my fifth-grade father-daughter dance? I didn't get to go because my dad wasn't a part of my life. Because you didn't want him to be my dad." Chelsea turned toward the door then back at Kate. "How could you *do* this to me?"

"Sweetie, I've always tried my best to be both mother and father to you—"

"But you're my *mom*. You can't be both. Not for everything, anyway. You should have let him be my dad." Kate tried to move closer to hug Chelsea and perhaps get her to forgive her, but the girl pushed her away. "I hate you for this!"

Even though Kate knew the words had been spoken out of anger and hurt, Kate felt them as a solid punch to the solar plexus. She'd been on the receiving end of her daughter's ire for going on a year now, but that had been nothing compared to the vehemence in Chelsea's voice now.

"I understand you're feeling hurt right now, but please know that I've done my best to raise you to be the wonderful girl you are, and I'll never stop loving you. But tonight isn't about our relationship. Travis is waiting downstairs."

Her eyes opened wide in horror. "I can't go down there, Mom." Chelsea's gaze drifted to the door before she looked at Kate again, pleading with her eyes. "How can you be sure he'll…love me?"

Kate smiled. "Because he already does and always will. What's not to love? You're a beautiful person inside and out, and he thinks so, too."

"How would he know? He just met me tonight."

"Because he's already asked me a million questions and looked over all the albums of you growing up. He stayed up most of last night looking at them." Her daughter cringed. "Don't worry. He loved each and every one. Now, he's dying to talk with you face to face to get to know you even better."

"I don't know what to say to him," she whispered. Tears that had been welling in her eyes spilled down her cheeks, breaking Kate's heart.

She opened her arms, hoping Chelsea would seek comfort there this time, but not wanting to invade her space again. Perhaps Kate hoped to gain a little comfort herself. At long last, Chelsea walked into Kate's embrace, and the two hugged as tears poured from her eyes now, too.

"Shh," she said, stroking Chelsea's hair. "You've had no trouble talking with him earlier."

"But he wasn't my dad then."

Kate chuckled. "Yes, he was. You just weren't aware of it yet."

"I did think it was kinda strange when he offered to pick me and my friends up after the movie and pizza."

"You'll see he's going to be a terrific dad. He's already been a great uncle to some kids in his life. Just be yourself. Let things progress naturally. He's very good at keeping a conversation going. And there's no need to rush things or try to say everything tonight. He's going to be here for a few days, and after that, we'll make sure the two of you get together as often as we can."

"But he lives in another state. What if I need him and he's not around?"

"He's only about four hours away by car." Kate had already mapped out online how long it would take to drive to Nolensville. She intended to go with Chelsea the first time she went down for a visit. The thought of sending her off without knowing where he lived or to be unable to picture her there while they were separated was unfathomable, so that first trip would definitely include Kate, whether Travis liked it or not. At least long enough for Kate to check out the house and make sure it was suitable for a tween. He'd been a bachelor a long time.

"And he has a phone—with text messaging. I'm sure you two are going to be able to find any number of ways to communicate."

Chelsea drew a ragged breath. "Oh, Mom, I'm so scared. What if he doesn't like me after he gets to know me? I can be…moody. It takes too much energy to be nice all the time."

Kate grinned. That she'd raised a daughter so self-aware made her proud. "He already likes you and will just grow to love you more over time. Why, look at me. Have I stopped loving you because sometimes you're a little…moody?"

Chelsea smiled, warming Kate's heart. "No."

Kate hugged her again, stroking Chelsea's back in long sweeping motions. "The two of you are going to get along great. And now you'll finally have the one thing I couldn't give you." *Well, I could have, but chose not to.* Guilt washed over her. Would Chelsea continue to resent her for keeping Travis away all these years? "Now, tell me what you need from me before going downstairs."

Chelsea pulled away and met her gaze. Kate wiped the tear smudges from her daughter's cheeks. "I don't want to go down there alone. It's not that I'm afraid of him. I like him a lot, but…well, would you stay with me?"

"Of course, sweetie. But if you decide you'd rather just the two of you talk, just wave me away. Now, why don't we go in the bathroom and wash our faces before we go down to see your daddy?" Kate especially didn't want Travis to see her own tear streaks.

Chelsea nodded, a tremulous smile on her lips, and they went into the bathroom across the hall to repair the damage. Neither was wearing makeup, thank goodness.

In a few minutes, she'd deliver her daughter into the arms of her father—twelve and a half years late. Chelsea appeared to be hopeful. Father and daughter needed to bond without Kate being in the picture, because in all likelihood, once Travis returned home, Chelsea's visits with Travis would be in Nolensville.

"Okay, I think I'm ready, Mom."

That makes one of us.

Chapter Twenty-One

Travis heard the angry shouts coming from Chelsea upstairs, and then things grew quiet. He glanced at the enormous unicorn straddling the armrest of the couch. Maybe he ought to put it back in the truck and head home tomorrow. It didn't sound like she wanted to have anything to do with him, although from what he could tell, most of her rage was aimed at Katie.

Several times, he stood and started to pick up the stuffed animal then came to his senses and sat back down only to jump up again to pace the floor. He felt like an expectant dad waiting for the news he'd just become a father in an old-time movie.

A door opened, and he turned to look toward the top of the stairs, anticipating that they would come down at any moment, but instead, it sounded as though they went into the bathroom.

Travis plunked down on the couch again and buried his head in his hands. He still had no clue what he was going to say to her. Could he find the right—

"Travis, I'd like you to meet your daughter, Chelsea Michaels Cooper."

His head jerked up as his gaze focused on the stairs. All he could do was stare wordlessly at his beautiful daughter. He hadn't heard them come down the stairs and still hadn't found the right words, so he simply stood and opened his arms for her, hoping the gesture would convey what he couldn't speak at the moment. Seemed like a lifetime passed by—but it might have only been seconds—before she timidly crossed the room and walked into his arms. His heart nearly burst as he wrapped her in the tightest hug he'd ever given anyone, except maybe her mother. Chelsea's body trembled, and he squeezed her even tighter.

"I didn't think I'd ever meet you," she said in a thick voice he felt vibrate against his chest.

"Baby girl, I didn't know my heart was missing such a huge chunk until I found out about you a couple days ago." She might not be a baby anymore, but she'd always be *his* little girl, so the endearment his own dad still used with Travis's three sisters rolled off his tongue naturally.

"I'm twelve," she giggled but didn't ask him not to use that name for her.

He glanced across the room at Katie, whose chin trembled. He wished he could convince her he had no intention of stealing Chelsea away from her. He only wanted to share.

While addressing Chelsea, he tried to offer Katie a reassuring smile. "Indulge me a little. I'll try not to embarrass you in front of your friends, though."

"It's okay. I kinda like it. My best friend's daddy calls her that."

Call me *Daddy.*

She wiggled out of his embrace, and he released her with reluctance. When she glanced up at him, her eyelashes were wet and clumped, but he was lost in those beautiful green eyes that reminded him of Mom's. "What should I call you now, Travis?"

Anything but Travis.

"Whatever you'd like."

She averted her gaze a moment then met his again with a tentative smile. "I know I'm probably too old, but whenever I talked to you my whole life, I always called you…"

She'd talked to him? How sad was it that he hadn't been around to hear her? His eyes stung with unshed tears, and he blinked rapidly.

"Um, would it be too weird if I called you…Daddy?"

His heart filled with so much love in that instant that it almost exploded. "I'd love for you to call me Daddy."

Her face erupted in the biggest smile he'd seen on her yet, and he drew her into his arms again. After a moment, she asked, "Can I ask you some questions?"

Travis separated but kept his arm around her back. "Absolutely. Why don't we sit down and talk? Nothing's off limits. You just ask away."

He took his place on the couch with his back to the hallway. "Is this for me?" She'd spotted the stuffed animal he'd forgotten all about.

"Sure is. Hope you like unicorns."

She pointed to the dragon on her T-shirt. "I love all mythical crea-tures!" He couldn't help but wonder if she'd thought of him as being a myth as well. She picked up the unicorn that was nearly as big as she and hugged it, burying her face in its mane.

"Glad you like it."

"Like? I totally *love* her! I'm going to call her Xena."

"From *Xena: Warrior Princess*?" It had been one of Katie's favorite shows growing up, she'd told him once.

"Mom and I have watched the series on DVD a million times. It's over there if you want to watch it sometime."

Ah, that explains it. "Only if you watch it with me."

"Mom, you probably won't let us watch without you, will you?"

They both turned to Kate who stood in the doorway hugging her-self, her face stained with tears.

"I think it would be a great thing to do together," she said.

He didn't remember how many seasons of the show there were, but bring it.

"I'm okay, Mom."

Katie nodded. "I have some things to do in the kitchen."

That she trusted him with her daughter—*their* daughter—meant a lot to him, but he had to wonder what was going through her head right now. He'd seek her out to talk later, but first, he needed to get to know his little girl better.

Chelsea sat at the opposite end and faced him with her feet tucked yoga style and the unicorn across her legs. At first, she played with the unicorn's mane without meeting his gaze. She'd grown cautious and shy again. There was no need to rush. They had a lifetime to talk.

Without looking up, she asked in a barely audible voice, "Do you love me?"

How could she ask that? He wanted to wrap her in his arms again, but wasn't sure if she needed closeness or more space. "Look at me, Chelsea."

She raised her head and waited expectantly.

"Baby girl, I love you more than I've ever loved anyone in this world." Oddly enough, even more than he did his parents and siblings. More than Danny. Even more than Katie, but they'd only known an immature love. What he felt for his daughter was so much deeper. She was a part of him. Hell, he couldn't explain it, but tried to say something meaningful. "I fell in love with the *idea* of you almost the minute I heard about you. Then I went through every single one of those photo albums over there"—he pointed to the stacks of albums on the shelf across the room—"and fell deeper in love. Your mom did an amazing job chronicling your life."

Not the same as me being here watching you grow up, though.

Chelsea buried her face in her hands. He thought she was going to burst into tears until she let out a dramatic groan. "Mom told me, but please tell me you didn't see the one of me with spaghetti sauce all over my face."

Travis chuckled, relaxing again. The girl had his emotions on a careening roller-coaster ride. "That was one of my all-time favorites. Absolutely adorable. But don't worry. I won't use it as blackmail with future boyfriends or anything. My mom has a similar picture in an album showing me at about eighteen-months-old on a vacation in Gatlinburg where I had the same spaghetti-plastered face, grinning like a nearly toothless Cheshire cat with my hand in the bowl to grab some more."

Chelsea sobered, leaning closer. "Is your mom still…" She glanced down at her hands a second before meeting his gaze again. "Will I be able to meet her?"

"Sure. My dad, too. They'd disown me if you don't get up to Louisville to meet them soon. That's where I grew up, by the way."

Chelsea somehow managed to bounce in place as she squealed. "Oh my gosh! I have grandparents, too?! This is way better than any Christmas present ever!"

He grinned at her enthusiasm. "You also have four aunts, an uncle, and two cousins."

Her jaw dropped as her eyes grew wider at the news. When she regained her composure, she asked, "Do they know about me?"

"Not yet. I've only known about you a short while myself, and I wanted to see how you felt about me being in your life before I got their hopes up. But they are going to be impatient to meet you once I tell them. I take it you'd like to meet them."

"Would I?! I don't remember my grandpa, and my grandma was gone before I was born." Had Katie told her the truth about her grandma or let her draw her own conclusion? "Mom's an only child, so I don't have any real aunts or uncles, just fake ones, like Aunt Lidia and Uncle Jason."

"Hey, nothing fake about them. They were there for you while you were growing up. I'm Uncle Travis to the kids of a number of coworkers and others, and I take that role as seriously as I do with my brother Clint's kids who are blood related."

At his stern rebuke—man, did he ever feel like a dad now—she sat up straighter. "Oh, I didn't mean fake in a bad way. I love them both to death. I just meant we're not related by blood." Her eyes grew wider again. "Tell me more about my cousins?"

"Yeah. Your uncle, Clint, and Aunt Susan have two kids—a four-year-old boy and an eighteen-month-old girl, Erik and Olivia."

"Wow. Sometimes I work in the nursery at church. I love babies. I can't wait to play with them."

"We'll have to talk with your mom about when might be a good time for you to meet the Cooper clan, but I'd like to arrange for a get-together as soon as possible. Mom loves having backyard barbecues."

"Mom can come, too, right?"

Travis didn't want to answer for Katie. "Why don't we go find her and ask?" Too late, he realized he'd be putting her on the spot. Reuniting with his family wouldn't be easy for her, not after the way they'd taken the news of their breakup and the resentment a couple of his sisters still held toward her. Mom had adored Katie and had been hoping for a wedding in a couple of years, and his sisters were outraged any girl would dump their big brother.

Thinking better of asking Katie tonight, he began, "Wait. Why don't I—"

Chelsea jumped up like a lithe cat, much quicker than he could move, and started toward the kitchen before he could stop her. When she turned to take his hand so they could walk together, worries about Katie fled.

"Mom! We need to ask you something!" she said, nearly dragging him into the hallway.

Katie came to the kitchen door, her brows furrowed. He couldn't read her expression due to the backlighting in the dark hallway, but even in the dim light, he thought he saw tear tracks on her cheeks. She clung to a dishtowel, but forced a smile when she saw them. Until she glanced down at their clasped hands, and her smile faded.

"What's that, honey?"

"Daddy wants to take me to meet his parents. Did you know I have grandparents, aunts, uncles, and even cousins?"

Katie smiled, but her eyes seemed filled with sorrow. "Yes, I do. I've met most of them, and they're wonderful people. You're going to love them, and they're going to be over the moon when they hear about you."

"I can't wait! Can we go this Saturday"—Chelsea looked up at Travis for confirmation—"if that's okay with them?"

He turned to Katie to see if that was okay with her. Her shoulders relaxed as if with relief, and she nodded at his unspoken question.

"Will you come with us, Mom?"

Katie's gaze collided with his. Her jaw tensed as if she'd clenched her teeth. With a quirk of his eyebrow, he waited for her to answer. "Chelsea, you know I have lessons all day Saturday. Besides, I think it might be best if you got together with your dad's family without me around, because I'm not really sure they—" Katie glanced at him as if trying to let him off the hook, he supposed.

"Nonsense." While they may not be a traditional family like Clint's, Katie was Chelsea's mother, and his folks would probably have a million questions about Chelsea he wouldn't be able to answer. "How about Sunday? Miguel will be back by then, right?"

"When do you have to head back home, Daddy?"

He shrugged. "Don't worry about my schedule." Jackson had told him to take as long as he needed. What's another week? After all, he was a short drive away, if needed.

He glanced at Katie. "Come with us. You and Mom always got along well. I know she'd love seeing you again." Mom never held a grudge. She still talked about Katie from time to time, no doubt hoping Travis would get in touch with her to rekindle something. Man, was she going to be surprised to find out about Chelsea.

Katie drew her trembling lower lip between her teeth. Unable to stand it any longer, he closed the gap between them and cupped her chin, forcing her to meet his gaze. Her eyes welled. "Come on, Katie," he whispered. "Chelsea and I both want you to be there." Whether as moral support for Chelsea or to pretend for a short time they were a real family, he didn't know, but having her there was important to him.

"Please, Mom," Chelsea begged from across the room. "It won't be so weird if you're there with me."

Apparently, his little girl had her own set of insecurities. Katie grinned at Chelsea's remark, and Travis waited for her to respond to his invitation.

"Well, if you're going to gang up on me, okay. I'll go. Miguel returns Saturday night and can keep an eye on things here while we're gone."

Travis grinned at Chelsea's squeal of delight. "Thanks. I'll call Mom tonight, and if Sunday's okay with her, too, we can leave after the barn chores are done. It's just a little more than an hour's drive. We should make it back in time to bed down the horses that night, if Miguel needs a hand."

An idea started to form in his head, even if they couldn't make a go of things romantically. He needed more time to think about all the ramifications, but Chelsea deserved to have both parents in her life.

First, though, he needed to smooth things over with his family. If this plan would have any chance, they'd need strong support behind them.

Chapter Twenty-Two

K ate's stomach churned at the thought of facing Travis's family again. If only they'd decided to do it on Saturday, she would have been off the hook. Travis made it sound like they were a typical family planning a Sunday visit with relatives. Would the Coopers hate her for not letting them get to know their granddaughter? She tried to remind herself that this wasn't about her comfort level. Obviously, Chelsea was ecstatic to meet her extended family. And the Coopers were good people. They'd love Chelsea in an instant and would treat her well. Kate would be there for Chelsea.

She forced a smile and stepped out of his reach to go to the counter and pretend she was busy cleaning. This Sunday would be for Chelsea. She owed her that much.

Her decision not to tell them about Chelsea suddenly sounded like the stupidest, most selfish thing anyone could have done. All she'd tried to do was to protect her daughter from being abandoned if Travis wasn't able to cut it as a father, and to keep Travis from feeling obligated to give up on his hopes and dreams. She and Travis had discussed getting married, but not until after college. There had been talk about holding off on having kids, but not until they were in their thirties so that he could establish his career.

What a different life they would have given Chelsea if Kate hadn't shut him out. He'd have made a wonderful father and loved every minute of it. Tears filled her eyes again. She was now the one with regrets concerning what might have been. For whatever reason, Travis's life had gone in an entirely different direction.

"Your truck has Towers Contracting on the side," Chelsea said, bringing Kate back to the present. "At first, I wondered why a construction guy was here from that far away. Now I know. What's contracting?"

"I coordinate the building of luxury homes, pricey condos, and the occasional high rise."

"Is that where you met all those country-music stars?"

He chuckled. "Pretty much."

"I still don't know what I want to be when I grow up, although I do like horses and mechanics. How'd you decide?"

Chelsea was all over the place about what career she might pursue—from healthcare to car mechanic. Kate was interested in hearing this, too.

"My dad owned a construction firm, so I learned a lot from working with him over the years. I guess it was ingrained in my genetic makeup."

But what about your dream, Travis?

"I enjoy bringing all the various tradesmen together rather than only overseeing one small part of the operation like I did with my dad." Travis chuckled. "Sorry. Best not to get me started on my career."

If he loved it so much, how long would he be able to stay away from it? Once again, doubt reared its ugly head.

"Once, I wanted to oversee the building of skyscrapers in New York City, but…"

Kate had been wondering for a long time why he hadn't returned to University of Kentucky after Manhattan. Not that she had finished her senior year, either. She'd had to drop out in November when she'd become too sick during her pregnancy. When he didn't seem to intend to explain further, Kate couldn't help but ask, "What happened to that plan?"

He met her gaze, sobering. "The Manhattan internship. I met a lot of survivors of 9/11, including some of the first responders." He shrugged. "Hearing them tell about how they witnessed metal structures that were supposed to stand the test of time, to protect those working and living within, come crumbling down around them....well, it made me change how I saw my future career."

Wow. "I can imagine that it would."

The two of them stared silently as each other until Chelsea said, "My social studies teacher talked about it last year. It made me cry." Chelsea hadn't even been born yet when it had happened. "Why are people so cruel to other people?"

Travis shook his head. "Search me. But my experiences that summer made me reevaluate my priorities." To Kate, he added, "I joined the National Guard immediately after I came home from my summer in New York City. Served eight years. I didn't return to UK for our senior year. Much later, I finished up at Vandy on Uncle Sam's dollar." He focused on Chelsea again. "I'm in the reserves now."

"Did you go to war?" Chelsea asked, her eyes solemn.

"Three deployments too many."

Chelsea grew silent for a moment. "I'm glad you made it back home. The dad of one of my fourth-grade classmates didn't." Kate could hear the thickness in Chelsea's words and was going to comfort her when Travis opened his arms and wrapped their daughter in his shield of protection and comfort. Kate had been up with Chelsea many nights after LaTasha's dad had been killed in Afghanistan. Now it was Travis's turn.

"I'm sorry about your friend's dad."

Kate longed to give them both a hug, but didn't want to intrude on their moment. "I'm going to go take care of the horses for the night." She doubted they needed anything more, but crossed the kitchen and set the dishtowel beside the sink before heading toward the door. Travis had everything under control here.

"Wait!" Chelsea came toward her and wrapped her arms around her. Kate reciprocated. "Good night, Mom. This has been the best night ever."

"Night. I love you, sweetie."

"Me, too, you. And thanks!"

"For what?"

She let go and met Kate's gaze before lowering her voice. "For giving me the best dad ever."

Before Kate could form any words, Chelsea pivoted and returned to Travis, grabbing his hand before dragging him out of the kitchen.

Kate couldn't help but smile on her way to the barn. Maybe things were going to turn out all right, at least for Chelsea.

She was in B.C.'s stall later when she heard someone enter the barn. She looked up as Travis came to stand in the doorway. Alone.

"Chelsea all right?" she asked.

"She said she wanted to take Xena up to meet her other stuffed animals." He grinned. "I think she wanted to call or text some friends and tell them what's going on, too. She probably needed some time to digest it all." He came closer to where she stood in the aisle with the empty water bucket. "How about you, Katie? None of this could have been easy for you."

"Nonsense. Seeing my daughter happy is all I've ever wanted." She stroked the horse's neck. Now what? Kate swallowed past the lump in her throat, unsure where to go from here.

When she said good night to B.C. and would have headed back to the house and the sanctuary of her room, Travis gently grasped her elbow and turned her toward him.

"Please don't..." she begged, not even sure what she was afraid he'd do. Kiss her again? Express his regrets over time lost?

"Katie," he said, cupping her chin with his warm hand and forcing her to meet his gaze no matter how much she wanted to escape. "Can we pretend for the sake of Chelsea that we enjoy each other's company? Especially in front of my family?"

"Of course. I think we only get into trouble when we're alone like this." She sighed. "It'll work out fine Sunday. By the way, you were wonderful with Chelsea tonight. I didn't know what to expect, but you're a natural father."

"Why do you look so miserable then?"

She did? Okay, probably more than a little. "I'm scared." Her life was changing in a huge way, although not as drastically as Chelsea's. Her daughter embraced the changes, but Kate, well, not so much. "I have always tried to plan everything out to ensure stability in our lives, and now I don't know what's going to happen from one minute to the next."

His thumb brushed across her cheek, and she inhaled sharply, not expecting the intimate gesture to affect her so. When she tried to pull away, he wrapped his other arm around her waist. "Katie, I'm not the enemy. How can I make you see that I have no intention of hurting you?"

"It's not you. Just give me time to process all that's happened."

When he started to lower his face to hers, she did wrench herself away. "Travis, kissing me isn't going to do anything but add to my stress right now." Why did their bodies have no problem reconnecting whenever they were alone? Sexual attraction didn't last, though. And her heart wouldn't be able to stand it if things didn't work out between them.

"I've enjoyed every single one of our kisses."

"Mom! Daddy! I have the best idea ever!" Both turned as Chelsea came bounding through the open barn door into the aisle. Kate took several steps from him to provide more distance. The last thing she wanted to do was have Chelsea think there might be a chance of them rekindling their old feelings for one another.

"What's that, sweetie?" she asked.

"Daddy should stay in Grandpa's old room so he can be part of our family for real. Besides, nobody ever uses that room. And now that Daddy's going to be coming here lots of times, he needs a nicer place to sleep than the barn apartment." Chelsea smiled up at Travis after making her pitch. Had Travis been aware she was going to ask that?

"Nothing wrong with the apartment. You should have seen some

Kallypso Masters

of the places I've slept."

Okay, maybe she was being overly cautious, but being under the same roof with Travis—on the same floor no less—didn't sound like such a great idea to Kate.

"Mom, it's just for a few nights this time, and whenever Daddy comes back to see me." The hopefulness in Chelsea's voice as she gazed up at him made Kate see there was no choice.

Do it for Chelsea.

"Forgive my manners, Travis, but she's right. You can move into the house tomorrow. I'll need to clean and air out the room first, though. Nobody's slept in there for years."

"Thanks for the invitation—both of you," he said, returning his gaze to Chelsea for a moment and smiling.

"But you're welcome to take the couch again tonight, if you want." Kate couldn't believe the words that just came out of her mouth. She was curious how he'd answer, but before he could open his mouth, Chelsea ran over to him and wrapped her arms around him. "Please, Daddy? This way, we can stay up late and talk about more stuff. I still have hundreds of questions to ask."

He smiled down at Chelsea. She'd already wrapped him around her little finger, an innate ability most daughters had a knack for.

"I appreciate that, but I'll wait until tomorrow. That will give me time to clean up some out here."

"Bummer." Chelsea's lower lip jutted out.

"But I can hang out until bedtime."

She fisted her hand in front of her mouth and gave a high-pitched squeal. "That would be awesome! And I'll help carry your stuff over to the house tomorrow, Daddy," Chelsea offered.

He laughed. "I don't have much. I think I can manage, but thanks."

Everything was happening so fast. Kate would have to get busy changing linens and straightening up in the guest room right away. It had become a bit of a storage room so she'd also have to find a place for several boxes of winter blankets and clothes. And the dust would be an inch thick. Usually, she only had time for the bare minimum of cleaning in the main living areas, so a room rarely used was hardly touched.

"It's getting late," Travis said. "Katie, do you need anything else done out here?"

"No, the horses are all settled."

She checked to be sure she'd closed B.C.'s stall door and started down the aisle as the image of Travis lying shirtless on the guest room bed flashed across her mind. Did he still wear boxers?

You aren't going to find out, Katie dear.

"Daddy, maybe we can watch a movie tonight or something. I won't be able to sleep for hours." Chelsea talked a mile a minute all the way to the house. She'd had more to say to Travis than she'd said to Kate lately. Chelsea was a different girl around him. What other changes would come over Chelsea as she grew closer to him?

Leaving daddy and daughter to their movie, she went into Daddy's old room to start preparing it for Travis. After she'd knocked down all the cobwebs and surveyed what else needed to be done, her thoughts went to her mom for some reason. They used to sit by the fireplace while she read Kate stories for hours on end. Through her teen years, Kate had often come in here to talk to her as if she were still here. Kate remembered how Chelsea had admitted to Travis that she'd often talked to him over the years, long after Chelsea had stopped bringing him up to Kate. The thought tugged at her heartstrings. She and Chelsea were alike in so many ways, both longing for a missing parent. Only her daughter's situation was different. She'd done nothing to drive her father away. Not the way Kate must have done, even if she couldn't recall what exactly had caused her mother to leave.

After moving some of the junk out of what would be Travis's room whenever he visited, Kate walked down the hallway toward the stairs and overheard the two of them talking in Chelsea's bedroom. A quick glance at her watch told her that it had been almost two hours since she'd left them in the living room. Light spilled through the open doorway into the hall. The poor man must be exhausted.

Kate didn't intend to eavesdrop, but peeked inside as she passed to find them standing in front of her bookshelf filled with photos of the times Chelsea had competed in 4-H at the fairgrounds and again this past May in nearby Shelbyville at the academy level, both classes for beginners.

"Your mom has taught you a lot about horseback riding."

"She has, but she doesn't think I'm good enough to compete in the big shows."

Kate stopped in her tracks, almost turning around to voice her disagreement, but remained silent so they wouldn't think she was invading their privacy. It wasn't a lack of confidence in Chelsea's talent at all. Perhaps if she'd been more honest with Chelsea concerning their finances and how hard it was to make ends meet, she wouldn't be thinking that way. Clearly, Kate needed to have a talk with her.

Kate always tried to be effusive in her praise of each student's riding abilities. Had she not taken her own daughter as seriously? No, she'd even used Chelsea to train some of the better horses to rider. Of course, those horses were eventually put up for sale.

One of the reasons her relationship with Chelsea had taken a turn for the worse a year ago was that Kate had sold one of the horses Chelsea had grown quite fond of. Chelsea's interest waned after that.

"I wish I had my own horse to perform on at big shows. But I don't want to train on one of Mom's horses again, because she'll just sell it to someone else when it gets good."

Chelsea's words broke Kate's heart. She wished she could let her keep one of them, but that would mean sacrificing a lot of income for them.

"Why not show on Princess Jasmine?"

"Oh, I'll love her forever, but she toes out."

"Speak in a language a non-horseman would understand."

Chelsea giggled. "Jazz has problems with her forelegs. Her elbows didn't form right so her hooves point outward. She does okay in 4-H shows, but could never compete above that level. But, boy, I would kill to show in the Lexington Junior League with Melissa."

"I've heard that one's tough to get into, but there are some good shows in Murfreesboro, not too far from where I live. Maybe we can get you in one of those."

Oh, Travis. Please don't—

"That would be awesome! I went with Mom to watch Melissa compete there in April. But I'd never qualify on Jazz." The disappointment in her voice when she said the last sentence broke Kate's heart. She had no idea Chelsea still wanted to compete. When Kate couldn't promise her a horse for keeps, she'd said she didn't really care anymore.

"I think there's another show this fall, actually."

She regretted getting him interested in Saddlebreds back in college. If Travis continued to get the girl's hopes up, he would set her up for disappointment. She'd better go in and break this up before it became impossible—

"Why don't we find you the best horse possible so you can compete there and anywhere you'd like?"

Chelsea squealed.

Travis chuckled.

Kate seethed.

"You would do that!? Omigosh!" It sounded as though she'd just knocked the air out of Travis as she hugged him. "I love you, Daddy!"

Kate clenched her fist while imagining his neck being squeezed in it. How dare he get Chelsea's hopes up or bribe her with such an extravagant gift? Besides, did he have any clue that a decent show horse would run ten thousand dollars, let alone a really good one that could be five times that much? She wanted to march in there and kill the idea immediately, but she had no business eavesdropping. Still, she needed to talk with Travis. Sooner, rather than later.

Chelsea giggled. "Would you come and watch me compete?"

"Try and keep me away." A long pause ensued. "What's wrong?"

"Do you think Mom will let me have another horse? I've been asking forever, but she always says no."

"I don't see why not. It'll be my gift. Then you both can focus on training so you'll be ready for the upcoming year of competition."

"This is so a-maz-ing! I can't wait!"

Oh, Travis. Why didn't you talk with me first?

While Chelsea had been in training for years, and Kate had taken her to the shows where Melissa and other students competed, Kate's first priority was with paying students. Preparing Melissa for the Lexington Junior League show in early July and for Louisville in August, if she qualified, would take every spare moment. Not to mention that the breeding season would soon be under way—her second-highest priority. Next year's foals would be a turning point for her if everything worked out with the stallion on loan.

She'd raised Chelsea to be levelheaded and not get her hopes up too high, and now Travis was throwing extravagant gifts and promises at the girl. If Chelsea had to choose one of them over the other, no doubt Kate would come up on the short end of that stick.

"What if I don't win any of my classes?" The sudden insecurity in Chelsea's voice broke Kate's heart. She was a fine rider, Kate's best. But she hadn't been given a lot of opportunities to prove herself in competition.

"Work your hardest. You can't expect to win them all, but with each show, you'll get better. I have faith in you."

Kate clenched her fists and turned to continue downstairs for a bedtime snack when Chelsea stopped her in her tracks.

"Can I ask you a question, Daddy?"

"Anything at all, remember?"

"Do you still love my mom?"

Kate should interrupt and make her presence known to them to let him off the hook for answering. Or perhaps just go to her room and leave them alone. But she remained rooted to the spot.

Kate might burn in hell for this, but she wouldn't take another step away from this door. She wanted to hear how Travis answered Chelsea's question.

*   *   *

Travis drew a deep breath, knowing he was stalling, but having no clue what the best way to answer Chelsea's question might be. Should he be honest with her and run the risk of making her think there was any hope of the two of them deciding to marry someday? Or hedge?

Vague. Just be vague.

Thanks, Danny. Knowing his friend was with him right now gave him a little more courage.

He glanced at the doorway, wondering if they could be overheard if Katie happened to walk by. She'd left them to their movie hours ago, saying she wanted to get started on the spare bedroom. Not that he could remember what film it was. Mostly, he and Chelsea had continued to get to know each other.

"I love that your mom gave me you. For that, she'll always have a place in my heart. Right there with you."

"Why did you break up in the first place?"

Hadn't Katie explained to Chelsea what happened? Was Chelsea testing him to make sure he told the same story she'd heard from her mom? "A misunderstanding, I'm sure," he began. "I can't even remember what it was about." *No lie there.* "I'm sure it was over some dumb thing." He shrugged. "It happens sometimes. You will probably go through similar things when you start to date."

Her shoulders slumped a little. "I thought grown-ups are supposed to have everything figured out."

He chuffed. "Yeah, well, age gives no guarantee of wisdom. Emotions, hormones, stress—a lot of things factor into decisions about who we fall in love with and who we stay in love with. I'm afraid your mom and I must've hit the perfect storm that spring." Would she accept that answer? He hoped she didn't ask for any specifics.

"Well, if anybody cares what I think, I wish you and Mom would make up again. Don't you?"

Instead of speaking aloud, he nodded.

Chelsea threw up her hands and squealed. "Then what are you waiting for?"

Good question. One he most definitely couldn't answer. But he liked that Chelsea was able to be so straightforward with him from the get-go. He'd rather she pester him with her questions about them than go to Katie.

"I think it's time for you to be in bed, squirt."

She rolled her eyes. "Total cop-out, dude."

He thought he heard something in the hallway but looked over to find the doorway to the hall empty.

While Chelsea moved her stuffed animals to various spots in the room, he did some thinking. Someday soon, he needed to clear the air with Katie and find out if there was any chance of them pursuing something again. Hearing Chelsea express a desire for her parents to work things out gave him the impetus to approach Katie on the subject. But not tonight.

Travis turned to his daughter again. They'd have the whole next week together. He wanted to be a part of as much of it as she'd let him be. But what about after he returned to his life in Nolensville? Even if he did want to be in on every day of her life starting now, he had responsibilities and obligations back home, too. A lot of people depended on him. And it wasn't easy to reestablish a contracting firm in a new location. It had taken years to develop the confidence of his clientele and for them to spread the word enough to make him one of the top homebuilding companies in the Nashville area.

On the other hand, no way would Katie give up the farm to move down there. Besides, Chelsea was in middle school. Being a part of her peer group with the friends she'd grown up with was important. His mom had been an Army brat and talked about how hard it had been when the family had moved halfway across the country just before her senior year in high school.

No, that kind of upheaval in a young girl's life was out of the question if it could be avoided. But how much would Katie be willing to share their daughter? Weekends and school vacations probably would have to suffice, but if Chelsea was serious about competing in horse shows, he could meet up with them there to watch and cheer her on rather than having her visiting him in Nolensville.

Chelsea pulled down the bedspread and turned to him. "Why couldn't one of you just apologize and get over it?"

Apparently, she wasn't finished with the discussion about a romantic reconciliation for her parents. He sighed, seeing that he wasn't going to get Chelsea to give up this conversation anytime soon. Katie didn't seem to have any interest in patching things up.

"Whatever happens between your mom and me will happen, with or without your meddling."

"Sorry." Chelsea grinned, telling him she wasn't the least bit sorry. Not that he could blame her. "But you came back because you loved her, right? Even before you knew about me, you wanted to see her again." Astute observation for such a young kid. "So if you love her, then nothing else should matter."

Travis shuffled his feet, unable to return her gaze for a moment. "Right now, my top priority is getting to know you better. Your mom and I are going to need more time. Things were a little crazy when I first arrived, and we haven't had a chance to talk about it yet." *Liar.* They'd talked plenty. And kissed some, too. He just wasn't making any headway at breaking down Katie's defenses. "Now, I'd appreciate it if you'd give us some time to figure things out for ourselves rather than say anything to your mom about what we talked about."

Coward.

As usual, Danny hit the nail on the head.

So when was he planning to broach the subject with Katie? Travis liked to fix things, but digging at an old wound would only make matters worse. Still, he was the one who'd been dumped, and if he could forgive Katie for that and for hiding Chelsea, then what did *she* have to stay mad about?

He supposed it all depended on why she dumped him in the first place.

Was there a chance of his having both Chelsea and Katie in his life?

Maybe. His heart raced at the thought of Katie being a part of his life again—and not only as Chelsea's mom. Lord knew he still had the hots for her, but he wasn't some wet-behind-the-ears twenty-one-year-old anymore. Sex was great, but it wasn't going to give them a basis for a lifelong commitment. And a commitment to her would mean uprooting himself and everything he knew to make a real family out of the three of them. He needed to be damned sure this could last.

He ran his fingers through his hair. What the hell was he going to do? A week ago, he'd only intended to come up here to check on Katie after that bizarre dream visit from Danny. Now he had a daughter's feelings and future to consider. He loved his crew, but Chelsea was more important than almost anyone else in the world to him right now. Besides, the men and women working with the contracting firm still had Jackson. Chelsea, and maybe even Katie needed him more.

So now what?

"Oh, I need to take a selfie of us to share with my friends. They can't believe what's happened, and everyone wants to see you."

A smile lifted the corner of his mouth as he wondered just how many people she'd called or texted while he was out in the barn.

Since his arms were longer, he decided to take the picture, not that he was all that good at lining them up on the screen. They were both laughing when he finally got a good one.

"Mind if I text it to myself?" He had a few people he wanted to share it with, too. After sending a few of the pics to himself, even the blurry ones, he said, "I'm going to head downstairs. You get some sleep. Night, sweetheart."

"Night, Daddy." She beamed up at him. "I like saying that."

He gave her a hug and kissed her on the forehead before leaving. Tomorrow, he'd be sleeping down the hallway from his two best girls. One was ecstatic; the other probably wished he'd just go home. He chuckled to himself.

More than ever, he was determined to figure out a way to get Katie to come around. He'd already melted her defenses a few times in the last week. This mission might take longer than he'd anticipated, but the prize would be well worth every minute of it.

Your days of hiding from me are over, Katie Michaels.

Chapter Twenty-Three

K ate couldn't continue to eavesdrop beyond Travis's answer about whether he still loved her. She surmised he couldn't have feelings for her in that way, not after what she'd cheated him out of.

Her faced flamed hot as she scooted down the hall to her own room. She still had feelings for him. Perhaps because she'd never gone out of her way to find a replacement. A single woman running a farm and raising a baby didn't have the time or energy to date. Being a good mom to Chelsea and keeping them afloat was all she'd had time for.

Until Travis showed up this week and reawakened yearnings best kept buried.

Would Chelsea be hoping for some kind of reconciliation between them now?

After stripping out of her clothes and before jumping in the shower, she stared at herself in the full-length mirror on the back of the bathroom door. She tried to see her body realistically through Travis's eyes. Her breasts weren't high and perky anymore. The silvery stretch marks marring her abdomen were a little unsightly. She'd read in novels that some men actually found them attractive, especially if *their* babies had caused them. Would Travis be one of those?

Oh please.

Who was she kidding? She stepped into the shower and let the lukewarm water cool down her body, while lingering dreams of a rekindled relationship with Travis washed down the drain along with the grime of the day.

She needed to focus on arrangements for him and Chelsea to have time together and stop her dreaming.

Kate stepped out of the shower, dried her hair, and slipped into her long T-shirt. Back in her room, she crawled into bed and was about to drift off when something Travis had said came back to her.

Why don't we find you the best horse possible so you can compete there and anywhere you'd like?

Kate bolted upright, tossing the sheet off. How could she have forgotten that outrageous promise he'd made? Clearly, she'd let her brain be addled by thoughts of love. Quickly pulling on her jeans and flip-flops, she crept down the hall past Chelsea's door. Her light was out, so Kate headed for the barn apartment. Travis was probably still awake because he couldn't have left the house more than thirty minutes ago. She pounded on the door, calling his name.

His muffled "Come in!" assured her he was inside.

Opening the door, she entered the studio apartment and glanced around. No sign of Travis until splashing from behind the bathroom door warned her where he was. She turned to leave when the door opened. He stood there half-naked with only a dark blue towel wrapped around his waist.

"What can I do for you, Katie?"

Water droplets clung to the hairs on his chest, and she swallowed hard to dislodge the lump in her throat. Kate's heartbeat thudded loudly, and he grinned, no doubt because he could hear it or at least knew the effect his body had on hers.

"We…" She cleared her throat. "We need to talk."

His smile faded. "Everything all right? Chelsea okay?"

"Chelsea's fine. Sound asleep." *I would be, too, if not for you.* She pursed her lips before forcing her gaze from his bare chest to his face. "Would you mind putting on some clothes so we can have a serious conversation about how we intend to parent our daughter?"

"At one o'clock in the morning?" In response, she glared at him. He quirked an eyebrow and shrugged. "Sure. Give me a minute." He crossed the room to the duffel bag on the coffee table and bent to pull out his clothes. So he wore boxer briefs now instead of boxers!

The towel already left little to the imagination, but when he unashamedly discarded it to pull on the formfitting underwear, Kate's jaw dropped as she stared below the tan line at his tight buns.

Sweet mother of God!

Realizing she was gawking and not wanting to be caught, she finally had the wherewithal to turn away so he could finish dressing in some semblance of privacy. But the image of his butt and those long, sculpted legs had been burned onto her retinas. He'd not only filled out in all the right places in his upper body, but had developed muscles below she didn't even know existed.

What was wrong with the women of Nashville that no one had snatched up this man?

Well, they can't have him.

What? Where'd that thought come from? Of course, they could! He'd only complicate her life.

So why did the thought of anyone else kissing him bother her?

Kate folded her arms as she waited for him to give her the okay to turn around again, not that he seemed in the least bit hurried or self-conscious. Was he trying to ignite her passions with his body?

Unfortunately, he'd done exactly that. Still, she refused to fall victim to the man's ample charms. She hadn't come out here for a tumble in bed, although now her mind tortured her with images of what that might be like with both of them now older.

Before she let herself be sidetracked yet again, she said, "How could you promise Chelsea an expensive show horse without talking to me first?"

"You were listening?"

Busted. She drew a deep breath, not allowing him to put the heat on her. "I was on my way downstairs and happened to overhear you two."

"Just how long were you listening?"

She cast her gaze to the floor. "That's neither here nor there."

He chuckled, which exasperated her even more, but he let that go.

"What's wrong with me giving her something she wants so badly?"

Not caring what state of dress—or undress—he was in, she pivoted around to see that he'd only put on his boxer briefs; his chest remained bare and wet.

Stop thinking about kissing away those droplets clinging to his chest hair, Kate.

Why was she letting him short-circuit her brain? Again, she had to force her gaze up to his face. "You don't know the first thing about how much a good performance Saddlebred horse costs. For a good one, we're talking many tens of thousands of dollars just to buy the horse. Then there's feed, entry fees, veterinary bills, transportation to and from shows and—"

He shrugged. "I spent sixty-five thousand dollars on a boat I only take out once or twice a month anymore. I'd rather spend my hard-earned money on something that would get a lot more use than that. I want Chelsea to have the best."

Was he implying that Kate couldn't? *Well, of course, I can't. Don't make me out to be the bad parent because I can't lavish her with extravagant gifts.* "You can't buy her affection, Travis. You don't need to anyway. She already adores you."

"I don't see what the problem is? She wants a show horse. I can afford one. Problem solved."

"You can't fix everything by throwing money at it."

He shook his head and grinned, which only infuriated her more. "Maybe not, but it sure can smooth over a lot of crap."

She wasn't going to win a fight about money with him. Time to try something else.

"I started training Chelsea on fine horses over a year ago. She could have shown on one if she'd wanted to, but she lost interest."

His eyelids narrowed. "Because as soon as she'd get attached, you'd let someone else come along and buy the horse out from under her."

"I'm a breeder and trainer of horses. That's how I make my living so I can keep a roof over our heads and food on the table." She was so close to making it where she wouldn't have to live worrying about every penny coming in or going out, but not if she gave her best horse to her daughter.

"And you're doing a great job, but you need to let Chelsea show you what she's got. Let her work with her own horse."

"You think you know what's best for my daughter after looking at photos of her and picking her up from camp?" Anger the likes of which Kate had never felt before surged through her.

"What? I can't believe we're fighting about this. I thought you'd appreciate the offer to help out with expenses. I heard how frustrated you were when we talked about this earlier, even though, at the time, I had no clue *my* daughter was the student wanting to compete who couldn't afford to."

He remembered that offhand conversation? Of course. He was so like Chelsea. No detail escaped either one of them. Still, she simmered at the thought of him charging in on the white horse and making everything a fairy tale for Chelsea. Life didn't work that way.

"With a decent horse of her own," he continued, "you'll be able to train Chelsea to a whole new level."

"I already know she has the potential to be my best rider, but she also has to learn that we don't always get what we want in life. Sometimes we have to make sacrifices." Her voice sounded shrill as it echoed around the room.

Travis winced. "Don't tell me about sacrifices, Katie Michaels."

He'd misinterpreted her words, or perhaps she hadn't chosen them carefully given her level of upset. "We aren't talking about what you or your buddies went through, Travis. Play fair."

"Neither am I. We're talking about parenting *our* daughter. *You* never gave me a chance to be a father to my own kid. You *stole* that from me."

She closed her eyes as her body absorbed his anger, which mixed with her own. She could never undo that. Kate counted to ten silently before meeting his gaze again. "I'm sorry, Travis. But please don't set her up to believe she's going to get everything she wants when she wants it, because the world doesn't work that way."

"Maybe not, but it happens a lot more when you don't always push away the things—and people—you want. Try it sometime. You might find that life doesn't have to be as dire as you always expect it to be, either."

When did *she* become the focus of the conversation? This conversation had veered to the edge of a cliff, and if she wasn't careful, she'd go over the side and have her heart crushed.

No matter how horrible she'd imagined this moment would be, she hadn't expected his anger to be aimed anywhere but on the issue of Chelsea. "We aren't talking about me here."

"Fine, then let's talk about what *I* want," Travis said, advancing toward her a few steps. "*I* want to watch her ride and compete. *I* want to see her smile with a sense of accomplishment after succeeding at something she's always wanted to do."

She sagged with relief that he wasn't continuing to pursue the tirade about her shortcomings. On safer footing once more, she said, "I think we both want to see Chelsea happy—"

"Tell me how much money you need for a good horse. I can post-date you a check tonight and move the money from savings tomorrow."

But she still wasn't going to concede this point. "What's the rush?"

"She wants to perform in Murfreesboro this October."

Why wouldn't he listen to her? "She might be ready for that next year, after doing the Spring Fling in Murfreesboro before tackling their season's finale. But Chelsea needs nothing from you other than your love. Stop trying to buy her affections." For God's sake, didn't he see he already had the girl's heart?

His nostrils flared, and he took another step toward her. "Look, I'm trying, but I don't know the first thing about being a dad—yet. Cut me some slack. It's not like I've had as much practice as you have." He raked his hands through his hair. "Why are you all bent out of shape about me wanting to help make that girl's dreams come true? Consider it long overdue child support, if that soothes your ego."

Kate clenched her teeth to keep her jaw from dropping. "This isn't about my ego."

"Bullshit." He moved closer yet, robbing her of the ability to breathe without smelling soap and…leather, although the latter might be because they were so close to the tack room. Still, she found the combination intoxicating.

Too intoxicating.

She needed to maintain her space. Poking her finger into his chest to stop him from advancing farther, but she quickly realized that wasn't the smartest move. His pecs were so hard the impact actually hurt. She wondered what it would feel like to fan out her fingers and caress his skin, trailing down to…

Her gaze dipped to his bare chest again before she stared into his eyes. When had his pupils dilated? Okay, it was rather dark in here. The heat radiating from his body made her want him to wrap his arms around her and pull her against him, erasing all the years apart. Her breathing became shallower, and her gaze flitted to his lips a half-second before his mouth descended upon hers.

Kate didn't fight it. Instead, she curled her arms around his neck a half-second before she molded her body against his. His erection hard against her abdomen ignited the flames inside her even more.

This is so wrong. But I don't care.

She'd gone without having this man inside her way too long. A niggling voice in the back of her mind told her she was only going to create more problems by giving in to raging hormones like this, but she didn't care.

Travis's comment about her not allowing herself to have what she wanted out of life made her desire this all the more. She'd sacrificed plenty. He cupped her breast and his breath hitched. He'd probably expected to encounter a bra under her shirt.

She turned her head to break contact with his mouth. "I was in bed already when I decided to come out here. Didn't bother putting on my bra."

"Did you hear any complaints?"

He pinched her nipple and crushed her against the door. The pressure of her body sandwiched between the door and the hard planes of his chest made her core erupt in molten flames. She lowered her hands to his waistband to nudge his boxer briefs down. He opened some space between their lower bodies to allow the underwear to be shucked. His erect member sprang free. Her hand squeezed his hardness, imagining the moment when he would take her completely. Then he took both of her hands and placed them above her head against the wooden panel behind her.

"No touching," he growled. "I want this to last more than a minute. I'm so damned hot for you right now, Katie…"

She kept her hands where he'd placed them, thinking he would lift her T-shirt over her head. He let it rest just above her breasts. His eyes grew steamy as he took in the sight of her bare chest. He didn't look away as he fumbled with the button and zipper of her jeans. She kicked off her flip-flops seconds before he crouched and lowered the denim down her legs. Grabbing hold of his shoulders to keep from falling over, she stepped out of them. Instead of standing again as she expected him to do, he kissed her hip bones then her thighs. He hooked his thumbs between them to nudge them apart.

His fingers delved between her folds. He chuckled, grinning up at her. "You're already wet." One finger dipped inside her and then another.

"Oh, Travis!" She didn't want to delay their coming together a second longer so she grasped him by the biceps to urge him upright. "Please! Don't make me wait another minute. I need you inside me."

In one swift motion, he stood, yanked her shirt off, and lifted her into his arms. He carried her to the double bed in the corner where he gently placed her on the quilt. She took in the sight of his nakedness as he did the same to her until her belly tingled under his scrutiny, and she splayed her hands to hide her stretch marks. "Could you turn off the light, please?"

Ignoring her request, he moved her hands over her head again before climbing onto the mattress beside her. His finger traced the ridges of the worst of the stretch marks, and she wanted to die of embarrassment.

"I wish I could have seen you delivering our baby girl."

The sting of tears made her turn away, not wanting to be condemned yet again in this moment for cheating him out of something he should have been a part of.

Her brain kicked in, and she started to roll over to get up when his hand to her shoulder pressed her into the mattress again.

"I didn't mean it that way. I only wish I'd been able to be a part of that moment when she gave her first cry."

"She didn't cry. Just opened her eyes and looked around."

"Always the inquisitive one from the beginning, I see."

Her heart ached at the thought of how different it would have been if he'd been with her, rather than Lidia.

His eyes smoldered as they bore into her half a second before he closed the gap and captured her lips with his.

His insistent tongue plunged inside her mouth and took her breath away. She should put an end to this before suffering the consequences, but she didn't want to call a halt. They'd deal with the aftermath later. Chelsea wouldn't find out, and tomorrow, they could go back to their separate corners. But for now, she had never wanted anything more in an extremely long time.

She wrapped her arms around his neck and held him close in case he, too, suffered second thoughts.

Chapter Twenty-Four

Travis was afraid to pinch himself and find out he'd fallen asleep in the bathtub to dream yet again about having Katie lying naked beside him. If so, he didn't want to wake up.

Her body was different than he remembered. New curves in all the right places and markings that gave proof—as if he needed it—that she'd carried a baby in her belly. *His* baby.

He trailed kisses down her neck to her chest and latched onto the peak of one breast, suckling as he grew harder himself. It had been a long time since he'd felt the urge to take himself in hand, let alone be with a woman. He didn't expect to last long this first time, either, but didn't want this moment to end.

His palm slid over her belly again before his middle finger slipped between her folds and spread her sweet honey up to the nubbin that caused her to gasp. She opened her legs wider.

Taking her nipple between his teeth, he stretched it away from her body until she met his gaze with a look that told him she wanted this as much as he did. Her pupils dilated. He released her, and her plump breast bounced back into place.

Her body said "yes, yes," but he needed to be sure she wouldn't have regrets later, fool that he was.

"Katie, tell me what you want."

She swallowed hard, her brows furrowing in anguish. "You. I want you inside me," she repeated.

He reached across her to the nightstand and opened the drawer to pull out the box of condoms he'd bought the other day, ripping it open and pulling out one of the foil packets. Handing it to her, he said, "Put this on me first."

He'd give her every opportunity to come to her senses—to consciously act, not simply react. Expecting her to grab her discarded clothes and run for the door, she surprised the hell out of him when her mouth curved into a wicked smile. She knelt beside him on the mattress, tearing the foil packet open with her teeth.

Lord have mercy, take me now!

He fell onto his back and watched as she bent over his long-neglected member, astonishing him yet again when she wrapped her mouth around him and sucked. *Hard.* Her warm mouth cocooned him as she applied gentle pressure with her lips covering her teeth as she went down on him. Afraid to distract her, he remained still except for his throbbing hard-on and reveled in the sensations. Could tonight get any better?

Her head bobbed up and down several times at a faster pace as she took him deeper each time. When his groin pulsated to indicate he was close to coming, he placed his hand on the side of her head to stop her. She didn't take her mouth off him. When their gazes met, he nearly lost it anyway.

"If you don't quit now, this is going to be over before it starts. Put the condom on me. I need to be inside you. Now."

She grinned as she slowly rolled it over his erection. Unable to wait for her to finish at this pace, he got the job done before tossing her onto her back on the mattress and covering her with his body. He kissed her swollen lips and reached down to lube the condom in her wetness, stroking her clit to hardness. Her smile faded as a look of intense need told him she was ready for him. She spread her legs wider, encouraging him to nestle deeper between them. With her ankles entwined above his ass, he dipped himself into the pool of her sex. Her heels dug into his back, spurring him onward. But he only teased her, entering her a little deeper each time before pulling out again.

"More. Don't make me wait."

"Are you sure you're ready? You're so tight."

"Yes!"

Needing no further assurance, he buried himself to the hilt.

"Oh, God!" she shouted, gasping for air. "Yes! I've waited so long."

He wondered how long, but all that mattered was this time, this moment. Bracing his hands on either side of her head, he pumped in and out slowly. So tight. As he increased his tempo, each thrust brought a grunt that sounded like pain from her, but her face was filled with ecstasy.

No way did he want this to end for him, but she'd been known to enjoy more than one orgasm when they made love, so he lowered himself to one elbow to reach between their bodies again. As he stroked her sensitive nubbin, she made the cutest kitten-like sound with each upward thrust of her hips.

"Yes! Please! Don't stop!"

"Wasn't planning to," he said, not realizing until then how short of breath he was. Man, he needed to start working out again so he could keep up with her next time.

Jeezus, let there be a next time. A thousand more next times.

He bent down to kiss her, cutting off her "Oh, yes!" just as her eyes squeezed tight. Forcing his tongue between her lips, he mimicked what his shaft was doing. When her vaginal muscles tightened around him, he nearly exploded, but raised his torso to watch her come. A primal look of pain crossed her face again as she screamed her release, but he kept stroking her until she begged him to stop.

Her chest rose and fell rapidly as she tried to recover. Then she opened her eyes and quirked her brow. "You didn't come."

"I don't want this night to end. Don't worry about me. How was your first orgasm of the night?"

She smiled dreamily. "Even better than I remembered." She met his gaze and grew more serious. "Hold on. First? Does that mean what I think it does?"

"I'd say we still have plenty of time before I have to send you back to the house."

"Good." She smiled and sighed. "I waited thirteen years and two months for that one—way too long. I don't want to wait for the next."

That she'd not only been with no other man in all that time—and remembered to the month how long it had been—gutted him. How was he supposed to process that? When she squeezed his manhood with her internal muscles, teasing him, he shook his head and grinned. "That feels incredible. You always amazed me at how soon you could be ready. I held off coming so I could keep up with you and take you over the top one more time."

If only they didn't have to worry about their daughter finding Katie missing from her bed… but he didn't want to have her thinking the two of them had reconciled. He may want that, but Katie had a way of pulling the rug out from under him whenever he got too close. No sense giving Chelsea false hope.

Intending to distract Katie, he traced a finger around her areola, watching her nipple bunch again. "I could lie like this forever." He bent to latch onto the peak and sucked. She gasped, clutched the back of his head as if making sure he wouldn't stop. *As if.* Flicking his tongue against her, again she squeezed him. If she kept that up, he wasn't going to last long enough for her to be ready.

When she lifted her hips, he took it as a sign and once again began moving inside her slick passage. "God, woman!" he grunted. "You're so tight."

"I haven't been with anyone since you, but after having Chelsea…"

Hearing those words, he rammed her harder, faster as he neared the summit again. She hadn't been with anyone else? *Dayum.* Her panting told him she was close again, too, without any additional stimulation from his fingers. His woman was so responsive.

His. Knowing there'd never been any other man to experience this with her made him feel like a king.

He pumped harder as her mewling sounds increased and she

screamed, "Yes! Yes! Oh, please, Travis!"

Her face tightened as she hung on the crest, waiting, waiting...and then she screamed. He couldn't hold back any longer, and as she spasmed around him, he roared his release, too. The moment seemed to go on for a lifetime—and was over all too soon. He'd never come so hard or so long.

"I love..." The words of love that came to the tip of his tongue scared him, and he finished with "...the way you explode for me." Thankfully, he had the wherewithal to keep any romantic declarations to himself.

His member throbbed, still surrounded by her tight sheath. He bent to shower her with kisses, their bodies connected skin to skin from her lips to her toes. "That was incredible, Katie. You're the only woman I've ever wanted to be with."

Her eyes opened wider. Clearly, she didn't believe him. Not wanting her to escape until they had time to talk, he pulled out. "Stay right there. I'll just get rid of this and be right back."

He hurried into the bathroom, keeping the door open to listen for signs that she might be escaping, but he heard nothing to indicate her imminent departure. After washing himself off, he wet a clean washcloth with warm water and returned to the bedroom. She lay with her eyes closed, sated with a half-smile on her face. At least the regrets hadn't piled in on her yet.

"Spread yourself open for me."

One eye opened in a question until she spied the washcloth, and she reached out. "Here. I can do that."

"I said, spread...your...legs."

Her cheeks flushed even redder. Why she'd think this was more intimate than what he'd just done to her body, he couldn't understand, but she did as he instructed.

When the cloth rubbed over her nubbin, she jerked her legs closed around his hand. "Careful. It's still pretty sensitive."

He grinned. "Sorry." *Not sorry!*

He'd finished, got up, and quickly discarded the cloth in the sink. Returning to the bed, he stretched out and wrapped one arm under her as his other hand settled on her breast, playing with her nipple with much less urgency than earlier.

"Why'd you break it off, Katie?" Oh, hell. Why'd he have to go and ask her that at a time like this?

"I messed up," she whispered, closing her eyes.

He'd expected her to pull away and leave, not to answer him after all the times she'd evaded the question.

"I thought I was doing the right thing back then, but nothing turned out the way I expected."

His finger moved up to stroke her lips. "Open your eyes and look at me."

She grimaced before complying.

"What are you talking about?" When she still didn't meet his gaze, he placed a finger under her chin and tilted her head toward him.

Her eyes sparkled with unshed tears. "I wanted you to finish college and make a name for yourself before we married and started a family. All I could think about was how much you would one day resent my tying you down if I forced you into an early marriage."

His body tensed. "Seriously?" He withdrew his hand from her face. "God, Katie. How could you think that you'd be forcing me into anything? It took both of us to make Chelsea. I wouldn't have deserted you when you needed me, and I sure as hell wouldn't have shirked my duty to you both."

"I didn't want to be yet another responsibility for you, Travis."

Okay, she'd said that wrong.

"You were pursuing a career that wasn't compatible with living on a horse farm in Midway. When you told me that your life had veered off in a totally different direction than planned, I was heartsick. I'd sacrificed a chance at our being together for something that didn't even come to be."

He sighed. "My early plans were immature nonsense dreamed up by a cocky guy who thought he was going to set the world on fire. I never looked back for anything I might have missed—other than you." He fell onto his back and stared up at the ceiling. "God, I couldn't wait to come home from New York and convince you that you'd been wrong. But your dad wouldn't let me see you."

"I'm sorry. I knew if I saw you again, I'd cave and make your life miserable. So I asked him to turn you away if you came by. He agreed that it would be wrong to tie you down just when your career was poised to take off."

"Your dad shouldn't have interfered. I think he secretly wanted me out of your life. He must have been afraid I'd take you away from him forever, even though he only had you a couple years after that. He screwed you more than me."

She exhaled slowly. He glanced away, running his hand through his hair. "I can't believe how much we missed out on, Katie."

Water under the bridge, but what about the future? He met her gaze, his fierce with a passion he'd never felt before, perhaps because he hadn't really thought they could turn this thing around until tonight. "The important thing now is, what do we plan to do to fix it?"

"Sometimes things can't be fixed."

"Bull. We both just exploded for each other, didn't we? I'd say we still share strong feelings for one another. And we've had some good times since I've been back. Why don't we stop fighting long enough to see what possibilities there are, if for no other reason than to be a family?"

*   *   *

She hadn't realized what a dreamer Travis was. Apparently, he hadn't lost that despite the way his life had veered off track. But she needed to keep her focus on what was best for Chelsea, not for Kate. They hadn't really resolved the issue of that damned horse yet.

"Let's get back to something that we need to fix right now. Chelsea's not ready to handle a horse of the caliber you're talking about buying her. Why set her up to fail?" Kate hoped that Travis would take the bait and move on to discussing Chelsea rather than their future. She needed to distance herself from whatever had just happened here.

"What if I'm setting her up to succeed?" he whispered, grinning as he grabbed her hand and held it against the beating of his heart. "On a level playing field with the kids whose families have more money?"

All the fight left her as she fought the urge to play with his chest hair. She'd tried to give Chelsea everything important in life. To have Travis show up and to see Chelsea happier than she'd been in a long while made her realize that perhaps this *was* about Kate's ego.

If only she could lay in bed with him for hours and pretend they were a married couple sharing in pillow talk following an intimate respite. But when she met his gaze, the fire reigniting in his eyes made her realize the time to return to reality had arrived. The only thing his throwing money at the problem would do would be to make her look inadequate in her daughter's eyes.

"I don't want us to get into a competition for who can give her the most." *Because I could never win.* "She needs to go up the ranks and start out with more academy-level shows. There's a national one held in Murfreesboro every November that I could prepare her for. If she does well and wants to continue, you could consider giving her a performance horse for her birthday in January. Can we agree not to rush into anything about the horse right away? She has enough change going on in her life at the moment."

"Fair enough." He nodded, his gaze lighting on her lips before returning to her eyes. "I'll admit I can be impulsive at times. When I heard what she wanted, I just blurted out my offer without thinking."

"We're going to have to decide how to deal with her expectations of getting a new horse now that the promise has been made. You'll have to tell her this isn't going to happen right away."

Travis's face grew grim again. "I haven't changed my mind yet, but I'll consider your request for better timing. We'll talk about it some more in the coming weeks."

Negotiating wasn't something she'd ever had to do when it came to Chelsea. "Will you agree to run major decisions like this one by me first in the future? Then we can discuss them together and decide what's best for her before dashing her hopes by taking something back?" At least that's what Kate assumed other parents did. She'd never had to share parental control before—and didn't particularly like having to start doing so now.

"Since her hopes are already up this time, why not just let me buy her a good horse with the stipulation that she doesn't ride it until you determine she's ready?"

Had he not heard anything she'd just said? Why did the man have to be so stubborn? So infuriating?

"Having a horse in my barn that she knows is hers for the taking is going to make it impossible for me to live with her begging me to let her train on it. She's many months away from being ready for that. What's wrong with waiting until January?"

"That's six months away."

Closer to seven, actually, since Chelsea's birthday was at the end of the month. "She'll be able to hit the ground running. I can train her to ride Chula in some upcoming shows—"

"All right, I don't want to have to disappoint her." He shrugged, hitching up the corner of his mouth for emphasis. "She's expecting me to come through for her on this, but you're making it damned hard for me to do that."

Clearly, he wasn't about to let this promise go or be the bad guy in Chelsea's eyes. Unable to say anything more, Kate sat up and swung her legs over the edge of the mattress. She stood and crossed the room to retrieve her clothes. She quickly donned the T-shirt, slipped into her flip-flops, and picked up her jeans before facing him, clutching them to her chest like armor. His gaze bore into her lower body, but she tamped down any response that might lead to more lovemaking.

"Travis, your life is four hours away. You can't just breeze in here every weekend, or however often you intend to visit, and throw money and promises at Chelsea to make yourself out to be some kind of hero. You're her dad. That's hero enough in her book. Just tell her you and I talked and you realize now that it was a mistake to make that offer to her."

"All you have to do is say the word and we can work on finding a way to blend our lives together."

"I have no intention of leaving this farm until they carry me off in a hearse. That hurdle isn't going away. But we aren't talking about us. We have a long way to go until we're on the same page as parents, first."

"I agree we have a lot to sort out there, but I'm not giving up on us getting back together. Especially after what just happened in here."

She'd made a colossal mistake to let her guard down with him. "Let's not bite off more than we can chew. Right now, I want you to focus on Chelsea."

* * *

Travis couldn't argue that there was a lot they'd have to work out, but if they didn't discuss things they weren't going to get anywhere. "Katie, tell me one thing."

She glanced toward the door, no doubt ready to make a hasty retreat, but met his gaze. "What?"

"Will you give this spark a chance?"

A wry grin spread across her face. "I'd say we just did, but sex obviously is not going to be enough."

"Yeah, but it's sure a great start." He probably had a silly-assed grin on his face, and she wasn't buying it judging by the narrowing of her eyes. He sighed. "Look, I want us to build a deeper relationship this time. For you to allow me inside that place you've shut me out of since the day we met."

She reached behind her for the doorknob. "I can't change who I am, Travis."

And with that, she was gone.

What the hell did that mean? How could they go from making passionate love to her battening down the hatches for whatever storm she always seemed to expect to blow into her life?

He almost got up to follow her, but thought better of it. Katie had been running from something her whole life, and until she faced it, they weren't going to get anywhere as a couple—much less a family.

Speaking of family, he hadn't called Mom yet to ask her about Sunday. Knowing she'd want to plan a feast and do deep cleaning in the house and yard, he got up to find his boxer briefs and put them on before retrieving his phone from his jeans pocket.

He texted her first to make sure she was awake. Mom never kept her ringer on at night, so he wouldn't wake her. Within seconds, though, she texted him back telling him to call her. She answered on the second ring.

"Hi, Mom. How's everything going?"

"Great. Just finished beating your dad in a late-night game of canasta. Speaking of which, isn't it a little late for you to be up on a work night? You okay?"

"Everything's…fine. I'm taking the week off."

"Well, it's about time. I hope you went somewhere relaxing. You work too hard."

Relaxing would be the least accurate adjective he'd give this past week—well except for maybe the last hour or so. "No, Mom, it's not a vacation. That's what I'm calling about. I'm in Midway…visiting Katie Michaels."

The silence on the other end made it impossible to judge her reaction. "Well, how is she? I always loved Katie. Most down-to-earth girl you ever brought home to us."

Other than a few girls he'd dated in high school and his freshman year in college, Kate was the *only* one he'd ever brought home.

"Well? Don't keep me guessing."

Mom, you'd never guess this in a million years.

"Are you seated?"

"Why?"

"Because I have some news for you."

"Joe, come back in here! Travis has some news!"

He waited for his dad to ask what was up and for Mom to put her phone on speaker.

"We're here. What's wrong?"

He grinned, knowing they were expecting the worst. "Nothing, actually. Everything's more right than it's been for me in a while." Since Danny's death for sure, but even before that. "Katie has a daughter. Her name's Chelsea. Mom, she has your eyes and Clint's high forehead. She'll turn thirteen in January, and…well, she'd like to meet her grandparents."

"Oh, dear Lord." His mom's voice had grown thick.

"What are you trying to tell us, son?" Dad asked.

"Appears that I left something behind when Katie and I split up."

"I can't believe what you're saying. You haven't been drinking, have you?"

He laughed. "No, Mom. I'm stone sober. I can't wait for you to see her, Mom and Dad. She's beautiful. Hold on! Let me send you a couple pics."

He texted them several of the selfies the two of them had taken earlier tonight.

"Oh, Joe, she's gorgeous! We have another granddaughter!" He waited for her to address him again but judging by the sniffles and blowing of her nose, she was crying. "When can we meet her?"

"Would Sunday be soon enough?"

"No, but if that's the best you can do, I'll round up everyone for a family cookout." His mother had probably planned half the menu already.

"Mom, Dad, I want Katie to come, too."

Silence again. "You know we'd love to see her again, but you also know your sisters don't think much of her after she dumped you."

Thanks, Mom. "Don't worry. I'll have a talk with each of them first.

If they can't be civil, then I'd rather they not be there."

His father's stern voice reminded him of some of his scoldings as a boy. "Son, you need to remember who your family is. They come first."

"Dad, Katie and Chelsea are my family now, too."

His dad hadn't said much at all about the break-up, but it sounded as though he might harbor some negative feelings toward Katie, too.

Travis may need to lay some groundwork before Sunday to make it go as smoothly as he possibly could. Last thing he wanted was for Katie to get skittish and run him off again.

"We'll talk to the triplets. And if you want Katie here, then she's welcome."

"Thanks. I do. I'll see you Sunday, late morning. Is there anything I can bring?"

"Chelsea, you, and Katie. We'll take care of everything else."

He still had nearly a week to build a stronger bond between him and Katie, not to mention getting to know Chelsea better. He hoped that, by the time they showed up in Pleasure Ridge Park, he'd have forged a family bond that would withstand anything his sisters could dish out.

Chapter Twenty-Five

E arly the next morning, Kate found herself standing on a stepladder in the guest room dusting and trying not to think about what had happened in the apartment last night.

Good luck with that.

She and Travis had come together as if all the years apart never happened. Her playfulness with the condom surprised her a bit, but they'd always joked about them after that first time in college when they'd made love without one. Neither of them particularly liked them, but she appreciated that he'd bought some, just in case. That he'd been thinking in that direction before the news of Chelsea came out made her wonder if perhaps they might have rekindled their romance if not for her keeping the secret from him.

Today, she planned to avoid the barn where Travis and Chelsea were working together. She had a couple of lessons after lunch, which should give her plenty of time to finish up and be ready for him to move in this afternoon.

Oddly enough, she now took comfort in knowing that, with all three of them on the same floor, it wasn't likely they'd have a repeat of last night's lovemaking.

She'd already removed all the family photos from the mantel and doused her cotton cloth with oil as she vigorously wiped away the dust of the past few years. Swiping at the edge of the frame around the mirror, she heard something and watched an envelope fall to the mantel. Had Chelsea tucked it behind there? Why? If she wanted to hide something from Kate, it would make more sense for her to do so in her room rather than in here. She picked it up. The mirror was an antique. Perhaps it had been tucked away for two decades, if not longer.

Staring down at the age-yellowed envelope, she was shocked to see her name and address on it. The thirty-two cent stamp had an Escondido, California, cancellation dated just before her twelfth birthday. Her heart thudded against her chest. Instinctively, she knew it was a letter from her mother.

Her chest grew tighter as she turned the letter over to look for a return address. The back flap was blank—and loosened. She had no memory of reading it, so who had? Daddy?

Her legs suddenly weak, Kate stepped down from the ladder and crossed to the bed where she sat on the edge of the mattress to lift the flap, remove the letter, and unfold it.

The paper shook in her hand so badly she had to set it on the bed and take some deep breaths before she could begin reading. Pink stationery. On a whim, she held it up to her face and could have sworn she breathed in the familiar scent she always associated with her mom. Something more herbal than floral. Earthy. Not unlike the subtle lemongrass scent Kate wore.

Mom had been a free spirit, a derogatory term when used by her dad, but Kate thought it sounded exotic and wild. Two adjectives no one would ever use to describe Kate in a million years.

Confused about why the letter had been concealed all these years, her mind quickly pointed to the only person who could have done it.

Daddy.

But why would he keep something so precious from her? He knew how much she missed her mother. Unless he... No. He wouldn't have done something so despicable on purpose.

Then how did a letter go from the mailbox to hidden behind a mirror in his room if not an intentional act?

The enormity of what she suspected brought bile into her throat. If Mom had tried to keep in touch with her, why wouldn't he encourage that?

Realizing she wasn't going to find any answers speculating like this, she picked up the letter again and tried to read the words through her tears.

Dearest Chula,

Oh God. I can't breathe!

The air was sucked from the room as she flashed back to her childhood. A distant memory she'd long ago blocked out came flooding back to her. When young Kate had asked her mom what *chula* meant, she'd said it reminded her of a song her mother used to sing to her as a child about a party on the beach. Kate had never been to Southern California where her mother had lived, but she pictured sunny beaches with mountains in the distance.

Mom had sung "La Chula" to Kate every night—in English except for the title. Her beautiful voice came through crystal clear as Kate blinked away more tears.

And my beloved siren has arrived

And my beloved brunette is here

My beloved and gorgeous baby has arrived.

Mom had also sung it on a picnic they'd shared with Daddy up at the springhouse. How could Kate have forgotten about that picnic all these years? While she'd been very young, it had been such a precious day to her, perhaps because it had happened shortly before Mom left.

Kate had even named a horse Chula without being aware of the word's significance—at least not consciously.

Letting the tears fall so she could read the words more clearly, a feeling of love and warmth cascaded over her as she remembered that lullaby and the emotions she'd experienced each night with her mother. With difficulty, she tried to make out the words on the first page of the letter, distinctly hearing her mom's voice. How much more of her mother's memory had she blocked out? And why? No doubt to cope with being abandoned by her own mother.

It's been so long since I've seen you that I wonder if you'd even remember me anymore. Today is your twelfth birthday.

That her mother hadn't forgotten about her even after all those years apart had Kate blinking rapidly until she could continue reading.

I wish things had been different and that I hadn't given in to the lure of the beach that summer so long ago. I was always searching for some elusive butterfly, I suppose, not realizing I had the most precious one on earth within my grasp if only I'd stayed around to nurture it.

Kate, you can't imagine how my heart aches to hold you, hug you, and kiss you once again. But I know from all the letters that have been returned over the years that you wanted nothing more to do with me after I left you.

What? He'd even returned letters addressed to Kate? What kind of monster would do such a thing?

I can't help but try one more time. It's been a few years. Perhaps you're older now. Or maybe you will find this in the mailbox before your daddy can send it back.

"No, Daddy," she whispered. "What did you do?" The only consolation she could gather was that at least her mother didn't think she'd been the one to send them back.

A tear dropped onto the letter, and she quickly pressed the precious paper to her chest to dry it before smudging the ink. Kate moved the page out of harm's way on the bed again as more tears flowed unchecked.

Years? Her mother had continued to write to her for years, and Daddy hadn't let her see any of them? Rage churned inside her, something she'd been taught by the same man not to express. How many other things had he convinced her were the norm while all the time doing such unthinkable things behind her back?

A sob escaped her as the truth became evident. She looked toward the heavens, no longer believing that her father deserved to be there. "Daddy, I'll never forgive you for this. You controlled and meddled in my life from the beginning, but I always respected you as my dad. But this"—she gasped for a breath—"*this* is beyond contemptible."

Hugging the letter to herself once more, she doubled over, rocking herself much as her mother had done in the chair in her parents' room. "She *did* love me." Clearly, her childhood had mostly been a lie, one story after another concocted by a self-centered man who wanted to make sure no one else got close to his precious daughter. Not even her own mother.

Kate gritted her teeth, anger replacing sorrow. "How *dare* you!"

"How dare I what?"

Kate jumped, glancing toward the doorway where Travis stood. His eyes narrowed with concern as he came around the bed to hunker down on the floor beside her, stroking her cheek. "What's wrong? Why are you crying? If it's about last night…"

"No," she uttered, unable to speak another word beyond the knot in her throat. She shook her head and held the letter toward him with a trembling hand. When he started to take it from her to look, she pulled the cherished treasure back and held it tight against her chest again. She didn't want anyone to take away this irreplaceable gift from her mother, not even for a second.

Getting up, he sat on the bed behind her, stroking her back in long sweeping motions. His touch calmed her somewhat. When he pulled her against his chest, she didn't fight him. Finally, she was able to say, "My mother wrote me."

"Your *mother?* After all these years?" He stroked her hair and cheek, further calming her.

She shook her head. "No. This letter was written almost twenty-two years ago. But I'm only seeing it for the first time today." Anger bubbled up, but she didn't want to express it in front of Travis.

"Where'd you find it?"

With the shaky hand holding the letter, she pointed toward the mirror over the mantel. "I was cleaning the mirror and it fell out. It's probably been hidden away since my dad put it there soon after it arrived. Strange, but I did deep clean this room a few years ago when Lidia and Jason stayed here during a remodeling project. Lidia's a neat freak, so I know she'd have probably dusted while here. Neither of us found it."

"You're sure your dad hid it?"

"We lived alone. Who else could have? He also was the one with the biggest stake in me not knowing or communicating with my mom." Fresh tears spilled. "What kind of selfish bastard would do something like this?"

He'd been determined to keep her all to himself.

Even with her emotions so raw, Kate saw that she'd done almost the same thing by not letting Travis know about his daughter. "Oh, God, Travis!" She turned around to face him, trying to breathe, but finding it difficult. "I'm no better. I did the same thing to you that he did to my mom. I never should have kept Chelsea a secret from you. How can you ever forgive me?"

He tucked a strand of hair behind her ear, letting his finger trail along her jaw line. "We can't undo the past, Katie. Dwelling on it over and over again isn't going to change it, either. The important thing is that we're taking steps to move forward and make things right for her now."

She nodded, but hated herself almost as much as she hated her father at the moment. "I've made such a mess of things for you and Chelsea. I intend to make up for it if you'll let me."

He cupped her face and closed the gap to kiss her tenderly on the forehead. Nothing urgent. Nothing carnal. But that kiss filled a void inside her and left her with such a feeling of peace that she almost started to cry again.

"Katie, I understand better now why you did what you did, knowing how profoundly you were affected by not only your mother's seeming desertion but your father's actions as well. Even if you didn't know he was keeping her from you, I would guess he's colored your view of men and the world just the same."

She sniffled. "I have a lot to process. Every day seems to bring some new revelation. Frankly, I'm exhausted at the moment."

"Well, if it helps, you can stop cleaning up in here. Everything looks great, and I can take care of myself."

She nodded, but her mind wouldn't let go of the enormity of the situation. At least Chelsea wouldn't reach the age of thirty-three wondering if both her parents loved her. She'd know because Travis would be a committed dad to her for the rest of their daughter's life. And Kate would keep trying to be there for her, loving her and perhaps finding ways to make amends for what she'd cheated both of them out of.

Speaking of which… "Where's Chelsea?"

"Softball practice."

"Oh, I forgot! I was supposed to take her!"

"Don't worry. I took her. She wouldn't let me hang around and watch, so that's why I'm here." He pointed to the letter. "So have you learned anything that might help my sisters in the search?"

"No. It was postmarked in…"—she picked up the envelope again—"Escondido, California. I've never heard of it."

"Let me google it." He pulled out his phone and pecked in the name with his thumbs, not nearly as fast as Chelsea texted. "It's in San Diego County, about an hour north of the city. In the mountains."

"Mom talked more about the beach than the mountains, but I haven't finished the letter yet. Maybe she'll say what she was doing there." When he didn't get up to leave, she hated to say it after he'd given her such comfort just now, but… "Would you mind if I read it alone? If I'm going to be a blubbering mess, I'd rather not have you witness it." She shrugged her shoulders and smiled wryly.

Travis shook his head and bent to kiss her on the cheek, whispering in her ear, "You keep too much bottled up inside, darlin'." He stood. "There's nothing wrong with showing strong emotion, Katie. Your tears would never be a mess to me. Although they do give me the urge to kiss them away and try to make it all better."

Kate laughed for the first time since she'd found the letter. At this moment, she could kiss him, too. "Thanks, Travis. I appreciate your support more than you could know."

Travis started toward the door. "Well, if you need me, just holler. I'll rustle us up some lunch. You've been up here an awfully long time, so I'll bet you haven't thought about eating."

"Guilty as charged. A sandwich and a small salad would be great. I'll be down shortly. Then you can move your things in after lunch."

He nodded and left her alone with her letter and her thoughts, but she couldn't dive back in right away. A realization came over her about her interaction just now with Travis. She'd allowed Travis to see her being vulnerable, and he hadn't run away from her or ridiculed her.

For years, she hadn't allowed herself to cry or show any strong emotion in front of those she loved, falsely believing all these years that she'd driven her mother away by being fussy or disobedient. She didn't really remember much before her fifth birthday, and her mom had left soon after.

Whoa, had she said those she loved? Well, she had to be honest. She did love Travis. How could he burrow into her heart again in such a short time? He'd made himself at home in her heart years ago and apparently had never been evicted. Rather than infringing on her space, he enhanced it. How had she progressed from wanting him to go away like a bad flu to wanting to make him a part of their lives here?

Well, maybe that was going a little too far. She didn't want to raise her hopes that his living here was even a possibility.

But she also didn't want to think about Monday coming and Travis heading home to Nolensville again. Chelsea would be heartbroken, and Katie would hurt for her. Maybe for herself, too.

With a heavy sigh, she forced herself to focus once more on the letter. The interruption had given her a chance to regroup. This time, when she began reading, much of the dread had departed, allowing her to simply enjoy the words as if sitting here having a visit with her mom.

Where had she left off? *Oh yeah.* So her mom had also surmised that Kate's dad had been intercepting the letters, although earlier in the letter she seemed to be feeling that Kate had rejected her. How many letters had been sent and returned? Knowing that her mother actually had reached out to her on multiple occasions sent Kate careening on an emotional roller coaster. Euphoric because her mother truly hadn't moved away without a backward glance. Devastated because the two of them had been separated unnecessarily all these years.

> *If by chance you read this letter, please call me anytime at the number below my name. My heart needs to hear your voice once more. Perhaps we will meet again someday, although my finances aren't very good right now, so it might be difficult.*
>
> *Know that I love you to the moon and back and always will.*

Love,
Mom

Kate stared at the phone number at the bottom, wondering if it was still a working number. With Travis downstairs, she decided not to call now. It would be awfully early on the West Coast. She'd give it a try later, maybe tonight.

Kate stood and tucked the refolded letter back into its yellowed envelope. On her way down the hall, she popped into her room and set it on the dresser. Later, she'd probably reread it a few dozen more times before ever dialing that number. Why was she so afraid of hearing her mother's voice again? It was what she'd dreamed of for years, but now, when she could be as close as a phone call, Kate was terrified.

Because what if she found out Kate had turned out just like her father? She didn't want to have her mother know that. Maybe if she could manage to get things to work out between her and Travis, she'd consider it, but not yet.

Once again, anger at her father bubbled up. She wished her mom had taken her with her when she ran off to California. Her entire life would have been different.

No, you don't.

True. If Kate had been taken away from here at five, she'd never have met Travis or had Chelsea. They were arguably the best things that had ever happened to her. Only she'd thrown Travis away in part because of the wrongful notions her father had instilled in her about being abandoned by those she loved.

He'd shut her mother out of her life all these years when they could have at least talked on the phone and written each other letters. Why had he stolen that relationship from her? She'd never know the answer to that now, but for the first time in her life, she despised her father.

And she knew that she had a lot of work to do to remedy the wrong she'd done. But remedy it she would so that she could despise her own actions a little bit less. She couldn't believe that Travis hadn't been angrier about what she'd done. He'd always been easy-going, but this was taking it to the extreme.

Perhaps he wasn't all that much better at expressing his emotions than she was.

* * *

Travis finished making turkey sandwiches to go with the small tossed salads and wondered how much longer Katie would be. Seeing her so broken up over what her dad had done opened his eyes to a lot of things. While he still harbored some hurt over all the years he'd lost with her and Chelsea, at least he was beginning to understand why Katie would keep her secret. It had nothing to do with not trusting him with their daughter or thinking him unfit. She'd just been screwed up by her father who'd fed her all kinds of paranoid ideas and lies. *The bastard.*

When Katie entered the kitchen fifteen minutes later, he smiled in her direction. While her eyes were red, she'd stopped crying at least. Probably best not to talk about her mom's letter while it was so raw, unless she brought it up. "Perfect timing." He carried the plates over to the table.

She moved across the room looking like she'd been visited by another ghost. Would Katie try and contact her mother? How much information did the letter give? As of Friday, Shania and Emmy hadn't been able to find her mother yet. Could he provide them with any new clues so Katie could get some closure, maybe even answers? Clearly, that damned letter was foremost on *his* mind.

"Thanks for making lunch." She went to the sink to wash her hands and did a glucose check before taking her seat, but only stared at the plate as though she didn't know what to do with it.

Travis squeezed her hand. "Eat. You'll feel better. I'll get you some water."

When he handed her a glass of iced lemon water and sat across from her, he noticed she'd taken a couple bites of the sandwich. With that vacant look still on her face, she picked up a blackberry from her salad and nibbled on it.

Maybe he could distract her from her thoughts. "Why don't we go for a ride this afternoon? I could load up a couple of the horses, and we can drive to a nearby trailhead. Chelsea won't be back from softball practice until suppertime." He'd been floored when Chelsea offered to cancel on her friends for the movie and pizza night, choosing to hang out with him instead. But they'd merely rescheduled for Tuesday. She must be pretty popular with them.

"No, thanks. I'll be busy working with Melissa this afternoon. She's getting worried about her performance in the Junior League show and booked extra sessions all week long."

He cupped her cheek, and she met his gaze. "I'm worried about *you*. In the last couple of days, you've been hit with a lot. I've become Chelsea's father, you've found out that what you've always believed about your mother is probably a lie, and then there was what happened between us last night. How are you handling all this?"

She finished chewing and swallowed. "You were always Chelsea's father to me, Travis. That's only news to you two."

He gave a half-nod. "True. But what about your mom?" He wanted to find out how she felt about their lovemaking, too, but one thing at a time.

"I'm still in shock from finding that letter. Part of me wonders if there might be any others hidden away. I'm going to force myself not to tear the house apart looking." She grinned, but her eyes remained sad.

"Any new clues as to where she might be living?"

Katie shook her head. "She did include a phone number. I'll call it later today to see if it's still good."

"Sounds like a plan. You could even try after we finish lunch. If it's not a working number, maybe my sisters can glean something from the letter that will help track down her whereabouts. I can call them again today if you have anything more to go on. Just say the word." He didn't want to tell her Emmy and Shania had hit a rock wall so far.

In all honesty, he wasn't keen on having to deal with their crap again about Katie now that Mom had probably told them what was going on. They'd better not make a scene at the cookout Sunday.

"Thanks, but I need to get my head in the right space before Melissa arrives. It helps knowing she wanted to stay in touch with me, though. I'm not as reluctant to try and find her. Unfortunately, I didn't see anything else in the letter that can help much."

"Well, we know she was in Escondido at some point."

She nodded, and they ate a few minutes in silence before she said, "How could Daddy keep those letters from me? I had every right to know..." Her voice broke, and he pushed his chair back and guided her by the hand onto his lap.

God, it felt good to hold her again, although he wished she wasn't in such pain. "People do stupid things sometimes. Maybe he was afraid of losing you to your mom. Without a doubt, he had no clue how to parent."

"I can't believe I did the same thing as he did without even knowing he'd done that to me. I was so afraid of losing Chelsea that I selfishly kept her all to myself."

Lots of people repeated what they knew. Travis would probably do the same, but fortunately he had great role models—two loving and supportive parents. Not that they didn't kick his butt when he needed it and kicked their kids out of the nest when the time came.

"Perhaps, subconsciously, you knew all along he'd been responsible for her not returning. Could be you blocked out some scene that was too difficult for you to remember."

She shrugged. "Hard to say." He stroked her arm, loving that she hadn't run from his affection this time. "I did find out that the name Chula wasn't random after all. Mom called me that and sang me a song called "La Chula" as a lullaby at bedtime."

"Wow. See? The mind sure is a powerful thing and who knows what other little tidbits it will release now that you know more of the truth."

Her chin began to quiver, and she sniffled. He wrapped his arms around her and held her closer as her body trembled uncontrollably. Clearly, he wasn't doing a very good job of taking her mind off the letter, but maybe she needed to talk about it.

"Reading the words in the letter was like hearing her voice and sitting with her again."

Tires crunching on the gravel outside made Katie sit up.

"I'm glad you found it, Katie."

She blinked a few times and stood up. He followed suit and brushed her hand away when she began clearing the dishes. "Anything you want me to work on this afternoon?"

"Nothing I can think of. I need to get ready for Melissa. She's a little early. If you want to see if she needs any help getting Miss Pickles ready, I want to send an email to make sure everything's set for the stallion I have on loan to arrive on schedule next week. I've fallen a little behind with everything that's going on."

She'd tamped down the emotions of a few minutes ago, but at least she'd leaned on him a little and shared some of what she was feeling, however briefly.

"I'll take care of things in the barn," he said. "We can talk later about whether there's anything you need to work on before the stallion shows up. In the meantime, I'll also head up to the old barn and bring down more hay and straw. You have my phone number if you need anything. I can get a signal up there." He stood and picked up their empty plates and bowls. "Hey, why don't I pick up some pizzas and rent a movie or something for tonight? Have you seen *The Longest Ride?*"

Katie shook her head. "Saw the previews, but most movies are long gone from the theaters by the time I see them. That's why my DVD collection is so extensive. It looked good, provided it has a happy ending. I don't think I need a sad Nicholas Sparks movie tonight."

Travis chuckled. "My sisters loved it. I think they have the hots for Scott Eastwood, though. I'll check with one of them to make sure it ends on a high note." It would give him a chance to tell them about the letter, even though he didn't have much more information to share.

"Great," Katie said as she crossed the room toward the hallway. "Chelsea only likes plain cheese pizza, so get two and make ours something more interesting."

"Sausage, onions, mushrooms, and..." He couldn't resist. "...green olives?"

She pivoted and glared at him before breaking out in a smile. "Busted. I thought I was going to die when you caught me about to toss a handful of those disgusting things over my shoulder and I was forced to eat them." She shuddered, but continued to grin. At least he'd lightened her mood. "Chelsea loves them. Which reminds me, you could put green olives on her cheese pizza, since I don't have any here. I need to get some more."

"I'll put it on the list for the next trip to the store." He tapped his temple since he played a game with being able to memorize his grocery list. Kept his mind sharp.

"I'll hold the popcorn bowl between you two." God, that sounded a lot hokier than he'd intended, but Katie smiled wider as she shook her head, making it worth a moment of embarrassment.

On his way out to the barn to greet Melissa, Travis couldn't wait for tonight to come. Maybe it would take Katie's mind off both the letter and Sunday's visit with his family.

Only thing that would make the evening better would be if they could be together as a family like this permanently, not just during his quasi-vacation. Of course, he couldn't stay away from his business forever, even if Jackson was doing a great job of running the place without him.

Already the tug of war between his two greatest responsibilities had begun. He was going to have to come to some decisions about the future—and soon. But not until after the meeting with his family.

He had no doubts that Chelsea would be accepted by them. Katie, on the other hand…well, that might be a different story. Oh, his parents would be welcoming, but he was worried about Emmy. She'd taken it particularly hard when Katie had dumped him. She tended to be fierce in her loyalty and protectiveness for family and had come to her older brother's defense on more than one occasion.

He'd set the tone for Sunday, which would probably mean making a few more phone calls before they showed up on his parents' doorstep. Travis didn't like leaving anything to chance.

Chapter Twenty-Six

"I've sure made a mess of things," Ben muttered to himself as he watched Kate walk down the hallway toward her office. Instead of going in, she went upstairs, her shoulders sagging under the weight of the day's revelations, he supposed. In her bedroom, she retrieved the letter from her mother again, holding the envelope up to her face as she breathed deeply, eyes closed.

Then she took the paper out of the envelope and her phone from her pocket. Was she going to call the number now? Hell, it probably wasn't in use any longer, but he wished Kate would at least give it a try. Knowing she was ready to reconnect with Gail would help him convince Gail to reach out.

She checked the number at the end of the message and punched it into her phone then pocketed the phone again.

Ben felt deflated after getting his hopes up. What was Kate afraid of? Gail, too, for that matter? That letter confirmed that her mother still loved her. Wanted to be a part of her life. What more did she need?

"It's been twenty-two years, man. Cut 'em some slack."

Ben turned to see that Danny had joined him. How much had he witnessed of the goings-on in here today? Did he know about the letter?

"At least you managed to get the letter in front of her."

Apparently so.

"But you sure were a piece of work, Ben. That was one of the most contemptible things I've ever seen anyone do to a loved one—and I've seen plenty, believe you me."

"You don't have to kick me. I'm already down."

"Well, just pick your ass back up because your mission won't be completed until those two reunite. How much time do you think we have left before…?"

Ben shrugged, but appreciated the *we* in Danny's question. He wasn't sure he could fix this mess on his own anymore. "Obadiah isn't letting on but reminds me every time I see him that I can't pussyfoot around."

"Sure doesn't sound good." Danny acknowledged.

Returning his focus to his daughter, he watched Kate pluck a tissue from the box on the dresser, dab at her eyes, and blow her nose.

"I'm afraid she's going to bury her feelings around Travis and Chelsea and pretend her world hasn't just collapsed. That's always been her method of functioning in the past."

"Gee, wonder where she got that from?"

Ben gave it some thought. "You're probably right. I taught her that, too."

"Why do you suppose you did that?"

Ben had never been one to analyze things in life, but the afterlife was all about going over what he'd done while incarnate and figuring out how to move his soul forward on its path. "Probably had to do with my own parents deserting me as a kid. My grandparents took me in on this very farm," he said, waving his arm to indicate the place, "and loved me as much as anyone could. I was eight. Spent a few nights in foster care before my grandparents could come to Cincinnati to get me. But growing up, I always felt like I had to toe the line and keep my emotions under control for fear I'd drive them away, too."

"What makes you think you were responsible for your parents abandoning you? Maybe they were just selfish bastards or clueless about how to raise a kid."

"Well, we've reconnected on this side to hash out some of those issues. They've apologized, swearing it wasn't anything I'd done. But how do you convince a little kid of that?"

Danny nodded. "Yeah. We have our own skewed way of looking at things at that age. You think Katie blames herself for her mom leaving?"

"I think so. At least, she did until she found that letter. Maybe things will get better now that she knows it wasn't her doing that kept her mom away, but mine."

"You're fighting on two fronts, you know. Besides her mom, you also messed with Katie's relationship with Travis. I hope to hell you can see how wrong you were about his ability to be an excellent husband and father."

"Now, wait a minute. I only did what Kate told me to do. She said, 'Send him away if he shows up. Don't tell him where I am.' I just followed her wishes."

"But you helped convince her that if she told him, he'd eventually resent being tied down, didn't you?"

"Oh, yeah, I guess I did." Was there no end to the lives he'd messed up? "I never saw how good they were together even before the split." The man sure did take awful good care of her now from what Ben could see. Looks like Ben had been wrong about him all along.

Kate laid the letter down again, and this time she did go into the office to send an email before heading out to the arena for an afternoon of lessons. Ben and Danny hung around the house. He just didn't want to see the hurt on his little girl's face anymore.

Something triggered his argumentative side. "If Travis is so into having a relationship again, when in tarnation is he going to make an honest woman out of Kate?" Ben wasn't sure yet that he'd be the man for her, but she'd obviously never shown any interest in anyone else in all these years.

"What are you—blind or merely oblivious? The man's been shot down once by her. Maybe he's a little gun-shy, although I get the feeling something big happened between them last night while I was in a session with my spirit guide. He's got a spring in his step I haven't seen in a while."

There certainly hadn't been a bounce in his daughter's step when he'd seen her earlier.

"Maybe I've been wrong all this time about Travis and Katie." Danny said.

"How so?"

"I'm beginning to think she's a mite bitter and distrustful for someone as saintly as Travis to be saddled with."

"Now, wait a minute, there!" Ben would have knocked the younger spirit on his ass if Danny had one. "They don't come any better than Kate. She wasn't always like this, you know. It's my own fault she goes around not trusting anyone with walls around her heart."

"She could change if she wanted to. She still has free will. If I can overcome the shortfalls of my upbringing, she can, too."

Ben wondered what he'd been through, but before he could ask, Danny continued. "Yeah, if he'd listen to me, I'd tell Travis to cut bait and run. Not from Chelsea, of course. He's never going to turn his back on his daughter." Ben seethed, but Danny wasn't finished yet. "When's Travis gonna see that Katie doesn't have the capacity to love him the way he deserves to be loved? Not if she keeps running away from him whenever he gets too close."

"Enough already! My Kate's never been good at dealing with messy things like emotions, thanks to me. Stop blaming her. Sure, she's running scared right now with so much on her plate—integrating Travis into their lives, deciding whether she wants to find her mother, and facing Travis's family on Sunday." Ben stood down. "Damn it, the only thing I can see that will break down her walls is for her to reunite with her mother. Somehow, Gail holds the key here. She'll need someone strong like Travis with her to face her fears." He couldn't believe he'd just admitted that she needed Travis Cooper.

Danny grinned and winked. "Then what are you standing here jawing with me for?"

Had Danny been provoking him into action and to get him to

sanction Kate and Travis being together? Maybe Ben needed to visit Gail again. Before he could act, Kate surprised him when she entered the kitchen. He had no concept of time, but it was still afternoon judging by the light. "I thought she told Travis she had Melissa booked for lessons all afternoon."

"Maybe they're taking a break."

Before he could speculate further, Kate pulled her phone out of her pocket and sat down at the table staring at it. At last, she punched the green button to connect a call. Immediately after, she hit the red one to cancel the call before it could have gone through.

"Dammit, Kate! Stop torturing yourself and me like this!" He swatted at and knocked the basket of mail to the floor. Wow. That was a lot easier than anything else he'd tried to move from this side.

Kate stared at it a moment, glanced around, and then picked it up and placed it back on the counter before squaring her shoulders and attempting the call again. This time, she didn't end it before it had begun. Ben held his breath. She had a white-knuckled death grip on the phone.

Instead of a ringtone, though, the screeching sound of a disconnected phone number blared in the air.

"Crap," Danny said.

"I figured as much."

When Kate buried her head in her arms as the sound of her sobbing filled the room, Ben's heart broke—again. "That settles it. See you later."

In a flash, he was back in Gail's house. Without preamble, he said, "You need to call Kate."

She paused in brushing her teeth and turned toward where he hovered nearby. "I told you, she doesn't need me in her life anymore."

"Like hell she doesn't. Right now, she's back in Kentucky crying her eyes out because she finally found that letter you wrote for her twelfth birthday."

She squinted at him in the mirror. "How on earth did she get her hands on that one? I thought you sent them all back, although I moved around a lot, so figured some were just lost in the mail. Question is, why'd you hang onto it?"

Ben looked away, guilt still raw despite his lack of a body. "It caught me in a moment of weakness. I hadn't intercepted a letter from you in more than five years and was curious."

"You read it?"

He met her gaze, expecting anger but simply finding curiosity instead. Ben nodded. "It was so beautiful that I decided to hang onto it." He wouldn't tell her how many times he'd re-read the letter, up until he'd been stuck in that damned bed and unable to retrieve it from it's hiding place. But they weren't here to talk about an old fool like him. "Kate was moved by the words in that letter, too. Then it took her half the day to get up the courage to call you, only to find the damned phone number doesn't work anymore."

"Well, of course it doesn't. I was living in the hills outside San Diego in some fleabag apartment then."

"Call her."

"I don't have her number anymore."

He'd forgotten that he'd changed it a few months after Gail left, worried she might call and that Kate would pick up the phone. She'd begun to get on with her life without a mom, and he hadn't wanted to disrupt her life again. Apparently, Gail had called, though, or how would she know it didn't work? "Call information. Or look on the computer. Kate Michaels in Midway. Come on, Gail. She needs you."

Gail rinsed the toothbrush under the water and replaced it in the holder. She walked right through him on her way to the bedroom, her movements slow and labored. "What would I say to her after what I did?" she asked as she sat on the edge of the mattress trying to catch her breath.

"There's only one thing she needs to hear—that you never stopped loving her." A tear trickled down her cheek, ripping his heart out. He hovered on the bed beside her and wrapped an ethereal arm around her. "Take out your anger and revenge on me, Gail. Not on Kate."

She went to the closet to pull out a long, flowing dress to wear. "How could I be angry at Kate? She's the other victim of your selfishness."

He'd hurt both of them beyond belief and might have to spend eternity atoning for what he'd done. "Then why won't you call her? She needs her mother right now."

Daggers shot from her gaze. "If I thought it would begin and end with a phone call, I'd pick up the phone in a second. But I told you I don't want her to know everything about my past. Let her live with the illusions of her childhood memories."

"What could you have done that's so bad?" She stared at him long and hard but remained silent. Had she resorted to drug abuse? Prostitution? What? She didn't seem to be doing either since he'd come back out here. "Whatever it was, that was a long time ago. Call her."

She walked behind the Chinese screen in the corner, tossing her gown over the top as she dressed for the day. He waited only to have her come around the screen to say, "I'm going to have to think about it."

"Well, don't take too long." He couldn't tell her that he suspected her time on earth was coming to an end or that he thought he'd been sent here, in part, to be around when she crossed over. She'd been disowned by her family when she'd chosen her hippie way of life. Kate and Chelsea were the only family she had left. Obadiah had told him this was his chance to make amends to her in some small way.

Pretty damned sad he had no more control than this. If only...

No sense mulling over all that again. His primary mission was to make sure these two reunited, whether by phone or in person, before it was too late.

How on earth had he ended up with two of the most stubborn women known to man in his life?

Chapter Twenty-Seven

The following Sunday, Kate had a knot the size of a basketball in her stomach when Travis pulled his Sierra into the drive of the familiar red brick house off Dixie Highway. Being here brought back memories of the times he'd brought her home with him to be with his family. Travis was the oldest, followed by Clint three years later and the triplets two years after that.

"I'm scared, Mom. What if they don't like me?" The quiver in Chelsea's voice sent Kate's heart rate into overdrive.

Kate turned toward the back seat, as Travis assured her, "They're going to love you."

She added, "How could they not? Just be yourself, sweetie."

She pulled the door handle before stopping. "Wait! What am I supposed to call them?"

Kate looked toward Travis. Well, Erik, Clint's oldest, calls them Gramma and Pop-Pop. How does that sound?"

She seemed to mull it over, then nodded. She took another deep breath and, when she opened her door, they did the same and climbed out of Travis's truck. He took Chelsea's hand as they walked to the front door. Kate lagged behind, wishing she could be anywhere but here. She'd sent up a dozen prayers in church this morning that today would be a good one, but didn't expect to be welcomed with open arms.

Inside the house, she stood back and watched as introductions were made. Tears flowed from the adults as Chelsea was wrapped into one hug after another. First, her grandparents. Then two of her aunts,

Emmylou and Shania. And lastly, her uncle, Clint; his wife, Susan; and their two toddlers. Chelsea's family had grown exponentially in a matter of minutes. Travis had told them earlier that Tanya, the third triplet, was away on business in Canada, or she'd have been here, too.

Once she'd met everyone, Chelsea took a deep breath. She gave Kate a deer-in-the-headlights expression at the enormity of the occasion. When Loretta asked her about her horses, though, she beamed a smile at her gramma and rambled for ten minutes about them. Kate relaxed somewhat. So much love in this room directed at Chelsea, who deserved every ounce.

Guilt washed over Kate again for having kept Chelsea all to herself all these years. But what's done was done. Moving forward, Kate would give them as many opportunities as they wanted to spend time with Chelsea. The Coopers were only an hour away from the farm, and allowing them to spend time with Chelsea would be one more way to make amends for Kate's fear-fueled selfishness that had kept Chelsea away from her father and his family.

Loretta crossed the room and opened her arms to Kate, who walked into them. "It's been too long, Katie." Wrapped in a bear hug from Travis's mom, Kate nearly lost it. The years apart evaporated. She returned the woman's embrace, and the two of them held on. Kate's heart overflowed, feeling as if she'd come home again.

When they separated, she saw tears in Loretta's eyes, too. "Chelsea's beautiful and so sweet. I can already tell you've done a great job raising her."

Kate forced the words around the lump in her throat. "Thanks for having us, Loretta." She glanced at Chelsea, who was talking to Travis's sisters and sister-in-law, her daughter's hands flying animatedly. "Chelsea needs you, Joe, and your family so much. I'm sorry I didn't tell you about her sooner."

Loretta raised her hand and graciously waved away the apology. "The important thing is that you've brought her to us now."

A strange whining made Kate spin around just as Mayze, the

Cooper's Great Pyrenees, bounded from the hallway into the living room to greet them. The dog whimpered as she jumped up on Kate, nearly knocking her down as she lavished Kate with love. "Hey, girl. You remember me?" After all these years, Kate couldn't believe it.

Loretta tried to pull the dog away. "Mayze, get off her. Sit!" The dog ignored her mistress as she continued to lick Kate's face. "I'm sorry, Katie."

Kate laughed for the first time in days. "It's okay, Loretta. I don't mind."

"What's gotten into her? At her age, she barely moves more than from her food and water dishes to her bed. Why, she's behaving like a puppy again." Mayze had been a puppy when Travis first brought Kate here for visits. Apparently, the dog had imprinted on her. "Clearly, she's missed you."

"I missed her, too." *And your entire family.* But she didn't say that aloud because it was her own fault she'd been cut off from them.

"If you'll excuse me," Loretta said, "I have to put something in the oven."

"Need any help?"

"Oh, no. You stay here and get reacquainted with everyone." Loretta left the room to go into the kitchen around the corner, patting Chelsea's shoulder as she walked by.

Kate stood and glanced around the room, making eye contact with Travis, whose smile faded before he broke away from the chattering crowd to head her way.

"You okay?" His hand brushed her upper arm.

Why'd he have to ask that? The backs of her eyelids stung, and she turned her attention to Mayze again before making a mess of her makeup in front of him. God, she hated wearing makeup.

Kate nodded curtly.

"Thank you."

His words caught her by surprise, and she met his gaze. "For what?" She'd hurt him and his family terribly. How could he be thanking her?

"I haven't seen my parents this happy since Tanya changed her mind about eloping two years ago."

"I'll bet your mother would have hated missing out on planning a big wedding for each of her girls."

He shook his head and grinned. "It wasn't the wedding so much as the fact that Mom didn't care for the guy." Loretta? Seemed out of character for her to interfere or take sides. "I have to agree he was a bit of a horse's ass. Some guy she works with in Chicago. I was glad she came to her senses in time, too."

Kate had to wonder how his family would feel if Travis ever asked her to marry him. Once again, guilt washed over her. She wouldn't blame them for holding a grudge against her. Not that Travis seemed to hold onto hurt or anger long. Perhaps that was a trait he learned from his parents.

Swallowing past the lump in her throat, she glanced at her daughter. Although Chelsea had asked her to come along for support, she didn't need her at all. In so many ways, she was stronger than Kate. Her "baby" was growing up right before her eyes.

Rubbing at the ache in her chest, Kate fought the urge to flee. She longed desperately to leave, but didn't want to be far away if Chelsea had a momentary meltdown.

Unfortunately, the only person in danger of that seemed to be Kate herself.

"You sure you're okay?"

She nodded quickly. "I'll go see if your mom needs any help."

Kate nearly raced into the hall and around the corner to the kitchen with Mayze plastered against her leg as if afraid she'd disappear again if she let Kate out of her sight. She had no idea Mayze had been so attached to her.

"Relax, old girl," Kate said, petting the dog. "I'm not going anywhere." Kate hadn't had a dog at the farm since George, the Border Collie she'd raised from a pup, passed away from cancer at fourteen.

She'd found it unbearable to lose him and hadn't wanted to adopt another furbaby since then. Maybe she should reconsider that now.

In the kitchen, she quickly ascertained that Loretta had everything under control. *Thank God.* "Surely there's something I can do to help."

Loretta patted her on the back. "Nonsense. You're our guest."

"Well, then, if you don't mind, I'll get out of your hair and go outside."

"You're never in the way." Loretta glanced toward the patio doors. "As for Joe, give him a little time. He's being a big old grouchy Papa Bear today, but I'm sure once he sees where your heart lies, he'll warm up to you."

With that warning, Kate had no intention of seeking out the man when she went into the backyard. She really just needed a breather and to hide away from everyone else. Large family gatherings for an introvert like her were physically and emotionally exhausting—and something she was wholly unfamiliar with.

The oppressive humidity smacked her in the face when she opened the door, but she didn't care. Thankfully, Joe was talking with Clint. Near the playset, Susan pushed Olivia on the swing while Erik scooted up the slide backwards on his butt using his tennis shoes for traction against gravity. Had Clint's wife needed to escape the packed house of in-laws, too? Maybe she should go back inside and find a place to hide.

"Katie!" Susan called, waving her over. *Too late.* She crossed the yard to where she was playing with her kids, Mayze tagging along by her side.

"Olivia is adorable," Kate said. It was always a good bet to steer the conversation away from yourself and to endear someone to you if you compliment their kids. Not that the toddler wasn't completely adorable. Her smile was infectious, lifting Kate's spirits. "I can barely remember Chelsea being that little." While she'd gone over the early photos with Travis the other night, it seemed like a million years ago Chelsea was a baby.

"She keeps me busy, for sure," Susan said.

Kate hadn't met Clint's wife before, as he'd been a teenager when Travis and Kate first started dating in college. She didn't detect an accent. "Where are you from?"

"Up around Florence. Clint and I met at the University of Kentucky."

"Really? That's where I met Travis."

Susan began pushing the swing again after Olivia fussed then met Kate's gaze again. "If you don't mind my asking, are you two going to get back together?"

"I honestly don't know. We've both moved on with our lives." Geography was the least of their hurdles, although a substantial one. Kate absent-mindedly dug her fingers into Mayze's thick white fur and scratched her back.

"I worry about Travis."

Kate's hand stilled. "Why?"

She smiled and shrugged. "He's so driven, but doesn't take time to enjoy life. I didn't know him…" She looked away again. "…before he enlisted, but I understand he came back…"—Susan grew serious—"…changed."

"Not hard to imagine how something like combat would change a person."

"Oh, for real. I know it sounds selfish, but I'm glad Clint didn't follow in his dad and big brother's footsteps."

"I don't blame you, and it's not selfish at all. It's hard to raise kids alone."

Susan stared at her a moment. "Then why didn't you tell Travis about Chelsea?"

At least Susan was forthcoming. "I knew he'd have accepted the responsibility of fatherhood, but I just didn't want to keep him from pursuing what I thought was his dream to become a civil engineer and live in the big city."

Susan's attention shifted somewhere over Kate's shoulder a half-second before she heard Travis. "Hey, Susan. I see you've managed to wrangle this little one for a while." He reached out to stroke Olivia's cheek, and the little girl raised her hands toward him, bouncing in the swing and squealing. "Unca Tab! Unca Tab!" Laughing, he picked her up.

She had her hands in his mouth immediately and giggled when he gummed her fingers and pretended to eat them. Seeing him with the little girl brought tears to Kate's eyes and closed up her throat. No doubt he'd have been wonderful with Chelsea, too.

"She loves her Uncle Travis, even if she can't say his name yet."

He kissed Olivia on the cheek. "This little princess can call me whatever she wants." Travis glanced over at Kate and sobered. "Susan, do you want to hold her or should I put her back in her swing?"

Susan reached out to take the baby. "I'm going to see if I can put them down for a nap before we eat." Erik went down the slide for the umpteenth time since Kate had joined them. "Erik, let's go in, and I'll read you a story."

"With dinosaurs?" he asked as he picked himself up and ran over to her.

"Of course."

"And tornadoes!?"

"Well, I'm not sure I can find both in the same book, but we'll see." Susan grinned with an aside to Kate. "He's obsessed with dinosaurs and tornadoes lately."

When Susan and her kids had left, Travis turned to her. "Everything okay?"

"Stop worrying about me. I'm fine. Susan's really nice."

"Yeah, Clint's a lucky guy. He's got it all."

She heard the regret in his voice, but chose not to dwell on what-ifs. "How's Chelsea doing?"

"She and her aunts are playing Clue."

"That's one of her favorites, but not much fun with only two of us."

His eyes narrowed. "Well, maybe when I come back for a visit, we can play."

She wondered how often he'd want to come up. "Still heading home tomorrow?"

He nodded. "I need to make an appearance on each of the job sites and check in with my subcontractors before letting my employees go on vacation for the first two weeks of July. But I should be able to come up again Saturday afternoon."

Kate had mixed emotions about his leaving as well as his returning. Having him around for almost two weeks had been both frustrating and oh so enjoyable, but Chelsea would be heartbroken the next four days. Kate would be tied up with Melissa all weekend in the final training sessions before the Junior League competition next week.

Needing some space, Kate said, "Why don't you go hang out with your dad and Clint? I'm just going to sit over there at the empty picnic table and check in with Miguel to be sure everything's all right."

"He seemed pretty capable. I'm sure he'll be able to handle anything."

She smiled unapologetically. "Indulge me."

Travis grinned. "Big families can be a bit overwhelming to an only child, I guess."

He always seemed to tap into what she was feeling. "Thanks for understanding."

She chose the table farthest away from the grill and, within a matter of minutes, had been assured that everything at the farm was fine. When she glanced up, she saw the three men standing around the grill watching the chicken cook and catching up.

Peering at the other picnic table, she noticed Chelsea deep in conversation with two of her aunts, Emmy and Shania. When had they come outside? Kate must have zoned out for a while, but the mental break from the Coopers had done her good. She could engage again now.

Chelsea was animated as she said, "Daddy's promised to buy me my own show horse as soon as we can find the right one."

Kate cringed inwardly, but forced a smile to her face. She didn't want to be the bad guy when the time came to tell Chelsea a new horse wasn't in the cards, but Travis had insisted she wait and let him find the best time to inform her that they'd decided there wouldn't be a horse in the near future. Truthfully, Kate suspected he was hoping to win Kate over to his side, but the longer Chelsea went on believing she was getting this expensive horse, the more difficult it would be for her to accept reality.

This was their first major challenge, and already Kate and Travis disagreed on how to parent Chelsea. How many other things would they clash on? It had been a lot easier when she had sole responsibility and made every decision concerning Chelsea. Not necessarily better, though.

Kate walked up behind Chelsea and squeezed her shoulders before taking a seat on the bench next to her daughter and facing Travis's sisters. Chelsea gave her a sidelong glance and smiled. "Mom's a great trainer. She's going to let me work with one of her best horses this week, Chula. This one might make it to Louisville someday." Kate had always dreamed of a run for the World Championship.

Hoping to keep the conversation light, Kate said, "Chelsea's one of my best students. I hope to have her competing regionally in the coming year." Kate had no shortage of horses like Chula who needed to compete in order to raise their potential for sale later on, and Chelsea should be able to bring home a number of ribbons. On this point, she and Travis could agree. Chelsea would begin competing this fall. "Perhaps you'll get a chance to see her compete sometime."

Emmy was the first to speak, directing her comment to Chelsea. "We'd love to be there to watch, Chelsea."

"For real?" Chelsea seemed shocked and excited at the same time. "That would be a-maz-ing! How about Aunt Tanya? When will I get to meet her?"

"She's the Chief Operating Officer for an international corporation in Chicago," Emmy said, "so she can only make it to Louisville a few times a year."

"But she already knows about you and is excited to meet you," Shania added. "Maybe she can make it to one of your shows, too, with enough notice. Especially if it's not far from Chicago."

"Mom, are there any shows I can do up there?"

"Sure. Lots are held in Illinois and even Wisconsin."

"Awesome!" Chelsea's excitement was contagious. She hadn't realized how eager Chelsea was to compete, but then it was probably because she expected to own a prestigious show horse any time now.

Shania squeezed Chelsea's hand. "As soon as you have show dates and times set, let us know so the whole family can block them off on our calendars. Trust me, the Coopers will be there in force."

Emmy added, "I hope we'll get to see you outside the horse arenas, too." She glared at Kate before schooling her features, taking her by surprise a moment. Up to this point, everyone had been extremely polite, but soon Emmy smiled at Chelsea again. "Anytime you'd like to stay at our place for a sleepover or girls' weekend, you're welcome."

Chelsea looked toward her mom, waiting for Kate to give a nod of approval. Once she did, Chelsea faced her aunts again. "Hanging out with you sounds like a lot of fun. We can play Clue again. I can't wait!"

"We have a ton of board games," Shania said. "And can play with makeup and hair. Maybe even go shopping."

Chelsea squealed with delight. "I can't wait!"

When Travis called Chelsea over to the grill, the girl jumped up without a second glance. "Be right back!"

Kate wrung her hands in her lap—out of their sight under the table. Hoping to ease her anxiety, she first met Shania's gaze before turning to Emmy. "Thanks for making Chelsea feel so welcome. She's over the moon."

Neither woman smiled back. "She's part of our family...finally," Emmy said.

Ouch. Not totally unexpected—or undeserved—but at least the rest of the family hadn't treated her with such scorn. The triplets were only five years younger than Kate. If she'd married Travis all those years ago, they'd have become sisters to her. She'd already been growing fond of the three of them while dating Travis. Probably not much chance of that bonding happening now.

Why not deflect their anger toward a more professional conversation?

"Travis says you're working on finding my mom. I guess no news is bad news in my case."

Shania's shoulders relaxed; she'd never been confrontational or around anyone who was. "I'm sorry, but we haven't been able to locate her yet."

Emmy chimed in, "We've tracked her to Reno in about 2000, but the trail ended with no clue where she went after that. She may not be using the same name." The two of them shared a knowing glance before turning to her again. "How far do you want us to take this search?"

Did they know something they didn't want to share? "Well, I'd love it if you dug up any information about her. I'd especially like to know if she's still alive. The last contact I had with her was a letter she wrote in the Nineties, and she lived in Escondido then."

Emmy nodded. "Yeah, she showed up in the utility records for about three years there. She seemed to move around a lot."

Which was one of the reasons her mom left her and Daddy in the first place.

"I can take bad news as well as good."

They merely nodded. "We'll let Travis know what we find."

"I'd prefer you tell me. Can I share my phone number with you?"

They conferred silently before Shania said, "Well, we found something this morning that we haven't told Travis about."

Kate's spirits lifted. "Really? What?"

They exchanged another cryptic look, making Kate more nervous before Emmy said, "Did you know your mother was a prostitute?"

"What?" Kate's heart pounded so loudly she didn't even hear the word she'd spoken, but when Shania opened her mouth to answer her, Kate knew she must have.

"She was arrested on the charge in Reno, but jumped bond before being convicted."

Her mother had a warrant out for her arrest? Somehow this was the last thing she'd expected to learn about her. Or was this some kind of sick game they were playing? Obviously, the two sisters were angry at how she'd broken it off with Travis, but surely they wouldn't concoct such a story out of spite. Their professional reputations were at stake.

"She completely disappeared before her trial," Emmy added. "My guess is that she's assumed a new identity, which is going to make it even harder to find her. If you still want to."

Kate's hands grew numb before she remembered to breathe. *Did* she still want to find her? What had her mother become—or had she been a questionable character all along that Daddy had tried to shield Kate from?

Somehow, though, Kate couldn't mesh the image of a street hooker with the fresh-faced, free-spirited, joyful woman in the photos she cherished.

"We'll have to tell Travis something. After all, your mother is Chelsea's other grandmother, so he has a right to know what she's like before he allows Chelsea to meet her." Emmy smirked as if she found some kind of sick joy in this.

"I'll inform Travis when you find out more."

"Keeping more secrets from him, Katie?" Emmy asked.

Perhaps she needed to clear the air with these two if they were going to remain civil for Chelsea's sake. Kate leaned forward, keeping her voice low. "I've apologized to Travis for keeping Chelsea to myself all these years. We've decided it's best for *her* if we move forward and not dwell on the past."

Emmy glanced in the direction of the grill—whether at Travis, Chelsea, or both, Kate didn't know—then directed her attention to

Kate again. "You broke him."

Travis was the most together person she knew, other than Chelsea. "What are you talking about?"

"He'd never have gone into the Guard if you hadn't dumped him. He hasn't been the same since."

Susan had said something similar, so apparently it was no secret to family members whatever had happened. Hadn't he told them about the 9/11 Memorial and the people he'd met in New York City who had influenced that decision to enlist? If not, it wasn't Kate's place to enlighten them. If they blamed her for putting him in harm's way, no wonder they had such animosity toward her.

"I suggest you talk to Travis sometime about his reasons for joining." The Army National Guard was one of the things he was most proud of. How dare his sisters make it sound as though he'd only joined on the rebound from their breakup?

Mayze whined as if sensing Kate's discomfort. She reached down to absently dig her fingers into the dog's thick fur and took a breath before saying anything more. Yet something gnawed at her. Hadn't Travis enlisted on the 9/11 anniversary? The internship would have ended six weeks earlier.

"He drank heavily for a month after he'd been sent home early from the internship," Shania said in a whisper, her eyes brightening with unshed tears. "We were afraid we'd lose him one night."

Wait. Early? "He didn't finish the internship?" Why hadn't he told her that?

"How could he?" Emmy said. "He was devastated. He'd planned this whole perfect life—one that included you. Suddenly, that was yanked out from under him."

No! They had it all wrong. They had to. "But all he ever talked about was that internship leading to something more. About moving to the city to make a name for himself." Kate had never promised to be a part of a life in the big city. Sure, they'd talked about marrying one day, but in truth, she'd never expected it would happen because their dreams led in opposite directions. One of them would have had to make a huge sacrifice so she'd decided to make it for him.

Perhaps breaking it off with him had more to do with her inability to commit to a life away from her farm than her trying to save Travis from giving up on his dreams.

Kate needed some space but would extend an olive branch before going inside. "If you'll excuse me, I'm going inside to freshen up before we eat." She started to climb off the bench. "Travis is probably planning to be at my farm most weekends. You're welcome to arrange visits around the same time." With her training schedule and a bit of luck, Kate hoped to be away during those times.

"We have a lot of lost time to catch up on," Emmy said, narrowing her eyes, "and we don't see Travis nearly enough anymore, either."

Kate forced a smile and nodded before starting toward the house. Mayze followed her to the patio and inside. She was determined to weather the bombardment of information just as she always did—by compartmentalizing her emotions and grinning until her cheeks ached.

Then she'd have a talk with Travis about what she'd learned.

As for Travis's sisters, future contact would be minimal. Chelsea would be the one to set the tone. She obviously adored her newfound family. Kate would do nothing to tarnish their image for her daughter.

Please, God, let the rest of this day hold no more surprises. She was done and just wanted to go home. How much more would she have to deal with before she could crawl into bed tonight?

Chapter Twenty-Eight

D ad insisted on showing Chelsea his trick to grilling the perfect hamburger. Travis had been given the same lesson a dozen times in his teen years.

"Daddy, why don't I come stay with you over the Fourth of July weekend?"

What would Katie say? Should he consult with her first?

"Please," she begged. "I want to go fishing with you on that lake you told me about."

"Not only is the fishing good there," Dad said, "but so's the swimming."

"Oh, I've never gone swimming in a lake before. And I'll bet the fireworks there are way bigger than the ones in Frankfort or Georgetown."

Travis glanced over at the picnic table where Katie sat with his sisters. They seemed to be talking civilly. He didn't want to intrude. He'd already gotten permission to see her that weekend at the farm. What difference would it make if they hung out in Nolensville instead?

"Sure, Chels. I don't see why not."

Chelsea squealed and wrapped her arms around him. He hugged her back and glanced over her shoulder at Katie. Judging by the rigidness of her back, something was going sour. Abruptly, Katie stood and walked toward the house with Mayze in tow. Emmy and Shania met his gaze and shrugged innocently.

Not good. Despite his warning them over the phone and Mom's assuring him she'd had a talk with them earlier, too, he feared they hadn't listened to either of them. Especially Emmy, who could be as tempestuous as a badger when riled up. Emmy had harbored a grudge against Katie since the day she'd heard that the relationship had been broken off. A lot of bitterness had built up inside her over the years.

When his sisters headed toward the house as well, he let Chelsea go. "Why don't you continue with your grilling lesson? I need to check on something with Mom."

He excused himself and was on the patio a minute later. Even with the kitchen window closed, he heard Emmy's raised voice yelling Katie's name. He opened the sliding door to enter the great room his parents had built across the back of their house years ago to find his mom, sisters, and Katie standing around the island in the adjoining kitchen. Katie's ramrod straight back was turned toward him, her hands clenched at her sides.

"Remember your manners." Mom glared at both of his sisters, so maybe Shania had gotten a jab in, too. Emmy opened her mouth to say more until she saw Travis standing behind Katie and promptly took a sudden interest arranging the sliced tomatoes on the fixings platter.

Travis wrapped his arm around Katie and pulled her close as he bent to whisper in her ear, "You okay?"

Katie nodded, pulling away from him. "Everything's fine, Travis. You should be with Chelsea."

One thing he'd learned about Katie was that, when she said something was fine, it was far from it. Today should be filled with love and happiness—hell, his family was complete at last. Instead, the harmony was being ruined by petty blame and sniping. He needed to fix this.

First, he'd neutralize the oldest of the triplets. "Emmy, if you have a problem, you bring it to me. Leave Katie alone."

Katie turned to glare at him. "Travis, I can handle this," she gritted out. "Go back out to Chelsea. We're just having a little family disagreement here."

"You aren't part of this family, Katie," Emmy shouted. "You made that choice a long time ago."

Katie cringed, the blood draining from her face, although Emmy probably couldn't see she'd made a direct hit on her target.

"Emmylou Cooper," Mom began, "if you weren't twenty-nine years old, I'd take you over my knee myself. Today is difficult enough for Katie without you making it impossible with your insensitive remarks. If you can't show our guest some compassion and understanding, then you need to leave my home and come back when you grow up. You weren't raised to—"

Emmy's eyes and mouth opened wide at the same time. "Mom, how can you pretend not to be hurt by what she did to Travis? To our whole family?"

Mom set down the head of iceberg lettuce carefully, as if afraid she'd crush it to a liquid, and took a deep breath. "Because today I met my oldest granddaughter for the first time, and *I* couldn't be happier. Don't you *dare* take away my joy by sullying this occasion in any way."

God, I love that woman.

"I will thank Katie to my last breath that she chose to have Chelsea." Apparently, Mom hadn't finished having her say yet. "She had other options, but chose to keep and raise her to be the fine young girl we've all welcomed into the family today. I'd say she did a finer job mothering Chelsea than I've done with you two girls, given your remarks today. But I want you to remember that Katie is just as much a part of this family as Chelsea is—or you are."

As his sisters sputtered apologies to their mother, Mom's words made one thing crystal clear to him. As soon as he could get Katie alone, he'd explore it…which might be sooner than expected. "Would you like to leave now or right after we eat?" he asked Katie.

"We aren't leaving until Chelsea's ready to go." Katie's words were slow, deliberate. "Your mom and dad went to a lot of work to have this get-together. And Chelsea's having a great time. If I get my feelings hurt in the bargain, so be it. I can deal with it myself."

So she *had* been hurt by his sisters. He turned to them. "You two owe Katie an apology, too." When they met his gaze, fire spit from their eyes, but he gave as good as he got until they averted their heads in shame. "Not tomorrow—now," he demanded.

"Travis, please, stop this," Katie pleaded. Her hand shook in his as she fought to pull away from him.

"Not until they apologize."

Mom cleared her throat. "Katie, I'm sorry that my daughters have made you feel unwelcome and uncomfortable in my home."

"Thank you for that, Mom," Travis said for her, "but you aren't the one who needs to say you're sorry."

The standoff dragged out as the tension mounted. When Emmy opened her mouth to speak, he didn't know if she'd erupt in more anger or do what he wanted. But peacemaker Shania was the first to spit out the words he wanted Katie to hear.

"I'm sorry, Katie. I don't want you to feel unwelcome here," Shania said.

Katie relaxed a little. "It's all right. No need to—"

"Your turn, Emmy." Releasing Katie's hand, he rubbed her back up and down in long strokes to try and ease her shaking. He just hoped things didn't go any farther south in here and that Chelsea stayed outside until this ruckus was over. He could never predict what would come out of Emmy's mouth.

Emmy shot a few more daggers at him then Katie before grudgingly directing her attention toward Katie. "I'm sorry if you're feeling hurt, Katie."

"None of that non-apology crap. Take responsibility for your words and actions, and do it right."

"What about *her?*" Emmy glared at Travis, jabbing the air in Katie's direction. "Doesn't she owe Mom, Dad, and all of us an apology for robbing us of Chelsea? Where's *our* apology?"

Katie tried to step backward, but he pressed his palm against the small of her back. Was she trying to escape from them or him?

"Katie apologized to me earlier," Mom said, "and I'm sure she's made her peace with Travis. But I don't see that she owes either of you anything whatsoever. You need to get over yourselves and focus on what's important—welcoming Chelsea and Katie into this family wholeheartedly."

Emmy fumed but didn't make eye contact with Mom.

"Apologize today, Emmy," Travis said.

"I'm sorry—but I can't forgive her for what she did to you, Travis. Not the way she—"

"That's enough, Emmy!" The last thing he needed was for her to open old wounds. Travis bent to whisper in Katie's ear. "I'm sorry about this. This isn't who we Coopers are."

"This has festered a long time." She lowered her voice. "Let them vent. I just want it all to blow over before Chelsea gets wind of any tension. But you and I need to talk. Alone."

He couldn't agree more. Not waiting for Emmy to come down off her high horse—or to say another hateful word—he tried to catch Katie by the hand. "Let's go."

But Katie dug in her heels. "I'm not leaving, Travis! We came here so that Chelsea could get to know her family better."

"You said we need to talk. I agree." She didn't balk this time, although she wasn't exactly walking without resistance. He tossed over his shoulder toward Mom, "We'll be back in time to eat."

"Should be ready in twenty minutes!" she called out, and he heard the humor in her voice. No doubt she looked forward to setting Emmy straight while they were gone.

He continued to propel Katie through the media room as they circled around the interior of the house the long way in order to avoid going through the kitchen. As they neared the front door, Katie sputtered, "Wh-wh-where are we going? Wh-what about Chelsea?"

He needed to calm down before he ruined it, but he'd never been more sure of anything than he was now. Outside, he ignored the humid air as he set off at a brisk pace to put some distance between them and the ugliness inside his parents' house. He was practically dragging Katie down the sidewalk and forced himself to slack off the pace.

Halfway down the block, Katie yanked her hand away from his and squared off with him. "I never should have let you and Chelsea talk me into coming here. This day should have been one for you all to welcome Chelsea into the family. I don't belong here."

"Bullshit, Katie. You're Chelsea's mother, and your place is by my side." This wasn't how he pictured this moment coming off, but he wanted more than anything to make them a real family. The only way he could see that happening would be for the two of them to have a solid commitment. Taking a deep breath, he said, "We need to get married." Well, crap. He hadn't intended to ask her like that.

She cocked her head and stared as if he'd just grown two more heads. "Are you out of your cotton-pickin' mind?"

The look of disbelief on her face made him realize he could have worded his marriage proposal a lot better than that. But what's done was done. "I've never been more sure about anything. Even more so than I was about my plans to propose when I came back from New York City."

Katie's jaw dropped, and her gaze grew distant. How could he salvage this wreck of a proposal before she said no?

The next words he spoke held more meaning today than they had the first time he'd uttered them back in college. He understood the importance of them now more than ever. "I love you, Katie Michaels. I always have, even when you didn't...love me back."

Don't remind her of that, asshole.

Butt out, Danny.

Katie continued to stare at him stupefied, and a niggling doubt lambasted him. Maybe she didn't share that level of feeling toward him now, despite what happened in the barn apartment the other night.

*   *   *

This careening roller-coaster of a day took a turn she hadn't expected in a million years. What on earth had gotten into Travis? Was he merely trying to fix the mess with his family? That was no reason to marry.

"You've got to be crazy if you think our getting married is going to change anything. Give them more time. They'll come around—and I'll just find something else to occupy my day the next time Chelsea wants to visit Louisville."

He raked his fingers through his hair. "This has nothing to do with Emmy and Shania. This is me finally stepping up and doing the right thing."

Katie rolled her eyes much like Chelsea would. God save her from a man on a mission to be honorable. Even his declaration of love seemed to be an afterthought. "Travis, I'm not marrying you to uphold whatever antiquated notion you have about responsibility and duty."

"Why not? It's what's best for Chelsea."

"Chelsea's stronger than you think. She's adjusting to everything perfectly well. Obviously better than the adults in her life seem to be."

"But she wants us to get back together."

"She also wants an expensive show horse, but she isn't going to always get what she wants."

He stared at the ground, breathing deeply as his nostrils flared. Was he trying to bring his temper under control—or perhaps think of how to counter her completely logical argument?

When he met her gaze again, the passion in his eyes struck her heart dead center. "Our being together as a family is what's best for us, too, Katie. After the other night, the way we picked right up where we'd left off, surely you can't deny that we still have feelings for one another."

"Sex and marriage aren't going to fix anything. If we married and wound up divorcing later, Chelsea would only be hurt worse. As it stands now, with us having separate homes, separate lives, I just think it's for the best. You can't tell me you're ready to give up your business in Nashville...or your home in Nolensville." Before he could argue further, she took his hand and said, "Why don't we head back to the

319

house? I don't want Chelsea to think we've deserted her."

Travis didn't budge. When he met her gaze once more, the torment in his eyes tore her apart. Something else was going on here, but she had no clue what. "Why now, Travis? Why can't this wait until we've had time to figure out what's best for us all?"

After a moment, he whispered, "Because I've lost too many of the people I've loved in this life. I don't want to lose you, too." His hand cupped her cheek. "Not again."

People he loved in the past tense. She closed the gap between them, rubbing her hand up and down his arm in comfort. Danny was at the top of that list. But an irrational fear of losing someone was no reason for them to marry, either. She gave him a lopsided grin. "I'm afraid you're stuck having me in your life, married or not, at least until Chelsea goes to college. Realistically, it will be much longer."

His thumb grazed over her lips, and she nearly lost her resolve and accepted his ridiculous proposal. With all the strength she could gather, she steeled herself so as not to cave into his charm.

"Katie, this isn't over. Granted, my method of proposing sucked today, but we're going to talk more about where we're headed when things aren't so emotionally charged."

Forcing a bigger smile, she pulled away from his touch, feeling bereft immediately. "Right now," she said, taking his hand once more, "we're heading back to your parents' house for a barbecue that I refuse to let be ruined. Your parents and Chelsea deserve that at a bare minimum."

"So do you," he said, before falling into step beside her. "If Emmy gives you any more lip and I'm not around, promise me you'll let me know."

"Travis, Travis. What am I going to do with you?" Katie shook her head sighed as they walked on in silence. "Let your sister blow off some steam. You should be thrilled to have a loyal sister who has your back." Should she bring up what Emmy had said in the backyard? Why not? "You know, it might help if you'd tell them you didn't join the

National Guard because you were rebounding from our relationship."

Travis stopped walking, and she did the same, turning to look up at him. "Is that what she said?"

"More or less. I think if you told them about the 9/11 survivors who influenced your decision…"

He squinted his eyes at her, as if trying to decide what to say. Kate swallowed hard, wondering what new bombshell was about to be dropped. "Breaking up with you was the hardest thing I'd had to face in twenty-one years of life. Emmy isn't completely off base."

He'd enlisted because of *her*?

"But I *was* influenced by the survivors I met and the time I spent at Ground Zero during my brief stay in New York."

"So you didn't finish the internship?"

He shook his head. "Only about a month, and I couldn't tell you the first thing I learned during that time. All I could think about was coming back to Kentucky and finding a way to win you over."

Kate raked her fingers through her hair, tugging the strands. They'd already been over this, but she hadn't understood how devastated he'd been until today. Emmy was right. "I could have gotten you killed."

He furrowed his forehead. "What are you talking about?"

"You joined the Guard and were sent to Iraq three times because of me."

He grinned. "No, I gave up my internship and spent a month wallowing in my sorrows because of you. Then I was watching the anniversary shows about 9/11 and saw someone I'd actually met while in New York, and the next day, I enlisted. I told you, I have no regrets about that. The Guard taught me a lot and I met some incredible people who became brothers and sisters for life."

She felt marginally better as they proceeded down the driveway and through the gate to the backyard. Mayze greeted her and Travis with enthusiasm, and Chelsea came over as well.

"I wondered where you two went. Pop-Pop said you took a walk."

She looked from Kate to Travis and back again, concern in her eyes.

Kate stroked her daughter's warm cheek, smiling, and searched her eyes to make sure she was okay, but all she saw was a happy sparkle in the girl's eyes.

"Grub's on!" Joe called.

"I see we came back just in time," Travis said, taking Chelsea's hand with his free one but hanging onto Kate's as well. "I want my two favorite girls on either side of me."

At his words, Kate saw Chelsea beam up at her father. Kate would need to have another talk with Travis about not getting the girl's hopes impossibly high and definitely insist that he not say a word about that ridiculous proposal he'd made a few minutes ago.

Needing some space to breathe, Kate excused herself. "Let me run inside and test before I eat." With her stress level through the roof, it would be hard to predict where she was on the scale. After injecting the necessary insulin, she went outside to join them.

The Cooper clan filled the two picnic tables, which had been butted up against each other. Kate saw there was no way she'd be able to squeeze in beside Travis. The only spot open was next to Emmy, and Kate felt her appetite disappearing despite how delicious everything looked and smelled.

"Katie, you sit here beside Travis." Clint winked at her and picked up his plate. Before she could tell him no, he'd already vacated the spot and moved down to the other end of the table next to Emmy. Gratefully, she took his seat.

Loretta was seated to Kate's right and Travis sat between Chelsea and Kate, just as he'd wanted. Joe sat across from Kate. After she'd filled her plate from all the dishes being passed around, Loretta leaned over and whispered, "Welcome back to the family, Katie."

Overwhelmed by the wild ride her emotions had taken today, Kate simply wrapped her arm around Travis's mom and patted her on the back. "Thanks, Loretta."

"Don't you worry about my girls," she whispered. "They're a little too spoiled by having had such an easy life, but you won't be the brunt of their mean-spirited behavior again. Not in my house, anyway."

Kate glanced down the table at Emmy and Shania, but neither met her gaze. She wondered what had happened while she and Travis were walking, but didn't want to ask.

"How's your sugar?" Loretta asked.

"Fine. I took some insulin so I wouldn't have to turn down all this delicious food. I see most things are okay on my diet, but then Travis told me you have diabetes, too." They compared stories about being diagnosed and treatments.

"Darlin', you've outdone yourself," Joe said, and Loretta beamed with pride.

Is that where Travis got the pet name darlin' for Kate? She glanced over at Travis to find heat smoldering from his eyes. Then he winked at her, and her heart dropped into her stomach.

"Y-yes, Loretta," Kate said, finding the words oddly comforting coming off her tongue. "Everything's wonderful. And, Joe, you and your helpers did a wonderful job at the grill. You'll both have to share your recipes."

Joe seemed slow to smile, but when he did, she knew it was genuine. "I have my newest apprentice to thank for these juicy burgers." Joe smiled at Chelsea, who blushed with a big grin.

"You've outdone yourselves, Mom and Dad," Travis said, followed by a chorus of praise from those at both tables.

The day was going to work out fine after all. Chelsea had gained a new extended family, one built on a strong foundation that could withstand whatever life threw at her. And by association, Kate was being adopted by that family, too. Well, by most of them.

"Chelsea's a lovely girl, Katie. I'm sure it couldn't have been easy for you, all alone."

Loretta's words were honest and real, just like her. She wasn't one to mince words or play games. Kate simply nodded. "My dad was around her first couple of years, but his health was already failing when

she was still an infant. Thankfully, Chelsea was an easy baby to raise."
Kate had been lucky in that regard.

"She must take after you," Loretta said. "Travis was one of those
colicky babies who never slept."

"Hey, Mom, don't ruin my image!" Travis said with mock distress.

Kate smiled as she turned toward him. "That explains a lot."

"What's that supposed to mean?" he growled in her direction.

"Just that you still don't sleep much at night. I've seen the light on
in the barn apartment well into the night." She hadn't shared that with
him before or asked why he couldn't sleep. Was it Danny? Such a
recent loss might result in a lot of torment. Did he blame himself?

As if caught in the act of doing something he shouldn't, his smile
faded and a look of desolation crossed his face. He glanced down at
his plate. "A lot on my mind lately, I guess."

She didn't understand the change in mood, but Joe asked her a
question about raising horses, and she spent the remainder of the meal
talking about Saddlebreds, always a safe subject.

Joe grew serious as he leaned forward. "Katie, you've raised a fine
young lady. Thank you for sharing her with us. I'll admit I had my
concerns when Travis called the other night, because I want what's
best for all my kids, but Travis couldn't do any better than with you."

She didn't know how to respond. Did he know Travis had proposed? Regardless, she was too choked up to say a word so merely
smiled with a nod.

Before she was ready, the meal came to an end. Because she'd had
little to do with the preparation, she insisted on helping to clean up.

In the kitchen, she divided leftovers to go to the various homes.
Judging by the amount of food not eaten, Loretta and Joe must have
prepared four times as much as they knew anyone would eat today, just
for this purpose. Afterward, while rinsing and stacking the dishes, she
turned to find Emmy staring at her.

"I'm sorry," she said to Kate. "I was upset imagining how hurt
Travis must have been when he learned about Chelsea, but if he isn't

upset, then I have no reason to be, either."

"Thanks, Emmy. Travis and I talked a bit about what you'd said, and I know if you ask him sometime, he can clarify some of your concerns about what happened back then." She didn't know what else to say, and their shaky truce wasn't to the point she was ready to hug her, but Emmy seemed more sincere this time. Some of the earlier tension evaporated. "And thanks for being so kind to Chelsea." That was all that mattered to Kate, that they love and accept her daughter.

Emmy smiled. "Chelsea's awesome. Smart. Talented. Grounded." She glanced away. "You did a great job."

Kate relaxed even more, giving Emmy a nod when no words would come to mind. At least she was making an effort. Maybe things would go more smoothly the next time they came together. She might actually be looking forward to that day—as long as it wasn't too soon.

Now that the day was almost behind them and she'd survived, she couldn't wait to head home. Tomorrow, after Travis left, Chelsea would be a little lost. Perhaps Kate could carve out some girl time just for them.

Chapter Twenty-Nine

As he took the exit toward the farm, Travis worried about how quiet Katie had been throughout the drive home. Chelsea sat in the backseat of his truck with earbuds in and her nose in her cell phone listening to music. The day had been a positive one for her, at least. Introducing her to his parents and the rest of his family had to be one of the proudest moments of his life.

But it had been hell for Katie. Emmy, who had a protective streak a mile long when it came to those she loved, had been particularly nasty. After dinner, while Katie and Chelsea were playing on the swing set with Erik and Olivia, Travis had pulled Emmy aside to remind her he could fight his own battles and take care of himself. Emmy surprised him by telling him she'd apologized to Katie. He wanted to ask Katie how she'd interpreted whatever Emmy said, but her eyes were closed with her head resting against the back of the seat. The stiffness in her posture told him she wasn't asleep. Softly, in case she'd fooled him and actually was asleep, he said, "Almost home. You okay?"

She drew a deep breath and stretched as if waking up. "I'm fine." Wasn't that Katie code for *I'm anything* but *fine*?

"I'm sorry about Emmy's behavior."

Her shrug seemed dismissive. "No need to be. She apologized while we were packing up the leftovers. We've called a truce."

Good. "Just know that, if it ever came to a choice between the two of you, she'd lose." He reached across to squeeze her arm, since her hands were folded in her lap beyond his reach.

Katie jaw dropped momentarily before she pressed her lips together. "I have no intention of standing between you and your family."

"I'm not asking you to. I just want you to know where I stand. Thanks for coming with us today. It meant a lot to Chelsea and me, even though it had to be rough for you." His parents seemed genuinely happy to see her again, though.

"I enjoyed most of the day." He pulled into the lane and drove up to park beside the house. He'd never been happier to see her place than tonight. It felt like home. He turned off the engine and sat there a moment simply staring at the wheel.

They removed their seatbelts. From the backseat, Chelsea said, "I'm starving, Mom."

She laughed. The kid had a healthy appetite. "We have no shortage of food in the cooler and all the bags back there." Katie picked up her purse from the floorboard and handed the house key to Chelsea over the backseat. "Why don't you open the door, sweetie?"

They exited as Miguel came out of the barn and greeted them. "Everything is fine. The horses are taken care of. I'll see you in the morning, Kate." He nodded in Travis's direction. "Travis," he said. The two had met briefly last night.

"Good night, Miguel," they said at the same time. Katie added, "Thanks for holding down the fort so we could get away."

"*De nada.*"

Chelsea came running back to the truck, saying loudly, "Daddy, I'll carry the cooler." Then she whispered, "I'll disappear tonight so you can talk to mom about my new horse."

Crap. Was there any chance of his convincing Katie after his first attempt failed? *Probably not.* But it was worth a try. The last thing he wanted to do was to disappoint Chelsea or have to go back on his word.

Chelsea carried the small cooler while Katie reached for the two bags from the backseat. "Here, let me get those." He followed them inside where Katie tested her glucose, she decided to have a late-night snack, too. Travis had an appetite like Chelsea's, so the three of them prepared leftovers and reminisced about the day until Chelsea yawned dramatically and claimed she was worn out and going to bed early.

After she kissed them both on the cheek and practically skipped out of the room, Katie said, "She certainly has more energy than I do if that's what she calls being worn out."

Travis smiled at her, hoping she didn't suspect anything was up, but then she grew serious. "Travis, earlier today, when I mentioned noticing you'd been up late at night while you were staying out in the barn, you seemed a little down. Was there anything you'd like to talk about?"

Side-tracked from thoughts of Chelsea's horse, Travis debated whether to open up to her about Danny. Maybe he'd gauge how much she might want to hear. "Actually, I don't sleep a lot anymore. Haven't for months. Three or four hours a night most of the time, then I may go for a couple of days where all I do is sleep so my body can catch up."

"That's not healthy, especially for someone working around construction sites."

"Yeah, I know." He'd been lucky so far, with the help of Jackson and even Sadie, Danny's dog. While not a trained service animal, Sadie instinctively alerted him when he was about to do something dangerous or careless. Maybe Danny was guiding the Golden Retriever from the other side. Whatever, more and more, he'd been spending time in the office to keep from hurting anyone. "Usually, it's thoughts of Danny that keep me up."

Not sure how much more he wanted to say, he stood and started clearing the table. Knowing Danny had found a way to communicate with him lately made his death not seem so final. And his buddy sure as hell had gotten through to Katie the other night, sharing information she wouldn't have known otherwise. When he'd tossed the paper plates and scraps, he turned to her. Drawing a deep, ragged breath, he admitted, "I'm ready to tell you more about Danny."

Meeting his gaze from where she was putting her water pitcher away, Katie closed the fridge. "I'd love to know more about him. He definitely has a strong, captivating personality."

Travis chuckled, some of the tension ebbing away. "One stubborn cuss, you mean."

She grinned back. "Let's say he's quite persuasive and won't take no for an answer."

God, I miss you, Danny.

Taking Katie's hand, he led her to the living room. He felt lost for a moment, but she prompted him to sit on the couch by choosing a spot on the end and tugging him downward.

"Tell me more about Danny."

Travis wondered where to start. "I was closer to Danny than I am with Clint in many ways, especially after serving in combat. We'd bunked together in boot camp. I was a few years older, but we both enlisted knowing it was a sure bet we'd be deployed—and served almost two tours together before he was injured. I had one more after that. Danny and I, we spoke in a kind of shorthand that cut to the chase of wherever we left off without skipping a beat."

"I'm glad you had each other."

"He was injured by the IED blast on a convoy between FOBs— forward operating bases—about halfway through our second tour. After his discharge from the hospital and the Army National Guard, he had a hell of a time getting back into the rhythm of civilian life."

"Small wonder. That's a lot for a kid to have to go through."

Hey, who's she calling a kid! I was almost twenty by then.

Travis smiled. Whatever Travis was about to say to Katie, apparently he'd be saying to Danny, too. "His back injury and leg amputation required a lengthy recovery and dozens of surgeries. When he lost his pre-deployment job, I hired him at my company, but I could soon tell he was struggling with an addiction to prescription pain meds."

Danny remained silent.

"I'm proud of you for hiring your fellow vets. Daddy would have appreciated that, too. He served in Vietnam and finding a job to supplement his farm income wasn't easy, especially after the tobacco growers' settlement. He admired anyone who chose military experience over civilian."

Old Man Michaels proud of him? *Yeah, right.* "It's not just their work ethic and skills, but there's a camaraderie and mutual respect among those of us who served that makes for a better work environment. We speak the same language. Of course, I can't discriminate against others, but vets rank a little higher in my estimation."

"Sorry I interrupted."

"No problem." Where was he? "Anyway, Danny never really let on how bad the pain was." *Something I can't quite forgive you for, Danny.* No response. Was he still listening? "He'd been legally prescribed too many opioids. May have even been stockpiling them, for all I know."

Travis raked his fingers through his hair as his heartbeat ramped up, robbing him of the ability to take a deep breath. "That day, when he didn't show up for work, I called to check on him." Katie's hand stroked his arm as if she'd guessed where this was headed. "Certainly not the first time he'd had a rough night and couldn't make it to work on time. I kept trying to reach him all day. By three o'clock, I became worried enough to knock off early so I could run by his apartment on the way home. He lived in Brentwood, about halfway between work and home." His lungs grew tight. "No one answered when I banged on the door, but we'd exchanged house keys long ago. We both lived alone and vowed to look out for the other and our properties. Jackson also has a key to my place."

Travis tried to drag air into his lungs, but no oxygen seemed to be left in the room. He'd never spoken in great detail about that afternoon before to anyone.

"So I let myself in."

*   *   *

Kate's hand stilled, as did her breathing. She waited for what she knew was coming, but didn't want to hear. Travis shouldered the burdens of obligation for family and friends, even when he had zero control over their situations and choices. Clearly, he was feeling a sense of responsibility—and guilt—over what happened. She squeezed his arm, hoping to reassure him that she was here to listen.

"I found him lying face down on the bed… I thought he'd passed out at first. I shook his shoulder to wake him up and knew immediately he was gone. Still, I called 9-1-1 and dragged him to the floor to perform CPR. Kept trying to bring him back until the paramedics showed up to take over and told me almost immediately it was too late. He'd been dead for hours, according to the medical examiner."

"Oh, Travis. I'm so sorry you had to be the one to find him like that." Tears filled her eyes. She wanted to wrap her arms around him, but decided she needed to be strong for him at least until he was able to get the story out. It had obviously been festering inside a very long time. But when she glanced at him, he didn't seem to be teary-eyed. She'd never seen him more deadly calm, in fact.

Poor choice of words.

He sighed. "Actually, I'm glad it was me who found him and not his sister. She's older than he is but has a form of autism. Peggy lives in a group home near him and sometimes visited his apartment unannounced."

He remained silent for a long moment. She wondered if he'd finished, but then he continued. "After his medical discharge, Danny received monthly benefits from the government. When he came to work for my firm, he had money deposited from every paycheck into Peggy's bank account. He knew that money would dry up when he quit working, though, so he took out life insurance policies from the government and my company in case anything happened to him. Of course, I'd have made sure Peggy was taken care of without it, but Danny was a proud man and wanted to take care of his own responsibilities."

"He sounds a lot like you." After having "met" Danny's spirit, she found it hard to refer to him in the past tense.

Travis shrugged, without remark. "Anyway, I have the same insurance policies he does…did. Neither would pay out for suicide within the first two years. About six years ago, during a particularly severe post-surgery depression, one of Danny's policies was nearing the date the clause would no longer affect a payout to beneficiaries. I worried he may take that route, so I confiscated his firearms. As far as I know, he never replaced them."

It sounded as though Travis had been pre-disposed to believing Danny might commit suicide; no wonder he jumped to the wrong conclusion. "I was so sure we'd gotten through to him."

"We?"

"Jackson, my foreman who served in Afghanistan, and me. The other vets on my crew, too. We try to be there for each other when anyone's having a tough time." He shook his head. "None of us saw this coming."

Kate remembered how adamant Danny had been about his death. "But I told you, he said it wasn't a suicide."

"Yeah. But I didn't know that back then."

"What made you draw that conclusion in the first place?"

"I found a half-empty bottle of prescription pain pills in the bathroom."

"Maybe he'd had it a while."

"Less than a week. Weird thing is we found other bottles in the apartment that were older and barely touched."

"Doesn't sound like he was overdoing it with pills. And he didn't take all the ones in the bottle you found?"

Travis shook his head.

"I agree with Danny. It sounds accidental to me," Kate said. Travis turned toward her and stared at her blankly. How could she make him see? "Don't you think if he'd intended to kill himself, he wouldn't have left anything to chance and would have taken all of them? Why leave himself hanging in a coma or with liver damage, especially if his sister depended on him?"

He raked his fingers through his hair. "I never thought about the fact that he hadn't taken all the pills in the bottle. Maybe you're right." Obviously, he had some kind of mental block on this, because he hadn't taken her message from Danny as evidence, either.

"And what about the alcohol?"

His eyes narrowed. "What do you mean?"

"Danny told me it wasn't so much that he took too many pills as the combination with alcohol."

"Jackson said the M.E. found both in his system. I'd forgotten until recently, but there was a bottle of tequila in the apartment."

"Maybe he started out drinking, and when that didn't help, he turned to the pain pills." She wished she knew for a certainty, but Danny hadn't spelled it out. Was Danny ashamed that he'd made such a deadly mistake? "Had he been known to combine alcohol and opioids before?"

He stared at her as if she'd grown two heads. "If I'd known he was doing that, I'd have kicked his ass into rehab. Maybe he'd still be around here if I had." He sighed, looking away. "When I found him, there was no doubt in my mind it was a suicide." His voice broke. "Why didn't he call me? I would have sat up with him and tried to take his mind off it."

"When's the last time you asked someone for help?"

He gave a curt nod. "Point taken." His voice grew raspy. "That's what's kept me awake at night. Thinking about those final hours, how alone he was, asking myself why he didn't reach out…"

She reached out to stroke his blue-jean clad thigh, wanting to hold him and make all the hurt go away. "Travis, I'm so sorry." She rested her head on his shoulder, needing to be close even if she did have to invade his space. Suddenly, he wrapped his arms around her and buried his face in the crook of her neck. "God, I miss him so much."

The anguish he'd kept bottled up released in a torrent, and she stroked his back as he poured out his heart's sorrow. "That's it. Let it out." Even knowing Danny's death hadn't been a suicide, the loss of a close friend still tore him apart.

When he seemed to have shed the last tear, she said, "You need to forgive him. I don't know if you sense him around you, but there's a good chance he does come around you if he visited me."

"Oh, yeah. He's always butting into my business." She could hear Travis's grin. "I'll have a talk with him tonight, even if it's one-sided." He pulled away slightly so he could meet her gaze. "Thanks for listening, Katie."

"Anytime you want to talk, I'm here."

A cloud passed in front of his eyes. "I don't know why all this erupted now."

"You can only ignore the valve on a pressure cooker so long before there's an explosion." She smiled, stroking his arm. "I'm just glad you trusted me enough to share with me." She wouldn't be with him most of the time, though. "Is there anyone else in your life you can open up to? Jackson, maybe?"

He chuffed. "Never. I'm supposed to be the leader. They don't need any sign of weakness from me."

"Who meets your needs, Travis?" The words came out sounding differently than she'd intended.

"My dad and I have talked about our combat experiences a few times. He never talked about it at all to my brother, but I think he felt I'd understand."

If he interpreted her words in a sexual way, he didn't let on. *Good.* Unsure about leaving him alone and vulnerable tonight, Kate wondered how she could keep him talking more before going to their separate rooms. She'd rather stay here with him.

"You think Chelsea'll be all right?" he asked. "She had a big day, too."

"Yeah," Kate smiled. "I'll check on her before turning in, but my guess is that she's already asleep." Travis was her biggest concern tonight. He seemed a little lost. How could she prolong their time together?

"Do you have any photos of Danny?"

"Sure. On my laptop upstairs."

"Would you share some of them with me?"

Travis cocked his head. "You want to see them?"

"Very much so. I'd like to know what he looks like." She grinned.

He paused a moment. "Tonight?"

"I'm not doing anything more important."

"Okay. Just let me go get my laptop from my rucksack, and I'll meet you back here."

Katie used the time alone to try and regain control of the inappropriate thoughts going through her head. Memories of when they'd made love in the barn apartment. Memories of his fingers caressing her breasts, his body pressed against hers, his hands bringing her to orgasm. Okay, this wasn't going to do anything to make it easier for her to breathe when he returned.

What was the matter with her? They were talking about his deceased friend. Sex had to be the furthest thing from the man's mind at the moment. When he came back downstairs, she forced herself to concentrate on Danny and Travis, waiting for him to pull up the first images with a mixture of dread and excitement wreaking havoc with her emotions.

Chapter Thirty

Travis worried about how he'd react going through Danny's photos with Katie, but joined her in the living room a few minutes later filled with an odd mix of anticipation and dread. Taking a seat close to her so they could both see the laptop screen, he opened the lid. While waiting for the computer to boot up, he surreptitiously inhaled the lemony scent radiating from her body.

Katie's body felt so right next to him that he had to fight the urge to crush her lips under his. That would be a preferred diversion, though. Despite the other night, his need for her was at an all-time high. Totally wrong, given they'd just been talking about Danny's death.

Get your mind out of the gutter, Trav.

Aw, admit it, Danny. You'd do the same if you were sitting next to her.

Danny bellowed with laughter. Where had he been while they'd talked about his death a few minutes ago? Here he was trying to share his best friend with Katie, and all Travis could think about was taking her upstairs…

Whoa, Trav! Your preteen daughter's sleeping up there. Better scratch that idea until you two tie the knot.

A little less apprehensive, he opened the folder labeled "Danny" on his desktop. Thumbnail images filled the screen. Travis drew a deep breath before setting it to slideshow. The first image was one of the two of them at boot camp graduation. His mind wandered back to that day, which followed fourteen grueling weeks of training. Neither of them had ever accomplished anything so difficult in their lives.

Several more photos flashed across the screen, dragging Travis into the past with both good memories and bad. The walls started closing in…

"You both look so young."

Katie's voice drew Travis back before he could sink too deeply into the abyss. "Maybe from my perspective now. Danny and most of the enlisted members of my unit were eighteen or nineteen with a few exceptions. But I was twenty-two by the time we reached Iraq. I was considered an old man."

"I can't imagine being thrust into a situation like that at such a young age."

He shrugged. "We were damned good at our jobs. Most units were deployed two or three times—one year out and one year home. You mature fast in the Guard."

The next image to fill the screen was one from a forward operating base well south of Baghdad. "That's one of his hero shots." Danny sat on top of a tank with a serious expression on his face, his M4 carbine in front of him pointed skyward.

"Hero shot?"

Travis paused the slideshow before it advanced to the next photo. The term had come out automatically. "Those are…" How to explain it without sounding crass? "They're shots taken that may be used by the media and the family in the event someone is…"

She stiffened beside him. "My God, you all seriously pose for pics with that purpose in mind? It seems so…morbid."

"Oddly enough, it lightens the mood. And for most of us, the photos become part of the memories of our service. I treasure all these with Danny in them, regardless of why we took them originally." It was hell seeing this one, though, because it had been placed on the table in the front of the chapel at Danny's memorial service.

"You posed for some, too?"

"Sure."

"Where are yours?"

"Mom has them." He shrugged. "She insisted. Although I tried to give her ones without me looking scared or armed to the teeth. When I posed for this type of shot, it was always with the thought about what my family and friends would see if confronted with my..."

Katie squeezed his forearm, and their gazes met. Her lips trembled, and he wanted to kiss her in the worst way. "I'm glad your family didn't have to face that. I'm sure they were worried sick about you every day of your deployments." Again, she pulled him away from any carnal thoughts.

"It's always been harder on the families waiting at home than it was on the ones serving in a combat zone. Still is. We stayed busy day and night then dropped into our racks to catch a couple hours of sleep. But our families sat home dwelling on what they imagined was happening to us. Most soon learned not to watch the news, worrying that they'd see reports of casualties where we were serving. They went straight to picturing the worst scenario."

"These photos give me a clearer image of Danny, in case he ever shows up in my room again." She shrugged as if she didn't expect that to happen, but he wouldn't put it past Danny.

One of these days, he wanted to do something to memorialize his friends—Craig, too, the only member of his team Travis hadn't brought home. He hadn't given any thought to that until now. Maybe he was coming to grips with his being gone. Perhaps a tattoo for each of them.

Bringing himself back to what he was doing, Travis started the slideshow again, watching the photos advance ever closer to that day. His mind moved in slow motion toward that day when—

He slammed the lid down on the laptop. He didn't want to see the photos taken of them shooting the breeze over breakfast that morning, not realizing their lives were about to change—or, in Craig's case, end altogether.

When his hand trembled, Katie covered it with hers and squeezed. Soon his entire body shook as flashes of light and the aftermath of the explosion impacted his body. He threw himself onto the soldier on the seat next to him, covering him.

"Travis! It's Katie. You're in my house in Midway. We're safe....you're safe!"

Katie? He blinked himself out of the flashback and saw that he'd slammed her prone against the couch, his upper body covering hers. *What the...* Filling his lungs with air, he tried to slow his erratic heartbeat as the scene from hell receded back into his memory, leaving his line of sight filled with sweet, innocent Katie. Her breasts pressed against his chest as she, too, struggled to control her breathing.

"I'm sorry," she said. "I shouldn't have asked you to show me those photos and relive this again."

"I didn't think I'd lose it like that." Usually when he was going over the photos, he stopped well before the place they'd gotten to in the slide show. "Did I hurt you?"

She shook her head. "I was just worried about you."

"I'm okay." He was no longer lost in the past. Katie was warm and real and life itself. Her clean, fresh scent mesmerized him.

When he didn't move to get off her, her forehead furrowed in worry. Time to send Katie up to her bed, even if he needed her more tonight than he'd ever needed anyone before. No way did he want her to have sex with him out of pity.

When she wet her lips and glanced down at his mouth, though, he felt a stirring that didn't bode well for keeping his libido in check.

His thumb traced her lips.

"Trav—"

He cut off her attempt at putting the brakes on this by closing the gap and crushing her mouth under his. Her body melted against the couch, as she wrapped her arms around his neck telling him she needed this, too. Travis backed off, nibbling at her full lower lip. "Just a taste..." He'd be leaving tomorrow. No sense complicating things any more than they already were.

If only Katie hadn't opened her mouth and tangled her tongue with his. He wanted to stretch out and strip her of every stitch of clothing, but his daughter's presence upstairs kept him from totally losing his self-control.

"Let me touch you." He eased off, and his hand stroked the side of her breast as his lips trailed kisses and bites along the column of her neck. She moaned, her fingers holding onto the sides of his head as though to keep him from stopping. Not that he planned to anytime soon.

Slipping his right hand between their bodies, he unbuttoned her shirt to give him more territory to cover. He shoved the flap aside and pulled away so he could make sure she was okay with where this might go. Her languid eyelids and sultry smile hardened him with anticipation. He glanced at the stairway, feeling like a teenager worried about his parents walking in on him necking with his girlfriend—only the roles had been reversed.

"Don't go anywhere." He crossed the room and pulled the wooden pocket door panels from the walls to close off the living room from the hall. At least they'd have a warning if Chelsea ventured down here before she could catch them in the act. When he returned to Katie, he saw she'd removed her shirt and was in the process of unclasping her bra. The exposed expanse of skin made him hard as a rock. He removed her shoes and then sat on the couch to get rid of his own. Standing, he undid his belt and shucked his jeans while she did the same from a prone position.

With far fewer clothes coming between them, he stretched out on the couch again, resting his weight on his elbows. "You turn me on like no woman I've ever known." He bent to kiss her smile away before continuing along his path of seduction.

* * *

Travis's words sent a thrill through Kate right to her core. The man could have any woman he wanted, but he desired her.

Something niggled in the back of her mind telling her that it was a bad idea to fool around like this, but Chelsea slept like the dead and Travis had shut the door. Ever since they'd made love in the barn apartment, she'd wanted more.

His mouth teased her earlobe before his raspy cheek grazed down the column of her neck to where his teeth nibbled at the hollow. Her hips bucked upward in response. A definite hot spot for her.

Kate raked her blunt nails over his back and elicited a similar response from his lower body. His hardness connected with her sex, and she gasped. How could she be ready for him so quickly?

But she wanted him buried inside her to the hilt. Now!

Travis, on the other hand, seemed to be in no hurry. He blazed a slow trail downward until his lips latched onto her taut nipple. Every time he flicked the tight bud, a ripple ran down her body all the way to her throbbing core. When his teeth clamped onto the hard peak and tugged, she moaned with need. She opened her eyes to find him staring at her, his teeth not letting go of her nipple. He continued to pull until she had to arch her back and then released it.

"Travis, we don't have all night. What if Chel—"

Ignoring her, he did the same with her other nipple. She held onto the sides of his head, afraid he'd stop. The swirling torrent inside her needed release—and yet she didn't want the moment to come to an end. However, when he ground his erect member against her, she could wait no longer. "Please, Travis. Don't torture me."

He only chuckled before releasing her nipple and trailing kisses and nibbles across her abdomen. Oh, no!

She lowered her hands to cover her stretch marks, but he held them captive at her sides. "Don't cover your body. It's beautiful."

His eyes smoldered possessively as if laying claim to her body a half-second before his tongue traced one of the stretch marks lower and lower still until he released her hands and tugged at the waistband of her panties. She lifted her hips to help him remove them, ready for him to lose his boxer briefs, too. But he didn't finish stripping. Instead, he reached for a pillow. "Lift your hips."

Knowing full well what he intended to do, she complied. He hadn't gone down on her when they'd dated in college. She wished she'd showered after they'd gotten back home, but…

"Beautiful." Travis stared at her until she felt herself growing wetter. Scooting to the end of the couch, he leaned forward, spreading her outer lips and opening her wide. "Hold on, darlin'."

There wasn't much to hold on to, but she grasped the seat cushion with one hand and his shoulder with the other. His breath was warm against her skin as he lowered his head until his tongue slid along her cleft.

"Travis!" The overload of sensations nearly made her come undone immediately. Need clawed at her insides as he slowly drove her insane. Why was he avoiding the bundle of nerves that would have taken her over the edge?

His finger slipped inside her, and she almost lost it then, but he still wouldn't give her the release she sought. "I want you inside me."

"Thought you'd never ask."

What? He was waiting for her to ask?

Travis stood and hooked his thumbs in his boxer briefs. She watched, ready to see him in all his glory—

Crash!

Something fell over in the hallway. She and Travis quickly pulled on discarded clothes before Chelsea could open the door. They tried to resume their innocent positions on the couch, Travis even picked up the laptop to pretend they were looking at photos still.

But there wasn't another sound.

He slammed shut the laptop with a groan. "You've *got* to be kidding me."

"About what?" She fought to regulate her breathing and the frustrating ache in her core.

"Not you. Danny. If he wasn't already dead, I'd strangle him."

"What on earth are you talking about?"

"He just told me that we'd thank him later for knocking over the umbrella stand, because we wouldn't want Chelsea scarred for life if she happened to come downstairs."

"You mean that wasn't Chelsea in the hall?"

"No." He sighed, dragging his fingers through his mussed hair. "But Danny's right. We need to wait. I can't picture my folks having sex more than the three times it took to get pregnant with the Cooper kids." He stood and looked down at her. "So I'm going to take his ill-timed advice and head upstairs. Unfortunately, I'll be leaving early tomorrow."

Kate had been taught not to speak ill of the dead and didn't possess a violent bone in her body. But as she fought to get her breath back to normal, she wouldn't mind helping Travis strangle Danny. Her body was screaming for release, and Travis was going to bed? Without her?

Well, of course without her. Okay, Danny was right. Damn him. She wasn't thinking clearly at the moment.

He held out his hand for hers, and she stood as he wrapped his arms around her waist and pulled her near. "I'm going to miss you, Katie."

"I'll miss you, too."

"Hey, I know I said I'd come up here Saturday, but Chelsea wants to come down to my place instead for the Fourth."

They'd already planned a weekend away from the farm? Not only a weekend, but *four days*? *Stay calm, Kate.* She shouldn't complain, after having deprived him of his daughter her entire life, but God she'd miss her. As hard as it was to say, she choked out the words. "I don't want to intrude on your plans to spend time with her. Besides, I have a lot of work to do here and wouldn't have been able to see much of you two anyway."

"I want you to come, too. You need a break, even if you don't stay through Tuesday. And it would give us a chance to finish what we started tonight." He bent to place a kiss on her lips and smiled.

"Chelsea would be in the same house there, too," she reminded him.

"But the master bedroom is on the first floor and I'm going to give Chelsea a room on the other side of the house and upstairs. I can put you in the guest room on the first floor with me then after she goes to bed…" He wrapped a loose strand of hair behind her ear, sending a shiver down her spine.

I want to. "I don't kn—"

"There's a lock on my bedroom door," he said, continuing his sales pitch. "While she won't want to picture us doing the deed, she'd love spending time with us both. What do you say?" When she hesitated further, he cupped her ass and ground himself against her. "Come on. Join us."

"But I promised Melissa I'd work with her Saturday and Sunday."

"Then change it to Monday. The Junior League show isn't until next Thursday. You can stay Friday and Saturday nights and be home early Monday." Not giving her a chance to answer, his mouth covered hers. When her mind was sufficiently vacant, he pulled away and stared down at her.

"Um, I suppose I could stay until Sunday afternoon."

He grinned. "Now you're talking."

He kissed her again, his tongue skimming over her lips as he tweaked her nipple at the same time. His hand lowered to her sex, and he stroked her. "And I'll get to finish what I started."

Sensations flooded through her body, almost causing her to ask if he'd like to go up to the springhouse or out to the barn apartment, but he'd be leaving tomorrow. Spending more time with him would only make her more frustrated.

How was she going to survive the week thinking about the promise he'd just made? She hoped she had some fresh batteries around here somewhere.

Then she remembered what had precipitated the scene on the couch. His flashback. She reached up to stroke his whiskered cheek again. "Will you be all right tonight?"

He chuffed. "Doubt I'll get any sleep. I ought to make use of your gym in the garage to work off steam, but I'll settle for a cold shower instead."

If he had no clue that she was talking about the flashback and the memories the photos had churned up, she didn't intend to remind him. He certainly seemed to be in a good mood.

She cupped his face and pulled him closer to hers to give him a rather chaste kiss on the lips. "Good night, Travis. Sweet dreams."

With that, she left him standing in the living room while she mounted the steps to her bedroom, giving him a cheeky wiggle of her backside. She heard him whistle softly, much the way he had when he'd seen her in that awful hospital gown. He made her feel like a woman again.

Had she just agreed to spend a couple of nights with him and Chelsea? *Yes, you did.* She'd call Melissa in the morning and see if she could even put her off until Monday by promising her every available lesson between now and the first class in the Junior League show. Of course, Kate knew the girl was already as prepared as she'd ever could be. Perhaps this could be turned into a vote of confidence for Melissa and ease some of her jitters.

But Kate had some jitters of her own. Was she ready to open the door wider to Travis?

Chapter Thirty-One

Travis noticed Katie's blush first thing the next morning when he came into the kitchen. Chelsea was already at the table, so he couldn't comment on the reason for it. "Sorry I'm late." He wasn't more than a couple minutes past the time Katie had said, but he still felt guilty. She'd agreed to serve breakfast early so he could hit the road and get to the worksite soon after lunch. Hell, in longer than he could remember, he'd actually overslept this morning. He hadn't gotten a decent night's sleep in forever.

"Right on time, actually." She remained intent on watching the bacon fry. Maybe she'd slept in a little late, too. She was usually ready to plate the food precisely when she said it would be served.

He couldn't resist stopping by her to give her a kiss on the cheek. "Breakfast smells great, Katie." In a whisper only she could hear, he added, "And so do you." She swatted him away, casting a worried look at Chelsea as if caught doing something illicit. Last night, she'd agreed to join them for at least part of the weekend. Could life get any better than this?

He grinned as he made his way to Chelsea's side and gave her a kiss on the cheek, too. "Mornin', sunshine. How's it going?"

"Good. But do you really have to leave this morning?"

The disappointment in her voice made him wish he could stay—forever. "'Fraid so. But we'll be together again Friday night, which'll be here before you know it."

"I can't wait! I wish I could go home with you today."

Travis cringed, not looking in Katie's direction this time. "I won't be home much this week. I have a lot of work to finish up before my crew takes its summer break starting Friday." When he snuck a peek in Katie's direction, her knuckles had turned white gripping the tongs, and her smile had faded. "But your mom has agreed to come for part of the weekend."

Chelsea turned to Katie. "We're going to have so much fun. Daddy's going to take me fishing, and we're going to watch fireworks from his boat on the lake."

Katie moved the bacon from the skillet to a plate lined with a paper towel. "I can't stay through the Fourth on Tuesday, because I have a lot of work to do here. But I'll drop you off Friday night and stay until Saturday night or Sunday morning." To Travis, she added, "I'd like to see where you live."

The prospect of having both of his girls at his place made him anxious for the week to pass, too. He took his seat across from her at the table, and Chelsea immediately shot him a questioning glance, in a lousy stage whisper, asked, "Did you talk to her yet?"

Damn. He'd been so preoccupied yesterday with the visit to his folks that he hadn't had a chance to talk with Chelsea.

And what about all the days before that where you didn't tell her, either, Trav?

Danny was starting to sound like a second conscience. When did he become so perfect? Okay, so maybe he *was* avoiding the issue. He didn't want to disappoint her—or break her heart—by telling her she couldn't have the horse right away.

Katie turned toward them, setting down the tongs as she glanced from one to the other. "Talk to me about what?"

He hated to ruin her good mood, but if she was going to be the one to kill Chelsea's dream, then she needed to own up to it in front of Chelsea and not make him out to be a liar.

"Chelsea wants to start showing horses, and I've offered to buy her a good performance horse to help get her off to a great start."

Not giving Katie a chance to respond, Chelsea said, "Daddy, do you think we could go looking for my horse while I'm down there?"

Crap. Chelsea sure could learn a little something about timing and social cues.

The hurt in Katie's eyes tore at Travis's gut, but dammit, he was Chelsea's dad and saw no good reason why he couldn't do this for her. He'd still hoped to be able to convince Katie to let him do it without waiting until next year.

"Not on a holiday weekend, baby," he hedged. When he tried to gauge Katie's response—the rigid way she held herself as she scrambled their eggs didn't bode well. How could he fix this? Obviously, he and Katie still had things to work on, despite how well they'd connected last night.

Turning to look over her shoulder, Katie glared at him before turning her attention to Chelsea, her face softening with her smile. "About the horse, sweetie. Your daddy and I spoke about this, and I don't think he realizes how competition and training work. I don't want you taking on more horse than you're ready for. But we can work on training you to one of my horses and competing in this fall's academy shows. If you show you're going to stick to it and not treat it as a hobby, then your father and I will discuss buying you a new horse."

Chelsea's mouth dropped. "But, Mom! I already ride some of your best-trained horses. And I won two ribbons at Shelbyville in April."

Katie closed her eyes and drew a deep breath. He probably should say something, but didn't want to complicate the issue any further. Besides, he'd also like to hear how she'd address the issue directly with Chelsea, especially after admitting to him that Chelsea was one of her best students.

Meeting Chelsea's gaze again, she began, "The atmosphere in front of judges is vastly different from being in the arena with only me and your mount. You need to participate in more academy shows so you can get used to being timed, as well as learn to control your horse's reactions and movements. And then there's learning to curb your nerves, which can be projected to your horse, making him or her antsy.

Not that you can control everything, but it takes practice to find ways to minimize the damage if your horse sneezes or does something unexpected while the judges have their eyes on you. Those skills will make it easier for you to compete at a higher level."

Travis hadn't thought about that. Chelsea was still unproven in the arena. Maybe he *was* trying to put the horse before the cart, so to speak.

"After the Junior League show is over next week, we'll sit down and work out a plan for where you can start showing. Chula's ready for more challenges now."

Chelsea narrowed her eyes. "You don't think I can do it, but I can! And I'm tired of falling in love with a horse only to have you sell it."

Katie winced as she picked up the plate of bacon and a bowl of eggs and brought them to the table. Travis couldn't sit silently by any longer.

"Chelsea, your mom knows more about this than the two of us combined. I think we should listen to her advice. What difference will it make whether you get a new horse next month or next year?"

Chelsea's eyes welled with unshed tears. *Great.* He'd only been a father for a week, and he'd already gone and made his little girl cry. "You *promised*, Daddy." Her lower lip trembled, making him feel like a heel.

Travis raked his fingers through his hair, breaking eye contact as he tried to figure out how the hell to fix *this*. When he met Chelsea's gaze again, the tears were flowing down her cheeks. "Honey, I should have discussed the matter with your mom first before making you that offer. I made a mistake." Perhaps showing he wasn't perfect would make an impression on the girl. He started to say he was new to parenting, but didn't want to give Chelsea any reason to think he wasn't cut out for the job.

Katie set a bowl of biscuits between them. "Your daddy's right, but let's talk more after breakfast, sweetie. Daddy needs to leave for Nashville soon." Sounded like Katie was anxious for him to leave as quickly as possible.

Chelsea's chair scraped the floor, and she stood abruptly. "I'm not hungry."

"Fair enough, but your daddy's leaving soon so say goodbye first."

He received a perfunctory hug and goodbye before she made a dash to the kitchen door and outside before he could say a word. No doubt she'd run to Jazz for consolation. Might be just what she needed. He'd give her a few minutes to calm down before finding her to say goodbye until Friday night.

Travis met Katie's stern gaze. Instead, she said, "This is exactly what I was trying to explain the other night. I thought we agreed that getting her a horse now wasn't a good idea."

"Well, that's what you decided. I pretty much hoped I'd be able to convince you otherwise." He grinned, hoping to lighten the mood. She blinked at him a few times without a smile or a word. "Katie, if you'd just cave in and let me buy her the damned horse, she'd simmer down. Worse comes to worst, she's not ready and you have another good horse in your stable to let one of your students ride. You'll see. Everything's going to work out."

"How can you be so sure? You get to waltz back to Nashville within the hour. I'm the one who has to deal with her resentment— and her mood—alone for the next five days."

"I'm sure it'll blow over by suppertime."

Katie reached for the bacon and put two slices on her plate. "You obviously don't know your daughter."

"Exactly, but I'm trying to fix that." And a lot of other things. How many balls was he juggling now?

She sighed, and he tried not to notice the rising and falling of her breasts. Maybe he wasn't taking this discussion seriously enough, but being near her reminded him of what they'd almost done in the living room last night while their daughter slept upstairs.

She reached for the eggs. "Owning and training a show horse needs to be something she'd be willing to devote most of her time to for years to come. If she shows a strong commitment to taking care of one of my horses and trains hard over the next few months at some of the academy shows, we can revisit this discussion. One sure way of convincing me would be for her to do at least four shows and compete in the National Academy Championship in November."

"What's that?"

"A charity event benefitting St. Jude's Children's that gives novice riders of all ages a chance to compete without having to own their own horse or wear the expensive outfits required at higher-level competitions. The first day's classes are open to everyone, but she'd have to qualify to continue on to the later classes. It's held near you in Murfreesboro. Your family might like to attend and watch her."

"You're right. So would I."

"If she's ready, there are several excellent equine auctions about that time of year. You may even pick up a real bargain for her and give it to her for Christmas."

Hearing her compromise a little bit on how long he'd have to wait brought his appetite back, and he filled his plate with bacon and eggs before buttering a biscuit. When he noticed she wasn't eating, he said, "We'll do it your way. Now, eat." He didn't want to keep reminding her to eat, but when she had a lot on her mind, she tended to forget.

Before he started in on his meal, he said, "Katie, I'm sorry if I'm creating havoc in your life, but I was blindsided by all this and am doing the best I can."

"We'll figure out how to navigate this new dynamic. After all, it's only been a week since you've met Chelsea."

Would he eventually get the hang of being a father? And what about him and Katie? Would their relationship continue to be rocky, or was there any hope of them having a future together as something more than Chelsea's parents?

*   *   *

Kate hoped they'd heard the last about buying the show horse for a while. Travis seemed to accept her plan for testing Chelsea's readiness. She probably should have suggested it before. Would she ever get used to having to explain and discuss everything concerning Chelsea now?

"Drive carefully. I'll bring Chelsea down Friday night for the weekend, and you can bring her home." She gave him a peck on the cheek before heading down the hallway to her office at the front of the house to see if Melissa had responded to her email of encouragement. If not, they'd see each other in half an hour, but she wanted to be prepared.

No response yet.

She became distracted by an email regarding an issue with one of the horses she'd sold last year, until she heard Travis's footsteps coming down the stairs. She hadn't even heard him go up.

Wanting to arrive at the arena before Melissa did, she picked up an apple from the kitchen and left the house. No sign of Travis, although his truck was still here. Must be in the barn where, no doubt, Chelsea was having a good cry in Princess Jasmine's stall.

No sense interrupting them, since she'd said goodbye and would see him again in a few days, so she headed to the pasture gate for her morning ritual. Oddly enough, Angus wasn't waiting at the fence to gobble down his morning treat.

Then, as if bidden by her thoughts, the stallion raced toward her. She held out the apple just as she heard the door to Travis's truck slam shut. Turning briefly to wave when her focus returned to the horse, she noticed Angus was saddled.

And *riderless*.

What the… Her first inclination would have been that Travis had decided to take one more ride on him before leaving, but he wouldn't have left a horse saddled. Then who?

Oh, dear God!

She dropped the apple in the dirt as she spun around and ran toward his truck, hoping to catch Travis before he left. He was turning around in a wide circle, the front of the truck facing away from her already. "Travis! Stop! I think something's happened to Chelsea!"

The vehicle started down the lane, and she frantically waved her arms in the air and shouted, but he continued driving away slowly. Placing her fingers in her mouth, she released a shrill whistle. A moment later, the brake lights came on, and the truck started backing toward her. Running, she met him a hundred yards away. Travis exited the truck with the engine still running.

"Where's Chelsea?"

"No clue. I tried to find her before I left, but Jasmine's in her stall alone. I couldn't find Chelsea in the barn or the house, but I couldn't put off leaving any longer."

"I think she went out for a ride on Angus."

"Has she ever ridden him before?"

"Never. But he came back saddled and without a rider."

"You sure Miguel didn't ride him?"

She shook her head. "He's afraid of that horse. Calls him Diablo, sometimes even Satan."

"Get in the truck." She scooted across the driver's seat to the passenger side, and he followed her in. Travis raced up the lane in reverse, surprisingly adept at staying on the gravel. When he reached the arena and barn parking area, he circled around then drove forward up to the pasture. "Dammit. I should have kept looking for her."

"It's not your fault." She shouldn't have left Chelsea alone so long to stew about the show horse.

At the gate, Kate jumped out to open and close it. Driving slowly through the field, they searched for Chelsea. Kate's throat closed off as fear consumed her. What if she'd injured herself? Or broken bones?

Travis reached out to squeeze her leg. "We'll find her. I'm sure she'll be fine. Maybe she'd gotten off Angus, and he hightailed it back to the house without her. We'll probably find her walking home over that next rise."

"What was she doing on Angus in the first place? She's never ridden him before. He's way too much horse for her." Her words from this morning echoed back to her. "Dammit. She did this because of what I said at breakfast."

"Don't beat yourself up. She's a kid. They do stupid things for no good reason sometimes."

Despite his attempt at reassuring her, she had no doubt this was her fault. Not that the words weren't true, obviously. Especially if Chelsea had been thrown by the spirited Angus.

"Where can she be?"

"There must be a hundred acres here, with lots of hills and dips. It's going to take time to cover the whole area, because I don't want to accidentally run over her."

"Her yellow blouse ought to show up. Thank God she didn't wear something green or brown." And thank God Travis was here. She wasn't sure she'd have the wherewithal to operate her truck given how frazzled her nerves were. A minute or two more, and he'd have been gone. And from her experience in the past week, Travis wasn't one to view texts or take phone calls while driving.

Each acre passed in a blur of Timothy grass and tall fescue. The minutes felt like a lifetime as they scanned the landscape for any sign of their daughter. Twice, she almost called out, only to realize the anomaly wasn't Chelsea.

"Hey, is that her?" Travis asked.

She searched with her eyes the area where Travis pointed and caught a glimpse of something yellow. "Maybe. Stop the truck!" She opened the door before he stopped and ran toward the spot where she found a crumpled Chelsea lying facedown against the ground, a limestone outcropping near her head. Kate knelt beside her lifeless body brushing back her hair from her forehead. While there was a bump, the bleeding had already stopped. Chelsea's back rose and fell to indicate she was breathing, albeit shallowly. Travis ran up beside her and checked her pulse. Why wasn't she wearing her helmet?

Because she was upset and trying to prove something to you.

"Go back to the truck and grab the blanket behind the passenger seat."

Grateful for something to occupy her mind, she did as he said. She'd trained in CPR and first aid for riding accidents, but couldn't for the life of her remember what needed to be done when it was her daughter who'd been injured. Thank goodness Travis remained calm, at least outwardly.

"You're going to be okay, sweetie. Daddy and I are taking you to the hospital to get everything checked out." She covered Chelsea with the blanket and checked her phone.

"Have a signal?" he asked.

"No. Maybe if I go farther up the hill." But she doubted it and didn't want to leave Chelsea here. The goose egg over her right eyebrow had grown larger. Her skin seemed so pale despite her tan. Pasty white.

Travis checked her arms and legs. "No obvious broken bones, but I'd be afraid to move her."

"Look, I'll take the truck back down toward the house and call 9-1-1. Stay here with her in case she comes to."

Kate ran to the truck and barreled down the hillside toward the gate. She was within a few hundred yards when she found she had service and slammed on the breaks to make the call. The dispatcher, a friend from school, insisted on keeping Kate on the phone while she waited for the ambulance. If she asked one more question Kate couldn't answer, she'd scream. How was Kate supposed to answer when Chelsea was half a pasture away? Still, the dispatcher's calm, authoritative voice helped to calm her.

Miguel came from the barn and ran toward her. "Is everything okay?"

She filled him in on what had happened. "See if you can find Angus. I don't want him to get out but I need to keep the gate open for the ambulance."

"Sure thing."

The sound of the sirens was the most beautiful one in the world, and soon Kate led them with the truck to where Chelsea had been thrown.

When the EMTs took over, Travis came to Kate and wrapped his arm around her. "She's going to be okay. They'll take good care of her." They placed a collar around her neck to stabilize her before carefully moving her to a backboard and into the ambulance. Seeing her baby as limp as a rag doll sparked new fears in her.

The EMT looked toward them. "Who wants to ride with her on the way to the hospital to answer some questions for us?"

Travis nudged her numb body forward. "You go with her, Katie. I'll follow in the truck." To the EMT, he asked, "Georgetown?"

He nodded before guiding Kate into the back of the ambulance and indicating where she should sit. Seeing Chelsea's pale face and still body made her afraid to touch her.

"Go ahead and talk to her. It might help bring her out of it."

Kate started a rambling dialogue about some of the things Chelsea cared about, including Princess Jasmine, as the ambulance bounced slowly through the field. The driver was probably trying to avoid the danger of jarring Chelsea by hitting gopher hills and tunnels. Once through the gate, they picked up speed down the driveway and onto the road. Travis would make sure the gate was closed. Her own concern now was her baby getting more advanced medical attention. They were being careful with their precious cargo, which Kate appreciated, but she just wanted to get there.

Before she knew it, they arrived at Georgetown. "It won't be long now, baby." Kate said, stroking Chelsea's forehead, brushing her hair back from the ugly swollen bump. Why was she still unresponsive? How long had she been unconscious?

The back door opened, and Kate scrambled out quickly to let them take care of Chelsea. Suddenly, strong arms were wrapped around her, the familiar scent of Travis's soap telling her she wasn't alone anymore.

They followed the stretcher inside and were greeted by two male emergency department staffers. "What's the patient's name?" one asked.

"Chelsea Cooper," Kate answered.

Travis squeezed her hand. She was still so numb she hadn't realized he was holding it. "Don't worry, Katie. They'll take good care of her." No matter how many times she heard or even said the words, she wouldn't believe it until Chelsea opened her eyes.

Inside a cubicle, Kate explained what she could about the accident, which was pitifully little. Travis wrapped his arm around her, and they watched as Chelsea was evaluated. He stroked her back, helping to calm her frayed nerves a bit.

Everything happened in a blur. People moved around the hospital bed, but all she could focus on was how still her daughter lay on the gurney.

"Is Chelsea allergic to any medications?"

"None that I know of. She's never been injured this badly before or had to take anything but ampicillin and Tylenol in the past." Chelsea's eyes remained closed, her face pale except for the red bump on her forehead. A nurse checked her blood pressure. "How is she?" Kate asked the physician, only certain she was one by her white coat.

"I'd say she has a concussion, but we're going to need a CT scan to see if there's any bleeding or swelling in the brain. We'll know soon whether she'll need to be transferred to Lexington."

Only the worst cases were sent to Lexington. Kate asked if she could kiss her before they took her out. "Sure. We'll let her stay here until radiology is ready for her."

The doctor and nurse left, and Kate walked over to the bed. She stroked Chelsea's hair, careful not to touch the bump. "Chelsea. Open your eyes. Your daddy and I are here."

Chelsea's eyelids moved but remained closed. Was that a positive sign? Travis went to the other side of the bed. "It's Daddy, sunshine. You're going to be fine. They're just going to do some scans. Squeeze my hand if you can hear me."

Kate waited, still stroking Chelsea's hair.

"She squeezed my hand!" Travis said, smiling at Kate before focusing on Chelsea again. "Do it again, baby."

Kate glanced at their joined hands and tried to tamp down a moment of envy that Chelsea had given him that sign instead of her. But joy soon won out. Chelsea had responded to a verbal command. This was no time to be jealous. She reached for the nurse's button. Now if only Chelsea would open her eyes so she'd know she was going to be okay.

Chapter Thirty-Two

C helsea squeezed his hand, giving him the first ray of hope since Katie had whistled for him to stop the truck. Coincidentally, the sound was the same one he'd heard that day when Angus had nearly bucked him off, although he'd become convinced that one had come from Danny. Had his buddy gotten his attention again today, or had it been Katie both times?

"Mr. and Mrs. Cooper, we're ready to take her to radiology now." Travis liked the sound of that and didn't bother to correct the man. He stepped back, releasing Chelsea's hand with reluctance. Glancing across the gurney at Katie, he saw tears streaming down her face as she let go of Chelsea's limp hand. He rounded the bed to wrap his arm around her and pull her away to give the nurses the space they needed.

"She's going to be fine. She squeezed my hand, didn't she?"

Katie nodded, but remained silent. Together, they watched their baby girl being wheeled away. He hadn't felt this helpless since he'd found Danny...

But this day wasn't going to end like that one. Chelsea was young and strong. She'd managed to communicate with him in some small way.

A staff member came in and asked them to follow her to the registration desk to take care of paperwork while they waited. Kate promised to drop off the insurance card later because she hadn't brought her purse.

After she'd given them what information they asked for, he stood. "Come on. Let's take a walk. She's going to be in radiology a little while." He didn't think waiting in the cubicle with the screams of another patient fraying their nerves would be the best place right now.

Travis led her through the automatic doors and out the exit. The air was oppressive, but felt better than the chill in the hospital. Removing his arm from around her, he took her hand in his. Katie walked along as if in a trance. He steered her to a bench outside the emergency department's entrance for her to sit. Worried about her, he watched her fidget with a loose thread on her jeans. She stood after a few moments, looking around as if unsure how she'd gotten here.

Out of the blue, she spun toward him. "If only you hadn't promised her that horse, none of this would have happened."

What did she just say?

"It was an accident!" he argued. "Horses are unpredictable. Especially that mean old cuss."

She squared off with him. "She's never ridden Angus before. Never even wanted to. It wasn't until she thought she had to prove she was capable of taking on a more spirited horse that she tried to ride Angus. She wanted to prove something to me this morning. Why'd you have to make that promise anyway? Why couldn't you have told her it wasn't a good idea after we talked the first time, long before her heart was set on it?"

"Hold on a minute. I'm not going to take the blame for something that doesn't need to have blame attached to it in the first place. All I want to do is make her happy." Hell, if he wanted to join the blame game, he could point out that Kate was the one who said she'd need to prove herself on a higher caliber horse.

Clenching her fists on her hips, she said, "A parent's job isn't to make their kids happy. It's to set limits and boundaries, guidelines that will keep them safe and help them grow into strong adults. You're her father, not her friend."

"Maybe if you'd let her experiment with new ideas—and sometimes fail at things—she wouldn't need to prove anything to you or herself."

Katie's eyes opened wide as her jaw dropped, but only for a second before she fired back, "How would you know what I do or don't do? You've only known her a few days."

"You parent the way your father raised you. Your old man never let you try anything, either, as far as I can tell. And you aren't able to let Chelsea out of the safe cocoon you've placed her in on your farm." *Jeezus, where'd that come from?* But her words had cut him, and he needed to unleash some of the anger that had been building in him since he'd found out about Chelsea.

Katie's chin quivered before she pressed her lips together, narrowing her eyes. "My father did the best he could as a single parent. He brought me up to be a strong, independent woman who was able to expand her family farm's business and raise a child by herself, too."

"And you did the best you could to remain that single parent, never giving me the luxury of deciding whether or not I wanted to be a father to my own kid."

"I said I'm sorry, and I'm trying to rectify it, but you aren't meeting me halfway. Stop making promises without discussing them with me first. I'm tired of having to be the bad guy when you don't think things through."

His gut twisted as she swallowed hard, blinking rapidly. Dammit, why the hell were they tearing each other apart when their daughter should be bringing them together? The anger and bitterness was beginning to eat him alive. They had a helluva rift to mend if they were ever going to be able to move on, whether as a couple and a family or simply parents sharing joint custody. Right now, though, Chelsea needed them to be strong for her—steadfast together and on the same team.

"Look, Katie, this is no time for us to be going at each other. Let's go back inside." She took several breaths before her body relaxed somewhat, but then she began to shake. He cupped her cheek. Surprisingly, she didn't pull away. "We're both beyond worried about Chelsea." Travis reached for her hand. "Let's go back inside and wait."

She shook her head. "You go ahead. Give me a few minutes, then I'll join you."

Travis wasn't going to leave her out here by herself, not in this state of mind. He took her hand again, and she didn't resist. "I'll walk with you."

An unspoken truce opened up between them, and they walked in silence until he couldn't stand being away any longer. "I don't know about you, but it feels like they've had long enough to do the scans."

She glanced at her phone. "It's only been fifteen minutes."

"Well, I want to be there when they bring her back."

She nodded. "Me, too."

In unison, they turned around and started back across the parking lot toward the entrance. "She's going to be all right, Katie." He squeezed her hand as if his words would make it so. Chelsea had to be okay.

Dammit, Katie's right. He'd started all this with his grandiose gesture to try and instantly win his daughter's love and by not consulting with Katie about such a major decision in their daughter's life. In the future, he needed to think before he acted, to discuss things with Katie before making any more promises. God, he had a lot to learn.

His phone vibrated in his pocket near the emergency department's entrance, and he pulled it out.

JACKSON: There's been an accident.

Was the man psychic now? "You go on. I need to let Jackson know I won't be back today after all."

Katie nodded and went inside while Travis texted.

TRAVIS: Yeah. Don't know when I can get back. Waiting for word from the doctor.

JACKSON: What r u talking about?

Wait. Jackson couldn't be aware of Chelsea's accident. So what was he talking about?

TRAVIS: **Chelsea had a fall. Head injury. What accident r u talking about?**

JACKSON: **Sorry. She okay?**

TRAVIS: **Unconscious. Waiting on brain scans.**

JACKSON: **Shit, man. Never mind me.**

Now he was starting to worry.

TRAVIS: **What the hell's going on down there?**

It was almost a minute before Jackson responded.

JACKSON: **I'm a jackass.**

Enough of this… Travis called Jackson, and he answered right away. "What happened?"

"Nothing, really. You have more important stuff to deal with now. We'll talk later."

"If you don't tell me within the next five seconds who's been injured, you're fired."

Jackson's laugh was long and hearty because he knew Travis would never get rid of him. "Yeah, well, you might want to fire me regardless."

Travis didn't have time for this bullshit. Raking his fingers through his hair, he counted down, "Three, two…"

"Okay, I pushed too hard. Trying to get us back on schedule before the summer break, and I—"

"Last we talked you were ahead of schedule."

"I didn't want to worry you or have you hurrying back here before you were ready. You had more important stuff to do up there. But…I screwed up."

Jackson never messed up. "Who got hurt?"

"Luckily me and not someone else. Not too bad. I'm fine so keep your focus on Chelsea."

Jackson was injured? "How badly?"

He sighed. "Doctor says I'm going to be laid up at least six weeks. I doubt it'll be more than three."

Weeks? "What kind of injury?"

"Besides my wounded pride, I fractured my left fibula. Just a stress fracture. Won't require surgery."

Six weeks, hell. The bones of a forty-two-year old didn't heal as quickly as those of a younger man. He could be out for months given the type of work he did.

"What happened?"

"Misjudged the height when I jumped down to help Smitty lift a joist."

If Travis had been down there, the crew wouldn't have fallen behind schedule and Jackson wouldn't have been losing sleep and pushing so hard doing both their jobs.

Travis stared up at the hospital building where his little girl lay unconscious. He had responsibilities to Jackson and his crew, but also to his daughter. How could he be in two places at the same time?

Travis had invested every ounce of his time and energy into his business for the past decade. When deployments were expected, he simply cut back on the number of projects they were involved in, and Jackson managed to keep things running smoothly in his absence. Until this time. He hadn't accounted for taking any time away because he never took time off. But for the first time since he'd started the company, he had other priorities. Chelsea and Katie had to come first.

"Listen, Travis, this is nothing but an inconvenience. We're within a couple days of finishing up this job. I can bark orders sitting as well as standing."

Jackson and Travis led by example, not by telling everyone else what to do. Both were hands-on.

"As soon as I know Chelsea's out of the woods, I'll get down there. In the meantime, let me see if Clint or one of Dad's foremen can spare some time to help out a few days this week."

"Sure. I'll do what I can, but we both know how important it is to have boots on the ground at a site. Clint knows how things should be run."

"And by the time we start the new job after the crew's vacation, I'll be back there full-time." Hell, there he went making promises again. He knew nothing of the sort. Everything hinged on Chelsea's condition and building a future with her.

"You just worry about your little girl. I'll be fine."

"Anybody there to help you out at home?"

Jackson chuffed. "I haven't had anyone taking care of me in a long time. No plans to start now."

Travis wondered if maybe Emmy or Shania could check in on him. They had mobile careers that could be done anywhere. He'd think about that later. Right now, though, he needed to get back inside. "Keep me posted, Jackson. And I'll call Clint next chance I get."

They said goodbye, and Travis went back inside the emergency department to wait with Katie for news about Chelsea's condition.

Talk about one screwed up day. Whenever life settled down, he had some thinking to do about his future.

* * *

Kate's body had grown numb, along with her mind. Chelsea had only been in radiology twenty-five minutes according to her phone, but it seemed like a lifetime.

"Any news?"

She shook her head when Travis came back into the cubicle and took a seat on the opposite side of where Chelsea's bed would be, whenever she returned. "What do you think is taking so long?"

"Hard to say. The Emergency Department is pretty busy, so there might just be—"

Before he finished, someone poked his head between the curtains.

"Is anyone here willing to claim one Chelsea Cooper?"

She heard Chelsea giggle before she saw her smiling face as the bed was wheeled between her and Travis. She was awake! Kate and Travis both jumped up to greet her before the aide could even put the brake on the gurney.

"Mom, Daddy, I wanna be a radiology tech like Noah when I grow up."

Kate released a nervous laugh as some of the pent-up anxiety was expelled hearing Chelsea had returned to the medical field again in her job aspirations. "You can be whatever you set your mind to, sweetie. More important, though, how do you feel?"

She furrowed her brows. "My head is killing me." She reached up to touch the bandage on her forehead. "What happened?"

"I'll leave you folks alone. Chelsea, y'all take care and no more stupid horse tricks."

Chelsea grinned at the young man with the Kentucky-blue spiked hair. "Don't worry! I learned my lesson. Bye, Noah! Thank you!"

"Yes, thanks for taking such good care of her," Travis said.

Kate thanked him as well, but couldn't take her eyes off Chelsea. She couldn't believe she'd been seriously injured barely two hours ago and now was smiling and happy. While she seemed to be back to normal, Kate would wait for reassurance from the doctor that there weren't any hidden issues to keep Chelsea from a full recovery.

"You scared twenty years off our lives, young lady. What were you thinking to go out riding Angus, and without a helmet?"

Kate wasn't ready to chastise her. "Travis, we'll talk about it later." She was thrilled Chelsea appeared to be okay.

Chelsea grew contrite at Travis's words, though, not meeting either of their gazes. "I don't really remember much. At breakfast, I got mad and wanted to show Mom I was ready for a more challenging horse."

"And how'd that work out for you?" he asked.

Why was Travis being so hard on her? Okay, Kate was upset about the accident, too. All three of them shouldered some of the blame for what had happened.

Tears welled in Chelsea's eyes. Kate started to tell him to back off then suddenly realized Travis was doing what she'd accused him of avoiding before. He was parenting. As if expecting her to interrupt, he halted Kate with his hand. Both of them waited for Chelsea to respond.

"I'm sorry. It was stupid." She looked imploringly at her dad. "Don't be mad. You won't leave me because of this, will you?"

Her daughter's words echoed thoughts Kate had harbored inside since she was five, only she hadn't been able to beg her own mother to stay. She'd left while Kate was in school.

"You messed up, Chelsea," Travis said, drawing Kate back to the present. "But we aren't going to stop loving you because of it. Not that you aren't old enough now to think things through before acting impulsively." Travis glanced at Kate and grinned, giving her a one-shoulder shrug with a quirk of his lips. Like father, like daughter. Then he returned his attention to Chelsea. "I still have to go back home this week, but you'll always be in my life, even when we're apart for short periods. I'll never leave you."

Travis had told her she and Chelsea would come first no matter what, and she was beginning to see that he meant it.

"Then you don't hate me?" Chelsea asked in a whisper.

"I sure as hell hate the choice you made, and I'll expect you to learn from this mistake so it isn't repeated." He cupped her cheek. "But I'll never hate you. I will *always* love you, Chelsea."

Kate felt herself transformed into the little girl who'd blamed herself for causing her mother to leave her all those years ago. How did she erase decades of self-blame over believing she'd been the reason her mom had left?

Not to mention figure out how she was going to share her daughter with Travis. She'd better work on it before she drove Chelsea away trying to keep her all to herself, the same way her father had done with Kate by lying to her about her mom and keeping the two of them apart. How had she turned into her father?

Kate blinked away the tears as Chelsea wrapped her arms around Travis's neck and sobbed more apologies. Clearly, Travis was going to be the most amazing daddy ever given how quickly he'd grown into the role. Sure, he'd made a mistake about the horse, but Kate hadn't been a perfect parent, either.

"Daddy," Chelsea hiccupped, as she tried to regain control of her emotions, "I want to stay with you the rest of the summer."

Already Chelsea wanted to leave her? Kate's heart hammered. Was she prepared for this? Had the two of them talked about this earlier, once again leaving Kate out of the discussion? Travis made eye contact with Kate, however, arching his brows and giving an almost imperceptible shake of his head. But how did Travis intend to respond to Chelsea's declaration? He'd told her he had some days off after the Fourth, but he'd already been gone the last two weeks.

Grateful she had her daughter back in one piece, she mouthed to Travis *"we'll talk later."* Kate forced a smile to her face, not wanting to let on how much she dreaded what decision they'd come to about this, but deep down, Kate knew Chelsea needed more time with Travis to make up for the lost years.

He set Chelsea away and grabbed a tissue for her to dry her eyes and face. "Sunshine, let's start with this long weekend coming up, and I'll have to discuss plans for the summer with your mom later. Besides, she and I talked this morning after you ran out, and she might have projects arranged for your summer already."

Chelsea turned toward her. "You do?"

Kate nodded, grateful to Travis for remembering. "If you'd like to work toward getting a performance horse, then I'll sign you up to show the rest of the summer and into the fall on the academy circuit."

Chelsea turned toward her, eyes open wider. "You mean you're going to let me do shows like Melissa does?"

Kate nodded. "She started out at the academy level, too, and worked hard to get to where she is today. It took years, but if you're willing to put in the time and effort needed to train, I don't see why you can't be where she is in a couple of years. And if you can show me…"—she glanced at Travis, who was a part of this—"…*us* that you're committed for the long-haul over the rest of the year, then we'll talk about acquiring a horse of your own to show on."

Chelsea wrinkled her brow as she contemplated Kate's words, looking from Kate to Travis, before gracing them with her beautiful smile. "Could I train on Chula? She's my favorite of all your horses."

"Chula's an excellent choice, far superior to what many of the riders will bring to the shows." Honestly, the horse was probably her most valuable one, so Chelsea had to know she'd be sold eventually. Would Kate have the heart to sell this horse once Chelsea became more attached to her, especially after finding out where the name *chula* came from?

"I'm going to show you both I'm totally ready for my own show horse."

Travis, who had remained silent during the exchange, said, "We decided to hold off talking about you owning a performance horse of your own until the show season ends in November." He'd picked up on Chelsea's penchant for selective hearing, again showing that he was a natural at parenting once he learned the ropes. "However, I don't want you to neglect Princess Jasmine. She's been there for you for six years now, and you have a commitment to her."

"Oh, Jazz will always be my special horse! I like riding her the best." She turned toward Kate. "And she's much better behaved than Angus!"

The three of them laughed, something Kate hadn't thought she'd be doing again for a long while.

"Do your best, and I'll take you to Murfreesboro in November for the National Academy Championship. The first day's classes are open to anyone. I'm confident that, if you put your mind and energy into it, you'll place high in the initial classes and easily advance to the more competitive ones with your abilities. Do you want to work on accomplishing that goal?"

"For sure! You'll see, Mom. I'm ready!"

Kate hoped so. Her daughter had talent, but Kate wasn't sure she had the perseverance necessary. A few minutes ago, she'd wanted to spend the summer with Travis in Nashville. Kate realized that probably wouldn't happen if she was serious about this training schedule.

Perhaps the possibility of having her own show horse one day would be the incentive she needed to mature.

After the physician delivered the results confirming that she had a concussion but thankfully no brain bleed, Kate was given a list of symptoms to watch for and Chelsea was discharged.

On the ride home, Kate had to deal with the consequences for Chelsea's reckless behavior. "The doctor said you won't be able to ride for the next week or so, but he didn't say anything about you being unable to do extra chores in a couple of days."

"But Mom, my head hurts really bad." Interesting considering she's been giggly not so long ago.

"That's part of your punishment, too, for doing such a careless and dangerous stunt," Travis said, backing her up. She smiled at him as he drove them home.

"The doctor said your headaches should clear up in a few days, and tonight I'm going to have to wake you up a few times to check on you. But there's no riding in the meantime. You'll be staying home until we leave for Tennessee on Friday."

"But I was going to the movies tomorrow night with my friends."

"You heard your mom," Travis said. "You're grounded."

Kate had never had anyone around to help with disciplining Chelsea before. Maybe sharing parental responsibilities wasn't going to be so bad after all.

"Why don't you watch me working with Melissa this week?" An idea occurred to her that Melissa might like to become a mentor to Chelsea, much like kids did in 4-H, but she'd discuss that later after talking with the girl.

Back at the house, she discovered Miguel had helped Melissa with her morning lesson. Kate had completely forgotten about the day's lesson. He confirmed that the girl knew where she needed to improve. Besides, they still had plenty of lessons scheduled for this week and the beginning of next week. Chelsea was Kate's first priority now.

Kate insisted that Chelsea take it easy today, and the girl had gone up to her room while Kate prepared her a late lunch. She'd complained of a headache still, but the doctor said that was to be expected.

Kate overheard Travis on the phone in the hallway, apparently asking Clint to help out at the company this week. Did Travis intend to stay here until he was sure about Chelsea's condition?

It didn't sound as though the response he received was the one he wanted. He went upstairs, and when he came back down to the kitchen, his lips were pressed tight.

"Kate, I hate doing this, but I'm going to have to leave tonight."

Well, so much for sharing the parenting.

"Look, I didn't say anything earlier, but my foreman was injured this morning and won't be back until August. There's no one I can get to take over for Jackson. If we don't finish this project on time, we forfeit a sizable chunk of money."

"Have you told Chelsea?" He nodded his head. "How'd she take it?"

He shrugged. "Said she understood. I think it helped knowing she'll be down there with me Friday night to spend four days."

Kate wouldn't put words in Chelsea's mouth, but fumed for a minute before muttering that would be fine and turning to the fridge for some green olives to add to Chelsea's plate.

"I tried to see if Clint could take over, but he's in the middle of a big project for Dad. I don't like leaving you two, but I need to oversee the crew for the rest of the week."

"You need to do what's best for you. I'll keep you posted on Chelsea's condition."

He scrubbed his face. "Chelsea's twelve, not two. She doesn't need someone by her side the whole time. I can check in via Facetime or Skype."

"I said that's fine. What more do you want me to say?"

"Yeah, I know what your 'fine' means." He closed his eyes and inhaled deeply before piercing her with a stare that stilled her hands from opening the jar. "Cut me some slack, Katie? I'm doing the best I can. She has you. If this had happened two weeks ago, you'd have had to handle it by yourself. At least I was here for her today."

Kate's body began trembling. Perhaps the adrenaline was crashing. Suddenly, Travis's arms were around her. "She's okay. Everything turned out for the best. I'd stay if I could, believe me, but missed deadlines come with steep penalties and that could affect my ability to keep my crew working in the future if jobs dry up."

She sniffled, feeling like a shrew. "I understand that accidents happen. I don't know what got into me."

"You've had a helluva day, woman. Wish I could stick around and give you a massage or something."

She grinned, her mind going straight to the gutter. No, actually, there was nothing wrong with the feelings she shared for this man.

"The offer still stands for you to join us this weekend, Katie."

After the blow-up in the parking lot and again just now, Kate was embarrassed to accept. They'd both said some hurtful truths, and she felt raw still. "We'll see."

Spoken like a true parent, Kate.

She didn't relish the idea of dropping Chelsea off at the door, either. What if Travis was called in to work and had to leave her alone?

Kate glanced up and met Travis's gaze. "Are you sure she should make the trip after what happened today?"

"I asked the doctor, remember? He didn't see any problem with it unless she shows some of the warning signs."

Clenching her teeth, she nodded curtly before saying goodbye and heading up to Chelsea's room with her lunch. Neither Travis nor the doctor took one important issue into consideration.

They're not her mother.

*   *   *

Kate looked up from weeding the tomato plants in her garden when she heard a vehicle pulling into the lane. She'd only been at it for thirty minutes, but already was sweating buckets. Chelsea wasn't due home from her friend's house until after supper. They'd worked for more than two hours after Chelsea had watched Melissa's morning lessons. Kate showed Chelsea various moves and techniques Chula was capable of. When Chelsea complained that her head hurt, Kate sent her into the house. However, she couldn't be more pleased with the girl's questions and attention to detail. Last night, they'd found a show in northeastern Ohio for Chelsea to enter and work toward over the next month. It would be here before they knew it. Chula also seemed happy to be working toward a show again, as if she understood. It had been a long time since she'd had a mount for a show.

So had Chelsea decided to come home early? Kate's spirits soared. The afternoon had become lonely for her since Chelsea left a few hours ago. She'd become accustomed to having Travis around to fill the gaps, but he'd left yesterday once they knew Chelsea was going to be okay.

But the unfamiliar black Range Rover driving toward her wasn't the SUV she expected Chelsea to come home in. It wasn't Lidia or Jason's, either. She shook off the dirt from her gloves and removed them. The kneeling pad had kept her knees clean. She walked toward what looked like a couple. The man exited first. He was almost as tall as Travis. The woman came around from the other side, petite with long, auburn hair.

"Hi, I'm Kate Michaels. Welcome to Michaels Bluegrass Saddlebreds." She extended her hand first to the woman.

"We're Tillie and Greg Buchanan," Greg said. "Saw your sign about offering riding lessons."

Ah, that explained the unannounced visit.

The woman added, "We were just at the winery down the road choosing some bottles for our B&B in Nelson County, Jesse's Hideout."

"I'm good friends with Lidia and Jason. I'm sure you found some great wines. And, yes, I do offer riding lessons. Which one of you is interested?"

They glanced at each other and laughed before Greg said, "Actually, my son. He's five, almost six. I share custody with his mother in Minnesota. That's where he is this week, but he's been wanting to learn to ride for a while now."

"That's the perfect age to start. I'd be happy to talk with you about what I might offer. Perhaps you'd like a quick tour if you have time."

"Sounds wonderful," Tillie said.

"Follow me." Kate always loved bringing in new students and hoped they'd be impressed with what she had to offer. She showed them some of the horses in the barn. "This one's only fourteen hands high and would be a good one to start your son with."

Greg patted the neck of the bay mare, Twilight. "She's gentle and takes to kids. My daughter started out on her. She's twelve now, so I've had her for quite a few years."

Twilight nuzzled Tillie, who giggled. "She's adorable. I can't wait to bring Derek out here to meet her and the other horses—and his instructor, too."

"That would be me. I do all the training and am also the riding instructor."

Greg asked, "When would he be able to start lessons? He'll be back in Kentucky for the rest of the summer starting on Tuesday."

"I have a show that will take up most of next week, but the week after would be fine. We'll begin slowly, teaching him about caring for the horse before and after the ride, and he may have an affinity for a different horse. As long as I feel he's able to handle it, we'll go from there. Why don't we go into my office so I can check my schedule?"

On the way, they determined that weekdays would be best given their schedule at the inn, which also worked out better for Kate.

They headed toward the main office in the arena. The way Greg wrapped his arm around Tillie as they walked made Kate miss Travis all the more.

After looking at the availabilities on their schedules, Tillie said, "Let's do Wednesdays, then if guests are staying over or arriving early, we shouldn't have any issues."

Once that was set, Greg sat back, "So you run this place all by yourself?" His fingers played with Tillie's auburn curls.

Kate nodded. "With the exception of my breeding manager, but my students help with some of the chores, and my twelve-year-old daughter pitches in, too."

"I admire you," Tillie said. "You sound like me when I had to run everything on my own, too." She looked up at Greg and they exchanged a smile. "But I don't know how I would run the inn without Greg now."

Travis had been a huge help to Kate as well, when he'd shown up here. But more important than mucking stalls, he'd also made life much more enjoyable and had even managed to get her away from the farm to have some down time once in a while.

She missed spending time with Travis, but words had been said that would make it difficult for them to ever build anything deeper than a string of sexual encounters.

Watching Greg and Tillie together, for the first time in her life, Kate knew she wanted more. So much more.

Chapter Thirty-Three

O n Friday night, Kate tried to calm the butterflies raging in her stomach as she turned into Travis's driveway. A boat sat in an extended parking area to the left of a two-car garage. The gabled house was a beautiful mixture of brick, stone, and wood with a bay window in front. The detail work clearly spoke of countless hours of labor. Travis most likely had designed and built the house himself.

"Why am I so nervous, Mom?"

Good question—at least Kate knew why she was nervous. She smiled at Chelsea. "You're going to have a lot of fun with your daddy this weekend." Leaving Chelsea here would be the hardest thing Kate had ever done, especially so soon after Chelsea's concussion. But she wanted the two of them to continue forming a strong relationship. The days of having Chelsea all to herself were over. She'd have to share her from now on. With the distance between their homes, dropping off Chelsea was going to become commonplace, at least until she could drive herself there—at the age of twenty-five or so.

The front door opened, and a smiling Travis came toward Chelsea's door. Kate's hands shook as she gripped the steering wheel and tried to hide her nerves from her daughter. Not that she needed to bother. Chelsea was out the door and in Travis's arms in about five seconds flat.

The heated words she and Travis had exchanged at the hospital and again at the house afterward still reverberated in Kate's mind, so she wasn't yet sure if she'd stay tonight. But the two of them would remain civil at least in front of Chelsea. Kate took a deep breath, giving father and daughter a moment alone, then opened her door and retrieved Chelsea's duffel bag from the extended cab. For now, she'd leave hers in the Silverado. By the time she joined them on the driveway, she'd steeled herself for the moment she'd have to say hello to Travis again. He'd consumed her thoughts this week, especially after the promises he'd made Sunday night before all hell had broken loose Monday morning.

Chelsea talked a mile a minute about her first official lessons working toward the Ohio show. Obviously, the girl had overcome her nervousness of a moment ago. She told him about her first academy competition on Chula in late July in northern Ohio. When Travis took out his phone to program in the dates, Chelsea beamed, which made Kate happy, too. She hoped nothing more important would come up now that Chelsea's heart was set on him being there.

Travis listened, smiling, until he pressed a finger against Chelsea's lips and said, "Why don't we get everything inside first? Then we can catch up. Who knew I'd miss so much in just a few days?"

Chelsea giggled. "Sorry." She turned to Kate who stood with Chelsea's bag slung over her shoulder. "I can carry that, Mom." She gladly handed it to her. Kate had noticed a change in Chelsea this past week, where she'd offer to help around the house and farm and to simply take care of herself a lot more now. The change could only be attributed to Travis. If he continued to affect such a positive transformation, Kate was all for him spending more time with her.

Having avoided eye contact with each other the past couple of minutes, when Kate met Travis's gaze at long last, her stomach dropped.

"Hi, Katie." His whisky-smooth voice washed over her as he came toward her smiling. "Can I get your bag?"

"I doubt I'll be staying long. I just want to take a quick look around before I leave, if that's okay."

His smile vanished. "Like hell you're leaving. It's after seven, and you've already been on the road for at least four hours." She wouldn't tell him she'd gotten lost and had to backtrack at one point, adding another forty-five minutes to the trip. "You're at least spending the night before heading out on the road again. Where's your bag?"

Kate gave Chelsea a sidelong glance. She was busy becoming acquainted with his dog—Sadie, wasn't it? Lowering her voice, she said, "Given how we parted company Monday, I expected you to want nothing more than to see my taillights headed down the street."

"We both said some things amid all the stress that I know we regret. But I haven't been the one putting the brakes on in our relationship, Katie."

True. Kate had done it in college and seemed to be looking for opportunities to do so again whenever he'd brought up the subject of something long-term. Did she have a problem with commitment? Perhaps she had a need to beat him to the break-up finish line before he could dump her? Whatever her reasons, she needed to stop rehashing the past with him and come clean with him about how she felt. Why did that terrify her? Was she afraid he'd reject her?

"Are you sure it's a good idea that I stay? I don't want to add tension to the weekend. Besides, I have horses to feed in the morning."

"Isn't Miguel there?"

She couldn't get away with her standard excuse for hurrying home. Travis knew too much about her operation now. She really was exhausted after worrying herself to death for the past several days. But staying with him wasn't a good option. Reluctantly, she nodded.

"Problem solved. You can still be home by early afternoon if you have any lessons to give."

"My next lesson isn't until Monday."

His face lit up again. Now why had she admitted that to him? "Perfect. Then you can go to the lake with us tomorrow. Afterward, we can play it by ear."

Without waiting for her response, he opened the rear door and pulled out her overnight bag. She shook her head slightly. He wasn't going to take no for an answer. Oddly enough, the grin he shot her way made her feel there might be hope they could bridge the gap between them since he'd left her and Chelsea a few days ago. Kate relaxed a bit. She'd stay the night, but still didn't want to intrude on what they had planned to do. Or had Travis factored her in, expecting her to agree to stay?

"We'll go out to dinner after I give you two a tour and get you settled in your rooms."

He started up the steps to the front entrance, wrapping his free arm around Chelsea's shoulder. It took everything in Kate's power not to feel a pang of jealousy. How could she be jealous of her own daughter? That settled it. She'd leave first thing in the morning and give them their time.

Sadie came over to greet Katie, wagging her bushy tail. "Hey, girl. Aren't you a beauty?" She petted her a moment before following Travis and Chelsea up the stairs and inside with Sadie in tow.

She was surprised to enter directly into a great room with a vaulted ceiling and white-painted beams. The room was light and airy with a cozy feel despite its size. Although two stories, it didn't look this large from the outside.

A river-rock fireplace dominated one wall, and the open-floor plan encompassed the living room and kitchen with a wide archway leading to a formal dining area.

"What a beautiful home," she said. Kate imagined being curled up beside Travis on a cold evening. Would there ever come a time when she would stop picturing him in her future?

"Thanks," Travis said, setting her bag on the floor next to the sofa. "I practically live in front of this fireplace in the winter, but I don't use it much this time of year. Let me show you around."

She moved closer to the mantel to see what pictures he had there and was surprised to see one of Chelsea that must have been taken the first night he met her. That he'd already made her a part of his home touched Kate.

"Over here is the kitchen." They walked past three high stools tucked up against the island. Stainless appliances, including a gas stove, were tucked in among white cabinets trimmed in greenish-gray that complemented the green quartz countertops.

"It's so modern compared to mine."

"Well, your house has a good hundred years on this one." He opened the fridge. "It's stocked with the things you both like—including your green olives, Chelsea." Travis winked in Kate's direction, catapulting her back to the hike in Red River Gorge. Mostly her memories of that day were fond. "Take a look, though, and if there's anything else you'd like, we can pick it up when we're in town tonight."

She peeked in. Not only had he stocked olives, but also the protein-packed Fairlife milk, Oikos Triple Zero Greek yogurt, and the fresh berries Kate loved. "Looks like everything I'll need for breakfast. Thanks." The countertop also had new boxes of the cereals Chelsea ate, so she'd be good, too.

"There's a patio where we could have our morning coffee tomorrow." An image of them sharing their plans for the day over coffee invaded her thoughts.

"Daddy, can I see my room now?"

"Chelsea, remember your manners," Kate admonished.

"She's fine. Besides, I'm anxious for you to check it out, Chelsea, because it'll be your room to do with as you please. Right this way." He led them to the stairs and up to the second floor.

Without hesitation, she went inside. "I love it!" Travis motioned for Kate to precede him. A cherry four-poster bed, clearly an antique, dominated the room. Its mattress was covered with a star quilt made with red, white, and blue calico fabrics.

"Two years ago," Travis began, "Mom started making quilt tops to shift from work to retirement, but she's busier than ever. A friend she met in the local quilting guild does the machine quilting. Mom just likes piecing the tops, but I think she's probably made two queen- and king-sized ones for each of us since then and smaller ones for Erik and

Olivia. As with everything she does, Mom dives in and it seems more like work than a hobby, but she has fun making them." Travis shrugged then bent close enough to Kate to whisper, tickling her ear. "She's working on one for Chelsea for Christmas, but it's a surprise."

Chelsea was so loved.

Needing to put some space between them, Kate walked over to the quilt to admire it. "She does beautiful work."

"I can't wait to tell Gramma I slept in the bed with her quilt." Chelsea placed her bag on it before going over to the dresser to look at the photos. From across the room, Kate spied another taken the same day as the one on the mantel downstairs, but this one was of both of them. "Who's in this picture?" Chelsea asked, picking up a frame.

Travis came closer to her and pointed out himself and each of his siblings. "That was taken when I was about ten, so the triplets were only five. We were at Barren River Lake State Park just north of here. We spent a week there almost every summer and lots of weekends, too. Dad built a cabin there in the Eighties. I remember that vacation we also toured Mammoth Cave and Kentucky Down Under."

"I've always wanted to go to those places!"

She had? Chelsea had never told Kate that. She had seemed content to be home except the trips with her church's youth group. Of course, they used to go hiking and do more outdoorsy activities before Kate's training and instructional services became more in demand and her horse sales picked up with the improved breeding stock she had available since hiring Miguel.

"Well, then we'll have to go there on your next visit. I have too much planned for this weekend to add another thing."

"Like what?" Chelsea asked. "Besides going out on the lake."

"You'll see. I'll let you anticipate it for a while. That'll just make it all the more special."

"But how can I anticipate something if I don't know what it is?"

Travis chuckled but didn't relent, repeating, "You'll see."

Chelsea rolled her eyes, and Kate shook her head, smiling. Actually, she would have loved to hear what Travis had planned as well, but Chelsea could fill her in when she came home Tuesday.

"Katie, let me show you to your room." He made it sound as though there actually was a room with her name on it, rather than merely a spare bedroom. Of course, Chelsea's room would become hers for all future visits. Next time, they could bring some of her stuffed animals and other creature comforts to put her stamp on it.

"Oh, look!" Chelsea shouted when they turned around. Kate looked up in the corner between the bed and what she assumed was the closet to find a net filled with all kinds of stuffed animals. He really had given some thought to the room being Chelsea's already. She reached up to pull out a dragon. "I'll have to bring Xena with me next time. Unicorns and dragons belong together."

Chelsea surprised her by opening her bag and pulling out several of her smaller stuffed animals, mostly zoo animals and mythical creatures. "You settle in, Chelsea, while I show your mom to her room downstairs. Your bathroom is across the hall if you need it."

Kate followed him back into the hallway. There were two other doors on the opposite side that must be the bathroom and another guest room. She wondered why a bachelor would have so many bedrooms then realized he must have family visit often.

At the bottom of the stairs in the great room, he led her to the opposite end of the house from Chelsea's room. He'd said he had a secluded master bedroom. "I hope you like this room."

She walked in and was stunned at all the University of Kentucky memorabilia in the room. The blue-and-white quilt had a UK print in the center of each block and alternating blue and white squares. "Is this one of your mom's?"

"No. The second one she made me is on my bed. I found this one online when I was decorating this room nearly a decade ago. I might have finished my degree at Vandy, but I consider UK my alma mater."

She nodded. "I didn't go anywhere else but UK always felt like home." With a baby to raise and a farm to run, going back to school hadn't even occurred to her.

Across the cozy room was a gas fireplace and a settee draped with an afghan in the same colors as the quilt. She crossed to the mantel and found a photo of the two of them in animal husbandry class. Surely he hadn't displayed that all these years.

"I pulled that photo out and framed it in honor of your visit." Definitely not as creepy in an obsessed sort of way.

"I'm surprised you kept it all these years."

He seemed startled by her words. "Why wouldn't I? You were an important part of my life."

Of course, she'd kept photos of him, too, with the intention of someday sharing them with Chelsea when she was old enough to understand. She supposed there was no need to keep them from her any longer.

Feeling awkward, Kate said, "I'm looking forward to dinner. Will a western shirt and jeans be appropriate?"

"More than. I texted Chelsea this morning asking if she preferred Mexican or burgers, and she said tacos. So we're going to a local cantina. Nothing fancy but really good food."

Kate's stomach growled. "Sounds great. I haven't eaten since lunch except for a protein bar in the truck halfway here."

"Then we'd better get going. Don't want to have you keeling over on me."

Kate rolled her eyes much like Chelsea might have. "Travis, I'm not going to pass out on you or anyone else. I probably have another hour before I need to eat something." She didn't like having him focus so much on her condition, although she couldn't blame him after giving him such a scare when he'd first shown up.

"Well then, why don't I give you a private tour of the master bedroom down the hall?" His smoldering gaze brought back memories of them making love in the barn apartment and, more recently, his leaving her frustrated in her living room. Her body grew languid. He waggled his eyebrows, making her grin. When he lowered his head to kiss her, all the stress and anxiety since Chelsea's accident vanished. Maybe this weekend would be just what they all needed.

Kate held on to his waist to remain upright as his lips captured hers, first teasing then demanding. She opened her mouth to him immediately, and he held on tightly to her as his tongue delved inside.

What was she doing?

She pulled away and smiled. "I don't think it's a good idea that we go to your bedroom. Let's see if Chelsea's ready to go."

He chuckled and motioned for her to exit the room first. She couldn't help but feel his eyes boring into her back—or perhaps her backside—as she retraced her steps down the hallway toward the great room. The thought of walking the opposite way into his bedroom for a late-night rendezvous crossed her mind, but that was more than she wanted to contemplate right now.

Knowing he'd once again be sleeping in the next room did something to her insides, though. If she wanted to avoid making a mistake, she'd set her alarm for six o'clock tomorrow and hit the road before Travis or Chelsea woke up.

Kate, stop your running.

Maybe Daddy was right. But this weekend wasn't about her and Travis. It was about Chelsea spending time with him. They'd enjoy dinner; then she'd make herself scarce until it was time to go home.

Perhaps if she swallowed her pride and opened up to Travis, he would reward her. On that thought, she headed toward the stairs.

Chapter Thirty-Four

The next morning as the sky started to pinken, Travis rolled over and punched his pillow. It was a wonder the feathers hadn't flown out the other end given the number of times he'd done that overnight. He'd hoped Katie would have come down the hallway to join him in here, but that didn't seem likely at this point.

Frustrated much, Trav?

"Go away, Danny. I'm not in the mood."

As if he'd actually complied, Danny didn't say another word.

Now how was he going to get Katie to lower the wall she surrounded herself with and let him in? She'd come back from dinner hellbent on giving him time alone with Chelsea, so she'd gone to her bedroom and missed out on the movie-and-popcorn binge he'd planned for the three of them. He and Chelsea had watched *Jurassic Park* and *The Lost World: Jurassic Park* until after midnight when they'd gone to bed. He'd only planned on watching one movie before having a little adult time with Katie, but didn't want to wake her up at that point. But he'd hoped to also have some time together as a family. He had the distinct feeling Katie was ready to run. So they might not have today on Center Hill Lake unless he could talk her into sticking around to join them rather than hightailing it back to her sanctuary.

Regardless of whether Katie stayed or not, he couldn't wait to take Chelsea out on his boat at least. How she could reach the age of twelve without having been fishing or swimming in a lake was beyond him. Hell, he'd lived in the city, but his dad had taken them to Otter Creek any number of times to fish, as well as to the family cabin. Would he be able to talk Katie into a family trip someday if the timing was right, what with work, training, and school schedules?

His life was going to be busy from now on if he wanted to fit in Chelsea's shows, but he was pleased that Katie had already signed her up for one he'd get to attend.

The sound of the toilet flushing down the hall made him glance at the alarm clock. Six-eighteen. He tossed off the sheet and grabbed a pair of drawstring sweatpants and the T-shirt he'd left at the bottom of the bed before heading toward the door. Katie was an early riser. Maybe he could talk her into that cup of coffee on the patio after all. He welcomed having this time just for the two of them.

But when he opened the door to the hallway, what he saw wasn't what he'd hoped for—Katie with her purse strap over her shoulder, overnight bag in hand, and fully dressed.

"Good morning," he said, halting her departure by a few seconds anyway.

"Oh!" She jumped and turned toward him. "You scared me to death."

He leaned against the doorjamb with his arms folded in front of his chest. "Didn't do anything but say 'good morning.' Maybe you're feeling guilty about trying to sneak out without saying goodbye. Does Chelsea know you're leaving?"

She refused to meet his gaze, which spoke volumes. So she really had intended to do that. He walked toward her, noticing that she backed up a step before holding her ground. "Why don't I make some coffee? If you'd rather not drink it with me, I can fix you up a travel mug."

"Um, it's not that I'm avoiding you or anything..." *Wasn't it?* "...I just didn't want to intrude on your weekend with Chelsea. I'm sure she'd much rather have some one-on-one time with her daddy. I'll see her when you bring her home Tuesday."

"Actually, I talked with her last night, and she asked me to beg you to stay and go out on the lake with us today."

"She did? To go fishing?" She wrinkled her pert nose. Not her favorite pastime, apparently. "I haven't been fishing since I was about ten. I'm not fond of putting worms on hooks."

"Neither is Chelsea. I pretty much figured I'd be the official bait man for the day. But we'll be going swimming, too. Did you bring a suit?"

Her face brightened. "No, I didn't. Besides I really do need to head back. It's a busy time for me."

"We can stop at a store and get you one." She knitted her brow. "Horses really tie you down, which I guess is convenient for getting rid of a guy you don't want to spend time with."

Katie stood taller, fire flashing from her eyes. "That's not what I'm doing at all. I have responsibilities, like you do. Besides, I don't need an excuse. It's not as though we're serious about each other anymore."

How could she deny what was between them sexually, despite their hot tempers? But that was just the tip of the iceberg? "Speak for yourself, but you and I share more than a daughter. In the past two weeks, we've proven that the attraction between us is as potent as ever. Why do you keep denying it?"

Katie pivoted and started toward the great room. "Let's discuss this over coffee."

Travis grinned as he watched her cute little ass sashay away from him before he followed. In the kitchen, they prepared their coffee and took the pot and their mugs out onto the patio, along with her yogurt and berries.

"Have a seat." The sun had yet to make an appearance over the wooded hills but the sky was bright. Should be a nice day. She took a seat on one of the deck chairs at the table.

"Katie, what are you so afraid of?"

Without missing a beat, she said, "Losing Chelsea."

"Losing in what way?" Hell, he had to admit the thought of anything happening to either of them worried the hell out of him, too, especially after the scare with Chelsea. But somehow he didn't think that was what Katie meant.

"Aside from the obvious, I'll admit I'm also…afraid of losing her to you."

He leaned closer. "We aren't in competition. She needs and loves us both."

Katie closed her eyes. "I didn't say it was logical or even rational."

Bingo! Now that she'd conceded it might not be a rational fear, could he get her to move on? "This has to do with your mom leaving you, doesn't it?"

She shrugged, glancing away. "I'm sure being abandoned by her at such a young age had a lot to do with why I've always tried to keep Chelsea to myself. Being raised by a father who was equally afraid of losing *me*, didn't help. Even after you came back, and I saw you would make a great father to her, I kept returning to the concern that I was going to lose everything."

"What I can't see is why you don't think you can have it all? Why can't you see there's more than one way? Say the word, and we could find a way to make this work as a family."

She met his gaze with an intensity that took his breath away. Fear still, but with something else mixed in. Could it be longing?

He leaned forward and brushed his thumb over her knuckles. She didn't pull away at first or quickly, but then eased back in her chair, breaking contact with him.

They sipped their coffee in silence and he watched the sun light up her face. So beautiful. Would she ever be able to trust him with their daughter's heart? And with hers?

"Come with us today, Katie. It would mean a lot to us both."

She shook her head. "You two need to spend time together—without me."

"Says who? Chelsea wants to spend time with us both." Besides, he wanted to share a glimpse of his world with both of them.

He saw a softening in her expression before moving in for the kill. "Give her this time having fun with all three of us. One day. Isn't it worth a day for our daughter's happiness after what we just went through with her injury?"

Katie nibbled her lower lip. Travis smiled.

* * *

Kate stared at Travis's shirtless back and realized where he must have gotten his tan. His legs below his swimming trunks were dark as well. The three of them were under the boat's canopy to help block most of the sun as he maneuvered the boat into a secluded cove.

"We won't feel the effects of the wake from the other boats in here," he said. He smiled at Chelsea, and it warmed Kate's heart to see how careful he was being with her after her recent concussion. Kate had nothing to worry about when it came to him taking care of their little girl when she wasn't around.

Chelsea wore a life jacket over her lime-green one-piece—and a smile that lit up her eyes. Her hair had blown wildly moments ago as she held on when the boat was moving at a faster clip. Travis had given Chelsea the swiveling co-captain's chair and a cute ball cap that read "Cap'n Chelsea." Kate sat on the side-facing bench behind Chelsea with a great view of Travis standing at the wheel. He'd had a "First Mate" hat made for her in Kentucky blue and white, reminiscent of their college days.

She couldn't help but comment on his "My Boat, My Rules" hat. "So what rules are there aboard *The One That Got Away*?"

He chuckled. "This hat's Danny's idea of a joke. He gave it to me a few years ago after I told him he'd better not come on my boat with a bad attitude."

Kate hoped she hadn't broken the rule, but she had adjusted hers after talking with him this morning. How badly would she have disappointed him—not to mention herself—if she'd gone home today? Over a hearty breakfast of bacon and eggs this morning, it hadn't taken long for Chelsea to twist her arm to stay. Kate surrendered without much of a fight.

Travis cut the engine deep in the Y-shaped cove and turned toward them. "Fish or swim first?"

"Swim!" Chelsea shouted, and both of the adults laughed at her enthusiasm. Kate was secretly happy because she didn't really care for fishing, not that she was that much more proficient at the other.

"Sounds good to me," Travis said. "I doubt the fish will be biting today anyway with all the traffic on the lake. They've probably gone deeper to avoid the commotion. But by tonight, they might resurface."

A short reprieve, at best.

The back end of the boat was made into a platform for them to get in and out of the water. Kate had found a simple black one-piece at the store, which would replace a similar one at home she'd had for almost a decade. When was the last time she'd been in a bathing suit, much less the water?

Chelsea sat on the back and dangled her toes. "It's warm!"

"Well, you'll find hot and cold spots, sometimes in the same place. But the cold will be refreshing when the sun gets hotter."

After Chelsea removed her life jacket they slathered each other with sunscreen. Kate asked Travis for a vest before she'd venture into the water. Her swimming skills were almost nonexistent.

"Last one in is a rotten egg!" Chelsea challenged as she slid off the boat and into the water. Kate held her breath until she surfaced and set off swimming. Chelsea had taken lessons from the ages of four to six because Kate hadn't wanted her to be afraid of the water, too. Travis dove in head first before surfacing and staring at Kate.

"Come on in! Water feels great!"

She didn't want to admit to him she couldn't swim. Of course, the life vest would keep her afloat. "You all go on. I'll just dangle my feet in the water first."

Travis tilted his head then shrugged. "Suit yourself. Chelsea, let's race from the boat over to the shore and back."

"One, two, three—go!" Chelsea took off and Travis swam after her. She nearly beat Travis to the shoreline, and it didn't seem that he was going easy on her.

"Eww! The rocks are slimy!" Chelsea said.

"Slippery," he corrected. "Just some algae, but we aren't leaving the water, so let's head back to the boat. First one to reach your mom gets to kiss her."

Why was he bringing her into this? Still, as much as she loved her daughter, she secretly rooted for Travis to win, because she'd love to kiss him again. "Come on, Chelsea! You too, Travis!" She didn't want to take sides out loud, but when Travis grabbed her foot first, she couldn't keep the smile off her face.

Chelsea was only a second later, and she beamed. "You have to kiss Daddy now, Mom!"

He grabbed a square flotation pillow from the back of the boat then tugged on her leg, gently at first, until she slid off the back of the boat and into his arms. She grabbed for his shoulders, wrapped her arms around his neck, and clung to him for dear life. Her heart pounded. "Don't worry. I've got you."

Embarrassed at her irrational panic, she told herself she wouldn't drown wearing the life vest then confessed, "I can't swim," and buried her face into the crook of his neck.

"Trust me, darlin'. I'm not going to let anything happen to you. Took me too long to find you again."

A sense of calm came over her, not only because he made her feel safe here in the water, but because she hadn't had anyone to lean on in such a long time and knew that Travis could be her anchor if only she'd let him. Bobbing in the surprisingly warm water, she lifted her head and stared into his eyes.

Chelsea giggled. "I promise not to watch." Kate had forgotten she was there. Glancing her way, she saw she'd placed her hands over her eyes, with the fingers over her left one splayed so she wouldn't miss a thing. Kate hadn't kissed Travis in front of her before, but refused to hide her feelings from either of them any longer. She didn't know what had finally clicked for her, but rather than one huge epiphany based on one incident, an accumulation of evidence over the past few weeks told her Travis was right for her. If they could be a family in every sense of the word, she welcomed him into their lives on a deeper level than they'd initially negotiated.

Turning toward him again, she looked into his eyes once more. This wasn't the time to let him know, but by God, she was going to enjoy the hell out of this kiss. She leaned closer and tilted her head. Her mouth nibbled at his lower lip, and he wrapped his legs around her hips below the vest and pulled her as close as he could into the cradle of his thighs. Chelsea couldn't see, could she?

Oh, who cares? She might as well get used to the fact that Kate intended to be demonstrative about her feelings for Travis from now on and not bottle everything up.

Travis's tongue traced her lips, and she opened wider to him, keeping her hands firmly on his shoulders even though she knew he wouldn't let her sink.

"Come on, Daddy! Kiss her!"

What did she think he was doing? Travis pulled away, though, and looked in their daughter's direction. "Why don't we see how fast you can swim back and forth to the shore?" Chelsea looked from one to the other, and Kate grinned, anxious to lose the audience, too.

Chelsea's face grew flushed and she nodded with a grin. "I know when I'm not wanted." She didn't seem the least bit upset, though, as she straightened out in the water and with a leisurely stroke swam away.

"Now, where were we?" he asked, drawing her attention back to him.

"I think you were kissing me."

Seemingly in no hurry, he leaned in, and she closed her eyes, waiting. He didn't disappoint. His lips captured one of hers and he placed tiny kisses there, until sucking her lower lip harder. When his tongue licked her upper one, she opened wider, tilting her head to give him better access. As his tongue mimicked lovemaking, she moaned. He squeezed her butt cheeks, pressing his erection against the apex of her thighs. Obviously, he was as turned on as she was.

One hand slid between their bodies and he stroked the bundle of nerves that had been neglected for too long. She pulled away, searching for Chelsea's whereabouts and saw that she was swimming parallel to the shore, just as slowly. Clearly, she didn't want to intrude and would give them their privacy, so Kate gave herself over to the moment. She hated that her fear of drowning wouldn't allow her to let go of his shoulders and touch him. Instead, she released his mouth and trailed kisses across his cheek to his earlobe where she nibbled. He groaned, his fingers stroking her harder. Would he bring her to an orgasm, knowing Chelsea was so close?

"How quietly can you come?"

Her hips surged against his hand. "Like a mouse."

He chuckled and his finger went in tiny circles against her, taking her breath away. She kissed his neck and whispered, "That feels so good. I've missed you so much."

"Me, too, Katie." Needing no further encouragement apparently, he increased the speed of his finger, taking her breath away. "Come for me." His lips covered hers again to capture any sound she might make, and she kissed him with a new sense of urgency. The tension she'd tried to ignore for so long burst through her and she grabbed the back of his head to make sure her not-so-silent moan couldn't be heard by Chelsea as she found her release.

Becoming aware of their situation far too abruptly, she pulled away. "That was incredible, but can we finish this tonight, in your bedroom?"

"Let's make sure we wear Chelsea out so she goes straight to bed when we get home tonight."

Fire surged through her. It was only eleven-thirty in the morning. How would she possibly make it through the rest of the day when all she wanted to do was to jump in bed with Travis?

He reminded her that she was still a woman, not just a mother. She had desires, too, and while she'd always take care of her daughter, she needed to let someone take care of her, too, sometimes. She also wanted to find out what Travis needed from her—not stopping with intimacy shared in stolen moments like this one, but long-term. Tonight, they needed to talk about where to go from here.

*   *   *

Travis reflected on how well the day on the lake had turned out—better than he'd expected. Oh, Katie had gotten quiet after lunch, making him wonder if she was tired or plotting her escape as soon as they returned to the house. But he'd been able to coax her back into the water and even had her swimming around the boat at one point.

A quick glance in the rearview mirror showed Chelsea fighting to stay awake. She'd enjoyed the hell out of swimming. After a few hours, they'd parked at the Fishlipz marina for an early dinner before he took them to one of his favorite coves for fishing. Both of them had tolerated more than enjoyed the sport, but Chelsea had been elated when she caught a six-inch bluegill. They'd released it again, but he hoped that had planted the seeds and that she'd want to go fishing with him again.

Katie and Chelsea had helped him towel dry the boat and trailer. He'd named the boat in reference to Katie, although most people simply thought "the one that got away" referred to a fish. Katie didn't seem any the wiser, either.

On the drive home, Chelsea asked, "Why don't you keep your boat at the marina, Daddy?"

"I like taking her to different lakes rather than always go to the same one. Might as well transport her myself."

He glanced over at Katie. He didn't know why she'd lowered her defenses earlier, but she'd laughed and become playful after that encounter this morning. Funny how a good orgasm could break the ice.

He chuckled to himself. God, the woman had exploded for him, albeit trying to remain quiet so Chelsea wouldn't be aware of what was going on. All day, he'd been anticipating getting her back to the house. To his bedroom.

At the house, he parked the boat to the side of the garage. They'd be going out to watch the fireworks on the lake, after all. After they'd unloaded the truck, he asked, "Would you ladies like anything to eat?" He unlocked the front door.

Chelsea shook her head. "I'm beat. Can I just go to bed?"

"Sure, sweetie," Katie said, wrapping her in a hug. "You've had a big day. But be sure and take a shower and wash your hair so you won't wake up smelling like the lake in the morning."

Travis had no clue what was wrong with that, but Chelsea gave her a squeeze then came to Travis. "It was the best day ever. Thanks, Daddy. I can't wait to go again."

His heart swelled as he opened his arms to her. "Anytime, but you're going to be busy the rest of the summer getting ready for your horse shows, and I'm going to have my hands full at work." He didn't know when the next time would be that he'd be able to go boating, given Jackson's being on disability for at least the next five weeks.

Travis had visited Jackson a few nights ago and, after finding out the man hadn't eaten anything but peanut butter and jelly sandwiches since the accident, he'd called Emmy to see if she'd be able to come down and take care of him for at least a couple of weeks. She'd jumped at the chance. He had a feeling she liked him. They'd met each other a number of times at the annual Veterans Day picnic Travis held, as well as the few times Travis had talked Jackson into coming to Thanksgiving dinner. She was an excellent cook and could help with other things around the house, too. Emmy might be a pain when she got something stuck in her craw, but there was no one else besides Mom that he'd go to in a time of crisis. Until now. He had Katie, too.

Of course, Travis was just about as stubborn and proud as Jackson was, so admitting he needed help wasn't easy for either of them. And he didn't take the offer until Travis threatened to demote him.

Stubborn man.

Takes one to know one, Trav.

Travis chuckled at Danny's assessment. Before they said good night to Chelsea, Katie pulled out her testing kit and alcohol wipes. Was her sugar okay? When she would have headed to the bathroom, he insisted she test in the kitchen. He certainly had no qualms about it. Katie needed to eat something, and he could go with a snack himself, so they split a turkey sandwich.

"Want to eat out on the patio?"

"That sounds great, if it doesn't rain."

"Not to worry. There's a section that's under cover with a table." They'd been lucky enough today not to run into rain. Then again, if it did rain, he could build a fire and cozy up next to her. But there didn't seem to be any imminent raindrops. He'd have to save that fantasy for when she came back the next time.

"Thanks for joining us today. It wouldn't have been the same without you."

She smiled. "I had a wonderful time. Now I'll be able to picture what you two are up to when she visits."

His spirits drooped a little. Was she distancing herself again? "You know the door's always open to both of you. I know you're going to be busy next weekend and that we'll be together in Ohio in a few weeks, but I hope you'll consider coming down here again in August."

"Chelsea starts school on the tenth."

He reached over the end table between them and took her hand. "This isn't going to work."

Her eyes grew wide and she met his gaze. "What do you mean?"

"I want to be a part of your lives, more than on the occasional weekend."

"I understand, but our livelihoods aren't going to give us a break for a while."

"Are you saying you'd be interested in something more if we could work it out?" She finished her sandwich and nodded, but he wanted to know what she had in mind. "Not just for Chelsea's sake, but to explore what we have between us?"

She shrugged, then grinned. "I spent most of today thinking about it while you were busy driving the boat and fishing."

Maybe that was why she hadn't been as enthusiastic about catching fish? She'd been mulling over their future? *Hell, yeah.* He'd take it.

Taking him by surprise, she stood and closed the gap, standing in front him. Taking his hand in hers, she indicated he should remain seated and knelt in front of him. He wasn't sure what was up, but didn't want to interrupt.

"Travis, a week ago at your parents' you asked if I'd marry you." His heart soared. "It's not fair of me to expect you to change everything in your life in order to make it work—"

He touched his finger to her lips and tugged her onto his lap. "Why don't you let me decide what I'm prepared to give up? All I want is for us to have a life together."

"But you have other obligations, too."

He nodded, wanting to kiss her in the worst way but she was being so damned serious. "I won't have much time for us until Jackson's healed and back to work, but you're going to be awfully busy with Chelsea's training over the next four or five months before the show season is over."

Her gaze dipped to his lips before she looked into his eyes again. "I'm willing to see if we can make this work."

"You aren't just saying that because of Chelsea, I hope, because I'll be there for her no matter what."

"No, this is about us. Not that she wouldn't love for us to figure this out at some point, but it has to be what we both want."

He slid his hand behind her neck and pulled her face toward his. "All I know is that I've been wanting to do this since I claimed that kiss this morning." His lips brushed hers lightly at first and then more insistently. She opened her mouth to him, but he pulled away. "Let's take this down the hall."

Her pupils dilated, and she smiled, scooting off his lap and holding out her hand for him. "What are we waiting for?"

They reentered the house and he led her toward his bedroom.

Two hours later, long after they had both found release, Travis heard Katie's breathing slow as her head became a precious weight against his shoulder. He could hold Katie like this forever. Tomorrow she'd go back home to Kentucky and he'd be left here in Tennessee. After this weekend, there was every indication they would work together to find a way to make their relationship stronger, but it was going to take time.

They belonged together, not only for Chelsea but for themselves. He wanted her to lean on him, but he'd need to be there physically for that to happen. He sure as hell had no desire to rattle around in this big house alone anymore. And, while he'd hate to admit it, he needed her, too. Losing Danny had taught him how alone he was, despite his friends at work and his family. He wanted someone he could confide in and be open with again on a daily basis.

Moving to Midway would mean selling his company, unless he wanted to be a figurehead owner—or open another branch and make Jackson his partner. Nah. He'd prefer starting over again. Now to find out if his foreman had any interest in owning the business. Jackson had practically run the day-to-day operations for the last six months, ever since Danny had passed. While Travis had physically shown up most days, his heart and mind hadn't been in it anymore. Not without Danny. Time to think about what he wanted to do for the next twenty or thirty years.

He'd also have to sell this house. Nolensville was a decent market. He shouldn't have trouble, but he'd put a lot of his heart and craftsmanship into the place. Having just anyone come in and live here would be difficult. Emmy raved about the place whenever she visited, so he'd give her first dibs on it. Having it remain in the family would mean a lot to him. She'd shown this week that she could pick up and move anywhere while she was taking care of Jackson. And she tended to prefer warmer weather, so Nolensville would be perfect for her new home.

One thing for sure, he had no intention of letting his boat go. Kentucky had plenty of lakes to fish and swim in. Chelsea and Katie had enjoyed being out on the lake, too, so he'd hang onto it for many more such days as a family.

Don't put the cart in front of the horse, Trav.

He smiled. *I've been wondering where you've been lately, Danny.*

Busy as hell. You'd better get used to me not being around. Looks like I'm going to have to move on soon for good.

Travis furrowed his brows. He wanted to ask what that meant, but didn't want to hold his friend earthbound if his spirit was ready to move on.

Oh, I'm going to be more earthbound than you think.

Travis grinned, forgetting Danny could "hear" his thoughts. He still had no clue what Danny meant, but understanding heaven speak was above his pay grade.

Take good care of Katie, or I'll find you and kick your ass.

"Don't you worry about a thing there," Travis whispered, stroking her hair when she stirred. *I'm not going to let anything bad happen to her.* Soon she settled into a deep sleep again. *But I'm gonna miss you, Danny.*

I'll miss you, too, man. Be good.

A few weeks ago, he hadn't thought the day would come when he'd be able to let Danny go, but the time seemed right now. "Oh, and by the way," Travis began. "I believe you that it was an accident that night."

He didn't hear a response and wondered if Danny had heard him. Regardless, Travis would find a way to honor his friend's memory properly. Sure, he'd put together a decent memorial service soon after Danny died and had given him a monument where some of his ashes had been buried in the Nashville National Cemetery, but Travis hadn't been all there then and barely remembered anything about it.

He placed a kiss on the top of Katie's head. Having her back in his life had helped him come to terms with the loss of Danny. His buddy had known just what Travis needed, even when Travis couldn't think straight. And Danny's sending him on the mission to reunite with Katie had enabled him to realize his friend wasn't gone. Danny would always have a strong presence in Travis's life.

Chapter Thirty-Five

Kate tried to control her anxiety as Chelsea entered the outdoor arena on a warm Sunday in late July. She was competing in the academy class for eleven to seventeen-year-olds. There was nothing more Kate could do to prepare her daughter. Chelsea and Chula had performed amazingly well in their earlier event this morning, winning first place in the walk/trot equitation class, but she wanted desperately to take home another blue ribbon in walk/trot/canter where the riders were of a higher caliber. While they'd spent all day yesterday watching the competition and Kate had given her pointers on things to watch for, these two were the only classes she'd been able to enter Chelsea in at that level of competition.

Kate was certain that if Chelsea remained calm, she'd excel. Her form was better than ever. She could see her daughter showing Chula, or any other horse, on the more advanced circuit next year if she kept this up. Clearly, Chelsea was more driven than she had been over the past year.

"You've done an incredible job with her, Katie." Travis placed his hand on her left shoulder and his thumb rubbed between her shoulder blades, distracting Kate. He wrapped his arms around her waist and pulled her against him.

"She did all the work. I was amazed at how quickly she was back in top form after such a long break."

"What are her chances in this one?"

"If she stays focused, she should ribbon, possibly even the blue, but it's always a crapshoot. Any distraction to her or Chula could throw them both off."

"I'm no expert and am probably more than a little biased, but I think she's going to win first place in this class, too."

Travis had been up at the farm the past two weekends to watch Chelsea prepare for the show. Yesterday, he and Kate had taken turns driving the truck hauling the horse and trailer to Ohio. Having another pair of hands to help load and unload made quick work of the process as well. She was going to enjoy having Travis around on show weekends.

"Oh, before I forget," Kate said, "Shania called last night to apologize for not being able to make it this weekend. She and Emmy are on a case that's going to require travel." Kate glanced over at the stands where Loretta and Joe were seated waiting for the class to start. Chelsea had been so excited to see them this morning when they came to the motel. "What happened with her taking care of Jackson, anyway? I thought she was going to stay until his leg healed."

Travis chuffed. "He threw her out after only a few weeks. Said he didn't need to have a fussy woman pestering him all the time. I'd say he's on the mend."

"That's good to hear." Perhaps some of the pressure would be off Travis then. "Anyway, Emmy asked me to brainstorm some possible names my mom might be using as an alias. They've really hit a brick wall." Kate didn't think they'd ever find her mother, but didn't want to give up, either.

"Funny you should say that because Danny told me the clues are right in front of our faces. We need to come up with some ideas to run by them."

He now accepted that Danny still talked to him, so much so that he took it matter-of-factly now. But it was time to solve this mystery if Danny wouldn't—or couldn't—tell them outright.

"I don't want to miss any great shots of Chelsea, so I'll make the list in my head and text it to you on the way home."

"Sounds good. Okay, she was in Escondido when she wrote me

the last letter. And Reno after that. Could she have picked up one of the names of the places she lived?"

Travis shrugged. "Could be anything."

"Diego, too, then, for San Diego." She thought a while waiting for Chelsea's turn. "She used to call me that. Perhaps she chose that as a name because it reminded her of me."

He didn't jot it down but pointed to the arena. "Here she comes," he said, and they leaned forward to watch. "Let me video some of it to show my brother and sisters what they missed." He held up his smartphone, pointing it in their daughter's direction.

Chelsea kept her back straight and eyes forward as she put Chula through the intricate steps that they'd practiced for hours every day for nearly a month. The horse's ears were pointed forward and her tail set at the perfect angle.

After several minutes, he lowered the phone. "I've never seen her this good, Travis. Look at the determination on her face. And the light in her eyes. Chula's on this morning as well. You might be right." What a boost to Chelsea's confidence it would be if she…

At the far end of the arena, Chula had a misstep and Kate tensed, holding her breath.

"What's wrong?" Travis asked.

"Her transition to the canter wasn't smooth, but I'm not sure the judge caught it with several other riders in the arena, too, so it might not be held against her."

"Man, this stuff is nerve-racking. How do you stay so calm watching her compete?"

She laughed, but didn't take her eyes off Chelsea. "It's a lot easier when Melissa's competing, even at a higher level, than when it's my daughter."

The horses and riders in this class lined up to await the judge's decision. Kate held her breath as the third-place ribbon was announced. Not Chelsea. Then the red ribbon. Again, no Chelsea.

Travis leaned down next to her ear. "Breathe before you pass out."

He pecked her on the cheek. Having him here made it so much more enjoyable than when she'd had to stand on the sidelines alone.

"And the first-place ribbon goes to…Chelsea Cooper on Michaels' Chula!"

Kate jumped up and squealed, turning around to hug Travis with all her might before directing her attention to Chelsea again. "She did it!"

"You both did," he said.

But the credit all went to Chelsea and Chula and their hard work. Chelsea patted Chula on the neck and bent down to say something to the horse before riding over to have the ribbon attached to the horse's bridle and taking her victory lap.

To Travis, Kate said, "I'm so glad you could be here to see this. It means a lot to me that you're taking such an active interest in her riding, even when it takes you so far from home at such a busy time."

"I wouldn't miss it for the world."

Chelsea rode over to them, beaming with pride, and they congratulated her. After they both admired the ribbon, she said, "I can't wait to show everybody in Louisville next week."

With school starting in a few weeks, Kate had promised to take her to Louisville for a long visit with her aunts, uncle, and grandparents. Kate would miss her, but would have enough to do with her new and former riding students wanting some extra lessons before the school year began. Chelsea would stay for about a week and then return in time to go school shopping.

Travis would be back in Tennessee. It was going to be a lonely time at the farm, despite all she had to do.

If only she and Travis could find a way to be together always. She hoped things would settle down when school started and Jackson's leg would heal so he could return to work. Maybe then the two of them could discuss their future.

*   *   *

"Katie, it's Emmy."

Kate set her fork down on the kitchen table and held her breath. "Is Chelsea all right?" she choked out.

"Oh, absolutely! She and Shania went shoe shopping at Oxmoor. I never understood the fascination; I tend to have three or four pairs at any given time, and that's plenty."

Emmy hadn't called to chat about shoes. Then why… "Have you found something about my mom?"

"Yes, I have. The brainstorming session you did with Travis last week helped us come up with some new combinations of names to try to find an alias for her, and we've cracked the case at last."

Kate's heart hammered to the point it became difficult to hear. "Is she alive?"

"Yeah, but going by another name—Serenity Chula."

Danny had been right. The clues were right in front of them all along. Her mom had assumed the middle name she'd given Kate as a baby along with a last name that had been her nickname for Kate. Both cemented the fact that Mom hadn't stopped thinking about her, despite all the years apart.

"She's living in Portland—Oregon's Portland," Emmy continued. So she'd remained out west. "But, Katie, there's something you need to know."

Her heart jumped into her throat. "What's that?"

"Her health isn't good. My source tells me she's been hospitalized for about a week." With the way insurance companies had people kicked out of hospitals so quickly these days, that sounded serious. "I'm really sorry, Katie. I don't know what her prognosis is, but you might want to go out as soon as you can if you're going to go."

Kate blinked away the sting in her eyes. She stood and started toward the office at the front of the house before stopping and glancing around at a loss for what to do next. Then her brain kicked in again. "I need to make some arrangements for the farm and book a flight out there."

"Would you like for us to keep Chelsea in Louisville until you get back or do you want her to go, too?"

Kate was torn between wanting Chelsea to meet her other grandmother and wanting to protect her in case it didn't go well when she went to see her mom. If it worked out, she could always take Chelsea out to meet her later.

"If you could keep her with you a little while longer, that would be wonderful, Emmy. Thanks so much. I'm sure it will be a quick visit and I'll be home before school starts on the tenth."

"Oh, Travis is here and wants to—Hey!" Emmy shouted a half second before a deep, sexy voice came on the phone.

"I'm going with you, Katie." He'd said he'd be in Louisville this weekend and would bring Chelsea home after visiting with his folks. She closed her eyes and tried not to imagine them both crammed into tight airplane seats for the long flight. "That's really not necessary."

"I'm coming with you," he repeated firmly. "I don't want you to be alone out there."

She didn't want to be alone, either, frankly. "Thanks, but this can't be a good time for you to be away from work."

"Keeping Jackson off-site lately has been impossible, and everyone knows what they need to do so they won't need all that much supervision. He can handle any last-minute crises as long as he keeps his leg propped up."

Knowing Travis would be there to help her face her mother gave her a bit more courage.

I'll be with you, too.

Kate closed her eyes at the sound of Daddy's voice. She ought to remain angry at him for the rest of her days after he'd kept her mother away all those years, but his presence brought her an odd sense of comfort. *Thanks, Daddy.*

"Katie, you still there?"

"Yeah." She took a deep breath. "I'll hang up and book the two of us on a flight."

"You pack. I'll take care of the airline tickets and hotel." To Emmy, apparently, he asked, "Which hospital is she in?"

Her heart tripped a beat. She hadn't been alone with Travis in such close quarters since the Fourth of July weekend.

"I'll pick you up in two hours or less. Would you prefer taking the redeye or to leave first thing in the morning?"

"Tonight's best. Can you put Emmy back on?"

"Sure." His voice was muffled when he said, "She wants to talk to you again. I'm going to text Chelsea and meet her wherever they are to say goodbye before I head out to Katie's." He always seemed to handle crises so effortlessly.

"Sounds good, Travis," Emmy said. "Be safe." Her voice was louder when she spoke directly into the phone again. "Hey, Katie."

"Emmy, can you see if your mom can stay out here with Chelsea if I'm not back before school starts?"

"Absolutely! Mom's been wanting a getaway but Dad won't slow down at work. I can come out, too, if she wants company. Do you want us to take her shopping for school?"

"Thanks. That would be great," she whispered before clearing her throat. "The list of supplies she'll need is on the school's web site. She can print it out. If she wants a new backpack, go ahead. She might think her old one is a little childish, so I'll donate it somewhere. Just let me know how much I owe you."

"Not a thing. I haven't been school shopping since I was in school myself. That kind of shopping I can get into."

Kate was overcome with emotion. "I don't know what I'd have done without you all."

"Hey, that's what families do." Kate truly felt like she was included in that sentiment this time. It meant the world to Kate that it was coming from Emmy, too.

"Thanks, Emmy."

"Now, go pack. I'll talk with you soon."

During the next ninety minutes, Kate called Chelsea to let her know what was going on, checked in with Miguel to be sure he was aware she would be gone for at least a few days, and packed a bag with enough clothes for up to a week, if need be, without having to do laundry. Not knowing what she would find or what kind of reception she'd receive, she probably was overdoing it, but…

"Katie! You up there?" Travis's voice called from the bottom of the stairs.

"Yes!" she called from her bedroom. "I'll be right down."

Seconds later, she heard his boots in the hallway and turned to find him filling the doorway, his broad shoulders tapering to a slim waist. Her heart fluttered before she went back to zipping up the suitcase on her bed. "I'm almost ready. What time is our flight?"

"Not until eight, out of Louisville, so we have time for a quick bite before we leave." She tried to lift the heavy bag until Travis crossed the room and took it from her hand, setting it on its casters. Facing her, he cupped her cheek. "How are you doing?"

The enormity of what was about to take place overwhelmed her, and she soon found herself cocooned in Travis's arms. A sense of security like she hadn't felt in a long while calmed her nerves. "Nervous. Petrified, actually." She pulled away from his arms and looked up at him. "Thanks for going with me. I would never have asked you to, but I'm so glad you offered."

He grinned, shaking his head. "I wasn't about to wait for you to ask." He bopped her playfully on the nose. "Now, let's get your things downstairs, grab a bite, and head to the airport."

Shortly after seven-thirty they boarded the plane. Travis had bought first class tickets, he said so Kate could sleep most of the way to Oregon. She wasn't sure that would be possible. "I haven't flown in I don't know how long." She'd gone with Lidia on a trip to New York City one Christmas during college. Was that the last time? Usually, anywhere she needed to go was within easy driving distance.

When she shivered, Travis asked the flight attendant for a blanket and a pillow. His solicitous manner made her feel like a princess.

"What can you drink?" he asked.

"I don't need anything but water."

"A little alcohol might do you good, as long as it doesn't spike your sugar."

"Actually, it probably would result in a drop in blood sugar. With the fluctuation of nerves to factor in, I'll have to test repeatedly for the next twenty-four hours to make sure I don't run into trouble. Water is preferable to making it worse, though."

He ordered her a water with lemon and a bourbon and water on the rocks for himself. By the time they reached cruising altitude, her eyelids were drooping.

"Feel free to rest your head and your pillow on my shoulder if you'd like."

"Thanks." She did so and then he rested his head on hers, once again giving her that sense of assurance that all would be well.

The next thing she remembered was the announcement that they'd be landing in Dallas momentarily. Travis was reading the in-flight magazine. "I'm sorry. I didn't mean to sleep through half the flight."

"You were beat. You don't have to worry about entertaining me."

In the restroom of the terminal, she tested and saw her sugar was low. So, on their way to their next gate, they stopped for a bite. "Do you think you'll have any trouble getting in to see your mom?"

She shrugged. "I hope she's conscious and will tell them who I am. Otherwise, I don't know. Privacy laws are pretty strict."

"I'm sure we'll find someone to help."

No doubt Travis could persuade the staff by simply marching in like he belonged. She'd have to employ a little bravado, if needed.

Their plane landed in Portland in the wee hours. He'd booked a hotel downtown near the hospital starting the night before so they could sleep until about nine then head over to see her mom. The room was enormous, with two queen-sized beds, but Travis turned down only one of them.

"I want to hold you tonight. Nothing more."

His last two words disappointed her, but she understood. They still hadn't reached a point in their relationship where they could agree to be more than friends sharing parenting duties, despite having made love twice this summer. Exhaustion set in and, after finishing up in the bathroom, she got into bed beside him.

"Come closer, darlin'. I won't bite—unless you ask nicely."

She shook her head, but couldn't help but grin. She nestled in the crook of his arm and rested her head on his pec. "Do you think she'll be happy I found her?"

"Hard to say."

She appreciated his honesty. No sense in going in there expecting the best and being devastated all over again. "Night, Travis." When she started to pull away to sleep on a pillow, he held her tighter. "Don't go anywhere. I like having you here like this. Makes me feel like…" She waited, but he didn't finish.

Travis kissed her on the forehead, making her feel protected and cherished. "Let's get some sleep." While she might have liked having something more happen between them, she knew this was for the best. She wouldn't be able to focus on anything but meeting her mom in the morning anyway.

Chapter Thirty-Six

K ate held onto Travis's hand as they walked up to the hospital's information desk to ask where she could find her mother. All they would tell her was that she was in the intensive care unit. Travis squeezed her hand reassuringly as they got off the elevator on that floor and went to the desk at the entrance to the ICU.

"I'd like to see Serenity Chula, please." Calling her mom by a different name than the one she'd known all these years sounded odd.

The woman looked up. "Are you a family member?"

"I'm her daughter."

She looked at Travis. "And this is?"

How should she identify Travis? He wasn't a boyfriend or fiancé. "…my friend."

The woman clicked some keys, staring at her computer screen. "We don't show any next of kin listed for Mrs. Chula." Hearing her referred to her as married struck Kate as odd. If she'd made up the name, which Kate assumed she had, there was no Mr. Chula, not legally, anyway. Did that mean, in Mom's mind, she thought of herself as married to Daddy still?

Before Kate responded, Travis said, pointing to Kate, "This is Katherine *Serenity* Michaels. Named for her mother. And she'd like to visit her. Please find us a nurse or someone who can help us."

The clerk looked up at him with a simpering smile, which faded under his intense scrutiny. She hit the buzzer on the door. Addressing Travis rather than Kate, she said, "Go through that door and the nurse's station is halfway down the hall on the right."

Travis gave her a curt nod, muttered a thank you, and took Kate by the elbow to guide her through the door. Kate's body shook, not so much from anger as from fear. She hadn't been this close to her mom in more than twenty-eight years.

"I can see you're going to come in handy," Kate said to Travis. He chuckled, but she remained serious. "I'm glad you're here. I've never been so scared in my life."

He stopped mid-stride and turned her toward him. "Take a deep breath, and look at me." Like the woman at the desk, she couldn't do anything but cave under his authority. "Now, repeat after me. 'I have every right to visit my mother.'"

"I have every right to visit my mother."

"'I belong here.'"

"I belong here."

"'No one is going to keep us apart another minute.'"

Kate repeated the words, beginning to believe them. Some of the tension lifted, and she smiled pulling her shoulders back and standing taller. "Let's do this," she said, smiling.

"I don't want to intrude on your time with her so once we find out where she is, I'll sit in the waiting area."

She grabbed his forearm. "No, please, Travis. You understand my needs better than anyone has in a very long time. I want you there."

"Then I'll be there."

Kate blinked a few times, trying to center herself. Taking his hand, they proceeded to the nurse's station. Two women in dark blue scrubs were intently typing into their computers.

"Excuse me. May I speak to Serenity Chula's nurse?"

The woman at the far end of the desk glanced over at her. "I'm Monica. I've been taking care of Mrs. Chula today. How may I help?"

Kate took a deep breath as she moved closer to her. "I know your records show no next of kin, but I'm her daughter." Her throat closed up as she said the words, desperately hoping the nurse would believe her. Travis stroked her back, centering her again. "I've been searching for her for a very long time." She blinked away the tears stinging her eyes. "I know you can't tell me anything about her condition without permission but you could verify who I am if you ask her. Please help me. Is she conscious?"

"Yes," she said, somewhat reluctantly as she looked from Kate to Travis and back.

Good. At least then there was a chance she could get in to see her. Kate opened her purse and pulled out the only proof she had that she was who she said she was. A birth certificate wouldn't work because Mom was using an assumed name. So she handed the nurse the photo of her and her mom on Kate's fifth birthday. "Please, show her this. Tell her Kate's here to see her."

She stood up, a hint of sympathy on her face, and accepted the photo, looking down at it. "That definitely looks like Mrs. Chula." Hearing that her face hadn't been ravaged by whatever disease had brought her here gave Kate hope that she'd see some resemblance in her. Would her mom remember her? She had to. How could a mother ever forget her child?

Coming around the desk, the nurse added, "Wait here, and I'll ask if she's up for a visit."

Travis continued to stroke her back, calming her nerves.

"I may need you to pick me up off the floor if I pass out."

His hand stilled and a look of concern crossed his face. "Do you need to test?"

She grinned. "I didn't mean from a glucose drop." They'd grabbed bagels and coffee in a café in the lobby. That would tide her over for a while.

"Ah." He smiled as he cupped her cheek. "You can count on me, Katie."

"I always could."

Before he could respond, the nurse returned. "Well, I didn't think it possible, but that photo left her speechless." Hearing someone talking about her mother was surreal. "She asked me to take you to her—after she had me brush out her hair. I think your visit is going to do her more good than anything we can offer her at this point."

Kate sagged in relief. *She wants to see me.* The moment she'd dreamed about since she was five was almost here, and Kate hadn't realized she'd expected her mother to refuse to see her. While more terrified than ever, she was now filled with hope as well.

Travis wrapped his arm around her and propelled her forward as they followed the nurse almost to the end of the hall and into a room on the left. His arm tightened as if he was afraid she'd collapse as she walked into the room. The air thinned, and she almost feared she would pass out. A frail-looking woman lay on the bed, her thin blond hair cascading over both shoulders and tears flowing down her cheeks. Kate's lower lip trembled and her vision became blurred, but when her mom reached out her arms to her, Kate broke free of Travis and closed the gap. The two women hugged as the tears spilled for all the years they'd lost. The scent of lemongrass permeated her senses, and Kate felt like she was five years old again being comforted in the arms of the woman who had given her life.

Her mom stroked her hair. "Oh, my precious *chula.* I didn't think I'd live to see you again."

Kate couldn't form any words but even if she could, she wouldn't have been able to speak past the lump in her throat. Her mother's arms around her at long last overwhelmed her. All the hurt and everything they had missed was swept away in this embrace.

After an unknown amount of time, Kate sat up, wanting to look at her mother. "Chelsea has your blonde hair."

"My granddaughter. I've been dying to see her picture ever since Ben told me about her." Kate cocked her head. Was her mom suffering from early dementia, too? No matter. Where was her purse? She turned around as Travis pulled out his phone and punched the screen a couple of times.

He extended the phone to her mother. "Hi. I'm Travis, Chelsea's dad. And this is your granddaughter, Chelsea."

Kate hadn't thought to introduce the two of them in her current state.

"Oh, how precious." Her voice grew husky. She stared at the phone, blinking rapidly.

Kate didn't know which photo he'd shared, but a fresh batch of tears flowed down her cheeks now, too. "I didn't bring her with me on this trip, but will make sure you two get to meet soon." Perhaps she could even ask Emmy to fly out here with Chelsea. But while her mother was older and appeared to be weak, she couldn't be in danger of dying anytime soon. Kate had only just been reunited with her. The fates wouldn't be so cruel.

Mom handed the phone back to Travis. "I suppose that makes you my son-in-law."

"No." Kate should have introduced them properly in the first place. "Travis and I aren't married." *Yet*. She wouldn't go into all that. "It's a long story."

"Well, I'm not going anywhere," Mom said with a smile that faded quickly. "Not today at least. Have a seat, Travis." He pulled over one of the two chairs. Kate, holding her mother's hand and sitting on the side of the bed, told her how they'd met in college and that circumstances—and a misguided Kate—had torn them apart, until this summer.

"The important thing is that you're together now. It'll work out between you this time. I can see the love in your eyes." She cupped Kate's face with both hands. "Your father's eyes."

Kate wondered if she knew what Daddy had done to keep them apart, but didn't want to put a damper on the visit. But she wanted Mom to understand why she hadn't responded. "Mom, in late June, I found the letter you'd written to me for my twelfth birthday. It had been hidden behind the mirror in Daddy's room. I had no idea you'd kept in touch."

"Most of my letters were returned, but I didn't know that one survived until recently." Kate wondered if she'd meant to say now, but

Mom continued. "I worried you'd want to have nothing to do with me."

"It wasn't like that at all!" More tears welled in Kate's eyes. "I didn't know you'd written to me until I found that letter."

"I'm so sorry I wasn't able to come back to you."

Kate might never have another chance to understand what happened between her parents. "May I ask a question?"

Mom seemed wary, but nodded.

"Why'd you leave?"

"I was young and stupid. I felt tied down on that farm and missed the ocean. When I left, I had every intention of returning a few months later, just as I had the two previous times I'd run off to try and prove to my parents that I was now a stable person worthy of their love."

"Wait—what?" Daddy had made it sound as though she'd run off to *find* herself, or to simply hang out on the beach. For years, Kate had tried to put herself in her mom's shoes to understand her reason for deserting her and Daddy, but nothing on earth would have made Kate leave her daughter behind. Not in a million years.

"You were going back to visit your parents?" Why had Daddy misconstrued that the way he had?

"I was pretty messed up in my head in those days. Thought I could win back my parents affection, but soon realized they were cold people who had no place in their hearts for me."

"Did Daddy know about that?"

She shook her head. "I was ashamed that my own parents would reject me like that."

So then you went and did the same thing to me?

Both her parents had been emotionally abandoned by their parents, but that was no legacy to carry on.

"I'm so sorry, Kate. The only real love I ever felt was first with Ben and then with you. Once I realized there was nothing for me in California, I begged your father to let me come home. "But," her voice broke and she cleared her throat. "He told you were better off without me. Stupidly, I believed him."

Was it stupidity, or merely a young woman who was truly messed up?

"Daddy lied—to us both. I hate that I spent so many years thinking I'd done something to send you away."

Mom's eyes opened wide. "He didn't—"

"Oh, no. That was just what my five-year-old brain came up with." She hitched the corner of her mouth. "I know now that wasn't the case, but as a kid, I was afraid to ask Daddy why you'd left me. He never let me talk about you. So many things were left unspoken and unresolved when he passed." Travis squeezed Kate's knee, grounding her in the present again. She smiled at him before returning her focus to her mom. "But that's all behind us now." Kate couldn't continue to harbor resentment toward the woman who had given her life. The healing needed to begin today. "Mom, I forgive you." Kate's eyes blurred and her mom let out a ragged sob. Blindly, they came together in a tear-filled embrace. "We're going to move on and not lose touch ever again."

Minutes later, Kate sat up, worried that she might be keeping Mom from breathing. She still had so many questions about her life in the years they were separated. "What brought you from California to Nevada and Oregon?"

Her smile faded. "You tracked me to all those places?"

"Well, not me personally."

"Two of my sisters work at finding lost loved ones," Travis explained. "They're the ones who finally found you."

"How on earth did they do that?"

Kate grinned. "It wasn't easy! A week or so ago, Travis and I brainstormed all the possible names you might go by if you created a new identity. Among them, Chula from the letter I found, and Serenity from my birth certificate turned out to be the ones they hit on."

"I chose Serenity for your middle name. I'd needed a sense of peace myself and thought giving you that name would provide some for you. If I'd only stayed in Kentucky, we both would have found that peace."

Kate smiled, happy she was finally able to start letting go of the pain. "Well, I didn't think that Daddy came up with it. He was such a traditionalist."

Mom shook her head, but the smile returned to her face. "That's a nice way of putting it, I suppose. He certainly was set in his ways."

But Kate didn't want to talk about him now. "Anyway, yesterday afternoon, one of Travis's sisters called to tell me they'd tracked you to this hospital."

Mom's smile faded. "I'm sorry to say it, but over the years I'd grown to fear being found by you and having you discover who I really was. I've done some things I'm not proud of."

Kate reached out to press her finger against Mom's lips. "Shh. That's water under the bridge."

Mom nodded. "I'm not sure how much time we have left together, but I want to make the most of every minute." Her voice had started off weak, but there was firm resolve as she finished.

Kate wondered for the umpteenth time why her mother was in here, but didn't want to ask. Wait a minute. Hadn't Kate spent a lifetime tamping down questions she should have asked? First with her dad and later Travis? If she'd asked Travis what he wanted when she found out she was pregnant rather than assuming she knew what his wishes would be, their lives might have been so different. Not asking important questions had left Kate with deep-seated insecurities and years of loneliness.

She needed to ask her question rather than continuing to make assumptions and living with regrets. Kate cleared her throat. Yet she still wanted to be tactful. "Mom, what are the doctors saying about when you'll get out?"

Her mom's lower lip trembled as she reached for Kate's hand. "There isn't much chance of that, *chula*, unless I'm moved to hospice or a nursing home. Two weeks ago, I was diagnosed with pancreatic cancer. There's nothing they can do other than manage the pain and treat the symptoms."

No! Kate's chest ached as if pierced with a dagger. She'd just found her mom again. How could she lose her again so soon? She blinked at the tears stinging her eyes.

Travis was suddenly behind her, rubbing Kate's arms and shielding her as best he could within his warmth, but even he couldn't make this shock, this intense hurt, go away.

"Thank God we caught the first plane west," Kate said. She wanted to hug her mom, but was suddenly afraid that if she did, it would cause her more pain. But Mom opened her arms and Kate was being cradled and comforted by her mom immediately, tears streaming down her cheeks again. Tears of sadness this time.

"I'm glad you did, too. Your daddy kept telling me to get in touch with you for the past month or so—even before my diagnosis a little over a week ago—but I…"

Kate sat up. "Daddy?" He'd visited Mom, too?

Mom gave a quirky smile and nodded. "Don't think me crazy, but he's visited me a number of times—mostly trying to convince me to call you."

While Kate swore she'd heard him yesterday, she hadn't said anything even to Travis. Until now. "I used to smell his pipe tobacco, the vanilla scented kind he liked so much. I think I hear him, too, sometimes. In fact, he told me he'd be here with me, although that might be wishful thinking on my part."

Mom glanced over Kate's shoulder at the same moment Kate felt Travis's hand pressing on her shoulder. "Oh, he's here, all right. Standing behind you."

Suddenly, she knew it wasn't Travis at all. "He just touched my shoulder, didn't he?"

She nodded. "His hand is still there."

Kate placed hers over where she felt his to be before reaching for Travis's and joining it with hers and Daddy's while taking her mom's frail hand with her other, welcoming Travis into the circle of her family. For the first time in almost twenty-nine years, she was sheltered safely between both her parents and the man she loved.

Mom's face became serious again. "Kate—you, too, Ben"—she glanced over Kate's shoulder—"I need to explain why I didn't seek you out over the past twenty years. Even knowing I don't have a lot of time left, I couldn't contact you. There's something that happened in Reno that I was so terribly ashamed of—"

Didn't Gail realize there was nothing she could do that would make Kate ashamed of her? Perhaps she'd never experienced unconditional love before. Kate pressed a finger against her mother's soft lips. "Shh. You have nothing to apologize for."

Mom kissed her finger before grasping her hand and lowering it to her chest, over her heart. "I need to unburden myself before it eats at me any longer."

"Just know that whatever you did doesn't matter now." Kate didn't reveal that she already knew about the prostitution arrest. Apparently, her mom needed to tell the story herself.

"While in Reno, I got in with the wrong crowd. Smoked too much pot. Got suckered in by the wrong man." She glanced over Kate's shoulder. As she continued, it was more as if she were confessing something to her husband rather than to her daughter, but Kate listened. "Then the drugs got harder and there are six months of my life I don't even remember...until I woke up in the county jail going through withdrawals from whatever drugs they were giving me and under arrest for...prostitution."

A single tear trickled from her mom's eye into her hair. "My pimp—and that's all he was, if only I'd realized that earlier—deserted me. Then some do-gooder from a local church took me under her wing. She bailed me out, helped me get clean, prepared me for my trial. But when my court date drew nearer, I panicked and ran." Her gaze returned to Kate's. "I hitchhiked to Portland, changed my identity, and never looked back. But I've lived in fear of being caught and sent back to Reno, so it hasn't been what anyone would call living by any stretch of the imagination."

"I'm sure no one remembers that case after all these years, Mom. Don't worry about it any longer."

"I know, but would you promise me something?"

"Anything I can do."

"If there's anything left from my life and cancer insurance policies, I'd like for fifteen thousand of it to go to the woman I stiffed on the bail money, which would pay her back with interest. I never had enough money to send her over the years and was afraid I'd create a paper trail to my doorstep if I tried."

"You know, Mrs. Michaels," Travis began, using a name Kate hadn't heard in connection with her mother in a long time. "...the statute of limitations probably ran out years ago on those charges."

Kate couldn't imagine the shame and guilt her mom had suffered all these years, not only from this incident but from leaving Kate and all the regrets that stirred up. If she could ease her mom's conscience at this time, she would. "I'll be happy to do that. Just give me her name and where she last lived. I'm sure Travis's sisters will be able to find her from that information."

Travis, whom she'd almost forgotten was seated behind her, said, "I'd be happy to make up any difference."

Mom shook her head. "This is my debt to pay. She's listed as a beneficiary on my life-insurance policy already for that amount."

"How'd you manage to get a policy with your new name, if I may ask?" Travis asked.

Her mom smiled sheepishly, avoiding eye contact. "It's not any harder to obtain fake IDs nowadays than it was when I was younger. I had a friend in Southern California set me up with a Serenity Chula driver's license, Social Security card, and even a birth certificate." She turned toward Kate again. "I couldn't use my birth name for fear of being sent back to Reno, which was a real concern at the time" That her mother had lived in such fear for so long, ruining the quality of her life and keeping her away from Kate when she might otherwise have finally tried to reconnect was heartbreaking. "I listed you to inherit the remainder, but there might be legalities given that I didn't use my legal name to take out the policy."

"Actually, Mrs. Michaels, I ran into this with one of my crew members not all that long after starting my business, and the insurance company didn't seem to mind at all about his name being fictitious. By law, they had to pay the beneficiaries listed because they were legal names and people whose legal identities could be easily proven."

"Well, that's quite a relief. But now I have a granddaughter." She turned to Kate again. "After I'm gone, please use some of the money for Chelsea, too. Perhaps pay for college or buy her something she really wants."

Kate blinked away more tears. "Mom, I just found you again. Stop talking about dying."

Mom squeezed her hand. "I've learned over the years to not ignore reality. I don't have a lot of time left."

Once again, strong arms surrounded Kate, and Travis's heat seeped into her body. She leaned back against him for support. She'd probably need to lean on him a lot in the months and years to come.

Her mom smiled. "You have a good man, there. Don't do anything foolish like I did and throw it all away. And please keep the lines of communication open at all times."

Kate nodded. She'd already repeated that mistake with him too many times. Reaching up to place her hand on his arm, she said, "I have no intention of letting him go again."

Realizing that her mom truly had loved her dad warmed her heart as well.

"I've been ailing for months. Nausea, indigestion, losing weight for no reason. I thought it was because of my diabetes…" She shrugged matter-of-factly. "But I guess not."

"You have diabetes?"

Mom nodded. "Insulin-dependent since my late thirties."

"I developed gestational while pregnant with Chelsea, but was diagnosed with Type I not long after. I didn't know where it came from because I knew nothing about your side of the family."

"I'm sorry if that's one of my legacies. My father had Type I diabetes from the age of fourteen until he died at forty-nine. It definitely runs in my family."

Before they could continue talking and get back to her cancer diagnosis, the nurse came in. "Mrs. Chula, you don't want to overtire yourself. Would you like to have your guests take a break and come back later?"

"No. I've waited too long to be with Kate again. I'm fine."

"Mom, if you'd like to rest, we haven't booked return flights and can stay as long as you need us."

"I'd never be able to sleep knowing you were waiting somewhere in Portland to come back and visit again. I'll let you know when I'm tired. But right now, I want to talk."

Kate glanced up at the nurse to see if there was any hospital policy that would necessitate them leaving, but she merely smiled at Kate. "She must be feeling better if she's this energetic. Enjoy your visit."

The nurse left, and they spent the next half hour discussing everything but cancer and dying. Kate still had so many questions concerning what the doctors had said about the prognosis, but could ask later. Right now, they chose to talk about the memories they shared, including some Kate didn't remember at all from when she was a small child, and she filled her mother in on her granddaughter's life.

"She shows horses?"

Travis spoke up, "Sure does. She's good at it, too." Again he pulled out his phone and showed her videos this time from the Ohio show of Chelsea going through her program and of her victory trot with her blue ribbon flying. "Perhaps my insurance money could help buy her a good show horse. I just wish I'd been able to see her perform."

Her mom probably had no idea what a horse would cost, but the wheels started spinning in Kate's head. What if she brought Mom home to the farm in Kentucky to spend her final days? She could at least arrange for her mom to get to see Chelsea ride, if not actually perform.

When Mom's eyelids drooped a little, Kate insisted that she and Travis grab some lunch and let her rest but assured her they'd be back in a couple of hours. She'd run her idea by Travis. He'd help her figure out what needed to be considered before making the suggestion.

* * *

Travis drove their rental car to a restaurant that had good reviews online and soon they'd ordered and were waiting for their meals. A sense of peace had come over Katie since meeting her mom. He'd been worried about how she'd handle the news her mom had terminal cancer, but she hadn't dwelled on that. Meeting her mom had filled a void, it seemed. Perhaps finding her mother gave her the piece to the puzzle that had been missing since she was a little girl.

Halfway through the meal, she leaned forward, her eyes earnest. "Tell me if this sounds crazy, but if Mom is willing, I want to bring her home to the farm."

"I'll support whatever you choose to do, but be sure you're pre-pared for the toll it will take on you physically and mentally."

"I took care of Daddy in his final months when he was totally bedridden, and I was chasing a toddler at the same time. So that doesn't concern me, but it could be difficult for Chelsea. She was too young to remember Daddy's final days. If it wasn't time for school to start next week. I could let her stay with you—"

He shook his head. "I'll help with Chelsea, even move in, if neces-sary."

"I can't ask you to do that. You have a company to run."

"You didn't ask—and let me worry about the business. Family comes first. I can also take care of the horses. Maybe you can take a break from training."

"No. I might need that activity as an outlet for my sanity. Melissa did so well at the Junior League that she's set her sights on the World Championships in Louisville later this month."

"That's a lot for you to take on all at once." His thumb brushed her cheek. "Promise me you'll ask for assistance from another trainer if you aren't able to handle it all."

Her eyes grew bright and she blinked rapidly. "I will. Thank you," she whispered.

He asked the server for the check. "If you're sure about this, let's suggest it to her when we go back up after lunch."

She bit her lower lip. "What if she says no? It wasn't her home for very long." Would Katie ever get over the sense of abandonment with her mom?

"You and Chelsea will be there. I think she'd like to get to know you both better."

Katie nodded. "I hope so. I'm already dreading the thought of having to leave her here. With school, though, there are only so many more times I can fly out here before…" Again, she couldn't say the words and took a sip of water instead. He worried about how she'd handle losing her mother when the time came.

If her mom needed the guest room they'd been letting him stay in, he'd take the barn apartment. Regardless, they'd be together in this.

"What if she doesn't want to die at your place?" he asked.

Katie flinched at the word die, but replied, "I know I can't force her to do anything. She's as independent as I am. But we have good hospitals nearby if she'd rather not…be at the farm when the time comes."

"I agree you might have a fight on your hands; she has a stubborn streak as long as yours and your dad's." He hoped she wouldn't take that the wrong way.

Katie smiled again. "I know! Isn't it fascinating to see how much we have in common?"

He shook his head, grinning. Having always known where he came from and who he took after, he couldn't fathom what it must feel like to just be discovering that at thirty-three.

"If she says yes, you're going to have to set everything up for her—hospital bed, hospice care, in-home nursing. I'll do whatever I can. Just don't be disappointed if she turns you down or decides to back out for whatever reason. She may not want you to see her at the end."

She pressed her lips together. "It won't be a burden at all."

"You have to convince her, not me."

She held her chin higher. "I will. As soon as we go back to the hospital."

"Just don't worry about the farm. Whatever help you need, I'm sure Chelsea, my family, and I can help. And you have Miguel as well."

If her mom was half as strong-willed and determined as Katie, the two were in for a dynamic relationship. But Travis admired the hell out of Katie for wanting to honor and care for her mother despite the past.

It was time for Travis to fish or cut bait; he'd call Jackson tonight. The thought of going back to Tennessee and leaving Katie to deal with all this on her own wasn't an option. If only he'd decided to propose marriage again sooner, then there'd have been no question about his being there with her. But damned if he'd propose to her at a time like this. Besides, he didn't need a marriage certificate to justify his right to be with Katie and Chelsea. As far as he was concerned, they were destined to be married. Just a matter of finding the right time.

Chapter Thirty-Seven

The following Friday, Kate held her mom's hand as she helped her step down from Travis's truck. Her hands were so thin that it felt like she held onto a skeleton with skin, but after making frantic arrangements for almost a week in order to bring her mother home to Midway, finally Kate could breathe.

Mom was home again.

Her mom paused to catch her breath and surveyed the house, arena, and barns. "I can't believe everything you've done with the place, Kate. It looks busy and prosperous."

"Well, I still owe a chunk of change to the bank, but the business should turn a corner in the coming year now that the breeding and training programs are taking off." They started toward the house while Travis followed behind them with their suitcases. "Travis's sister and his mom are here. They've been staying with Chelsea."

At the steps, Travis set down the bags and reached for her mom's other hand. "These steps are a little steep. Let me help, or would you prefer I carry you? I'll work on adding a ramp as soon as we get you settled." While the steps weren't really steep, Kate appreciated his gracious way of offering assistance to her mom.

"No. Just let me lean on you a bit. I can manage."

Together they guided her up to the porch and into the kitchen.

Loretta greeted them at the door with a smile. "Welcome back, everyone!" The words encompassed them all. A sense of peace descended on Kate. She was home, surrounded by family—including Travis and his.

One day, they'd make it permanent, but she was satisfied now knowing he'd chosen to be here with her during this difficult time. One thing she'd learned from this experience with her mother was that no one has an infinite amount of time. She wanted Travis to be a part of the rest of her life. And for her mother to leave this world knowing Kate was happy.

"Mom…"

Both Loretta and her mom answered, "Yes?"

Kate laughed. "I've done the same a million times around Chelsea's friends."

When her mother leaned more heavily on her arm, Kate said, "I'm going to take my mom into the living room to get her settled."

"Everything's ready," Loretta said. "The hospital bed was delivered two days ago. We found a terrific shelf at Goodwill and set up a makeshift nurse's station with the medical supplies the hospice folks indicated their nurses might need."

Kate gave her a smile. "Loretta, thanks so much for all you've done."

She shushed her words. "That's what family does." Kate sure was learning that was what the *Cooper* family lived and breathed, anyway. She was happy to be accepted as part of the family, unofficially.

Speaking of which… "Where's Chelsea?"

"She and Emmy ran to the store for a minute to get some things for supper. Hope you're in the mood for sloppy joes. Guess I was homesick for that man of mine." Everyone but Kate's mom got the joke and grinned.

Travis kissed his mom as they walked by on the way to the living room. Kate couldn't help but think everything was going to be okay and that her mom's final days would be filled with love and family.

She'd just managed to get Mom tucked into the bed with her earbuds in place so she could listen to the New Age music that seemed to help her relax. Travis was coming out of the office where he'd been checking his emails, smiling broadly.

"Spill. I can use some good news."

"Just heard from Jackson. He accepted my offer."

"Your offer to do what?"

He beamed. "He's going to become my partner, with him being completely in charge of the Nashville operations while I open an office in Lexington."

Lexington was only half an hour away, a shorter commute than the one he made now. But this had deeper implications. "You're moving here permanently?"

"Well, that's contingent on whether you'll marry me or not."

Whether!?! She launched herself into his arms hugging him around the neck. "I'm not going to make the same mistake three times. Yes, I'll marry you!" He squeezed the air out of her before lowering her feet to the floor and his mouth to hers.

All too soon, the kitchen door slammed. "Mom! Daddy! Are you here?" Chelsea was home. She'd missed her so much and couldn't wait to share the news.

Pulling away from Travis, she overheard Loretta tell her they were in the hallway and to keep her voice down while her grandmother slept.

Looking up at Travis, Kate asked, "Can we tell her now?"

"I think she'll figure it out herself if we don't, but sure."

Kate smiled and turned toward the kitchen doorway as Chelsea entered. Soon they were enveloped in a group hug. After each of them dispensed a few kisses on their daughter, before they could tell her the news, Chelsea glanced toward the living room. "Is Grandma Michaels here?"

Kate nodded. "I just got her into bed. She's resting now."

"I'm awake! Bring me my granddaughter," Mom said, her voice sounding stronger than it had been just a few minutes ago. "I want to see her."

Kate's eyes misted up as she took Chelsea's hand. "Are you ready?" Kate asked Chelsea. She'd tried to prepare her for this moment over the phone these last few days.

"I think so."

Kate hugged her. "Don't worry," she whispered. "Mom's probably as nervous as you are."

Kate led her into the living room, pride welling up inside her. She'd been picturing this moment since she'd first gotten Mom to agree to come home with her, which had been more difficult than even Kate had anticipated. But reminding Mom that Kate had a daughter back home and couldn't remain in Portland indefinitely seemed to do the trick.

Mom had propped herself up in the adjustable bed and the earbuds lay on her chest. Apparently, she didn't want to miss a thing.

Chelsea seemed hesitant at first, but when her mom extended her arms toward her, Kate squeezed her hand and encouraged her to go forward. Tears filled her eyes, but she could hear Chelsea's meek voice.

"Hello, Grandma Michaels. It's nice to meet you." Kate couldn't blame her for being a little reluctant. The woman was a total stranger to her. But when her daughter bent down to kiss her mom on the cheek, Kate lost it and let the tears fall. Travis appeared out of nowhere to wrap both arms around her. He could always anticipate when she needed him to lean on.

Her mother patted the mattress, and Chelsea sat on the edge of the bed. "Honey, you have no idea how wonderful it is to finally set eyes on you. I've only known about you a short time and have only seen you in photos until now. I hope you'll forgive me for taking so long to get here." Mom glanced up at Kate, as though the words might also be intended for her.

Kate's heart grew warm. Thank goodness she'd persisted despite the many times Mom had said she didn't think the move was a good idea. Mom talked to Chelsea about her own childhood in southern California. Chelsea told her about Princess Jasmine and Chula. The two hit it off immediately.

Travis kissed the top of Kate's head, and she turned slightly to press her cheek against his chest. "You okay?" he whispered.

"Surprisingly, yes."

"Maybe tomorrow I can go out and watch you ride some," Mom said.

"That would be awesome! Chula and I are getting ready for our next show. This time, Mom said I could enter in a regular class, not just academy."

Mom met Kate's gaze once more. "You named one of your horses Chula?"

Kate nodded, too choked up to elaborate, but happy that memory had stayed with her, even if she didn't know where it had come from at the time.

Chelsea reached out and stroked her grandmother's hair. "We have the same color hair." The tender scene brought more tears to Kate's eyes. Kate and Travis wouldn't need to help Chelsea and Mom bond. And eventually to let go as well. *Better to have loved and lost...*

Bringing her mom here was the right decision. Her final days would be spent surrounded with love and family, and Kate couldn't help but feel her father was here, too, perhaps waiting for Mom on the other side when the time came.

"*Chulita*, I want you to have the wedding ring your grandpa gave me when we married. Your mom will keep it for you until the time is right."

Mom had made sure Kate knew about the ring when packing up her apartment, and Kate had brought it home with her rather than leave it in the boxes being shipped. She'd see that Chelsea had it when she was responsible enough to take care of it.

In a voice much weaker than the one Kate remembered from her childhood, Mom began to sing "My Chula" to her daughter, bringing back poignant memories for Kate.

Wanting to give the two of them a chance to be alone, she said softly to them, "We'll be in the kitchen if you need anything." Mom smiled blissfully up at her making Kate's eyes sting yet again.

In the kitchen, she didn't see Mom Cooper or Emmy and turned to Travis while they had a moment alone. "Thanks for everything, Travis. You've been my rock this past week."

"You're the one who's been handling everything." He placed a kiss on her forehead. "But you'd better let me know if you need anything at all," he warned. "I know you aren't one to ask, and I can't always anticipate."

"You've given me everything I need with just a touch or a shoulder to lean on."

He tucked his finger under her chin and tipped her head back. Her heart tripped a beat. They'd been together every day for the past week, even sharing the same bed at the hotel, but were too exhausted each night to make love again. Whenever he'd come up from Tennessee to see Chelsea before that, he'd barely had thirty hours before having to turn around and go home again. Those hours had been consumed with Chelsea and her activities.

She wrapped her arms around him and welcomed his kiss. His lips were warm and reassuring, giving her energy to keep up her own strength for whatever was coming.

"Now that's a sight that does my heart good," Loretta said as they turned to watch her and Emmy set four bags of groceries on the table. She hadn't even heard the door open. "Son, when do you plan to ask Katie for her hand? I'm not getting any younger."

"Neither am I!" Mom shouted from the living room. How on earth had she heard Loretta's words? Was Daddy relaying messages between here and the living room? Kate smiled at the thought of the two of them making amends. Perhaps it was never too late.

Everyone in the kitchen shared a laugh before Kate became serious. "Oh, he already has, Loretta. And just a little while ago, I finally gave him my answer."

Kate turned to Travis, whose eyes smoldered. She poured her heart out to him. "There has never been anyone but you, and I'd be honored to go through the rest of my life with you by my side."

Chelsea's footsteps came bounding down the hallway into the kitchen. "You're getting married?" Kate and Travis caught her as she launched herself at them. "I can't believe this. Now you'll not only be my mom and dad but we'll all be family."

At last.

*   *   *

When the congratulations and hugs faded away, Travis asked, "Can we help?"

"Nope, this is everything," Emmy said as she began putting groceries away.

Katie went over and gave his sister a hug. "Thanks for being there for Chelsea this week." Travis was happy that the initial tension between the two of them was gone now. And with Katie's agreeing to marry him, and Jackson becoming his partner, Travis couldn't think of anything else that needed to fall into place.

He crossed the room to Emmy, too, hugging her and planting a big-brother kiss on the top of the head. "You've been great, Em. First with Jackson, and now Chelsea."

"Believe me, Chelsea is a lot more fun to be with. Jackson was a pain in the—"

"EmmyLou!" Mom said. "The man was injured and probably not himself."

Emmy rolled her eyes, probably a habit she picked up from spending so much time with Chelsea. Travis had no clue what had happened between the two of them, but didn't really want to know, either. He credited Emmy for getting Jackson on his feet faster than the doctors had anticipated, probably because Jackson wanted to show her he didn't need any help so he could send Emmy back to Louisville and out of his hair.

The next couple of hours were a whirlwind of preparing and eating dinner, catching up with Chelsea, and meeting with the hospice nurse. When it came time to go to bed, he wasn't quite sure yet where he'd be sleeping. Yeah, they were engaged, but with his mom, sister, daughter, and future mother-in-law in the house, he didn't think joining Katie in her bed was a prudent idea.

Alone with Katie in the barn after mucking the stalls, he asked, "Would you prefer I sleep in the apartment out here?"

She hung the stall fork on the wall. "Your mom and Emmy have the guest room, so it's probably best."

But he *wanted* to sleep with Katie again, truth be told. He'd never slept better than those nights they'd spent at the hotel in Oregon together, exhausted and curled up in each other's arms.

"But we can change that arrangement in the coming days, if you're open to what I want to suggest," she said.

He turned to face her, setting his gloves on the table in the tack room. Perhaps a little romp in the tack room? "What's that?"

"How would you feel about us marrying in the next few days, here at the house, with Mom and whoever from your family is able to attend on short notice?"

Well, not exactly what he'd expected to hear, but he worried about pulling it off on such short notice. Clearly, Kate wanted to have her mom there to witness the occasion, and he had no problem with that. "Are you sure you have enough time to pull it all together?"

She grinned as she walked toward him. "I'm a simple country girl. As long as we have a bride, a groom, a couple of witnesses, and a minister, that's all we need. Unless you want a church wedding or something, Lidia is an ordained minister and can perform the ceremony."

He framed her upturned face with his hands. "When I'm this close to you, I can't think logically, but I think you've covered all the bases. Whatever you want, I'll do. Weddings are more for the brides and if you don't mind the minimalist approach, let's do it." That didn't come out sounding the way he intended, but he lowered his head and captured her lips in a kiss to seal the deal. Moments later, he heard running footsteps down the barn aisle.

"Mom, Daddy! Come quick!" Chelsea ran into the tack room and glanced from one of them to the other, worry in her eyes. "Grandma Michaels is in pain, and we don't know what to do."

Katie took off running first, but he took a moment to make sure Chelsea was okay.

She nodded. "We were just talking and then she gasped for breath, grabbed her right side, and screamed in pain."

"You did the right thing to come and get us. Your Mom has instructions from the hospice nurse on what to do in times like this." Sadly, there were going to be many more of these times in the days to come as the disease took its toll on her body. "You okay, Sunshine?" He worried how Chelsea was going to handle being this close to death. If he and Katie felt it was becoming too much for her to handle, they'd send her to Louisville to stay with Shania.

"I'm okay. It's Mom I'm worried about. She's going to be really sad when Grandma Michaels dies."

He hugged her again. She had a big heart and empathy for those around her. "We're going to be here for your mom and together we'll get through this. Now, let's see if there's anything we can do tonight."

Inside the house again, they made their way to the doorway to the living room.

Kate bent over her mom's bed. "Take this. It will help with the pain." Katie measured the correct dose into the oral syringe and Mrs. Michaels opened her mouth to take it, squeezing her eyes shut as she swallowed. The narcotic patch they'd put on two days ago must be wearing off early, unless the dosage wasn't enough to keep up with the pain any longer.

Travis turned to his mom who stood looking on, clutching a wet washcloth. Was she remembering back to taking care of her own mother in her final days? To Chelsea, he said, "Why don't you go up and listen to some music for a while? Everything's under control here." He wished he could shelter her from witnessing what was coming.

Chelsea shook her head. "I want to sit with her until she falls asleep." He gave her a hug. She had a lot of compassion. "Grandpa Michaels told me she likes having me hold her hand."

Ah, so Old Man Michaels was here, too. Made sense, if the end was imminent. No doubt he'd be waiting to welcome Mrs. Michaels to the other side when the time came. The thought gave him comfort, but he wondered who had been there for Danny the night he crossed over. He hoped someone had been.

Mom handed Katie a wet washcloth, and Katie ran it over her mother's forehead and cheeks. The furrows in the woman's brow gradually smoothed out, and she seemed to be resting. Travis felt helpless, but knew that his role here was to support Katie, so he'd continue to find ways to do just that.

If that meant arranging a wedding before time ran out for Katie's mom, then so be it. He didn't care how they managed to tie the knot either, only that they did so. Katie didn't seem to care about the celebration so much as the ceremony.

"Mom, can I have a word with you in the kitchen?"

She nodded, wiping away a tear, and he motioned for her to precede him. Chelsea pulled up her chair again on the opposite side of Katie at the bedside. When Chelsea's little hand took her grandmother's, he had to blink away the moisture in his own eyes. Katie sure had raised her right.

In the kitchen, first he hugged his mom and made sure she was okay. He'd rarely seen her cry in all the years growing up.

"Just hits close to home. I miss my mom so much."

"I know." After a moment, he let her go and told her what Katie wanted to do.

"Do whatever she wants. I don't want her to have any regrets." He wondered if his mom had been left with regrets, although he couldn't imagine. She'd taken excellent care of his grandmother when she was in her final months.

"Can you call Dad, Clint, Shania, and Tanya and see if we can get them out here tomorrow or the day after? Katie's got a friend who can perform the ceremony."

Mom blinked rapidly and wrapped her arms around him. "I'm so happy for you, Travis. I know how much you've wanted this, just wish it could be under happier circumstances."

"Mom, when I hear her say, 'I do,' it will be the happiest day of my life. And if we can make it happen before her mom passes, that will give her some small sense of comfort, which is even better."

"I'll see what I can do. Tanya will be the toughest one. She works around the clock as it is. It's all I can do to get her home for Thanksgiving and Christmas each year."

He gave her a peck on the cheek. "We'll videotape it for anyone who can't make it." He just wanted to have this wedding and to finally be able to call Katie his wife and partner in life.

* * *

Ben took in the touching scene with his daughter and granddaughter at Gail's bedside. Everything had come together beautifully. He'd never imagined Gail's final days being filled with so much love.

Gail opened her eyes and met his gaze over the top of Chelsea's head and smiled at him. He returned one to her.

"Bet you didn't expect that to happen in a million years," Danny said.

"More like ten."

"How much longer?"

"Obadiah won't say, but my guess is only days."

"Man, Katie didn't find her a moment too soon." Danny paused. "But what about those two lovebirds?"

Ben had overheard Kate's conversation about having the wedding sooner than later. Gail had been excited about the possibility when Ben told her. "Yeah, maybe more good will come of all this than we thought. I want Kate to be happy, and if Travis makes her happy and takes good care of her and Chelsea, then I'm all for it."

Danny laughed. "Never thought I'd hear those words from you."

"Well, a person can change, can't he?"

"Maybe, but not usually this late in life—much less in the afterlife." Danny sobered, furrowing his brows. "Think they'll tie the knot before Gail crosses over?"

Ben shrugged. "Heck, they've been hinting that Gail could be joining me since about June in earth time, and here it is August already. Either way, no doubt she and I will find a way to watch as they exchange their vows. Wouldn't miss it for the world."

"Yeah, but you know how people think on the physical plane. They forget that those who have passed over remain a part of their lives in spirit."

"At least Kate seems to hear me now, and accepts that her mother and Chelsea do, too," Ben said before turning to Danny. "What's the status of your reassignment?"

"Obadiah says it could happen anytime. Just have to wait for someone to agree to make the switch. As I understand it, once I'm alerted, I'll meet the other spirit to negotiate the terms. If we agree, then bam. I'm back."

"You're not going to screw it up this time." It wasn't a question.

"Damn right. I have no clue what kinds of issues I'll face or what struggles the other person has, but I'll deal with them as they come. I'm told I do have to make an effort to fit into his life, and that there might be a period where I don't remember the person I was before. Hopefully that won't be a permanent condition, but it's not uncommon for a walk-in soul to show up and those around them know immediately they aren't the same."

Ben laughed. "Well, you're one of a kind. I'm sure you'll charm whoever you meet." He sobered. "But I have to say I'm going to miss hanging out with you here, Danny."

"Yeah, we've had some interesting times, haven't we?"

Ben didn't know what the chances would be of his ever seeing Danny again once he left, but had no plans to stray far from Gail's side for a long while. He didn't know how the laws of atonement and the universe worked, but he damned well needed to make amends.

Gail closed her eyes. Ben knew she was only sleeping, and decided to take this chance to round up some of her loved ones for when she'd breathed her last.

Over the next two days, Ben witnessed a lot of hustle and bustle. The Coopers had been arriving throughout the morning, all except the sister living in Chicago who was away in Japan and couldn't return on such short notice. But still not a bad outpouring of love and support on such short notice for a wedding.

But Ben worried about Kate. The dark circles under her eyes spoke of her exhaustion. Gail slept more now that the nurses had increased the dosage of morphine, but Kate rarely left her mother's side. She'd been that devoted to him in his last days, too. He couldn't be prouder. At least she'd put off her riding students the past few days.

Travis came over to check on her. "You okay? When's the last time you ate?"

"I'm fine. Let me run upstairs and change. Lidia should be here in the next half hour. We'll start when Mom wakes up from her nap."

He brushed his finger over her cheek. "I'm worried about you."

She smiled. "I'm fine. Really." Without waiting for him to respond, she took the stairs two at a time.

Ben drew closer to Gail. She didn't seem to acknowledge his presence at first, then opened her eyes and smiled. When her disembodied arm reached out to him, he feared that they had waited too long for the wedding. But he didn't hesitate to take her hand and lift her from her tired, diseased body as he pulled her closer to him.

Her eyes opened wider. "The pain's gone. I can breathe. It doesn't hurt anymore."

Ben wrapped her in his arms. "No more pain, sweetheart."

"But I didn't tell Kate goodbye."

"Sure you did. Lots of times in the past week."

"I need to go to her. I'll only be a minute." Before he could stop her, Gail floated upstairs and into Kate's bedroom with him following.

"Nooo!" Ben heard Kate's cry of anguish followed by a loud thud. No doubt she's seen her mother and knew it was too late.

He watched as Travis ran into the room a moment later to find Kate lying on the floor, dressed in a pretty white lace gown.

He picked her up and sat on the edge of the bed with her. Cradling her with one arm, he tapped her cheek with his free hand. "Katie. Wake up." Toward the door he shouted, "Somebody call 9-1-1! Katie's passed out."

She blinked her eyes a few times before staring up at him. "I'm okay." Ben saw the desolation in her eyes. "But it's too late. Mom's already gone."

He cocked his head. "Your mom?" She nodded, tears flowing from her eyes. He held her tight against his chest. "I'm so sorry, baby."

Gail moved closer to them and placed her hand on Kate's shoulder. "Don't worry about me, *chula.*"

"But I wanted you at my wedding, Mom." Kate could hear Gail? It had taken him forever to get her to hear him, but it must be true that a mother's love knew no bounds.

Travis shushed her, apparently unaware of Gail's presence.

"I'll be there whenever it happens, but you need to go to the hospital and get checked out. You've run yourself ragged."

"Don't worry, Katie. She'll be there in spirit." Travis was a good man. Ben had no reservations about the two of them.

"He loves her so much," Gail said to Ben. "Travis will take good care of her and I know I should be content with that, but do you think I'll be able to stick around closer to earth for a while? I've missed out on so much already."

Ben turned to the woman he'd fallen in love with at first sight all those decades ago. "But this won't be the end. You'll be able to look in on them anytime you'd like."

She smiled, reminiscent of the one she'd bestowed on him that first day at the Kentucky Horse Park when he'd seen her petting one of his horses after a demonstration. "If I'd known how wonderful I would feel, I might have let go sooner. But I'm glad I stayed long enough to reunite with Kate and to meet my granddaughter and future son-in-law. I didn't expect the end to come so quickly, though. I reached out to you, and suddenly it was all over."

"No, not over. This is our new beginning. I have some mistakes to correct and lost time to make up for."

Gail took his hand. "We have all the time in the world now, but in case I didn't say it, I forgive you. And I hope you'll forgive me, too, for not being honest with you about why I kept running back to California—and for leaving you to raise our precious daughter alone. I just didn't see that what I needed and wanted most was right here on your beautiful little farm in Kentucky."

She leaned forward to place an ethereal kiss on his cheek, warming his soul to the core. He knew Kate was going to have some difficulties in the days, weeks, and months to come as she dealt with losing her mother, but perhaps they'd be able to convey to her that they were together and all was well, starting with the funeral. Right now, though, he wanted to give Gail a quick tour of where she'd be for eternity with him.

Chapter Thirty-Eight

Travis had never been so nervous in his life. Why? He was finally about to marry the only woman he'd ever loved. He drew a deep breath and blew it out forcefully as he stared at the wall of glassware in the tasting room, waiting for his cue.

The girls were getting ready in another part of the winery. Lidia would be performing the ceremony in the garden gazebo since it was unseasonably warm for Thanksgiving Day. They'd decided to wait a few months from their last attempt to marry, in order to allow for a mourning period and for Katie to deal with the added business she'd received since Melissa had done so well at the World Championship Horse Show. Chelsea had continued to compete on her level through the end of October and was the grand champion at the academy nationals in Murfreesboro earlier this month. By then, it was so close to the holidays, they decided to plan their wedding around Thanksgiving. The wedding had brought together his entire family, including Tanya who had ridden down with Daniel Morgan, the guy she used to date and still worked with. Luckily, he'd gone to visit his own family in some small town on the Ohio River near Owensboro, dropping Tanya off at Mom and Dad's first.

Travis looked up at the clock again and started pacing.

"Calm down, man, before you have a stroke." Jackson said.

He glared at his partner. Despite all the plans he and Katie had made over the last few months to make this day happen, he wouldn't relax until he slipped that ring on her finger and she said, "I do." They'd come so close before.

"Those girls love you to the ends of the world, you know," his friend reminded him.

Travis nodded. In his gut, he had zero doubts Katie wanted to marry him, but then his brain engaged and he started worrying again. "What if—"

"Enough. You've got this. Just give it a chance to happen while you're still alive to enjoy the honeymoon." Jackson looked around. "This is some fancy place. You'd think you were in Napa—or even Tuscany."

"Yeah. Good wines, too," Travis said absently. He'd been feeling Danny's presence all morning, but hadn't heard a peep out of him. Not like Danny at all. Why did he get the feeling this was goodbye for some reason? Like he wanted Travis to know he was here, but not to get too attached.

"Maybe if you'd partaken of the wine that flowed here last night at the rehearsal dinner, you wouldn't be so stressed out today."

Jackson brought him back to the moment. "No, I don't need to have my faculties impaired today. I want to experience and remember every single moment."

Jackson shook his head and chuckled as he clapped Travis on the back. "Good thing you aren't planning to tie the knot ever again—but as your friend and partner, know that I've got your six. This mission will end in victory."

Travis grinned, understanding for the first time how ridiculous he was being. It wasn't as if Katie had stood him up at the altar before. Yeah, she'd kicked him to the curb thirteen years ago for no good reason as far as he could tell, but that happened before he'd had the chance to propose. He'd been so sure of a "yes," though, that it felt like she'd jilted him. The first time he'd actually proposed had been outside his parents' house five months ago, but that was an act of desperation. She wasn't ready yet.

But when they'd decided to marry in August so that her mom could be there, they'd been dressed for their imminent wedding when

Mrs. Michaels had passed away. Then they'd had to rush Katie to the hospital with another dangerous drop in her sugar levels, despite his attempts to make sure she ate regularly during those chaotic days. He couldn't do much to predict or alleviate her stress or to get her to sleep more.

But last night, she'd been all smiles. Nothing was going to interrupt their plans this time!

He needed a diversion before he puked. "I noticed you and Emmy talking pretty heatedly last night."

Jackson's eyes shuttered before his mouth was set in a straight line. "She just likes to rile me up. I challenged her right back, and she didn't care for it, I guess."

Travis snickered. "Her bark's worse than her bite. She might be a little spoiled, but it's always best to have her in your corner."

"I thought triplets were supposed to all have similar personalities."

"Hell, no. Emmy, Shania, and Tanya are as different as they come, not so much in looks as in personality and temperament." Travis grinned.

"What?" Jackson asked.

"Just thinking that if anyone could handle Emmy, it would be you."

"Not on your life. She's beautiful and all, but as her big brother, you really should clue her in on the fact that she'd catch a guy a lot faster using honey than all that piss and vinegar.

"What makes you think she's looking to catch a guy?"

"Well, now that you mention it, she didn't make any moves on me or anything, but I try to send out a vibe to women so there's no confusion. Just saying, if she ever decided to go after a guy, she's going to have to quit being so bossy."

Travis chuckled, but wouldn't share what Emmy had said about him. Probably best that the two of them went their separate ways. With Emmy living in his house in Nolensville now, the chances of them meeting by chance were still pretty remote, given that they both lived about an hour from Nashville in opposite directions.

"Perhaps she needs somebody like you to straighten her out, Jackson," Dad said, coming up behind them.

"No disrespect, Joe—but *hell*, no. I have no intention of taking on her or any other woman. At forty-two, I'm a confirmed bachelor whose happy with that status and intends to keep it."

"Famous last words?" Dad asked. Dad almost sounded anxious to marry off the first of his three daughters now that his two sons had tied the knot—or soon would.

"Don't curse me. I've got no time for women now that I am a partner in a kickass contracting firm. But I'm thrilled your son fell so hard for his girl that he had to move up here and sold me a 50-percent stake in his company."

"Well, I couldn't very well move Kate's horse farm to Nashville, now could I?" Travis asked.

"Hey, I'm not complaining. To be honest, I like being the boss of the entire Nashville operation."

Perhaps that's part of the problem with Emmy—two head-strong alphas who both want control in all aspects of life. But Travis wouldn't have entrusted the Nashville branch of his company to anyone else, not even Danny. Jackson had good business sense. "You've always done a great job as my foreman, but you've blown me away with how you're running things down there. I know the crew likes and respects you, too."

"So when will you be opening up the second branch of Towers Contracting?"

"Any week now. We have our office set up and all the licenses we need. Should be in full swing by January."

Clint, his best man, poked his head inside the door. "Ten minutes, brother! Are you ready?"

"Readier than I've ever been for anything in my life." It wouldn't be long now.

"Erik! Don't untie Olivia's bow again!" He turned back to Travis and Jackson. "I promise to settle him down before the ceremony starts."

Travis laughed. Susan was pregnant with their third and feeling a little queasy, so his best man had been left to supervise the ring bearer and flower girl instead.

He wondered if more children would be in the cards for Katie and him? If not, it didn't matter. They had Chelsea. His family was perfect.

*   *   *

"Chelsea, you're beautiful. Wait 'til Daddy sees you."

Her daughter sashayed in front of the dressing mirror, making the skirt of her deep purple dress swish. "You think Daddy will like it?"

"Well, he might complain about the amount of skin showing if you take your jacket off"—Kate pointed to her daughter's bare shoulders—"but I'm more inclined to think he's going to be mesmerized instead."

Chelsea giggled. "Oh, Mom. He won't look at anyone but you. I can't wait for him to see the dress we picked out!" She stepped aside so that Kate could see herself in the mirror.

She'd pulled her hair into a soft and simple chignon with loose tendrils touching the back and sides of her neck. A small band of baby's breath had been tucked inside forming a partial wreath on her head.

The sleeveless, semi-lustrous satin weave dress made Kate feel like a modern fairy princess. The calf-length skirt's curvy, fluttery matte chiffon tiers had her sashaying around her bedroom this morning making the flounces swirl. Perhaps later, she'd do it again before taking it off in front of Travis. He hadn't seen her all morning as he'd chosen to stay here at the vineyard as Jason and Lidia's guest. Her heart skipped a beat in anticipation.

A quick rap on the door had both of them turning as Kate told whoever it was to come in.

"Kate!" Lidia said. "And Chelsea! You both look amazing!"

As Kate slipped on the lace jacket with its three-quarter sleeves, she tried not to let her nerves get the best of her, but was losing the battle. "How much time do I have?"

"None. We're ready when you are. Travis is waiting for you at the gazebo." She turned to Chelsea. "And we have the space heaters cranked so you won't freeze." Even though it was unseasonably warm, it was still in the low fifties.

They'd found their dresses in September when the temperatures were still hot, and she and Chelsea both chose sleeveless dresses thinking the wedding would happen sooner than November. She'd decided not to wear the lacy dress she'd picked out for their planned August wedding, not wanting to jinx the day since they seemed to have had a lot of bad luck as it was.

No doubt, when Travis seared her with his smoldering gaze, her skin would heat to tropical temperatures. But she couldn't wait for her wedding night. Once Kate's grief over the loss of her mother began to abate, they'd taken advantage of a few trysts in the house, barn, and springhouse while Chelsea was at school. But with an impressionable daughter in the house, they'd chosen not to sleep together until they married.

She couldn't wait.

Knowing everything was a go was probably for the best. If she had any more time to think about it, she'd throw up. Planning their first wedding had been stressful enough and it wasn't this elaborate. Still, she regretted that her parents wouldn't be physically here to witness this day. But she'd felt them both around her for days now, and knew that when she walked down the aisle toward Travis, they would be on either side of her. For that reason, she'd respectfully declined an offer from Travis's dad to walk her down the aisle. She explained and believed Joe when he'd said he understood completely.

"Did you test recently?" Lidia asked. "With your stress level up and what little you had for breakfast, I don't want you keeling over during the vows."

"How would you know how much I did or didn't eat this morning?"

Lidia grinned. "Because I know you!"

"Fair enough." She hadn't been able to eat much at all. "But I just had a protein bar before brushing my teeth. I'm ready to do this."

Lidia hugged her carefully, apparently worried about wrinkling her dress, but Kate wrapped her arms around her friend tighter. When they separated, Lidia gave her the once over again. "You're absolutely radiant. He's so right for you, Kate." She then addressed Chelsea. "And for you, too. You're all so happy together—just remember to embrace life head-on and love each other with all you've got."

Lidia hit the nail on the head, as usual. Today would be the beginning of their lives together as a family in every sense of the word—a bond that would endure whatever life threw at them. Kate had no qualms about saying her vows today, or living by them the rest of her life. But first she had to get through the stress of the ceremony. She wasn't used to having everyone watching her, and hoped she wouldn't trip on something.

"Let's do this," Kate said.

"I'll cue the music." Lidia left the two of them alone.

"Mom, will I ever find someone as strong and good as Daddy when I'm ready to get married?"

"Oh, honey, you will. Just don't rush it. When the right one comes along, you'll know." Katie wrapped her arms around Chelsea for one last hug before they both picked up their bouquets and started for the door.

Given the holiday, the guest list was small, with only Travis's family, Kate's best friends, Jackson, and Miguel attending. Travis insisted that his crew enjoy Thanksgiving with their families and avoid spending that many hours on the road.

Clint and Susan's children would be the ring bearer and flower girl and Chelsea the maid of honor.

Travis had chosen the processional song and told her to listen to the lyrics as she made her way toward him, because they were the words of his own heart. Kate peeked from her hiding place to watch Chelsea send Erik and Olivia down the white runner through the room where they would hold a brief reception after exchanging their long-overdue vows. Afterward, they'd move to Lidia and Jason's dining room where Travis's mom and Beckie Pritchard, a caterer recommended by Tillie Buchanan, would be serving a complete Thanksgiving dinner.

Soon.

Big brother Erik had to remind Olivia to scatter the rose petals as she meandered along until he finally traded her, giving the toddler the ring pillow to carry as he scattered rose petals with abandon. Kate grinned, wondering if there would be any left by the time they made it through the French doors and outside to where everyone waited near the gazebo. But the knots in Kate's stomach eased away at last.

When the opening notes of Keith Urban singing "Your Everything" sounded, any remaining butterflies flew away. Kate smiled. It was one of her favorite songs, and her entire being absorbed the words as though Travis himself serenaded her. Chelsea started forward. So grown up, with her hair styled similarly to Kate's, but without the baby's breath.

As Chelsea disappeared through the doors, Kate drew a deep breath. Time to begin her slow march to Travis's side. She wanted to run headlong into his arms, but forced herself to take the dreadfully slow steps Lidia had made her practice, not wanting to arrive at the gazebo before the singer had finished the poignant lyrics.

As she exited the building onto the patio, a blast of cold air shocked her at the same moment she spied Travis standing beside Lidia, dressed in a charcoal tux. He was the most handsome man she'd ever known and the only one she'd ever been in love with. She picked up the pace of her steps a little, keeping her gaze locked with Travis's.

He smiled, warming her insides to molten jelly. Tonight they'd have the house to themselves as Chelsea was spending Thanksgiving weekend with her Aunt Shania in Louisville. Not having to worry about her overhearing them making love would be liberating, although she was going to have to lose her shyness about it. Having sex was a natural part of showing your love to your spouse.

And I can't wait.

About halfway through the garden, a sense of warmth and peace washed over her, halting her steps momentarily. *Mom, Dad, I'm so glad you're here.*

Travis took a couple of steps forward to take her arm, concern in his eyes. She smiled, and he guided her the rest of the way to stand in front of Lidia. He smelled woodsy, overloading her senses. When he curved his arm around her back, they faced Lidia and she appreciated having him to lean on as her knees suddenly became wobbly.

Lidia's mouth moved, but Kate had to fight to hear her words. When Lidia asked who gives this woman, she distinctly heard her parents say, "We do," with an echo from Travis's parents.

After speaking their vows to each other and exchanging their white-gold rings, Lidia picked up the wine goblet from the pedestal beside her. Kate and Travis had found it in the Dirty South Pottery shop in Winchester, Kentucky, while stopping after hiking all day at the Red River Gorge last month. Kate had chosen a dry cabernet sauvignon from the winery for this moment, wanting to experience this symbolic bonding with her husband without spiking her sugar.

Holding it up before them, Lidia began,

Wine, like the life-blood that pulses through our veins,
is a symbol of life, that has been
created through the work of hands and minds.

Life is a series of contradictions.
It is said that all things end, and yet all things continue.
All things change, and yet all things remain the same.

The beautiful words touched Kate to her very soul. She gave Travis a sidelong glance and saw that he had sobered as well.

Love lies in the soul alone.
Just as wine stimulates the body
and enriches the life within it,
Love stimulates our souls.
As you share this glass of wine on this special day,
may you be joined in a love as fluid as the drink itself,
yet as solid as the hands that made it.

Through her tears, Kate watched as Lidia handed her the glass first. "Drink to the love you've shared in the past." Raising the glass to her lips, she took a sip before handing it to Travis. Their fingers brushed, sending a zing up her arm. After he took his sip, he handed it back to Lidia.

"Now," Lidia said as she continued to pass along her blessing, "drink to your love on this, your wedding day." Again, they each sipped in turn, returning the glass to Lidia. "And lastly, drink to your love in the future and forevermore!" After their final sip, they handed the glass back to Lidia who set it on the pedestal again. Kate couldn't tear her gaze away from Travis's as Lidia pronounced,

From this day forward, the two of you become one,
two parts become whole,
two paths intertwine,
each separate, yet united by love.

"As you have shared the wine from this cup, so may you share your lives. Travis, you may kiss your bride."

The grin on his face stole her heart as he lowered his face to hers. She closed her eyes and leaned her head back seconds before he crushed his lips to hers, capturing her breath and making her knees shake again. As if in tune with her body, he wrapped her in his arms and held her upright as the kiss deepened.

Chelsea giggled, breaking the spell and causing heat to flood Kate's cheeks. She'd completely forgotten that they had an audience. Regardless, Travis continued to kiss her, obviously not caring. She grinned against his lips, not able to focus any longer, and Travis broke away. The smoldering heat emanating from his eyes made her insides melt.

"Family and friends," Lidia said, "it gives me the greatest pleasure to introduce to you our newlyweds, Travis and Kate Cooper."

Kate *Cooper*.

At last.

Applause broke out and Kate turned to those gathered to witness this special moment. Kate's heart overflowed with love.

Now to get through the reception and dinner so they could make love for the first time in her bed. *Their* bed.

After one night at the farm, they'd spend Friday and Saturday nights at Jesse's Hideout B&B in Samuels. She couldn't wait to see Tillie and Greg again, and hoped her newest student, Derek, would be there, too. A short honeymoon, perhaps, but she couldn't be away from the farm too long.

Short or not, somehow Kate knew she and Travis would spend the rest of their days—and nights—making love as if newlyweds. They had so much missed time to catch up on.

Chapter Thirty-Nine

A long three hours later, Travis led Katie around the living room of Lidia and Jason's house to say their goodbyes after having way too much cake and champagne at the reception followed by the Thanksgiving feast Mom and Beckie had prepared and served. He'd tried not to overeat so he wouldn't fall asleep on his bride tonight, but he wasn't sure how successful he'd been. "Mom, you outdid yourself again—especially with taking your dinner on the road this year." He kissed her and gave her a hug.

"I know whose house we'll be visiting for our next Thanksgiving dinner, Mom," Katie said.

"Oh, it was such a treat to cook in Lidia's kitchen." Mom eyed Dad. "I think I might have to talk your father into a remodeling project this winter, but not until I get through the rest of the holiday season. I'm falling behind on my quilts."

Dad shook his head in mock dismay then grinned. He'd do anything for her, and since he'd finally turned over much of the day-to-day business to Clint recently, this might be just the thing to keep him happy over the long winter months ahead.

"Can I get you anything else?"

Travis turned to Beckie. "Not a thing," he said, rubbing his belly. His trousers already felt tight.

Katie added, "We can't thank you enough for coming here on Thanksgiving to work your magic for our reception and dinner. Tillie was right—you're incredible."

"And you helped Mom be able to enjoy some of the festivities without spending the day in the kitchen," Travis said.

Beckie laughed. "Well, since Tillie isn't as busy at the inn on Thanksgivings anymore, I needed a new gig."

"Miss Beckie, everything was *muy bueno*," Miguel said. Travis had noticed she and Miguel seemed to have hit it off. There was something about a wedding to bring out the romance in everyone.

"Katie," Mom said, "I'll say it again, you're such a lovely bride, inside and out. I am so happy to welcome you into our family officially now, but you've always been a part of my heart since the first time Travis brought you home to meet us. I saw the spark in his eyes and knew he'd found the one."

Katie's chin quivered before she wrapped Mom in her arms. "Mom, you've always made Chelsea and me feel so welcome. Thanks for everything, not just for today."

Katie had told him last night how special it was having her as a second mom. He was glad the two got along, unlike some spouses with their in-laws.

Dad kissed Katie on the cheek. "Always happy to welcome another daughter into the family."

Next, they said goodnight to Chelsea who was beyond excited to be spending the weekend at what was now Shania's condo since Emmy had moved to Nolensville. Somehow, he had a feeling his sisters' bank accounts would take a hit on Black Friday, what with all the doting on their niece they planned to do, but they'd insisted, and who was he to argue? He wanted this time alone with his wife to start their marriage off right.

He and Katie turned toward the door to see that the rest of their guests had formed a gauntlet of sorts for them to walk through. He wasn't sure what they intended to pelt them with, but when Chelsea pulled a small bottle from behind her back, everyone else did the same. Soon, the path they were to walk to the exit was filled with floating bubbles.

Only Chelsea would come up with something like this. *God, I love it.*

And her.

He couldn't wait until Christmas when he and Katie would give her Chula. When he'd overheard someone offer Katie thirty thousand for the horse after the academy nationals in Murfreesboro earlier this month, he'd outbid the guy with an offer of thirty-five. No way did he want Katie to have to give up a horse whose name held so much meaning, but the stubborn woman still wouldn't let him infuse any money into her business. After some wrangling, he convinced her to sell Chula to him before the horse got too valuable with the many wins she'd accumulate in competition next year. And this way, everyone came out a winner.

They weren't quite ready to present the horse's papers to Chelsea yet. First, they wanted to set up a bank account with some money from Gail's inheritance that Chelsea could use to pay the expenses on her horse and learn to take responsibility for the animal. Her 4-H experience would help with that. This would provide important lessons in finances for the girl. Who knows? Maybe someday, she'd want to be a partner in Towers Contracting.

A bubble blew into his face, bringing him back to the present. He glanced down at Katie, smiling. "Shall we, Mrs. Cooper?"

"I'm ready when you are, Mr. Cooper." Katie giggled as she squeezed his hand, and the two of them sprinted through the blizzard of bubbles, Katie reaching up to pop a few along the way. Seeing Katie so giddy made him happy, too. He knew it wasn't from the wine or champagne, because she'd only had the few sips during the ceremony.

He couldn't wait to get her home and out of that dress. While she was gorgeous in it, she'd be even more beautiful naked. Outside, he helped her up into his Sierra. No doubt Clint and Jackson had led the charge decorating it with shaving cream on the windows, saying "Just married."

"Wait right here."

He scooped some of the cream from the window and went to Jackson's truck and wrote, "You're next." Anyone so adamant that women had no part in his happy bachelor life needed a reality check. Travis wanted Jackson to be as happy as he was at this moment.

Travis jumped inside the Sierra and, as they drove off, the aluminum cans hanging from the back bumper clanked on the pavement.

Rattling all the way down the driveway, they exited and made their way the short distance to their home. "Home at last. While that was one fantastic meal, I thought it would never end."

"Me, too."

"Stay put." He opened his door and exited before going around the hood of the truck to open her door. His hands spanned her waist and he helped her down, sliding her body along his, making him hotter than ever, if possible. He bent to kiss her forehead and then tilted her chin up until he could capture her lips in another kiss. Would he ever grow tired of this?

Never.

He kissed her again, but not as hastily as he had at the end of the ceremony. They had all night, and he intended to keep her up all night, too. With all the preparations and excitement of the last week, they hadn't been able to steal away for even a quickie. He had no intention of rushing things tonight.

"I love you, Travis," she said, her eyes sparkling in the reflection of the yard light. "I always have."

"I know. Just glad you finally came to your senses." How'd he get so lucky? Grinning and unable to wait another minute, he scooped her into his arms and walked across the yard to the front door. Without releasing her, he unlocked and opened the door then carried her over the threshold for the first time as husband and wife. "I can get used to this."

"But I'd rather you put me down so we can go upstairs."

"Are you saying I can't carry you all the way to our bedroom?"

"Oh never!"

Sadie came bounding in from the front of the house, no doubt where she made her bed in the living room when Chelsea wasn't around to sleep with. Kate reached down to return the dog's greeting, but Travis refused to set her down.

"Sorry, Sadie. Go back to bed. We'll play later."

Kate giggled as he ascended the stairs with a bounce in his step until they reached the room they would share for the rest of their lives.

Inside, he finally set her on her feet. "Turn around. I want to watch you loosen your hair." She pivoted, her hands fumbling to remove the band of baby's breath from her upswept hair. Was she nervous? All he'd been able to think about during the reception and dinner was watching her shake it loose for him tonight. Now he wanted her to hurry so she could remove her jacket and the dress, but he forced himself to enjoy the slow tease.

At last, the pins plopped to the floor, and she shook out her hair until it cascaded down her back and across her shoulders. He couldn't wait to run *his* fingers through it—but first... "Now face me and remove the jacket." He'd caught glimpses of her bare skin under the see-through covering all day, but she hadn't removed it once. Grinning at him, she opened the pearly button at the top, spread the panels to reveal the form-fitting V-neck of the dress, and let the lacy garment slide down her arms to puddle at her feet.

He bent down to kiss the creamy expanse of skin revealed, and she threw her head back to give him better access. Trailing kisses over her collarbone and up the column of her neck, he paused over her pulse point. Judging by the hammering of her heart, she was as excited as he.

He forced himself to control the barbarian tendencies that urged him to rip the dress off her body. Chelsea might want to wear the dress at her own wedding someday.

A day far, far into the future. Chelsea could wait until she was thirty-four, too, just like her mom.

His hands gravitated to her back where he grappled to determine if the dress had a zipper or buttons. All he encountered were pleats, smocking, and tiny beads. How was he supposed to take the damned thing off of her? Maybe he'd have to rip it off after all.

"Should I call Chelsea home to get me out of my dress?" She giggled.

He playfully swatted her ass, loving the feel of the silky material between his hand and her curves. "Careful, woman. If you intend to wear this dress again on our fiftieth anniversary, you'd better show me how to get you out of it...now."

"Oh, I intend to wear it on *every* anniversary, unless I gain too much weight," she said.

With her meticulous diet, the only way she'd gain weight was if she were pregnant. They hadn't discussed having more kids, and he'd need some serious assurances from her doctors that a pregnancy wouldn't cause undue stress on her body. So why couldn't he banish the image from his head of Katie's belly swollen with his baby—his *second* baby? Only this time, he'd be here to watch the baby grow from conception.

"It just lifts over my head," Katie said, reaching for the hem before he took her hands and raised them upward.

Travis wouldn't admit where his thoughts had strayed, but her teasing laughter made him harder. Taking her by the shoulders, he turned her around and, trying to show some finesse, lifted the dress over her head.

He tossed it on the chair near her antique secretary desk and stared at the scraps of peach-colored lingerie she wore beneath that were so close to her skin-tone it was as if she wore no bra and panties at all. He pressed kisses across her bare shoulder blades until goosebumps broke out on her flesh. Her throaty moan was followed by a shiver.

Oh yeah, darlin'.

They were going to get absolutely no sleep tonight—and that was just the way he wanted it.

* * *

Kate's heart raced as his lips burned a path over her skin. A tug at her bra hooks loosened the material, and his hands skimmed around her sides to cup her breasts a moment before his calloused fingers pinched her nipples.

She gasped, not expecting him to move in so quickly, but smiled as the neglected peaks became swollen with need. After he slid the silky bra down her arms, he turned her around to face him and lowered his head to her breast. As he sucked the swollen nipple into his mouth, she held onto the back of his head for balance and to keep him from stopping. His tongue flicked against the sensitive nubbin robbing her of breath. All too soon, he stopped, but merely moved to do the same to the other.

"Travis, I need you inside me."

He pulled away and met her gaze. Would he deny her, prolonging that moment for some twisted need to exert control over her feverish body? His wicked grin gave her no indication until he bent to lift her into his arms and carried her to the bed where he placed her gently on the edge of the mattress. She'd half turned down the quilt this morning in anticipation of making love here tonight but as she watched him discard his jacket and vest, she tossed the quilt and sheet lower.

His tanned hands slowly removed the silver cufflink on one wrist, then the other, placing them on the nightstand. His gaze never left hers. Next came the shirt buttons. She wished he'd let her do it because she'd have ripped it open and let the buttons fly to end the agony of waiting. Why was he tormenting her so?

At long last, he spread the shirt open to reveal his tanned chest, lightly furred with hair. Her fingers itched to run through the soft curls, but again he seemed in no hurry.

"Please, Travis. Don't keep me waiting any longer."

A sardonic brow lifted, telling her not to say another word or he'd only prolong the exquisite torture longer. Then again, perhaps…

With her right hand, she let her fingers skim her abdomen and up to her nipple that had been in his mouth moments ago. She plucked at it to make it swell again, and his eyes grew smoky. When her left hand slid over her abdomen to her mound and slipped inside her panties, he shucked his trousers and boxer briefs and joined her on the mattress, stretching out beside her before giving her ample time to fully appreciate and adore his body.

Taking her other nipple into his mouth again, he clamped his teeth over it and tugged. She stretched out her hand to run her manicured nails, a rare indulgence for her, over his skin. He hissed. "Keep that up, and this may not last long."

"We have all weekend. I'm okay with having a quick release then we can go for the slow burn when we get to Greg and Tillie's inn." She caressed his erection, evidence that he was as ready as she. "It's been too long, Travis."

In one swift move, he stood between her legs at the side of the bed and yanked off her panties. Had she heard the fabric rip? He stretched over the length of her body, his erection pressing against her opening and his upper body a delicious weight on hers. She framed his face and pulled his mouth to hers for a searing kiss.

He pressed inside her, then retreated. "Damn. Let me put on a condom."

She grabbed him by the shoulders. "Unless you have an aversion to babies, let's stop using them."

He furrowed his brow. "I'd feel better talking it over with your doctor before—"

She pressed a finger to his lips. "I discussed the possibilities with both my endocrinologist and my gynecologist, and both said they would monitor me carefully and that I'd have to be on a strict diet and exercise, but there was no reason I couldn't have a healthy baby and remain well myself."

His erection throbbed against her, and she grinned. He smiled back. "Then what are we waiting for? Wrap your legs around my back," he said as he tugged her body closer to the edge of the mattress.

She did as he'd instructed, and he entered her wetness with one stroke. Her eyes opened wider. So full. Intense. He let her body adjust to him, then he pulled out slowly before ramming inside her again.

"Faster," she begged.

He let his body answer her plea, and they soon set a pace that had her panting on the cusp of an orgasm within mere moments. When his fingers dug between their bodies to find her sensitive bundle of nerves, he sent her over the top in seconds as he grunted his own release.

Kate lay spent, while Travis tenderly washed her and then himself, wondering if they'd taken the first step toward making a baby tonight.

"What are you thinking about?" he asked.

"That I'm the luckiest woman alive—and wondering when we're going to make love again."

Epilogue

K ate stared up at the old Federal-style brick house the next morning from the passenger window of Travis's truck. Tillie Buchanan hadn't done the place justice when she'd described her inn. "It's gorgeous! I'm so excited to stay in a haunted house."

Travis cupped her chin and turned her face toward him. "Not as excited as I am to spend two nights with my gorgeous bride, protecting her from nefarious spirits."

Her eyes opened wide and then wrinkled her brow. "Protect me? I'm actually excited to see if I have a connection with them like I did with your friend Danny."

"As long as they stay out of our bedroom, I'm okay with that." He shook his head, grinning, then leaned down to kiss her, taking her breath away.

When their lips parted, she struggled to remember what they were talking about. "I think we might have to be sociable with the Buchanans for a little while at least before we can escape to our bedroom."

"We'll make it quick. Now, let's get inside before I embarrass you out here in their driveway."

Kate smiled. They'd had sex just about everywhere she could imagine—and some places she'd never have thought of—and that was only since the wedding yesterday. But he was right. If Tillie or Greg caught them making love in the truck, she'd die. After all, their little boy, Derek, was one of her riding students.

Fortunately, they made it out of the truck and were removing their overnight bag by the time Tillie opened the middle door on the side of the house. Kate took one look at her, and her eyes nearly popped out. Greg had brought Derek to his lessons during fall break from his school in Minnesota, so she hadn't seen Tillie since August. But there was now a sizable baby bump under her 1940s-style, navy-blue silk dress.

Kate hurried over to her. "Tillie! Congratulations! When's the baby due?"

"February 18, if I last that long." She laughed. "At least I'm past the morning sickness now. That was rough."

"Oh, I hear you. That's the absolute worst part—only I think mine lasted all nine months with Chelsea."

"You poor dear! Where are my manners? Welcome to Jesse's Hideout! We've been so looking forward to finally having you and Travis as our guests. And congratulations on your wedding!"

"Thanks!" Tillie tried to insist that they should stay as friends, not paying guests, but she and Travis had quashed that idea. She didn't want to take advantage of their budding friendship. And, after all, they paid Kate for Derek's riding lessons even though he was a joy to have at the farm.

She turned toward Travis, who had followed her, setting their shared roller bag beside him and greeting Tillie before he wrapped his arms around Kate and whispered, "I can't wait to see you swollen with my baby, darlin'." His words made her heart flutter wildly.

Tillie held open the door for them, and they entered into the warm dining room, which smelled of cinnamon and pumpkin spices. A horn of plenty spilled its bounty onto the table, and a small Christmas tree was lit on the sideboard. Travis shut the door behind them to keep out the late November chill.

Greg came through a doorway on the right. "Great to see you again, Kate and Travis." He gave Kate a kiss on the cheek as he hugged her, then shook Travis's hand, clapping him on the bicep. "Tillie just baked a fresh batch of my grandmother's oatmeal-raisin cookies. Why don't you come into the kitchen and warm up by the fire. We've had quite a drop in temperature since yesterday."

"The weather held off just long enough for us to exchange our vows at the winery's gazebo," Travis said.

"Congratulations to you both."

Tillie chimed in. "And don't you worry, Kate! I baked a special batch for you, taking your advice on how to adjust the recipe, so it shouldn't spike your sugar."

Kate was touched that she'd go to so much trouble. "No wonder it's so hard to book your place, if you cater to your guests like this." She and Travis had asked about availabilities for this weekend back in September, but the only suite they rented out had been booked solid. Luckily, they had a cancellation about a month ago, and Tillie offered it to them. They'd snatched it up immediately. Since this weekend would be their only honeymoon, they were thrilled to be able to spend it in such a charming, romantic place. After all, hadn't Greg and Tillie fallen in love here?

In the kitchen, Tillie donned an apron and removed cookies from the baking sheet before glancing at Greg and turning to Travis and Kate with a smile. "Greg and I will be closing the inn to paying customers after New Year's weekend, except during the Bourbon Festival and some weekends during the holidays each year. We're going to have our hands busy with our daughter," she rubbed her belly, "and with Derek when he's here." As an afterthought, she smiled at Kate. "But as our friends you two are always welcome here."

As if he'd heard his name, Derek came bounding through the doorway, his cheeks rosy from playing outside. In his hand, he held a banded woolly bear caterpillar.

"Daddy, look what I found!"

Greg scooped it into his hand, apologizing to Kate.

"Oh, please. I live on a farm." To the boy, she said, "Hi, Derek!" He glanced at Kate and then Travis as though not quite understanding what they were doing here. "Miss Kate, did you bring Twilight for me to ride?"

Kate laughed. "I'm sorry, no. We're here on our honeymoon. Mr. Travis and I were married yesterday."

"I was bestest man at my daddy's wedding to Momma Tillie."

"I'll bet you were an outstanding best man," Kate said.

He puffed out his chest. "I only dropped the ring one time. But I found it really fast!"

Kate smiled, wondering if perhaps she and Travis would have a boy this time. Derek was her only male student, after Tony quit before he'd barely started, but she'd fallen in love with Derek from the start.

Greg ruffled Derek's hair before turning to them. "Why don't I show you to your room and give you time to get comfortable before we enjoy these cookies in the parlor," Greg said. "What can I carry?"

"We packed light. Just lead the way." They followed him into the dining room.

Tillie shouted from the kitchen, "Give them the nickel tour, Greg!"

"Right this way, folks."

In the next room, she looked around at the cozy furniture for reading or sitting by the fire, noting this one was ablaze as well. According to the website, they'd have one in their room, too.

"We call this the birthing room. My grandfather was a country doctor here for decades, my grandmother his nurse—and Tillie's grandmother was born right in here."

What a charming history! "I'm fascinated by the stories old houses can tell. My own has been in the family quite a while, although not as long as this one must have been in yours."

"I might as well warn you—if you're attuned to spirits, sometimes the walls do still talk here. But not nearly as often as they used to."

"As long as they give us our privacy tonight," Travis said, "I'm fine with a few spirits."

"Speaking of which, the liquor cabinet is through that door, in the office. Help yourself to anything you'd like. And if hot buttered rum is your thing, I'll fix us all one tonight. Well, not Tillie. She's sworn off all alcohol until after the baby arrives."

"I think I'll pass on one, too, but you two gentlemen feel free to enjoy one if you'd like."

"Oh yeah. I'll bet alcohol can spike your sugar, too," Greg said.

Kate smiled and nodded, even though that wasn't her reason for not having it this time.

"I'll pass, too," Travis said, grinning at Kate with a gleam in his eye. "I'll need all my wits tonight to keep up with my bride."

Greg chuckled and Kate couldn't believe it when heat crept into her cheeks. Since she wasn't carrying anything more than her purse, she couldn't blame exertion.

"Right this way. This door will be closed tonight to give you added privacy—and to keep Derek out. He usually sleeps in the small room that's part of Amelia's Suite, named for my grandmother, but he's looking forward to sleeping in the attic room above our bedroom tonight." Kate was about to insist they not put the boy out when Greg laughed. "Don't worry. He loves it up there. We've actually put guests there when we've had a full house. Kids love it. There's even a special plaster wall with the etched names of children who lived here over the centuries. My mother's name is there and, not too long ago, we let him carve his next to hers."

"If you're sure," Travis said.

Greg continued the tour. "The two sides of the house don't connect. It was built originally as a travelers' inn and they kept their living quarters separated by locked doors. Only we rent out what was once their living quarters and are living in the rooms once reserved for guests. This way, you have full use of the parlor, kitchen, and dining room anytime you'd like. Our house is yours during your stay."

In the foyer, she noticed a fanlight over the front door and rainbows scattered across the checkerboard floor. How delightful!

"The parlor is a great place to read or play chess, if you're so inclined. There are cards and other games on the shelves."

"Thanks, but I don't think we're going to be bored." Travis said, wriggling his eyebrows at her.

He must be determined to keep her blushing constantly. She glanced around the room. The fireplace burned brightly with what appeared to be a wood fire, warming the large room despite its at least fourteen-foot ceilings. A towering twelve-foot tree blazed from top to bottom with lights of every color in the rainbow. She walked closer to admire some of the vintage ornaments. Each must tell a story of Christmas past. "Your tree is so beautiful!"

"Tillie's responsible for that. Although I don't let her go up on the ladder after she…well, because of the baby now, mostly."

The furniture was antique, but comfortable looking, with a divan and wing-back chairs surrounding the fire in an intimate set-up.

She'd expected the house to feel like a museum at first sight, but instead found it to be cozy and homey. "Be sure to check out the initials carved into the mantel on the right-hand side. Tillie and I still can't decide whether the JH was carved by my grandmother's last beau or by Jesse James himself, who spent a lot of time here in the house and sometimes went by the alias John Howard."

"Either way," Kate said, "it must be special to be surrounded by so much history, whether your family's or that of the famous outlaws who hid out here." She'd read up on the lore in anticipation of their stay. Simply fascinating. Jesse's brother Frank had surrendered after the Civil War within a few hundred yards of the house.

"We're lucky. Tillie took care of it after my grandmother left it to her." Interesting that a non-family member had inherited it rather than Greg. Perhaps its current owners had stories to tell, too. "Shall we go upstairs to Amelia's Suite?"

"Yes, by all means." Travis said, as anxious to get upstairs, frankly, as she was.

The men indicated for Kate to precede them up the stairs, then she waited at the landing for Greg to take the lead once more, although there were only two doors to choose from. "This will be your en suite bathroom," he said, opening the one to the right.

Travis set down the bag in the hallway beside the door and briefly devoured her with his eyes before scooping her into his arms.

"What are you doing?"

"Carrying my bride over the threshold."

"But you already did that at home last night."

"This will be home for the next two nights, and I want to do this right."

The only regret she had now was that they'd promised to come down to have cookies soon. She'd never wanted anything less at the moment, not with the way Travis burned a hole to her core with his steamy gaze.

Inside the room, Travis kissed her and set her on her feet as Greg cleared his throat. She'd forgotten about him altogether and didn't make eye contact as her cheeks flamed. Undoubtedly, they'd had newlyweds and other couples here before. It wasn't as if Greg and Tillie hadn't had sex before, either. Thankfully, where the Buchanans would sleep was far removed from this room, although she intended to restrain herself from screaming the walls down this weekend, no matter how hard that might be to achieve.

"This is a rope bed," Greg said, "like most of the beds in the house." She'd always wanted to own one.

Greg moved to the gas fireplace and instructed Travis how it worked. "Sorry that we don't have wood-burning fireplaces in the bedrooms, but the insurance company prefers that we're in charge of building any wood fires in the house."

"No complaints from me. This will be quick and easy."

"Everything else here is pretty much self-explanatory, but feel free to ask for anything you need." Greg made his way to the door. "And take all the time you need to settle in." She blushed wondering if he knew they'd be naked about a minute after he left the room. "Dinner's not until six. Unless you're hungry now, why don't we save the cookies for dessert?"

"Sounds perfect," Kate said. More time alone.

Travis chuckled, and no sooner had the door clicked shut than he reached for the hem of her sweater and pulled it over her head. "I don't think he expects us to make an appearance until dinnertime, but that only leaves us two hours. We'd better work fast."

A smile spread across her face. She knew how Travis liked to take his time, but she couldn't wait. "Let me help." She unhooked her bra and tossed it on the back of the chair next to the fireplace.

His hands cupped her breasts and squeezed her nipples, making her wince. They'd gotten a workout last night, and were supersensitive. He sucked one, and she grabbed onto the back of his head to keep from crumbling at his feet. Without warning, he released her and tossed the appliquéd butterfly quilt back, along with the top sheet and probably a blanket. He then lifted her into his arms again, laying her gently on the high mattress before removing her slacks and underwear and his own clothes in great haste, his gaze never leaving her body, causing her nipples to remain pebbled and her sex to throb.

He positioned her near the edge of the bed. When she held out her arms to him, he ignored them and spread her legs wide before sinking into her in one swift move. She wasn't aware she was ready for him, but seemed to stay in a state of readiness anytime he was near.

After they'd both climaxed, he crawled into the bed and rolled on his back, his arms wrapped around her waist as he cocooned her to him. She rested her head against his chest.

"I bet I could make you come once more before dinnertime," he said.

She giggled. "That's the last time I challenge you to go faster."

He grinned. "We have a lot of time to make up for."

Kate wouldn't let the regrets over the past ruin the moment. They'd both made their peace with the secrets she'd kept and the opportunities they'd lost.

Travis kissed her. "We have everything anyone could ever dream of. I love you, Katie."

"And I love you, Travis. The best is yet to be."

The next two days were filled with lovemaking and copious amounts of good food. They were seated in the dining room Sunday morning enjoying brunch when Travis pulled his phone out. "Excuse me. It's Mom. It must be important."

He must have had it on vibrate because it hadn't made a sound that she could hear. She watched him go into the birthing room to answer it and tried to listen in, but Derek was regaling her with stories about the wonderful waterfall near his former home. She'd begun to relax when Travis entered the room again, his face drawn. Something was wrong.

"Katie, we need to go to Louisville."

Her heart pounded in her ears. "Chelsea?" She jumped up from the table, nearly toppling her chair. "Is she all right?"

He nodded curtly. "Chelsea's fine. But Tanya's been in a serious accident in southern Indiana and they've brought her to a hospital in downtown Louisville."

She felt guilty at the sense of relief knowing it wasn't their daughter, but her heart ached for Travis and her new family. Even though Kate didn't know Tanya well, she'd had a number of interesting conversations with her about her travels at the rehearsal dinner and on their wedding day.

"Tillie, Greg, I hope you'll excuse us for rushing off."

Tillie rose first. "Not at all. Let me wrap up some cookies to take to the hospital with you while you all pack."

"We're already packed," Travis said as he disappeared toward the foyer.

"Thanks, Tillie. That's very sweet of you." Kate followed Travis dreading what they were going to find when they made it to the hospital. Tanya was young and healthy, though. She had to be okay, once they were able to evaluate her condition.

But she worried about Travis, being the big brother. What on earth had happened? They'd all been together just a few days ago.

*   *   *

Danny couldn't believe his luck.

After months of planning and waiting, they'd found him a match. The man had been lying in a coma for hours before seeking out

Obadiah who then approached Danny's spirit guide with an offer of an exchange.

He didn't know a lot about him, but if the higher powers thought they would be a good match, then who was he to argue. Danny had been hovering near the man's bedside for the exchange to take place, but Daniel said he couldn't leave until a special someone came to his bedside.

In the meantime, Danny became restless and went out into the hallway near the ICU nurse's station just as Travis and Katie came running toward him. What the... How could they know he'd...

"We're here to see Tanya Cooper," Travis said to the nurse who asked his relationship to the patient. "I'm her brother and this is my wife."

What were the chances that he'd be granted this opportunity to see Travis again, but under what circumstances? What happened to Tanya to land her in ICU? The way he talked, she was a workaholic. Heart attack? Stroke? Happened to younger and younger people all the time.

"Follow me, sir."

Danny fell into line behind Travis and Katie as they were led to a room several doors away. Inside the room, he found Tanya attached to all kinds of monitors and IVs. Her head was bandaged. An accident?

"Tanya, can you hear me?" Travis asked.

Katie stood beside him rubbing his back, her brow wrinkled in concern. Thank goodness he had her. He probably wouldn't lean on anyone else.

"Daniel Morgan's going to pay for this," Travis muttered under his breath.

Wait. What did he say? Danny's gut twisted. He didn't believe in coincidences. So Daniel and Tanya had been together in the accident that landed the man in a coma? Tanya's eyes were closed. Travis brushed the side of her cheek avoiding the bruising.

If Danny went through with this, would he find out he was responsible for the injuries suffered by Travis's little sister? Travis already seemed to think Daniel was to blame.

"Is there a problem, Danny?" He turned to see Obadiah standing beside Danny's spirit guide, the two of them awaiting his answer.

"Is Tanya going to be okay?"

"That's not for us to say."

Fury bubbled up inside him. "Then who the hell do I ask? Travis needs to know that everything's going to be all right." He was on his damned honeymoon, for heaven's sake.

"His journey is of no concern to you now. While it's not too late for you to end this contract and wait for another, remember that it has been determined that this opportunity will give you the greatest potential for soul growth and enable you to complete several of the missions you've set forth in your chart."

Did he care about that now? Hell, yeah. But…

Obadiah waited, staring pointedly.

Danny ran his fingers through his hair. "I didn't expect it to happen this way."

How was this Morgan fellow tied to Tanya? What if Danny discovered the man was responsible for the accident that injured Travis's little sister? he wondered again.

"Of course, once you've accomplished what Daniel asked that you agree to as part of the exchange, you've mapped out several turning points in your chart in which you may choose between continuing life in Daniel Morgan's body or returning to spirit." Obadiah waited once more. "Well, Danny? Your decision?"

Danny's gaze moved away from the guides back to the three Coopers in the room. He had only one choice to make.

The "End"

Keep up with news about my writing journey for book three in the Bluegrass Spirits series—*Danny's Return*—as well as watch for release and preorder information at my website.

Books by Kallypso Masters

Rescue Me Saga (Erotic Romance)

Kally has no intention of ending the *Rescue Me Saga* ever, but will introduce some new series with new characters in the years to come. The following *Rescue Me Saga* titles are available in e-book and print formats on my web site and at major booksellers:

Masters at Arms & Nobody's Angel (Combined Volume)
Nobody's Hero
Nobody's Perfect
Somebody's Angel
Nobody's Lost
Nobody's Dream
Somebody's Perfect

Rescue Me Saga Box Set Books 1-3 (always e-book only)
Rescue Me Saga Box Set Books 4-6 and Western Dreams (always e-book only)

Rescue Me Saga Extras (Erotic Romance)

This will be a series of hot, fun, short-story collections featuring beloved couples from the *Rescue Me Saga*.

Western Dreams (Rescue Me Saga Extras #1)
(Contains new scenes with Megan & Ryder and Cassie & Luke)

Roar
(a *Rescue Me Saga* Erotic Romance Spin-off)

(Erotic Romance with Secondary Characters from the *Rescue Me Saga*. *Roar* provides a lead into the upcoming trilogy with Patrick, Grant, and Gunnar's stories. No clue when that series will be written. Kally is waiting for Grant to open up.)

Bluegrass Spirits (Supernatural Contemporary Romance)

(Contemporary Romance…with a Haunting Twist)

Jesse's Hideout

Kate's Secret

kallypsomasters.com/books

About the Author

Kallypso Masters is a *USA Today* Bestselling Author with more than half-a-million copies of her books sold in e-book and paperback formats since August 2011. All her books feature alpha males, strong women, and happy endings because those are her favorite stories to read, but that doesn't mean they don't touch on the tough issues sometimes. Her best-known series—the Rescue Me Saga—features emotional, realistic adult Romance novels with characters healing from past traumas and PTSD, sometimes using unconventional methods (like BDSM).

An eighth-generation Kentuckian, in spring 2017, Kally launched the new *Bluegrass Spirits* series, supernatural Contemporary Romances set in some of her favorite places in her home state. *Jesse's Hideout* (Bluegrass Spirits #1) is set in her father's hometown in Nelson County and includes a recipe section with some of Kally's treasured family recipes, most of which are mentioned in the story. *Kate's Secret* (Bluegrass Spirits #2) takes place in horse country outside Midway in Woodford County. Local flavor abounds in both novels.

Kally has been living her own "happily ever after" with her husband of more than 35 years, known affectionately to her readers as Mr. Ray. They have two adult children, a rescued dog, and a rescued cat. And, as her friends and fans know, Kally lives for visits from her adorable grandson, Erik, who was the model for the character Derek in *Jesse's Hideout* and Erik in *Kate's Secret*. (He insisted on having his real name used in the second one!)

Kally enjoys meeting readers at book signings and events throughout North America and is on a mission to meet with at least one reader for a meal, signing, or other event in all 50 states. She's staying closer to home these days, but expects to have KallypsoCon in Virginia or

Maryland in 2019. To keep up with upcoming events, check out the Appearances page on her web site! She's always open to having signings in her home state of Kentucky, too!

*For timely updates, sneak peeks at unedited excerpts, and much more, sign up for her e-mails or text alerts on her website at **kallypsomasters.com**.*

To contact or engage with Kally, go to:
Facebook (where almost all of her posts are public),
Facebook Author page,
Twitter (@kallypsomasters),
InstaGram (instagram.com/kallypsomasters)
Kally's Web site (KallypsoMasters.com).

And feel free to e-mail Kally at kallypsomasters@gmail.com, or write to her at
Kallypso Masters, PO Box 1183, Richmond, KY 40476-1183

Get your Signed Books & Merchandise in the Kally Store!

Want to own merchandise or personalized, signed paperback copies of any or all of Kallypso Masters' books? New *Bluegrass Spirits* series items will be coming soon, but there's already a line of t-shirts and other items connected to the *Rescue Me Saga* series and KallypsoCons. With each order, you'll receive a sports pack filled with Kally's latest FREE items. Kally ships internationally. To shop for these items and much more, go to kallypsomasters.com/kally_swag.

And you can also purchase any of Kally's e-books directly from her now, too! Just click the "Kally's Shop" link for any of the books listed on her website. Or go here for a complete list of available titles. New releases will be published exclusively in Kally's Shop at least two weeks before being available on other retailer sites. kallypsomasters.com/buy-direct

Bluegrass Spirits Series
Jesse's Hideout
(First in the *Bluegrass Spirits* Supernatural Contemporary Romance series)
Read Greg and Tillie's Story Today!

Jesse's Hideout

Tillie Hamilton is the latest person to use her 180-year-old house in rural Kentucky as a hideout—taking her cue from the infamous outlaw Jesse James who frequented the place. The house she converted into a bed and breakfast is the only sanctuary she's known, ever since the old woman she inherited it from rescued her from neglect as a small child.

However, sparks fly when her benefactor's handsome grandson, Greg Buchanan, accuses Tillie of exploiting his grandmother's memory for her own ends by claiming Gram haunts the inn.

While reading his grandmother's private journals, Greg learned Jesse James returned to this house in the 1930s, half a century after historians believed he'd been shot dead. Vowing to debunk the charlatan's claims of ghosts and to prove his grandmother correct, Greg quickly discovers the charming Tillie is not at all what he expected. Embarrassed to admit he's another of the conspiracy theorists she scoffs at, he hides his secondary reason for showing up at her B&B.

Yet his attraction to Tillie keeps him torn between setting history right and forging a new history of his own in Tillie's arms. Tensions mount, leaving his grandmother's spirit to think her dying wish—something she's wanted since Tillie and Greg were children—may never come true.

Can Gram and Jesse make the two lonely overachievers see they belong in each other's arms before time runs out for them to seize this opportunity?

Made in the USA
Monee, IL
03 June 2024

59066684R00272